REAWAKENED BY THE SURGEON'S TOUCH

BY
JENNIFER TAYLOR

MILLS &
BOON

D0243472

Published in Great Britain 2016
By Mills & Boon, an imprint of HarperCollins*Publishers*
1 London Bridge Street, London, SE1 9GF

© 2016 Jennifer Taylor

ISBN: 978-0-263-91519-8

Our policy is to use papers that are natural, renewable and recyclable
products and made from wood grown in sustainable forests.
The logging and manufacturing processes conform to the legal
environmental regulations of the country of origin.

Printed and bound in Spain
by CPI, Barcelona

Dear Reader,

I planned this book several years ago but, as sometimes happens, life got in the way and I put it aside. However, the central characters never quite left me, and I knew that one day I would have to tell their story. At the end of last year the time was right, and Jude and Claire stepped out of my imagination and onto the page. And what a journey they took me on!

Bringing these two together at last was a real joy, even though I probably worked harder on this book than on any previous one! Although I said at the beginning that I had planned Jude and Claire's story, that isn't quite true. Oh, I knew the basics—who they were, what obstacles they needed to overcome—but that was it. I am not a planner; I wait to see how my characters want to 'behave' and this pair kept on surprising me. Suffice to say it was an emotional journey. I hope after reading this book you feel that they deserved their happy-ever-after. I did!

If you want to know more about the background to this book then please visit my blog: jennifertaylorauthor.wordpress.com. I would love to hear your comments.

Love to you all,

Jennifer

In memory of Jean and Bob Taylor.
The best parents anyone could have had.

**Praise for
Jennifer Taylor**

'A superbly written tale of hope, redemption and
forgiveness, *The Son that Changed His Life* is a
first-class contemporary romance that plumbs deep
into the heart of the human spirit and touches the soul.'
—*CataRomance*

CHAPTER ONE

WHAT IN HEAVEN'S name was he doing here?

As the plane began the final stages of its descent, Jude Slater was struck by an unexpected rush of panic. Up to this point anger had buoyed him up. He had been so furious when his former mentor, a man he greatly admired, had accused him of choosing the easy option that he had set out to prove him wrong. Maybe it wouldn't have stung quite so much if Jude hadn't had the sneaking suspicion that the other man was right. He *had* been coasting for the past few years, although he had refused to justify himself by explaining why. He tried not to think about that period in his life; it was too painful. Suffice to say that he had paid his dues, even if it didn't appear so to an outsider.

Nevertheless, the accusation had spurred him on so that almost before he knew it, he had signed up to work for Worlds Together, a leading medical aid agency. True, he had been a little disconcerted when he had been invited for an interview a couple of weeks later and offered a post. He hadn't expected things to move quite so quickly but he had been determined not to back down. Nobody would be able to accuse him of losing sight of the real issues once he had done a stint overseas, he had assured himself. He would be accorded his true standing within the medical fraternity and that was all he wanted. It had all sounded so perfect in theory but now that he was about to land in the tiny central African country of Mwuranda reality had set in.

What did he know about the problems of working in the developing world? Jude thought a shade desperately. He was London born and London bred, and he thrived in the constant bustle of city life. When he travelled abroad, he visited other cities—New York, Paris, Rome—places where he felt at home. Wherever he went, he stayed in five-star luxury hotels too; however, recalling what he had been told at his interview—something about Mwuranda recovering from the effects of civil war—it appeared that five-star luxuries were going to be very thin on the ground here!

The plane rumbled to a halt and Jude unfastened his seat belt. Ten hours spent squeezed into a gap between piles of packing cases hadn't made for the most comfortable journey but, hopefully, things would improve from here on. The one thing he mustn't do was panic. Conditions couldn't be that bad or nobody would volunteer to work here, so it was just a question of putting everything into perspective. Maybe luxuries would be few and far between, but so long as he had the basic necessities he would cope. He was only here for three months and he could put up with a bit of hardship for that length of time.

Jude felt much better once he had reasoned everything out. He had been told that he would be collected from the airfield, so as soon as the ramp was lowered, he made his way out of the plane. His heart sank as he stepped onto the runway and looked around. All he could see in every direction was khaki-coloured landscape, the few scrubby trees which were dotted about providing the only relief from the monotony. It was mid-afternoon and the air was blisteringly hot. Apart from the plane he had arrived on, the airfield was deserted. He couldn't see any sign of a car waiting to collect him and his spirits sank even further at the thought of having to hang around in the heat until his transport arrived.

'Dr Slater?'

The voice was female but that was the only indication of the speaker's gender, Jude discovered when he turned around. The figure standing before him was dressed in a bulky old boiler suit which completely disguised the wearer's shape. Heavy boots on her feet and an old baseball cap pulled low over her eyes completed her ensemble.

Jude could just make out the lower part of her face—a softly rounded chin and a mouth which was bare of any trace of lipstick. He had no idea if she was young, old or somewhere in between, and it was unsettling when it meant that he wasn't sure how to pitch his response.

'That's right. I'm Jude Slater.' He held out his hand and smiled charmingly at her. 'And you are—?'

'Your driver.'

The woman ignored his outstretched hand as she stared past him into the hold and Jude felt himself bridle. Quite frankly, he wasn't used to women of any age ignoring him. The older ones wanted to mother him, the younger ones wanted to sleep with him, while those in between could go either way.

'If you've brought any luggage with you then you'd better fetch it. There's a truck on its way to pick up our supplies, but there's no guarantee it will make it back to town tonight. It all depends how long it takes to unload the cargo.' The woman treated him to a cursory glance and he could tell how unimpressed she was by his attempts to charm her by the sneering curve of her unadorned lips. 'We don't drive around after dark. It's far too dangerous.' Jude's chagrin faded in the face of this fresh snippet of information. He managed to hide his dismay but the situation seemed to be going from bad to worse at a rate of knots.

'I'll get my bag,' he said shortly.

'You do that. I just need a word with the pilot and I'll be right with you. The bike's over there.'

Jude stopped dead, wondering if he had misheard her. It had been extremely noisy in the plane and his ears were still ringing from the throbbing of the engines, but he could have sworn she had said something about a... 'Bike?'

'Uh-huh.' She pointed across the runway. 'That's it over there. There's some rope under the seat, so I suggest you tie your bag onto the back. It should be safe enough so long as we don't hit too many potholes.'

Jude's jaw dropped when he spotted the battered old motorbike propped against the perimeter fence. Its bodywork was pitted with rust and even from this distance he could tell that the tyres were completely bald of any tread. She didn't *really* think that he was going to travel on the back of that thing, did she?

'This is a joke, isn't it? Some sort of a...*stunt* you pull on new recruits like me?' His good humour returned in a rush as he realised what was going on and he laughed. 'You wind us up by telling us that we're expected to ride on the back of that heap of junk and I, in my innocence, very nearly fell for it!'

'I hate to disillusion you, Dr Slater, but it isn't a wind-up. We'll be travelling back to town on that bike, so I suggest you get your belongings together.' The woman pushed back her cuff. 'It's almost two o'clock and I haven't got time to waste, hanging about here. If you don't want to spend the night sleeping in the plane then you'd better get a move on.'

With that she walked away. Jude watched her make her way over to where the crew were standing then realised that he was holding his breath. He breathed out and then in, but not even a fresh shot of oxygen made him feel any better. His gaze went to the rusty old motorbike and his mouth thinned. Given the choice, he would have refused to get on the blasted thing but he didn't have a choice, did he? He was a stranger in this country and one who knew very little about what it took to survive here too. He might be able to hold his own in any city in the world but he was as vulnerable as a newborn babe out here and it was galling to admit it.

He was used to running his life the way he chose these days. It had taken him a while to get back on track after he had quit working for the NHS and he had no intention of relinquishing his autonomy ever again. Maybe he was at a disadvantage here but he still intended to be in charge of his own destiny.

Jude took another deep breath and used it this time for a specific purpose, i.e. shoring up his anger. He would start as he meant to go on. No way was he going to be ordered about by some overbearing, pushy woman!

* * *

'I'm sorry about the delay but our usual driver didn't show up this morning and we had to find a replacement.' Claire Morgan glanced at her watch again and frowned. 'The truck should have been here by now, though, so I don't know what's happened to it. I'll have to check back with base and see if they've heard anything.'

She left the crew to begin the task of unloading the cargo and made her way over to the bike. Dr Slater had just finished roping his very expensive leather holdall onto the back and he looked round when he heard her approaching. Claire pulled the peak of her cap lower over her eyes, hating the fact that she felt it necessary to hide beneath it. She had hoped that she had got over this fear but as soon as she had seen Dr Jude Slater disembarking from the plane, her internal alarm bells had started ringing.

She knew what the problem was, of course: he reminded her of Andrew. There was something about that air of self-confidence he exuded that put her in mind of her ex so that it was an effort to carry on walking towards him. The thought of having to live with this fear gnawing away inside her for the next few months was more than she could bear, so maybe she needed to focus on the differences between the two men rather than the similarities?

It was worth a try, so Claire tested out the theory as she crossed the runway. Jude Slater was tall like Andrew, but whereas Andrew was heavily built, Jude had the lithely muscular physique of an athlete. Both men had dark hair, but Jude's hair was jet black with the hint of a wave to it whereas Andrew's was a rather muddy shade of brown and poker-straight. Jude's eyes were a different colour, too, Claire realised as she drew closer—a warm hazel with flecks of gold in them. Andrew's eyes were pale blue, very cold and frosty. In fact, if she had to choose one feature which she had disliked it would have been Andrew's eyes. Even when they had been sharing their most intimate moments, his eyes had never held any real warmth.

Claire sighed. With the benefit of hindsight, she could see that she should have taken it as a warning but she had been too besotted at the time to read the signs properly. It was a mistake she wouldn't make again. If she ever reached a point where she could consider having a relationship with a man again then she wouldn't choose someone who looked like Andrew or Jude Slater, for that matter.

'Is everything sorted out?'

'Nearly.' Claire's tone was clipped as she stopped beside the motorbike. She didn't look at him as she lifted the seat and took out the two-way radio transmitter. She had done her best—flagged up the differences—but it hadn't helped as much as she had hoped it would. She still had this deep-seated urge to run away and hide, and it was painful to acknowledge how little progress she had made in the past two years.

'Nearly? So do I take it there's a problem?' he persisted, obviously not satisfied with her less-than-fulsome reply.

Claire ignored him as she tuned the radio to the correct frequency. Although most of the rebel fighters had been driven out of the area, there were still pockets of resistance and keeping in touch with base was vital.

'Hello!' He stepped forward and bent to peer under

the peak of her cap. 'I asked you a question. Did you hear me?'

Claire immediately recoiled. 'Do you mind,' she snapped, twisting the dial this way and that in the hope that it would disguise the fact that her hands were trembling. She hated it when anyone invaded her personal space. It was a trick Andrew had used to intimidate her and even though there was no reason to think that Jude Slater was trying to do the same, she resented it. Bitterly.

'I'm sorry. I just find it frustrating when people won't answer a simple question.'

He stepped back, folding his arms across his chest as he leant against the fence post, but Claire knew that he had sensed her discomfort. Colour ran up her face as she bent over the radio. Nobody knew about her past. Not even her family or her friends knew what she had been through. She had been too devastated to tell them the truth, that Andrew had forced her to have sex with him, that he had raped her. Women like her—intelligent, independent women—were supposed to be able to look after themselves. They weren't supposed to put themselves in a situation whereby something like that could happen. If they did then the consensus was that they were to blame for leading the man on.

It had taken Claire a long time to accept that she hadn't been at fault and that it was Andrew who was the guilty party. However, she knew how fragile her confidence was and there was no way that she was going to risk undoing all her hard work. Maybe Dr Slater wasn't cut from the same cloth but she wasn't going to test out *that* theory. For the next three months she intended to keep her distance from him and, more important, make sure he kept his distance from her.

'I need to contact base,' she explained as coolly as she could. 'The truck that was supposed to collect our supplies should have arrived by now and I need to find out what's happened to it.'

'It could have broken down en route.' Jude shrugged when she looked at him. 'If it's the same vintage as this machine then I'd say it's more than likely, wouldn't you?'

'It's possible. But I drove along the route the truck would have taken on my way here and I didn't see any sign of it—' She broke off when the radio crackled. The reception was terrible and she winced when a series of ear-splitting shrieks erupted from the handset. Twisting the dial, she tried to find a better signal, but it was no clearer.

'Here, let me have a go.'

He reached over and took the radio off her before she could object. He turned the dial the merest fraction and the next moment, Claire heard Lola's voice flowing across the airwaves. He handed the handset back to her with a smile that immediately set her teeth on edge. She knew it was silly to get upset over something so trivial, but his actions smacked of condescension and it was the one thing guaranteed to rile her.

Andrew had displayed the same high-handed attitude towards her. He had treated her with a mixture of charm and contempt from the moment they had met only she had been too naive to realise it. The way he had taken over at every opportunity had seemed touchingly gallant and she had enjoyed having him take care of her. It had taken her a while to realise that there was nothing gallant about his desire to rule her life, and definitely nothing gallant about the way he had reacted when she had told him that she no longer wanted to see him. Sickness roiled inside her at the memory and she forced it down. She had nothing to fear because she wasn't going to put herself in that position again.

'Thank you,' she said coldly, turning so that she could speak to Lola without having to look at Jude. 'Hi, Lola, it's me—Claire. I'm at the airfield and the truck hasn't arrived. Have you heard anything?'

'Not a word, hon. Give me a second and I'll see if I can get hold of the driver.'

Claire waited while Lola tried to contact Ezra, the truck driver. The heat was stifling that day and she could feel sweat trickling between her shoulder blades. The boiler suit she was wearing wasn't the most comfortable outfit in these conditions but all the women on the team made a point of covering themselves up whenever they left the hospital. Although the Mwurandans were lovely people on the whole, there had been a few unpleasant incidents recently, and it was safer to err on the side of caution.

'I can't raise him, Claire. I'll keep trying but at the moment I can't get a reply.'

Lola came back on the line. Claire frowned when she heard what the other woman said. 'Maybe his radio's down. Some of the sets are on their last legs, so that could be the problem.'

'Could be. Anyway, you'll be driving back along the same route, won't you, so you should pass him on the way.'

'I suppose so. Thanks, Lola.' Claire switched off the radio and stowed it under the seat then turned to Jude, trying not to let him see that she was concerned about what might have happened to the truck. 'We'd better make a move. There's no point hanging around here. The driver will just have to bed down in the plane if it's too late for him to drive back to town tonight.'

She straddled the scooter and started the engine then looked round when she realised that he hadn't moved. 'Are you coming or not?'

'Do I have a choice?' He sighed as he swung his leg over the seat. 'It's either a ride on this contraption or a night in the hold. Not much of a choice really, is it?'

'What did you expect? A chauffeur-driven limousine?' Claire retorted, letting out the clutch. The motorbike bucked as the gears engaged and she heard him swear as he grabbed hold of her around the waist.

'Do you have a licence for this thing?' he demanded, leaning forward so she could hear him above the roar of the engine.

Claire gripped the handlebars, her heart pounding as she felt the weight of his body pressing against her back. It had been a long time since she had been this close to a man and the memories it evoked weren't pleasant ones, either. It was all she could do to behave with apparent calm as they set off. 'No, I don't have a licence as it happens. However, I've not had an accident yet, so you should be safe enough.'

She increased their speed as they left the airfield, weaving her way around the potholes that peppered the road, and felt Jude's grip on her tighten.

'You really know how to reassure a guy, don't you?'

'I try,' Claire retorted.

She skirted around a particularly large hole, grinning to herself when she heard his breath hiss out as the rear wheel clipped the edge. Maybe it wasn't a kind thing to do but she had to admit that it felt good to be in control. She had a feeling that Jude Slater rarely allowed other people to order him about and she may as well make the most of it while she could. Once they were back at the hospital, she was going to do as she had said and steer well clear of him. It wouldn't be a hardship. From what she had seen so far, he was more trouble than he was worth!

CHAPTER TWO

THEY DROVE FOR almost a quarter of an hour in silence. Claire suspected that it was a combination of the noise from the engine plus a fear of her driving which was keeping Jude quiet, not that she was sorry, of course. When he suddenly leant forward she had to steel herself not to react as she felt the solid length of his body pressing against her back.

'What's that over there? Is it the missing truck?'

Claire slowed so that she could look at where he was pointing and felt her stomach sink when she spotted the truck partly hidden by some trees. All their vehicles were old and riddled with rust which was why the truck had blended so perfectly into the background; in fact, she wouldn't have noticed it if Jude hadn't pointed it out.

'It looks like it,' she agreed, bringing the motorbike to a halt at the side of the road. She kept the engine idling while she looked around, but there was no sign of movement from what she could see. The area appeared to be deserted, although she wasn't about to take that as proof there was nobody about. It could be a trap set by the rebel fighters and she needed to be on her guard. Switching off the engine, she climbed off the bike, nodding to Jude to indicate that he should get off as well. Opening the seat, she took out the pistol.

'You carry a *gun*?'

The shock in his voice would have been comical in other circumstances but not right then. Claire was starting to get a bad feeling about this and she didn't need him kicking up a fuss.

'This isn't Mayfair, Dr Slater. This is the middle of Africa and there are rebel factions active in the area.' She nodded at the bike. 'Stay here while I go and see what's happened.'

She didn't wait to check that he was following instructions. She just headed towards the truck, sure in her own mind that the handsome Dr Slater would prefer not to risk his *oh-so-handsome* skin. Anyway, she needed to keep her wits about her instead of worrying about him...

'Shouldn't we find some cover? We're sitting ducks out here in the open.'

Claire spun round when she heard him hiss the question at her and glared at him. 'I thought I told you to stay with the bike!'

'You did,' he said shortly, staring past her. His hand shot out when she went to walk away. 'Wait! I thought I saw something move— Yes! There! Just to the left of the truck—did you see it?'

Claire screwed up her eyes against the glare from the sun as she stared towards the truck. 'I can't see anything.'

'It could have been a bird, I suppose.' He turned to her and she could tell from the set of his mouth that it would be a waste of time ordering him to go back to the bike. 'OK. Shall we do this, then?'

'Yes, but stay behind me.' She gave him a grim little smile. 'I wouldn't like you to get between me and any potential target.'

'And here was I thinking that you would love the chance to put a bullet in my back.'

He gave her a mocking smile then set off, ignoring her instructions as he led the way towards the trees. Claire muttered something uncomplimentary under her breath as she hurried after him. Why, for two pins, she would haul him straight back to the plane and have the crew lock him in the hold! Didn't he understand how dangerous the situation was and that they were both at risk of walking into a trap? Yet he had to get all gung-ho about it, playing the big, tough hero protecting the helpless little woman…

'If you're going to curse me then may I suggest you wait until later?' He stopped so suddenly that Claire cannoned into his back. Muscles rippled as he absorbed the impact and she hastily disentangled herself, not wanting to run the risk of storing away the memory of all that warm, hard flesh.

'All that hissing and spitting under your breath is going to be a real problem when we reach those trees.' He glowered at her. 'I need to be able to hear if there's anyone moving about and your mutterings and mumblings will only hamper things.'

'Oh, well, excuse me! I didn't realise you were such an expert in these matters. Maybe you'd like me to walk downwind so I don't interfere with your olfactory processes?'

'Funny. If you're as good with that gun as you are with your tongue, lady, then we should be safe enough.' He treated her to a smile that was all flashing white teeth and very little warmth. 'However, from the way you're holding it—like a freshly skinned rabbit—I very much doubt it. So no more muttering until we know for certain there are no bogeymen lurking in the woods, eh?'

With that he started walking again, ignoring her as he headed towards the trees. Claire glared after his retreating back before she forced herself to follow him. If they hadn't been in such desperate need of another surgeon at the hospital then she would have left him here and to hell with the consequences. So far as she was concerned, the rebel fighters were welcome to him!

They reached the outer rim of the trees and stopped. Jude cocked his head to the side, obviously listening for any sound of movement. Claire held her breath because even though the rebels might be welcome to him in theory, she didn't really want him to come to any harm. He glanced at her and there was no trace of laughter on his face this time. He seemed completely focused on the possible dangers and for some reason, she felt almost ridiculously pleased that he was taking her concerns seriously.

'I'm going to skirt round towards the truck through those trees,' he explained in a whisper, pointing out the route he planned to take. 'I want to see if the driver's still in the cab.'

'I'll keep you covered,' she replied equally quietly, quelling a shiver as she looked around. The thought that someone could be hiding in the scrub, watching them, wasn't a pleasant one.

'You do that.' He gave her a quick grin. 'But if you do see anything untoward then make sure it isn't me in your sights, will you? I don't fancy taking a bullet home as a souvenir.'

'I'll do my very best to miss you,' she agreed sweetly, and he laughed.

'Promises, promises—sounds like the story of my life!'

He slipped away before she could say anything, not that she could have come up with anything apposite. Claire sighed because it was the story of *her* life that she could never come up with a witty response when she needed it. She waited in silence, wondering how she would know when he had reached the truck. He was hardly going to holler, *Yoo-hoo, I'm here*, was he?

Was he?

Her heart sank at the thought that he might not be taking this as seriously as she had thought. After all, Dr Slater knew nothing about the dangers of working in this country. Although the majority of the Mwurandans were kindly, God-fearing people, the rebel fighters stopped at nothing to achieve their aims. In the past two months they had stepped up their campaign of terror and everyone working in the country had been warned to be on their guard.

Claire knew that the Worlds Together team would be pulled out if the situation worsened and that she would have to leave with them if that happened. Although she wasn't officially part of their team, she worked alongside them and there would be no excuse for her to stay if they left. Although her visa expired shortly, she wanted to remain here for as long as possible. The thought of going back to England didn't appeal, so she tried not to think about it.

There was still no sign of Jude and she could feel her anxiety rising. Where on earth was he?

All of a sudden she spotted a movement near the

rear of the truck and her breath hissed out in relief when she realised it was him. He was crouched down beside the back axle and, as she watched, he began to creep forward, using the truck as a shield as he made his way to the cab. He disappeared from view and she held her breath, praying that nothing had happened to him. If it was a trap, she had let him walk right into it...

He suddenly reappeared and she saw him lift up his hand and beckon to her. He pointed towards the trees, obviously indicating that she should follow the route he had taken. Claire gripped the pistol more firmly as she began to make her way through the undergrowth but her palm was slippery with sweat. Twigs snapped and grasses rustled and her heart pounded harder than ever. She was making so much noise that it would have been far simpler and a whole lot quicker just to run across the clearing. Anyone watching was bound to have heard her!

She reached the truck at last and gasped when she saw that Jude had found Ezra, the driver. He was lying on the ground beside the cab with Jude crouched down beside him. She ran forward and dropped to her knees, staring in horror at the bloody mess that was the man's head.

'Is he dead?'

'No. He's hanging on—just.'

Jude's tone was grim as he elbowed her aside so that he could finish examining the man. Claire didn't protest as this was hardly the time to worry about the social niceties. Long, dexterous fingers tested the man's scalp with a delicacy she had witnessed only a couple of times before in her nursing career. Surprisingly, a lot of surgeons had big, clumsy-looking hands, but Jude's hands were as finely tuned as a pianist's as he felt his way across the driver's skull. He looked up and something warm and sweet rose inside her when she saw the concern in his eyes. Despite appearances to the contrary, Jude Slater possessed more than his share of compassion for his fellow man, it seemed.

'His skull's a mess. There's at least two deep depressions, so heaven only knows the extent of the damage. It looks as though he's been clubbed over the head because he certainly didn't get injuries like these from sitting in that truck, minding his own business.'

'It must have been the rebel fighters,' she said shakily, struggling to get a grip. Thoughts like that certainly weren't ones she wanted to encourage. 'Maybe they thought he was transporting equipment to the airport and that's why they ambushed him. They've been doing a lot of work on the runways recently.'

'You could be right.' He sighed. 'I don't know how we're going to get him to hospital but it certainly won't be on the back of that motorbike of yours. It looks as though I'll have to drive the truck back—if it's still working.'

'I wonder why the rebels didn't take it,' Claire said, frowning. There had been a number of similar incidents recently and on each occasion the vehicle had been stolen.

'Probably because it doesn't work,' Jude suggested with a grimace. 'In which case, we're up the proverbial creek without the proverbial paddle.'

He didn't say anything else as he stood up and climbed into the cab. Claire heard the engine screech as he attempted to start it and her stomach tightened with fear. If there was anyone hiding in the trees then now was the time they would show themselves.

The thought had barely crossed her mind when there was a loud cracking noise and she felt the air shiver as a bullet whistled past her ear. She dropped flat on the ground, her heart pounding as more shots were fired at them. Some hit the truck, others ricocheted off the trees, and all were far too close for comfort.

'Hell's bells! These guys really do mean business, don't they?'

The shock in Jude's voice as he dropped down beside her made her smile despite the precariousness of their position. 'This isn't a theme park experience, Dr Slater. This is the real thing, bullets and all. We really *are* being shot at by the bad guys.'

'That tongue of yours is going to get you into serious trouble one of these days.' He ducked as another volley of shots whined over their heads. Rolling onto his side, he glowered at her. 'OK, Ms Know-it-all, what do you suggest? Do we wave the white flag and appeal to the goodness of their hearts? Or do we try to outmanoeuvre them?'

'I don't think they're very big on the milk of human kindness,' she retorted. 'We have a choice. It's either fight or flight, and I know which I prefer.'

'I'm with you there, although I don't know if this thing is up to it.' He shot a disgusted look at the truck. 'That engine doesn't sound exactly tuned for speed to my ears.'

'Probably not if you're used to something more luxurious but we're not so choosy here,' she snapped, pressing her face into the dirt as more shots whined over their heads. Her voice was muffled as she continued. 'We only have one criterion when it comes to a vehicle: does it work?'

'In that case, we have the prince of trucks at our disposal. It works, although I can't guarantee how fast it goes.' He ducked as another bullet hit the truck then scrambled to his feet. 'I'm going to get the driver into the cab.'

'I'll help you.'

'No, you won't. You stay there and keep your head down. I don't want to have to rescue two casualties, thank you very much.'

Claire fumed as he scuttled on all fours to the cab and wrenched open the door. As the newbie member of the team, he seemed rather too keen to hand out orders. She started to get up then dropped back onto her stomach as another hail of shots pierced the side of the truck just above her head. She could only watch as Jude dragged the driver to the cab and somehow managed to bundle him inside. Sweat was streaming down his face by the time he had finished and there were damp patches on his shirt but he still managed to grin infuriatingly at her.

'So, are you coming, then? Or are you going to stay there and enjoy the scenery?'

Claire gritted her teeth as she belly-crawled to the cab. She wasn't going to fall into the unseemly habit of trading insults with him. Fortunately their attackers didn't appear to know that they had moved because they were still firing at the rear of the truck. It meant they would have surprise on their side when they set off.

Jude gripped her arm as she went to climb into the cab. 'I want you to get into the footwell and stay there. Understand?'

Claire did understand and she wasn't happy about

it, either. 'So you can play the all-action hero and get us out of here?'

'Yes.' He grinned at her, a lazy, sexy grin that managed to slip past her defences before she realised it. 'There's no bigger boost to a guy's ego than being able to save a damsel in distress, so don't spoil this for me, sweetheart.'

'I am not and never shall be your sweetheart,' she shot back, hunching down so she could scramble aboard the truck without giving the gunmen an easy target.

'"Never say never" is my motto,' he replied, putting his hand under her backside to give her a boost up.

Claire would have slapped his face if the situation hadn't been so dire. Not just for the cocky remark but for manhandling her as well. She shot into the cab, rolling herself into a ball so she could squeeze into the footwell. The driver was slumped in the passenger seat, mercifully unconscious. That was the one and only good point she could find about the situation, in fact; they wouldn't have to deal with a hysterical patient when they beat a retreat. How they were going to outrun the rebels in this clapped-out old truck was anyone's guess but they didn't have a choice. Handing themselves over to the rebels was a definite non-starter and there was no point trying to fight when…

'I'll take that.' Jude leant down and took the pistol out of her hand. He placed it on the seat then put the truck into gear, swearing colourfully when it failed to engage at the first attempt. There was a hail of shots and the windscreen exploded, showering glass all over the cab, but by that time he had managed to get the truck moving.

They shot out of the trees and careered towards the road as Claire desperately tried to wedge herself into the footwell *and* hold on to the driver to stop him falling off the seat. They hit a rut and she yelped when her head connected painfully with the underside of the dashboard but Jude didn't even spare her a glance. His face was set as he steered the truck across the rutted ground and she shivered. He reminded her of how Andrew had looked that night when he had forced himself on her; he too had been determined to get his own way. It was an effort to push the memory aside as they reached the road and Jude glanced down at her.

'How far is it from here?'

'Five miles, give or take,' she told him, trying to subdue the sickness that had welled up inside her. He *wasn't* Andrew, she reminded herself sharply because she couldn't afford to fall apart.

'Let's hope it's more give than take,' he muttered, jamming his foot down on the accelerator. The rear end of the truck fishtailed before the tyres got a grip and Claire bit her lip. She wasn't going to make a fool of herself by letting him see how scared she was...

'It's going to be OK.' Jude took his hand off the steering wheel and touched her shoulder, and there was a wealth of understanding in his eyes when she looked at him in surprise. He grinned down at her, his handsome face lighting up in a way that made her breath catch but for an entirely different reason this time. 'We're going to make it, Claire. Cross my heart and hope not to die!'

He laughed as he made a cross on his chest then put his hand back on the steering wheel, but Claire didn't say a word. She didn't dare. If she said anything then she was afraid it would be far too revealing.

Her stomach rolled and she had to force down the

wave of panic that rushed up at her. For the past two years, she had felt quite comfortable around the male members of the team. They were simply colleagues and she'd never had a problem working with any of them. However, she knew that state of affairs was about to change. There was just something about Jude Slater that made her feel more aware of him than she'd felt about any man in a very long time. He might not be anything like Andrew but he could prove to be just as dangerous.

Jude could feel the sweat trickling between his shoulder blades. He was scared witless although he had done his best not to let Claire see how he felt. Maybe it was ego which demanded that he mustn't let her know how terrified he was, but he'd be damned if he would start whimpering like a craven coward even though it was what he felt like doing.

He glanced in the wing mirror and felt his stomach try to escape through his boots when he discovered that they were being followed. There were three vehicles behind them and they were gaining on them, too. He jammed his foot down so hard on the accelerator that the engine screeched but he ignored the sound of ancient pistons being put to the ultimate test. If those guys got hold of them then he didn't rate their chances!

'Are they following us?'

He glanced down when she spoke, seeing the fear in her soft grey eyes. He had a better view of her face from this angle and he realised in surprise that she was younger than he had thought, somewhere in her late twenties, perhaps. The cap had been pushed back and he could see strands of honey-gold hair peeking out from under its brim. He'd always had a thing about blondes and he would bet his last pound that she was a natural blonde, too. He would also bet that she had a great figure once she was out of those appalling clothes, although if he didn't keep his mind on the job, he might not get the chance to prove that theory.

'Yep,' he replied laconically, determined not to let her know what he was thinking.

'In that case then can't you make this thing go any faster?' she demanded, glaring up at him.

'If I press down any harder on this pedal, my foot's going to go through the floor,' he retorted, not sure that he appreciated having her demean his efforts to save them. 'It's not my fault if this outfit of yours is too damned mean to buy itself any decent transport, is it?'

'If you mean Worlds Together then it's not my outfit,' she snapped back, bracing herself as they hit another pothole.

Jude grimaced when he heard the crunch of metal because the last thing they needed was a broken axle. He kept his attention on the road although her comment had intrigued him. 'So you don't work for the agency?'

'No. I work with them but not for them.'

He wasn't sure he understood the subtleties of that distinction but it didn't seem the most propitious moment to ask her to explain. The rebels were gaining on them and he grimaced when he heard shots being fired. 'How much further is it now?'

'About a mile, maybe less,' she told him, peering over the edge of the dashboard.

'Get down!' He pushed her head down as a bullet whined through the cab. He could hear more shots pinging off the chassis and hunched over the steering wheel, hoping that none of them would hit him. He groaned. Yesterday he had been sitting in an upscale London restaurant, enjoying dinner, and today he was in a beat-up old truck about to get fried. Talk about the difference a day made!

'Will you *stop* ordering me about! I've been here a lot longer than you and I know the drill.'

He risked another glance at her when he heard the anger in her voice and felt his heart give an almighty lurch. Her cap must have been dislodged when he had shoved her head down and now all that honey-gold hair was spilling over her shoulders. It was so thick and shiny that he physically ached to run his fingers through it. It was only the thought of them careering off the road if he gave in to the urge that kept his hands on the wheel.

'In that case, what do you suggest?' He raised a mocking black brow, not sure if he appreciated feeling so ridiculously aware of her when the sentiment obviously wasn't reciprocated. 'I could stop the truck and ask them nicely not to shoot at us any more, but somehow I don't think they would be keen to cooperate, do you?'

'Oh, ha-ha, very funny. It must be wonderful to have such a highly developed sense of humour, Dr Slater.'

'I've found it very useful at times,' he replied blandly, then ducked when another volley of shots rained over the cab. The rebels were just yards behind them now and they were gaining fast. He had to do something although his options were seriously limited.

'Here, grab hold of the steering wheel and hold it steady,' he instructed. 'The road's relatively straight from here on, so all you need to do is hang on to it.' He grabbed her hand and clamped it around the base of the steering wheel then picked up the gun.

'But I can't see where we're going!'

'Just hold it steady—that's all you need to do,' Jude said shortly, leaning over so he could see out of the window. He had a clear view of the vehicles that were pursuing them and smiled grimly. Raising the pistol, he took aim and squeezed the trigger—

Nothing happened.

'There aren't any bullets in it.'

It took a whole second for the words to sink in. Jude pulled his head back into the cab and stared, open-mouthed, at the woman in the footwell. 'What did you say?'

'The gun's empty.' She glared up at him, her previously soft grey eyes like shards of flint. 'We're in the business of saving lives, Dr Slater, not taking them. That's why there are no bullets in the gun.'

A dozen different retorts flew into his head and flew back out again. There was no point asking how or why or even giving vent to his frustration. Jude took the wheel from her and rammed his foot flat on the accelerator, forcing the truck to formerly undiscovered speeds. They rounded a bend and he let out a sigh of relief when he saw the town up ahead. There was an army patrol stationed just outside it and he stamped on the brakes when the soldiers flagged him down. The woman scrambled out of the footwell as the soldiers approached them with their rifles raised.

'We've an injured man on board!' she shouted out of the window. 'We need to get him to hospital.'

The soldiers obviously recognised her because they immediately raised the barrier and waved them through. Jude felt his spirits start to revive a little as he drove along the road. Not only had he managed to outrun the rebel faction, but he would get their patient to hospital as well. Not bad going for his first day in the country, all things considered.

'Take a right at the end of the road and drive straight across when you reach the crossroads. Sound your horn in case anything's coming but don't stop.'

Jude frowned as he glanced over at her. He would have expected her to be pleased at having got back to the town but she looked almost as edgy now as she had done when they were being pursued.

'You can relax,' he said, injecting an extra-large dollop of honey-coated reassurance into his voice. It was a trick he employed when dealing with particularly nervous patients and it always worked. He was confident that it would work just as well now too. 'We're perfectly safe now.'

'I hate to disillusion you, Dr Slater, but we won't be safe until we're at the hospital.' She smiled thinly as she pointed to a gang of men standing on the corner of the road. 'See those guys over there? They're just waiting for someone like you to come along.'

'Someone like me?' Jude repeated, unconsciously slowing down.

'Keep moving!' She tapped him sharply on the knee so that his foot hit the accelerator and sent them shooting forward. 'You never, *ever* slow down when you're driving through the town. And it goes without saying that you never stop. Those guys will have this truck off you before you can blink.'

'Oh, come on! You really think I'm just going to hand it over to them?' he scoffed.

'If they hold a gun to your head then yes I do. You'd be a fool not to.' She looked him straight in the eyes and he could tell immediately that she wasn't simply trying to alarm him. 'Vehicles of any description are worth a fortune here. They're far more valuable than a human life and I suggest you remember that.'

She didn't say anything else but she didn't need to; she had said more than enough. Jude's heart plummeted as he drove through the town. He had known it wouldn't be a picnic working here, but he had never imagined it would be *this* bad. By the time he pulled up in front of the hospital, he was beginning to wonder if he should have got onto the plane twelve hours or so ago.

'Stay here while I find a porter,' the woman instructed, jumping down from the cab.

Jude took a deep breath as she disappeared inside, determined to get himself back on even keel. Maybe the situation was far worse than he had expected but he would cope. He had to. Quite apart from the fact that he had been warned at his interview that there was only one flight per month in and out of Mwuranda, he had a lot to prove, didn't he?

When he had left the NHS he had been completely burnt out. The pressure of working the kind of hours he had done, added to the daily struggle to find sufficient qualified staff to allow a scheduled surgery to go ahead, had ground him down. Every time he'd had to explain to a patient that an operation couldn't take place, it had taken its toll on him. It had seemed nothing short of cruel to raise someone's hopes only to dash them.

He'd had such high expectations when he had gone into surgery, too, a genuine desire to help those who had needed it most, but he had become disillusioned. Nevertheless, he would have carried on if it weren't for

Maddie, but her death had been the final straw. He had left the NHS and gone into the private sector. It had been either that or give up medicine altogether which he couldn't quite bring himself to do. He had always believed that he had made the right decision, so why did he feel this need to vindicate his actions?

'Right, let's get him out of there.'

Jude swung round when the woman opened the cab door and felt his heart jerk like a puppet having its strings pulled. In that second he realised what was happening and bit back his groan of dismay. It was no longer enough that he proved his worth to his old mentor. Neither was it enough that he proved to himself that he could still hack it. For some inexplicable reason he needed to prove to *her* that he was a damned good surgeon!

CHAPTER THREE

'WE'LL HAVE TO use the triage bay. Resus is full.'

Claire guided the trolley past the queue of people waiting to be seen and elbowed open the door to the triage room. Myrtle, one of the cleaning staff, had just finished mopping the floor and Claire smiled at her. 'Thanks, Myrtle. Can you see if Dr Arnold is anywhere about? We could use his help in here if he's free.'

'I will go and find him for you, Sister.'

Myrtle left the room at her usual sedate pace. None of the local staff ever hurried and they seemed to find it highly amusing when they saw the foreign doctors and nurses rushing around. Claire had found their attitude frustrating when she had first arrived in the country, but she had grown used to it by now. She didn't turn a hair when Benjamin, the porter, took his time positioning the trolley beside the bed although she could tell that Dr Slater was impatient to get on with the job.

'On my count,' she said quietly, determined not to let him know how unsettled she felt by his presence. She grasped hold of a piece of the blanket then checked that he and Benjamin had hold as well. 'One. Two. Three.'

They transferred the injured driver onto the bed and then Bill Arnold arrived.

'You were supposed to be fetching us back a new surgeon not another patient,' he grumbled as he came into the room.

'Stop complaining,' Claire retorted, well used to the middle-aged Yorkshireman's dry sense of humour. 'I could have left the surgeon and just brought you the patient!'

'In other words, count my blessings, eh?' Bill laughed as he came over to the bed and held out his hand. 'Bill Arnold. Nice to have you on board, Dr Slater. What have we got here?'

The two men shook hands before Jude briefly outlined the man's injuries. 'He'll need a CT scan for starters,' he concluded. 'Once I have a better idea what I'm dealing with, I'll want an MRI scan doing as well to check the full extent of soft tissue damage...'

'Whoa! Steady on.'

Bill held up his hand and Jude immediately stopped speaking, although Claire could tell that he wasn't pleased about being interrupted. He was probably more used to people hanging on to his every word, she thought cynically as she began to remove the patient's clothes. Some surgeons seemed to think they ranked second only to God in the pecking order and if that were the case, Jude was in for a nasty shock. The surgeons on the team were treated exactly the same as everyone else, i.e. they were expected to knuckle down and get the job done without a fanfare.

'Is there a problem, Dr Arnold?' Jude asked coolly.

'It's Bill. I dispensed with the formalities a couple of years ago when I retired,' the older man told him. 'And yes, I'm afraid there could be a problem in so far as we don't have access to the equipment you mentioned.'

'What do you mean that you don't have access to it?' Jude demanded. 'Is the radiographer not on duty today?'

'Oh, the radiographer's here all right,' Bill explained easily. 'The problem is the equipment. We don't have a CT scanner or a Magnetic Resonance Imager in the hospital.'

'You don't *have* them,' Jude repeated, looking so stunned by the news that Claire almost felt sorry for him. Obviously it had come as a shock to him to learn that the hospital wasn't equipped with all the usual technology, but had he *really* expected that it would have been? Deliberately, she whipped up her indignation, not wanting to fall into the trap of sympathising with him.

'No. We don't have a CT scanner or access to MRI or PET scanning either, Dr Slater,' she repeated coolly. 'Mwuranda has undergone years of civil unrest and there's no money available for equipment like that. It's difficult enough to maintain an adequate supply of basic drugs, in fact.'

'Then how do you suggest we do our jobs?' he snapped, glaring at her as though he held her personally responsible for the state of the country's medical facilities.

Claire made herself return his stare but the chill in his eyes was unnerving. She couldn't stop her mind darting back to the way Andrew had looked at her whenever she had done something to annoy him. She had to make a determined effort to focus on the present moment. 'The old-fashioned way—through good diagnosis. Isn't that right, Bill?'

'Harrumph, well, yes.' Bill looked uncomfortable

about being drawn into the decidedly frosty discussion. He sighed when Jude looked sharply at him. 'I understand your concerns, of course, but in the absence of any modern technology, we just have to do the best we can.'

'I see.' Jude turned and glared at Claire again. 'Well, I want it putting on record that I'm not happy with the situation. Is that clear?'

'As crystal. I shall make a note of your comments in triplicate, Dr Slater, and ensure that the appropriate authorities are informed forthwith.'

Bill looked even more uncomfortable when he heard the sarcasm in Claire's voice but Jude ignored it as he plucked a pair of gloves out of the box. He bent over the patient, his hands moving over the injured man's skull with the same skill and dexterity which Claire had admired earlier. Maybe he was upset about the lack of modern aids, but he was able to contain his emotions while he got on with the job. And it was a salutary reminder of the way her former boyfriend had been able to emotionally detach himself as well.

Claire quickly excused herself and left. She knew it was unprofessional to leave in the middle of an examination but she simply had to get away. Fortunately one of the local nurses was standing in Reception, so Claire asked her if she would assist in triage then made her way to the office to sign in. Every member of staff had to sign in and out whenever they entered or left the building. Although it was a bit of a bind, they all understood how important it was to know where everyone was in case of an emergency. Now Claire sighed as she realised that she hadn't explained the procedure to Dr Slater. It meant that she would have to speak to him again and that was something she had been hoping to avoid. She'd had more than enough of the man for one day!

Lola was sitting behind her desk when Claire opened the office door and she grinned at her. 'I see you made it back safely, then, hon.'

'Only just.' Claire scrawled her name on the sheet then poured herself a cup of coffee. Walking over to the one and only easy chair, she flopped down onto its lumpy cushions. 'We found the truck on our way back. And the driver.'

'And?' Lola prompted when she paused to sip some of the muddy brown brew that passed for coffee.

'*And* we ended up starring in our very own version of the shoot-out at the OK Corral.' She grimaced as she put the cup on a pile of medical journals which served as a coffee table in the absence of anything else. 'That coffee is disgusting! How long has it been stewing in the pot?'

'Who knows?' Lola dismissed the coffee's pedigree with a wave of her hand. Anxiety was etched all over her face as she looked at Claire in concern. 'Are you sure you're all right? It must have been real scary for you, so don't think you have to pull that stiff-upper-lip routine you Brits are famous for. If you want to bawl your eyes out then go right ahead.'

'I'm fine. Really,' Claire assured her. 'OK, so it was a bit hairy at the time, but I was too angry to be really scared.'

'Angry?' Lola repeated. 'You mean with the guys who were shooting at you?'

'No. With Dr Jude Tobias Slater!'

Claire stood up and started to pace the room, her

temper rocketing as she thought about all the things he had done that day. Ignoring her instructions to stay with the motorbike had been his first offence and his second had been the high-handed way he had taken charge. Maybe they were only minor misdemeanours in most people's eyes but they were far more than that to her. Jude Slater had tried his best to undermine her at every turn and she had too much experience of the harm it could cause to allow that to happen to her again.

She turned and glowered at Lola. 'The guy is a liability! He's pushy and overbearing and, what's more, he seems to think that he knows everything about what it takes to survive out here when he knows nothing at all. Would you believe that he actually expected there would be an MRI scanner in the hospital?'

'It's his first mission, though, hon.'

Lola shrugged, obviously trying to defuse the situation, but Claire didn't want it to be defused. She wanted there to be tension between her and Jude, and lots of it, too, because it would help to blot out everything else. The one thing she mustn't allow herself to do was to like him.

'So?' she scoffed. 'I remember when you arrived, Lola. It was your first mission as well, but you didn't expect there to be all kinds of fancy equipment here, did you?'

'Ah, but I came straight from an inner-city public hospital, so my expectations were already fairly low.'

'I suppose so.' Claire gave a grudging smile. 'From what you've told me, conditions there weren't all that much better than they are here.'

'You got that right, hon.'

Lola laughed. However, Claire knew that her friend

was wondering why she had taken such an obvious dislike to the newest member of their team. There was no way she could explain that Jude reminded her of Andrew, not when she had told nobody about her former partner, so she remained silent and, after a moment, Lola carried on.

'Dr Slater doesn't have my kind of background, Claire. I checked his file while you were out and discovered that he's been working in some fancy private hospital in London for the past five years. How's he going to have any experience of real life when he's been mixing with rich folks like that?'

'In other words, I should cut him some slack—is that what you're saying?'

'I guess so. OK, so maybe you two didn't hit it off, but don't let first impressions colour your judgement. You guys are going to have to work together and it's going to make life extremely difficult if you're at each other's throats all the time.'

Claire knew that Lola was right. However, the thought of having to work with him was too disturbing to deal with right then. She bolted down the rest of her coffee, fixing a smile into place when Lola looked at her in concern.

'Don't worry. I'm not about to do anything rash. I forgot to tell Dr Slater that he needs to sign in, so I'd better go and do it before I forget.'

'You do that, hon. And I bet you find that he isn't nearly as bad as you thought he was.'

Claire didn't say anything. It would serve no purpose to argue with Lola. However, as she left the office, she knew that the one thing she wouldn't do was try to improve her opinion of Jude Slater. She intended to keep him at arm's length and the more things she could find to dislike about him, the easier it would be.

'I'll remove this section of bone. Then we can see how extensive the bleeding is.'

Jude bent over the operating table as he carefully eased the shattered section of bone from the man's skull. It was delicate work and even the tiniest slip could have the most horrendous consequences for the patient but he knew that he possessed the necessary skills. He was a first-rate surgeon despite the fact that he spent most of his time these days stripping out varicose veins.

The thought that he wasn't utilising his talent as he should be doing was unsettling. He had always believed that opting for the private sector had been the right decision. The perks which came with the job were all too obvious: an excellent salary; working hours which allowed him a healthy social life; an environment in which to work where the very best facilities were always available. However, he had to admit that he had become increasingly bored of late. Most of the work he did was purely routine and there was very little that stretched him. An operation like this was completely different. One slip and the patient could be left severely incapacitated and the thought put him on his mettle. As he suctioned away the massive haematoma that had formed inside the man's skull, Jude realised in surprise that he was *enjoying* himself.

'Clamp.' He rapped out the instruction, nodding when the nurse at his side slapped the instrument into his palm. He clamped the damaged blood vessel then carefully removed two minute splinters of bone. Fortunately the meninges—the protective membranes which covered the brain—hadn't been pierced, so once he had cauterised the vein, the bleeding stopped. Nevertheless, it was another hour before he was satisfied that he had done all he could. It was out of his hands now and up to nature to run its course.

Jude glanced at Bill Arnold, who was acting as his anaesthetist. 'I'm going to call it a day. There's not much more I can do for him.'

'From what I saw, you did more than most would have attempted,' Bill replied as he began to reverse the anaesthetic. 'Good work, son.'

Normally, Jude would have bridled if anyone had called him *son* but for some reason he was touched by the compliment. 'Thanks,' he said lightly, not wanting the older man to guess that it meant anything to him.

He left Theatre, dropping his disposable cap into the bin on his way out before making his way to the changing room only to stop short when he opened the door and found Claire sitting on one of the benches. She immediately sprang to her feet when she saw him and he couldn't help noticing how defensive she looked.

'I forgot to tell you about signing in,' she said quickly, and he winced when he heard the hostility in her voice.

It had been obvious when they were in Triage that he wasn't exactly flavour of the month and he could only conclude that it was because of what had happened earlier in the day. Maybe he should have deferred to her instead of taking over like that, but in his own defence, he had been more concerned about their safety than her injured feelings. He had been right, too, he assured himself, so he would be damned if he would apologise when he had got them safely back to the hospital.

'So tell me now,' he said flatly, stripping off the top of his scrub suit and tossing it into the dirty-linen hamper. There was a stack of clean towels on a shelf, so he picked one up and flung it over his shoulder then glanced round when she didn't reply. 'Look, I don't want to rush you but I would like to take a shower this side of Christmas, if it's all right with you.'

'Yes, of course. Sorry.' A rush of colour swept up her face as she hurried on. 'You need to sign in every time you come into work and sign out again each time you leave. The sheets are kept in the office, so if you could sign out after you finish up here that would be great.'

'And what do I do after that?' He shrugged when she looked blankly at him. 'Am I supposed to stay in the hospital, or what? I've no idea about our living arrangements.'

'Oh, I see. I should have explained it all to you before, but things got a bit hectic after we found the truck—' She broke off, obviously reluctant to talk about what had gone on earlier.

Jude sighed as he realised that his assessment had been spot on. She *did* harbour a grudge about the way he had railroaded her and it was going to make life extremely stressful in the coming weeks if she didn't get over it. He was just debating whether he should rustle up some sort of apology when she continued.

'The Worlds Together team doesn't actually live in the hospital. They use the old college as their base, so you'll be staying there.'

'I see. And how do I get there? Do I walk, in which case I'll need directions. Or is there transport available?' he asked, deciding there was no point worrying about what might happen. He would just have to take each day as it came and hope that she would do the same.

'You'll be ferried to and from the hospital in one of the trucks. It not only saves time but it's safer.' She glanced at her watch and frowned. 'In fact, the day shift should be leaving in about ten minutes' time, so you can catch a lift back to the college with them.'

'It doesn't sound as though it's going to be a whole lot of fun working here if we have to sign in and out, *and* use only the official form of transport,' Jude observed dryly. 'The last time I had restrictions like these imposed on me, I was at boarding school.'

'We aren't here to have fun, Dr Slater. We're here to help the people of this country. It certainly won't help them if you get yourself killed.'

'It wouldn't be too great from my point of view, either,' Jude retorted. She had the knack of making him feel as though he was lacking in some way and it wasn't a feeling he enjoyed. 'Anyway, I'd better take that shower,' he said, swinging round. 'I'd hate to blot my copybook again by keeping everyone waiting.'

'You'll be picked up outside the main doors. I'll let the driver know you're coming,' she said shortly, ignoring his final comment.

Jude sighed as she left, aware that it had been extremely childish to say that. There was no point antagonising her when they were going to have to work together. It was just that he wasn't used to people taking such an obvious dislike to him and definitely not a woman. Despite the fact that he made no bones about the fact that he wasn't interested in commitment, most women seemed to enjoy his company and were eager to spend time with him, but not this woman. He'd got the distinct impression that she had only come to find him out of a sense of duty and the thought rankled. He turned on the water, wondering why he was so bothered about her opinion. It shouldn't have mattered a jot what she thought of him but it did. He wanted her to like him—how pathetic was that?

Jude finished showering and dressed then made his way to the front entrance. There was a group of people sitting on the steps, obviously waiting to be collected, so he went and joined them. One of the women grinned at him as he sat down.

'So you're the new guy, are you? I heard that Claire was going to the airport this afternoon to collect you.'

'Jude Slater at your service.' He smiled as he held out his hand. 'And you are?'

'Lesley Morris. One of the nurses,' the woman explained as they shook hands.

'Nice to meet you, Lesley. So far I've met Bill Arnold and a couple of the local staff but that's basically it. How many of us are there on the team?'

'Nine at the moment, although it can and does fluctuate. There are five nurses and four doctors now that you've arrived.' Lesley pointed to a group of women in front of them. 'That's Kelly, Amy and Sasha—they're all nurses. Lola, who's our administrator, is also a nurse and helps out whenever necessary. Javid and Matt are the other two doctors on the team. Matt's working tonight, so you'll meet him at dinner before he goes on duty. And Javid should be along any second now.'

'What about Claire?' Jude frowned as he looked at the women. 'You said there were five nurses, so where does Claire fit in?'

'Oh, she's not part of our team,' Lesley explained. 'Although I don't know how we'd manage without her. If you need something doing around here then Claire's the woman to ask. We call her our very own miracle worker!'

'Praise indeed,' he replied lightly, wondering who Claire worked for if she wasn't part of the Worlds Together team. Although his knowledge of the agency's set-up was pretty sketchy, he didn't recall anyone mentioning at his interview that they would be working with another aid agency, yet who else could she be working for? He was just about to ask Lesley when the truck arrived and everyone stood up.

Jude followed them down the steps and waited his turn to board. Lesley had moved to the front. She patted the seat, indicating that he should sit next to her, so he climbed over everyone's legs and squeezed into the gap. The driver was just about to fasten the tailgate when Jude saw Claire coming out of the hospital and he felt his heart give an almighty lurch. She had shed the ugly old boiler suit and was wearing a light grey dress with a prim little white collar and cuffs. She had also got rid of the baseball cap and her blonde hair was caught back at the nape of her neck.

Jude's pulse began to drum as he took stock of the gently rounded curves of her breasts and hips, the purity of her profile. There was no doubt that she was a very beautiful and desirable woman and he would have needed to be dead from the neck up *and* down not to notice that fact...

'Do you want a lift, Sister? I can call at the convent on my way back if it will save you having to wait.'

Jude heard what the driver said but it was a full

minute before the words registered and he gasped. It felt as though everything was happening in slow motion as he watched Claire walk over to the truck and climb on board. She was obviously popular because everyone greeted her with a smile although he didn't. He couldn't. He could neither smile nor speak as he watched her take her place on the bench. He closed his eyes, wondering if his mind was playing tricks. It had been a stressful day and it was understandable if he was a little…well, confused.

The truck set off with a lurch and Jude opened his eyes, expecting that the scene would have changed. It hadn't. Claire was sitting serenely on the bench, her hands lightly clasped in her lap. A breeze suddenly blew into the truck and he saw her lift up her hand to tuck a loose strand of hair behind her ear. Jude felt a huge great wave of regret wash over him. Even though he knew he had no business feeling that way, he couldn't help it. It just seemed like such a terrible waste. Claire might be beautiful and desirable but she was also strictly off limits to him or to any other man.

The fact was that *Sister* Claire was a nun!

CHAPTER FOUR

CLAIRE COULD FEEL Jude Slater staring at her although she didn't look at him. Seeing him standing in the changing room had awoken feelings that she had never imagined she would experience again. She had honestly thought that she was incapable of feeling desire after what Andrew had done, but there was no point pretending. The sight of Jude's leanly muscular body had unlocked a whole host of emotions and now she just wanted to forget about them.

When Javid Khan asked her what had happened on the way back from the airfield, she sighed under her breath. She would have preferred not to talk about what had gone on but she could hardly say so in case it started people speculating. The last thing she wanted was everyone thinking that she had a problem with Dr Slater even if it were true.

'It was a bit of a rough ride,' she said lightly, trying to avoid going into detail. 'Basically, the rebel fighters had set up a trap and we walked straight into it. We were lucky to get back here.'

'That's an understatement if ever I heard one.' Javid grinned at her. 'I saw the state of that truck. There were so many bullet holes in it that you could have used it as a colander!'

Everyone laughed, although Claire noticed that Jude didn't join in. She shook her head when Kelly asked her how the driver was doing. 'I wasn't there during surgery, so you'll have to ask Dr Slater.'

Kelly repeated the question to Jude and Claire felt her heart skip a beat when she heard the edge in his voice as he explained that although the driver had come through the operation, the next twenty-four hours were critical. She shot him a wary glance but for some reason he seemed reluctant to look at her. Claire frowned as she studied the rigid set of his jaw. He hadn't looked this uptight when they had been fleeing from their attackers, so what was wrong with him?

The question nagged away at her for the rest of the journey. When the driver pulled up in front of the college, Claire realised that she wouldn't be able to rest until she found out the answer. Maybe it had nothing to do with her but the least she could do was to ascertain if Jude had some sort of a problem. After all, she was supposed to be helping him settle in and, so far, she had done very little towards that goal.

She told the driver that she had decided to spend the night at the college and followed the others out of the truck. She had stayed there many times before, mainly when there had been a problem getting back to the convent. There was no real reason why she should continue living there, in fact. Her role as an observer for the WHO had long since ended but it had seemed easier to stick to the arrangements. She knew that the nuns had come to rely on her. Most of them were elderly and she helped out as much as she could with the children they cared for. What would happen when she left Mwuranda was open to question but she knew that the nuns wouldn't be able to continue running the orphanage if they didn't get extra help.

'Oh, great! You've decided to stay over, have you?' Lesley looped her arm through Claire's as they walked into the building together.

'I thought it'd be easier than asking the driver to take me all the way back to the convent,' she explained, skirting around the real reason for her change of plans. She glanced round when Jude and Sasha followed them inside and couldn't help noticing that once again he avoided looking in her direction.

'I don't know why you don't move in with us,' Lesley declared. 'Oh, I know you like to help the sisters, but they're going to have to do without you at some point, Claire. You're due to return to England soon, aren't you?'

'I suppose so.'

'Don't you want to go home?' Lesley demanded, frowning. 'I'd have thought you would have had more than enough of this place by now. How long is it since you first came out here?'

'Almost two years.' Claire replied distractedly as she watched Jude drop his bag by the door then wander into the communal sitting room. If she was to find out what was troubling him then it would be best to get it over sooner rather than later, she decided. If he did have a problem then she knew from experience how quickly it could affect the smooth running of the team and that was something she wanted to avoid. They were under so much pressure as it was that even the smallest problem could rapidly turn into a major issue.

She turned and smiled at Lesley. 'I just need a word

with Dr Slater—make sure he's up to speed about what's expected of him. I didn't get chance to run through all the dos and don'ts with him before.'

'No wonder. You were too busy dodging bullets from the sound of it,' Lesley retorted.

Claire laughed. 'Something like that. Anyway, is it OK if I use the spare bed in your room?'

'Be my guest. Another pair of hands to swat the bugs is always welcome!'

Lesley sketched her a wave and headed up the stairs. The rest of the team had already disappeared and Claire guessed that they would be using the time to shower before dinner. It was the ideal opportunity to speak to Jude on his own.

She went into the sitting room, feeling her pulse leap when she found him standing by the window. He had his back towards her and there was an air of dejection about the way he stood there, staring out across the grounds. Had he suddenly realised what he had let himself in for? she wondered. From what Lola had told her, this type of work was a million miles away from what he was used to and she couldn't help wondering what had prompted him to apply for the job in the first place. Had it been just a desire to help his fellow man? Or had there been another reason?

He suddenly turned and Claire hurriedly squashed the thought when she saw him stiffen as he caught sight of her. He seemed less than entranced to see her and she found herself wishing that she hadn't bothered seeking him out. So what if he had a problem: why should she care? However, deep down she knew that she owed it to the team to find out what was troubling him.

'I just wanted to check that you're all right.' She

shrugged. 'I didn't get chance to discuss any issues you may have earlier, I'm afraid. There was too much going on.'

'Don't worry about me. I'm fine.' He moved away from the window and she could see a nerve beating in his jaw as he crossed the room.

'Oh, right, well, good. I know it must seem a bit restricting to have to stick to all these rules and regulations, but we have to be careful.'

'Of course. And I'm sure I'll get used to it.' He stopped, one dark brow arching when she failed to move out of his way. 'Was there anything else you wanted to say to me?'

'Er...no, not at all.'

Claire hurriedly stepped aside to let him pass, wondering why she had the feeling that he was upset about *her*. She gave herself a mental shake because now she was being ridiculous. He was probably tired and stressed after everything that had happened that day and the best thing she could do was to give him some space. A lot of new recruits found it overwhelming to be thrown in at the deep end, and Jude Slater had been thrown into deeper water than most. The fact that he had coped so well was to his credit.

The thought was more than a little alarming in view of the fact that she was determined not to find anything good about him. Claire hurried from the room and headed upstairs. Lesley was in the bathroom when she got to their room, so she sat down on the spare bed and waited for her to finish. She didn't have a change of clothes with her but she knew that her friend would lend her something to wear.

She sighed as she pulled the clip out of her hair and

shook it free. She couldn't remember the last time she'd had anything decent of her own to wear. Normally she wore scrubs in work and either overalls or one of the nuns' dresses after she finished her shift. It was safer not to draw attention to herself when she was travelling to and from the hospital and the plain grey dresses the nuns wore allowed her a certain anonymity. However, all of a sudden she found herself wishing that she had something pretty to wear that night, something that would make her feel like a woman. And it was such a shock to want to proclaim her femininity that she felt fear sweep through her. She had honestly thought that she would never feel this way again, so what had changed? Was it the fact that the scars had started to heal and she was feeling more confident, or was there another reason?

Unbidden a face sprang to her mind and her heart began to pound when she recognised Jude Slater's handsome features. Did she want to look pretty and feminine for *his* sake? Hadn't she learned her lesson, learned how foolish it was to allow a man that much power over her? Obviously not. However, there was no way that she was going down that road again. No way at all!

Jude collected his bag from the porch and made his way upstairs, pausing when he came to the first-floor landing. Sasha had told him that he could choose whichever bedroom he fancied but he didn't want to invade anyone else's territory. He had made enough gaffes for one day.

Jude's mouth thinned at the thought as he made his way along the landing. The doors to most of the rooms were standing open and it was obvious from the clutter lying around that they were in use. He came to a room halfway along the landing and glanced inside, pausing when he spotted Claire sitting on one of the beds. She had removed the clip and her blonde hair cascaded over her shoulders like a silken waterfall. Jude's palms began to tingle as he stared at the shimmering mass of gold. How he ached to touch her hair, to bury his face in it and savour its softness…

He forced himself to move on, feeling like the lowest kind of lowlife. She was a nun, for heaven's sake! A woman who had taken a vow of chastity. Thoughts like that were totally abhorrent and needed to be nipped in the bud yet it was far more difficult than it should have been. Crazy though he knew it was, he couldn't help wondering if she might be persuaded to change her mind about her chosen vocation…

'Idiot!' Jude didn't realise he had spoken out loud until a head poked round a door further along the corridor.

'Far be it from me to disagree with you, but that seems a tad harsh. Who or what is the idiot in question?'

'Me.' A couple of strides took Jude to the room and to the owner of the head who turned out to be a man roughly his age with dark red hair and what looked like a million freckles on his face. Jude held out his hand and grinned ruefully. 'I'm the idiot. I'm also Jude Slater, the new recruit. How do you do?'

'Nice to meet you, Jude.' The man uncoiled himself and straightened up, towering over Jude's not inconsiderable six-foot frame. 'Matt Kearney at your service. As well as being one of the doctors, I'm the general dogsbody around here—I do a bit of this and a bit of that, plus a lot of the other. If there's anything you need then I can usually get it for you. Within reason, of course.'

'That's good to know.' Jude laughed, taking an immediate liking to the other man. He glanced into the room, taking note of the colourful rugs on the bare floorboards and the bright cotton throw on the bed, and nodded. 'Hmm, not an idle boast from the look of it. You've made it very cosy in there, I must say.'

'It all helps, doesn't it?' Matt looked around with an air of satisfaction. 'Everything is locally made, so it's a win-win situation. I get to enjoy some home comforts while I'm here and at the same time help to boost the local economy. The best thing we can do to help the people in this country, apart from patching them up, of course, is to provide them with a living. That's why I'm hoping to get one of the big designer stores on board when I get back to Blighty. I mean, the Chelsea set would go a bomb for stuff like this, wouldn't they?'

'They would indeed,' Jude agreed, thinking how very true that was. Indigenous arts and crafts were very much of the moment with those who had the wherewithal to pay for them. Why, he himself had spent a small fortune on some rugs very similar to the ones on Matt's floor. He had never given any thought to who had produced them, just liked them and handed over the money for them. How much of it had gone to the people who had made them? he found himself wondering. Probably very little, he decided, and the thought made him feel uncomfortable. Maybe he needed to think more about the ethics of what he bought in future.

'Right. I'd better go and find myself a room. Is there one free on this floor or should I try the floor above?' Jude said briskly because he was becoming heartily sick of all these reminders as to his shortcomings.

'Oh, stick to this floor unless you're a fan of bats and don't mind sharing with them.' Matt grinned. 'They're not bad roommates, especially when you're on nights as they prefer to sleep through the day. However, their personal hygiene does leave a lot to be desired.' He pointed along the corridor. 'The end room is free, so help yourself. The women prefer to bunk up together, but we guys don't go in for communal living in quite the same way. Dinner's at seven but don't bother with the black tie. We're very informal. So long as you're wearing clothes, you'll do.'

Matt went back into his room, leaving Jude to get settled in. He unpacked his bag and laid out his shaving gear on the old marble-topped washstand. He hadn't noticed a bathroom on his travels but he would track it down at some point. Glancing at his watch, he kicked off his shoes and lay down on the bed as exhaustion caught up with him. He had been on the go for the past twenty-four hours and a nap would help to recharge his batteries. He was certainly going to need them charging too. From what he had seen so far, this definitely wasn't going to be a walk in the park. No, he would be kept busy from dawn to dusk which wasn't a bad thing if it stopped him thinking thoughts he had no right to harbour.

Closing his eyes, Jude let his mind drift, his heart sinking when it immediately sailed off towards the one direction it was banned from taking. Claire was off limits! If he repeated it often enough then surely it would sink in?

CHAPTER FIVE

DINNER THAT NIGHT was a lively affair. Whether it was the fact that they had someone new in the form of Jude Slater to entertain them, but everyone seemed in very high spirits. Claire collected her plate from Moses, their cook, and carried it to the table. They always ate together of an evening, gathered at one end of the huge refectory table that ran the full length of the dining room. Lesley had lit the storm lantern and she placed it on the table. She grinned when Jude looked at it in surprise as he came back from the serving hatch.

'It's less for atmosphere than practicality,' Lesley informed him. 'It's rare we ever get through an evening meal without the power going off, so we follow the old Girl Guide motto and make sure we're prepared.'

'Oh, I see.' Jude glanced round but there was only one seat left, the one next to Claire. His reluctance to sit in it was obvious and it stung. For some reason she had become persona non grata in his eyes.

Claire edged her chair away as he sat down, not wanting to risk coming into contact with him. Lesley had lent her a dress, quite a pretty one too, made from pale pink cotton with short sleeves and a modestly scooped neck. She hadn't bothered fastening back her hair, just left it loose around her shoulders, and she was aware of Jude's eyes skimming over her but determinedly applied herself to her meal. What he thought of her appearance was neither here nor there!

'This is rather good. What is it exactly?'

She glanced round when he spoke, feeling her heart catch when she found herself staring straight into his eyes. A rich warm hazel with flecks of gold around the irises, they seemed to draw her in and hold her spellbound. It was only when she saw one elegant black brow arch that she remembered he was waiting for her to answer.

'Mutton stew. It's one of Moses' signature dishes, so he tends to make it quite often,' she gabbled. She forked up a mouthful of the spicy concoction to give herself time to calm down but her heart was still behaving in a highly erratic fashion. 'Apparently, his mother used to make it for him—it's her recipe.'

'Clever mum. And clever Moses for getting the recipe off her.' Jude forked up some of the vegetable that had been served with it and grimaced. 'I'm not sure about this though. It's a bit like sweet potato but incredibly dry and stringy.'

'It's yam. I wasn't too keen on it either but I've got used to it now. The trick is to never eat it on its own. Mix some gravy into it to make it more palatable,' she advised, feeling a little easier now that the conversation was centred on such mundane matters.

'Mmm, better, although I doubt if I'll be adding it to my shopping list when I get home.'

Javid claimed his attention then and he turned away. Claire continued to eat, letting the conversation flow over her. Normally, she would have joined in but for some reason she felt strangely detached that night. When the lights suddenly went out, plunging the room into darkness apart from the glow from the hurricane lamp, it was a relief. There was less chance of anyone noticing how quiet she was now and remarking on it.

They rounded off the meal with fresh fruit and coffee, although Claire passed on the coffee. Experience had taught her that it was better to avoid the malodorous brew that Moses concocted with such delight.

'My heaven!' Jude put down his cup and shook his head. 'That stuff is lethal. I mean, I like strong coffee but that's in a league of its own!'

Everyone laughed and started to regale him with tales of their own experiences with Moses' pièce de résistance although Claire didn't join in. All of a sudden everything that had transpired that day seemed to have caught up with her. She felt a shudder run through her and then another...

'Are you all right?'

A lean, tanned hand closed around hers and her heart seemed to stop. Now it wasn't just the fear she had felt when they had outrun the rebel fighters that was causing her such distress but other memories, far more terrifying: Andrew holding her hands as he forced her down onto the bed; trapping her there with his weight as he ignored her pleas to stop...

A moan escaped her lips, like the tiny cry of an animal in pain, and she felt Jude's fingers tighten. 'If you're going to faint then mind the table. You don't need a lump on your head to add to your woes.'

It was so ridiculous that Claire laughed. She laughed and she laughed until she couldn't stop. Everyone had stopped talking and they were staring at her but all she could do was laugh. Jude was worrying about her getting a bump on her head while she was remembering being raped!

'That's enough now, Claire. You need to stop.' Jude felt a wave of alarm engulf him as he gathered Claire into his arms. She was trembling uncontrollably and his hold on her tightened a fraction more. What had caused her to behave this way was a mystery; however, he was less concerned about why it had happened than how he could stop it. She was going to make herself ill if she carried on like this.

'Come on, Claire. Take a nice deep breath.' Holding her at arm's length, he looked into her eyes, feeling more concerned than ever when she stared blankly back at him.

'What's wrong with her?' Lesley came over and crouched down beside them, her pleasant face filled with concern.

'I've no idea but she'd be better off upstairs.'

Jude stood up and helped Claire out of her seat, swinging her up into his arms when her legs buckled. There was silence in the dining room as he carried her into the hall and up the stairs. Obviously what had happened had come as a shock to everyone.

'Here, put her down on the bed.' Lesley had followed them upstairs. Scooping up the dress Claire had worn earlier, she unceremoniously tossed it onto the floor. 'You don't need to stay, Jude. I'll look after her.'

Jude reluctantly laid Claire down on the bed, unable to understand why he was so loath to surrender her to Lesley's care. He had vowed after he had left the NHS that never again would he allow himself to become emotionally involved and he had applied that doctrine to every aspect of his life, too, not just to the patients he treated but the women he dated as well. Oh, he did everything that was expected of him and more, but he always held part of himself in reserve. It was a system that had worked well, one that he'd had no intention of changing, and yet all of a sudden all his protective urges were rushing to the fore. Relinquishing Claire to someone else's care was the last thing he could do, not even if his life had depended on it!

'Has anything like this ever happened before?' he said roughly, ignoring Lesley's offer as it was easier than explaining his need to stay. Admitting that he could no more abandon Claire than he could fly to the moon was the last thing he intended to do.

'No. Never. Claire is normally so calm and controlled. Nothing ever seems to faze her.' Lesley shook her head. 'I really don't understand what's happened tonight.'

'Could it be the stress of the attack?' he suggested, reaching out to smooth back a strand of silky blonde hair before he realised what he was doing. His hand fell to the pillow as a feeling of despondency engulfed him. He had no right to touch her, no right at all. 'It was pretty tense,' he continued thickly. 'I have to confess that I didn't think we were going to make it at one point.'

'It's possible, I suppose, although it isn't the first time that she's been involved in an incident like that. A couple of times the truck ferrying her to the convent has come under attack.' Lesley sighed. 'Maybe it's been building up for a while. I mean, she's been out here for two years now and that's a long time to be under such constant pressure. What happened today could have been the final straw.'

'It sounds likely,' Jude agreed, darkly. Maybe it was expected of the nuns but to his mind there was only so much any human being could take. And Claire had obviously reached her limit.

He stood up abruptly, knowing that now wasn't the time to kick up a fuss. It didn't mean that he intended to let the matter drop; however, he would wait until he could speak to whoever was in charge of the convent before he made his views clear. Once again the realisation that he was allowing his emotions to get the better of him was very hard to swallow and he turned away. 'I've some sleeping pills in my room. I'll go and fetch them. The best thing for her now is a good night's sleep—'

'I don't want any pills. I don't need them.'

Jude glanced round when Claire spoke, relieved to see that she seemed far more alert. Although she was extremely pale still, her eyes were focused when they met his. 'I apologise for making a scene,' she continued huskily. 'It won't happen again, I assure you.'

She went to get up but Jude stopped her. As his hand closed around her wrist, he found himself marvelling at how slender it was. He could, quite literally, encircle it with his little finger and thumb. Once again all his protective urges rushed to the fore and once again he felt shock hit him in the gut.

He didn't do this! He didn't allow himself to feel this strongly any more. If he hadn't cared so much then it would never have hit him so hard when Maddie had died. He had learned a valuable lesson then, learned how to detach himself and feel only on the surface, never deep down; yet it was different where Claire was concerned. He couldn't seem to take that essential step back. What was going on here? Why had he, Mr Deliberately Indifferent, suddenly turned into Mr Overly Protective?

Jude had no idea what the answer was but it scared him to know that he had undergone such a massive change in such a short space of time. He had been in Mwuranda for less than a day and already he was turning into a whole different person, so help him!

Claire could feel the coolness of Jude's fingers on her hot flesh and shivered. Now that the memory of that dreadful night had started to fade, she felt better able to cope, although how she was going to explain her behaviour was another matter. Maybe it would be safer to settle for Lesley's explanation, that she had been under pressure for so long and tonight it had caught up with her. Telling everyone what Andrew had done was out of the question. She only had to recall what he had said when she had warned him that she would go to the police in an attempt to stop him. He had laughed in her face as he had stated that it would be her word against his, and who was going to believe the word of an embittered woman who had been dumped by her boyfriend?

'You need to rest even if you won't take a sleeping pill.'

Jude's voice cut through her thoughts and she shuddered. She mustn't think about the past. She must focus on the present and that meant making sure nobody found out what had happened to her. Even if everyone believed her, did she really want to become an object of pity in their eyes? Someone who needed to be treated differently? A victim? Was that how she wanted *Jude* to view her?

The thought was more than she could bear for some reason. It was an effort to concentrate as he continued. 'I suggest you take a few days off and give yourself a breathing space. If you want me to have a word with whoever's in charge then I'm more than happy to do so.'

'That won't be necessary,' Claire said quickly. 'And as for taking time off, well, I'm afraid that's out of the question. We're working at full stretch as it is and if I take time off then it will put the rest of the team under even more pressure.' Easing her wrist out of his grasp, she stood up before he could stop her. 'I'm fine, Dr Slater. There's no need to worry about me.'

'I disagree. It's obvious that you're far from fine.' There was an edge to his voice now but why should he feel angry about her desire to forget what had happened tonight? Why should he care? Before Claire could work it out he continued in the same biting tone.

'I appreciate that you consider your work a voca- tion rather than a job but it would be foolish to risk your health. I shall speak to the Mother Superior and explain that you need to rest, Sister.'

Sister? Claire wasn't sure why Jude had called her that until she saw the dawning comprehension on Les- ley's face. She bit back a gasp. He thought she was a nun! Oh, she could understand how he had reached that conclusion. Between her choice of clothes and the fact that she lived at the convent, it was an easy mistake to have made. She was about to set him straight when it struck her that it might be better if she allowed him to carry on believing it.

Even though she hated to admit it, Jude Slater *dis-*

turbed her. He made her think about things she hadn't thought about in a long time, made her aware of her own femininity in a way she didn't welcome, and it scared her. She had thought that part of her life was over, that never again would she be attracted to a man. Although she worked with the male members of the team on a daily basis, she had never had a problem with any of them—they were colleagues, no more than that. However, Jude was different. *She* felt differently around him. More vulnerable. More aware. Maybe it would be better if he continued to think that she was off limits.

'Oh, but Claire isn't—' Lesley began, but Claire cut her off.

'I shall speak to Sister Julie myself,' she said firmly, shooting a warning glance at her friend. 'There's no need for you to become involved, Dr Slater.'

'Fine. It's your decision, Sister.' He nodded dismissively, his face devoid of expression. 'Just make sure you get some rest. You obviously need it.'

He didn't say anything more before he left. Claire listened to the sound of his footsteps echoing along the corridor, followed by a door closing, and only then let out the breath she hadn't even known she was holding. There was definitely something about Jude Slater that set all her internal alarm bells ringing…

'OK, so what exactly is going on?' Lesley placed her hands on her hips and fixed Claire with a hard stare. 'Why did you allow the gorgeous, *sexy* Dr Slater to think you're a nun?'

'Because he is gorgeous. And sexy. And because I don't want him practising his gorgeously sexy charms on me.'

'Why ever not!' Lesley exclaimed. 'Oh, I know we're not supposed to form relationships but that's never stopped anyone, has it? I mean, look at Sasha and Javid. They're totally smitten but it hasn't affected their work. So what's to stop you and the gorgeous Jude indulging in an *affaire de coeur*? You're both young, free and single, plus it's obvious that he's interested...'

'Of course he isn't interested!' Claire denied hotly. Colour ran up her face when Lesley treated her to an old-fashioned look. 'He isn't. He's just one of those men who can't stop themselves hitting on a woman. That's all it is.'

'If you say so,' Lesley replied, making it clear that she didn't believe her. Reaching under her pillow, she pulled out her pyjamas. 'Right, time for beddy-byes, I think. There's clean jammies in the top drawer of the chest, so help yourself.'

She headed off to the bathroom, leaving Claire to sort out her night attire. Opening the drawer, she took out the first set of pyjamas she came to. They were made from plain white cotton, very prim and virginal, perfectly in keeping with her new persona, in fact. She smiled wryly as she undressed and slipped them on. *Sister* Claire wouldn't feel the least bit uncomfortable wearing these.

Claire went to the bathroom once Lesley came back and availed herself of the facilities. It was very quiet and she guessed that everyone had settled down for the night. She sighed as she headed back to their room. All she could do was hope that nobody would question her about what had gone on that night. She wanted to forget it and, most important of all, forget what had triggered that bout of near-hysteria. The less she thought about Jude Slater, the better.

As though thinking about him had conjured him up, he suddenly appeared. It was dark in the corridor with only the light from a single hurricane lantern to lift the gloom and he didn't seem to have seen her. Claire felt her breath catch as he ground to a halt when he spotted her. There was a moment when neither of them moved, when the very air seemed to have stilled, packed so full of thoughts and feelings that it could no longer move. And then Jude took one slow step then another until they were facing each other.

His eyes swept over, burning through the thin cotton of her borrowed pyjamas, scorching her. And even though he didn't say a word Claire knew. She knew what he was thinking. Feeling. She knew because it was what she was thinking and feeling too. He carried on, disappearing into the men's bathroom, but it was several seconds before she could move. She went into her room and lay down on the bed, listening to the hammering of her heart. It knew what had happened, knew and was reacting to it even though she didn't want it to.

Closing her eyes, Claire tried to blot out everything except the thought of sleep but it didn't work. How could it when her body was aching, throbbing, begging for fulfilment? For two whole years the thought of being intimate with a man had been repugnant to her but not any longer. Jude had awoken her dormant emotions and now she felt more vulnerable than ever.

How could she be sure that her mind wouldn't conjure up the memory of that dreadful night if she slept with a man again? That she wouldn't relive the horror of what had happened to her? It had been so hard to put her life back together and find a reason to carry on, and she couldn't do it again. She didn't have the strength. Maybe Jude had aroused feelings she had thought long dead but she couldn't allow them to grow and flourish. It wasn't worth the risk of being plunged back into the abyss.

CHAPTER SIX

A SOFT MIST shrouded the landscape when Jude awoke shortly before six the following morning. He hadn't slept well, and he felt tired and out of sorts as he tossed back the mosquito net and climbed out of bed. Gathering up his wash bag, he made his way to the bathroom, thinking about what had happened the night before.

Meeting Claire in the corridor had been the main reason why sleep had eluded him. Every time he had closed his eyes, he could picture her standing there in those oh-so-prim pyjamas. The women he knew back home wouldn't have been seen dead in an outfit like that but Jude knew that no amount of satin and lace could have had the impact those pyjamas had had on him…

He forced the thought aside as he stepped under the shower. The water was on the cold side of tepid but he preferred it that way. Maybe a cold shower would achieve what all his rationalising had failed to do. Claire wasn't for him, he told himself once more. She wasn't for any man. Her life had been promised to a far higher authority.

By the time he went down for breakfast he felt a little better, more positive about his ability to cope. Maybe he was way out of his comfort zone but he could do this. He only needed to get through the next three months and then he could go back to the life he knew, the comfortable existence he enjoyed…

Did he enjoy it, though? Did he derive any real satisfaction from the luxuries he bought and the expensive restaurants he frequented? Weren't they more a means to compensate himself for doing a job that bored him? Weren't there times when he longed for something more taxing, something that would make a difference to people's lives?

As he helped himself from the breakfast buffet, Jude was suddenly beset by doubts again, and he resented it. Bitterly. Maybe he did want to prove his worth but he hadn't realised it would mean him re-evaluating his whole life!

'Skip the coffee if you value your health.'

Jude glanced round when Matt Kearney called over to him. He nodded when the other man held up a flask and waggled it at him. Picking up his tray, Jude went to join him, forcing himself to smile. Maybe he was starting to have doubts about the life he'd led for the past five years but he would keep them to himself. Pride dictated that he present a confident front.

'I take it that's a tad more palatable than Moses' special brew,' he said lightly as he picked up a mango and started to peel it.

'Too right.' Matt poured a small measure of coffee into a plastic cup that he produced from his canvas holdall. 'Wrap your taste buds round that and see what you think.'

Jude's brows rose as he took a sip. 'Delicious! Where on earth did you get it?'

'Let's just say that I have my sources.' Matt tapped the side of his nose and winked.

Jude laughed. 'In other words, ask no questions and hear no lies.' He took an appreciative swallow of the coffee and sighed. 'I hope you can get some more. I may just survive the next few months with coffee as good as this on tap.'

'I'll do what I can but I can't make any promises.' Matt refilled the cup. 'There's a lot of stuff only available on the black market. Oh, I know we're not supposed to buy from the racketeers but it's part of everyday life over here. If you want something badly enough then you have to pay the going rate for it.'

'Well, I'm more than happy to contribute, although I only have dollars with me, I'm afraid. I was told that it wasn't possible to get hold of the local currency outside the country.'

'That's right. The government put a stop to it being traded but dollars are fine. Folk prefer them, in fact. There's less chance of the dollar being devalued,' he explained when Jude looked questioningly at him.

'Oh, I see. In that case, then, just tell me how much you want.'

'Will do, once I know what my contact is charging. Prices tend to fluctuate according to demand, if you get my drift.' Matt screwed the lid back on the flask and stood up. 'Right, I'm off to bed. Have a good one.'

'I'll try.'

Jude sketched him a wave and turned back to his breakfast, savouring the sweetly tangy flavour of the mango which tasted so much better than the ones he bought at home. The bread was rather solid and chewy but he made himself eat a whole slice. He didn't want to risk passing out from lack of nourishment, definitely not if he was in Theatre this morning. Why, who knew what he might have to deal with?

The thought of what the day might bring sent a rush of excitement coursing through him. He was smiling as he picked up his tray and took it over to the rack where the dirty dishes were stacked. There were several trays there which meant that most of the others had eaten already. He had better get a move on, he decided. He had no idea what time they were due to be picked up: Claire hadn't told him that.

Bang! That was all it took, just the thought of her and his pulse was off and running again like an Olympic sprinter. As Jude made his way outside, he tried to tell himself that it meant nothing, that it was merely the result of him and Claire having been thrust together into that highly dangerous situation the day before. Why, it was common knowledge that even professional soldiers formed a close bond when they were forced to face untold dangers together, so it was no wonder that he was having all these crazy thoughts after what had gone on.

Jude did his best but no matter how hard he tried to convince himself that was the real explanation, he didn't actually believe it. Somehow, some *way*, Claire had cast a spell over him and no amount of rationalising seemed able to break it.

Claire was relieved when no one mentioned what had gone on the previous night over breakfast. It seemed that everyone had decided to ignore her outburst and she was relieved. Although she knew that folk would be sympathetic if she explained what had caused it, she couldn't bear to go down that route. She didn't want the people she worked with to behave differently around her, to be constantly on their guard in case they said the wrong thing. She just wanted to be treated the same as everyone else.

That was one of the reasons why she hadn't told anyone at the time. It wasn't only what Andrew had said about the police not believing her but the thought of the effect it could have on her family and friends. It had made her see that staying in London was out of the question. Not only would she run the risk of bumping into Andrew but there was also the fear of somehow letting slip about what had happened to her. When the job with the WHO had come up she had immediately applied for it. No matter what dangers she faced, she would feel safer in Mwuranda.

That was why she had decided to stay on when the WHO job had ended. However, the time was fast approaching when she would have to leave. Her visa was due to expire shortly and she couldn't remain in the country without it. The thought of returning to London weighed heavily on her. She had honestly thought that she had turned a corner but what had happened last night had rocked her confidence. Was she really ready to put the past behind her and get on with her life?

Thoughts tumbled around her head as she went outside to wait for the truck. The early morning air was pleasantly cool although the temperature would start to rise soon. All the nurses were wearing cotton scrubs the same as she was wearing. Lesley had lent them to her and Claire was grateful for her kindness. She would miss Lesley and the others when she left Mwuranda. She would miss Jude too.

Her heart lurched even though she knew how stupid it was to think such a thing. She had known him less than a day, so why on earth should she miss him? She tried to dismiss the idea but it wouldn't go away. She was going to miss him whether she liked it or not.

A movement caught her attention and she glanced round, feeling her heart lurch again when she saw Jude standing on the steps. He was wearing khaki chinos and a white T-shirt, and Claire bit her lip. The soft cotton chinos emphasised the muscular length of his legs while the T-shirt highlighted the midnight darkness of his hair. He looked exactly what he was, an incredibly handsome and sexy man in his prime. Even though she didn't want to be aware of him, she couldn't help it.

His eyes suddenly alighted on her and she saw him frown. Striding down the steps, he came straight over to her. 'I thought you were going to rest,' he snapped, his deep voice grating with annoyance.

'I did.' Claire shrugged, hoping that he couldn't tell how keyed up she felt. Now that he was standing right beside her, she could feel the warmth of his skin and smell the citrusy scent of the shower gel he had used that morning. All of a sudden it felt as though her senses were being swamped by him, that he was invading every atom of her being…

'I had a good night's sleep and I feel fine this morning,' she said, quickly quashing that thought. She wasn't a character in some fifth-rate film. She was a qualified nurse and she knew for a fact that ideas like that were a load of nonsense. Sight, hearing, taste, touch, smell— it needed a lot more than some man's proximity to affect all of them.

'Really? So you're not going to throw another wobble like last night?' Jude folded his arms and regarded her with open scepticism. 'You can swear to that, can you?'

'Yes, I can!' Claire snapped, glaring up at him. Everyone else had had the decency to let matters lie but not him. Oh, no, he had to go raking it all up and make her feel even more unsettled. 'I am perfectly fine, Dr Slater. Thank you for your concern but it is unnecessary, I assure you.'

Fortunately, the truck arrived just then. Claire climbed on board, patting the seat beside her when Lesley followed her inside. Everyone took their places and she was relieved to see that Jude had opted to sit by the tailgate. They set off with a lurch and she grabbed hold of the bench, shaking her head when Lesley apologised as she cannoned into her. It would have been a very different matter, of course, if Jude had been sitting next to her...

Claire erased that thought and concentrated instead on what her friend was saying. Apparently, Lesley had received a letter from her fiancé and wasn't sure what to make of it. She handed it to Claire to see what she thought. Claire's heart sank as she read through the tersely worded paragraphs. Quite frankly, the tone of the letter didn't bode well and she hated to think that her friend might be heading for a major disappointment.

'I've no idea what Tom means about us needing to talk when I get home,' Lesley said as she took the letter back. She frowned. 'I mean, everything's sorted. We've booked the wedding venue and the honeymoon, *and* we've put down a deposit on a house that's being built in an area we both particularly like. What's there to talk about?'

'I don't know,' Claire said carefully. 'You don't think he's having second thoughts, do you?'

'Tom?' Lesley laughed. 'No way! We've been together since sixth form, so I reckon he knows me inside and out the same as I know him. No, I honestly can't see it's that.'

'Then I have no idea what he wants to talk about.' Claire summoned a smile, not wanting to upset Lesley, hopefully, unnecessarily. 'Mind you, I'm no expert when it comes to relationships. My track record is abysmal.'

'Is that why you're so wary of Jude?' Lesley lowered her voice. 'It's as plain as the nose on my face that he's interested in you, Claire, yet you've batted him into touch in the most effective way possible. No way is he going to try anything now he thinks you're a *nun*!'

'Good. I don't want him trying anything.' She shook her head when Lesley rolled her eyes. 'No. It's true. I'm through with handsome, *charming* men like Jude Slater after what happened the last time.'

'Is that why you've remained over here?' Lesley asked curiously.

'Yes. I got well and truly burnt, and I needed time to get over it. Being here has helped enormously,' Claire said quietly.

'Helped but not killed off all the demons,' Lesley said astutely. She patted Claire's hand. 'If you ever need a sounding board then you know where I am.'

'I do. Thank you.'

Claire was touched by the offer even though she knew that she would never take Lesley up on it. Her friend let the subject drop and Claire was glad. She didn't want to think about the past, especially now when she felt so vulnerable. She glanced at Jude and sighed. Was he interested in her, as Lesley claimed? She wasn't sure, not that it really mattered because she definitely wasn't going to get involved with him. Maybe she was far more aware of him than she wanted to be but it didn't make any difference. She still wouldn't risk getting involved with anyone after what had happened.

'I'm pleased with his progress, although it will be a while before we can be sure that he's over the worst. In the meantime, I want him kept sedated. It will allow the swelling in his brain to subside and, hopefully, lead to a better outcome.'

Jude handed Ezra's notes to Amy, who was accompanying him on his rounds that morning. Without wanting to appear boastful, he knew that it would be down to his skills as a surgeon if Ezra pulled through. As he followed Amy to the next bed, he felt his spirits lift. He had felt a little deflated after speaking to Claire earlier that morning but this had helped put things into perspective. Even if his reasons for coming to Mwuranda hadn't been as noble as everyone else's, he could still make a positive contribution while he was here.

The rest of the ward round passed quickly. Jude made a couple of minor adjustments to various patients' medication but on the whole he agreed with his colleagues' recommendations. He had been told that there was a clinic that morning which he would be taking, so after he left the ward, he made his way to the main hall where it was being held. He ground to a halt when he saw the queue of people waiting to be seen. He had never imagined there would be this many!

'This way, Dr Slater.'

Jude spun round when he recognised Claire's voice but she had already turned away. He followed her over to where old-fashioned screens had been set up in the corner to form a cubicle. Inside there was an old wooden table—presumably his desk—a couple of equally elderly chairs, plus a battered couch with a trolley beside it holding an ancient sphygmomanometer. Jude's eyes rested on the single piece of equipment. Was this it, then? Was this museum piece the sum total of his diagnostic aids?

He turned to Claire, unable to keep the incredulity out of his voice. 'You must be joking. You surely don't expect me to diagnose patients with only that to help?'

'Of course not.' Claire reached over and opened a drawer in the table. She brought out a stethoscope and offered it to him. 'There's this as well, Dr Slater.'

Jude took the stethoscope off her and stared at it in disbelief. How could he be expected to function with such a pitiful lack of equipment! Opening his mouth, he started to tell her in no uncertain terms what he thought when he suddenly thought better of it. What would she think if he kicked up a fuss when everyone else simply got on with the job? It was obvious that her opinion of him wasn't all that high and it would only make it sink even further. Was that *really* what he wanted, to be scraping the absolute bottom of the barrel in her eyes?

Jude took a deep breath as he walked around the desk and sat down. Maybe it shouldn't have mattered a jot what Claire thought of him but it did. It mattered a great deal, although he refused to go down the road of won-

dering why. Looking up, he met her eyes, determined
to project an aura of confidence even if his stomach did
seem to be suffering from a bad case of the collywobbles.

'If you could show in the first patient, please, Sister.
We may as well get started.'

'Of course, Dr Slater.'

There was grudging approval in her voice and Jude
was heartened by it. Maybe he did have his doubts but
the fact that Claire approved made him feel much better. He sighed, wondering why she had such an effect on
him. It wasn't as though she was going to play a major
role in his life, was it? Once he had done his stint here,
he wouldn't see her again—their lives were destined to
go in completely different directions. For some reason
the thought filled him with a deep sense of sadness.

CHAPTER SEVEN

'THIS IS JEREMIAH. He's ten years old and lives at the convent. As you can see, his leg was broken and healed badly, causing problems when he walks.'

Claire ruffled the little boy's black curls. Of all the children the nuns cared for, Jeremiah was her favourite. His parents had been killed when rebel fighters had attacked his village. Although Jeremiah had survived the attack he had been badly injured. His left leg had been broken in several places and as there had been no medical aid available, it had set badly, leaving him with a severe limp. However, he certainly didn't let it slow him down.

'Right. Let's take a look at you, Jeremiah. Can you hop up onto the couch or do you need a lift?'

'I can do it, Mr Doctor.' Jeremiah scrambled onto the couch and sat there beaming happily.

Jude laughed. 'Well done. So let's have a look at this leg and see if there's anything we can do to make it better for you.'

Claire moved aside as Jude donned a pair of gloves and started to examine the child. She had been rather surprised by how well he had got on with their patients. Even though she knew that he was way out of his comfort zone, he had an easy and relaxed manner that people responded to. Now she watched as Jeremiah happily answered his questions. There was more to Jude Slater than she had thought and it was unnerving to admit it. She had to make a conscious effort not to let him see how alarmed she felt when he turned to her.

'Can we get X-rays of his leg? I really need to see how the bone has set before I can determine if there's anything we can do.'

'Of course.' She frowned. 'Sister Anne brought Jeremiah in along with a couple more children from the orphanage. She will need to stay with them, so is it all right if I take him to X-Ray? I can ask Lola to stand in for me,' she added hurriedly.

'I can't see why not.' Jude helped the boy off the bed and smiled at him. 'OK, Jeremiah, you go with Sister Claire and have some pictures taken.'

'Will you be able to make my leg better, Mr Doctor?' Jeremiah asked eagerly. 'So I can play football with the other boys?'

'I don't know.' Jude bent and looked into the child's eyes. 'All I can do is promise that I shall try my very best, but it could turn out that your leg is just too badly damaged.'

Claire heard genuine regret in his voice and once again was surprised. As she led the child out of the cubicle, she couldn't help thinking that Jude was turning out to be very different from what she had thought. Not only did he have a definite rapport with their patients but he genuinely seemed to care about them too. The thought sent a warm little glow through her as she stopped at the office to ask Lola to cover for her. She did her best to ignore it as she accompanied Jeremiah to Radiography but it proved surprisingly difficult. The fact was that Jude wasn't the self-obsessed individual she had believed him to be and it was worrying to admit it.

Once the X-rays were done, Claire took Jeremiah back to the hall and handed him over to Sister Anne. The X-rays wouldn't be ready until later in the day, so she told the elderly nun that she would arrange for Jeremiah to be seen again later in the week. The rest of the children had been seen by then, so she waved them off and went back to the cubicle. Lola turned and grinned at her when Claire parted the screens.

'Ah, here's *Sister* Claire back again. Right then, I'll leave you two to carry on.'

Claire flushed when Lola winked at her as she left. It was obvious that Lola knew about the misapprehension Jude was under as to her true status and she couldn't help feeling guilty. She busied herself rounding up their next patient, trying not to think about the trick she was playing on him. She wasn't doing it out of a sense of malice, she assured herself, but purely because it made life simpler. If Jude *was* harbouring any ideas about her then it was far more sensible to nip them in the bud than allow them to develop and create a problem.

It was another couple of hours before they finished. It was the middle of the afternoon by then and the temperature inside the hall was stifling. Claire lifted her hair off her neck as she fanned herself with a spare folder. If she didn't get out of here soon, she might very well melt!

'Is it always this hot?' Jude stood up, easing his damp T-shirt away from his body.

Claire hurriedly averted her eyes when she realised that the cotton had turned semi-transparent in places. The sight of all those finely honed muscles visible through the damp fabric made her feel very on edge.

'It's the hottest part of the day,' she replied huskily, then cleared her throat when she saw Jude glance at her. She certainly didn't want him guessing that she had a problem about the way he looked. 'Of course, it doesn't help that we have to hold the clinic in here. There's very little ventilation in the hall despite its size.'

'Couldn't we hold the clinic outside?' Jude suggested. He frowned thoughtfully. 'If we had an awning or something similar then it would make life easier not only for us but for our patients as well. The last thing sick people need is having to wait around in heat like this.'

'It's an idea,' Claire agreed, wondering why no one else had thought of it. They all complained about the heat when they were rostered to work in the clinic and Jude's suggestion could be the solution they needed.

'Do we have such a thing as an awning, do you know?' Jude queried, then grinned at her. 'Or am I hoping for the impossible, like I did before?' He glanced ruefully at the ancient sphygmomanometer and Claire laughed.

'There's more chance of us finding an awning than any modern diagnostic aids,' she told him with a smile.

'Then what are we waiting for?' Jude returned her smile, his handsome face alight with amusement, and Claire felt her heart skip a beat.

'I've no idea,' she replied, trying to inject a matching lightness into her voice, not the easiest thing to do when her heartbeat was all out of sync. 'If there is anything like that then the only place it can be is in the storeroom round the back. Shall we try there?'

'We most certainly shall.'

Jude pushed open the screen then stood aside for her to lead the way. Claire was conscious of his gaze on her as they left the building. What was he thinking? she mused as they made their way along the path. Was he wondering what they would find in the storeroom or thinking about something else, her perhaps?

She bit her lip as panic assailed her. She didn't want him thinking about her—it was too dangerous. Thoughts led to actions and that was the very thing she wanted to avoid. Something warned her that if Jude ever made a play for her then she might not be able to resist.

My heaven, but she was lovely!

As Jude followed the slim figure in front of him, he was struck all over again by her beauty. It wasn't just the way she looked but the way she moved. Oh, there was nothing overtly sexual about it; she certainly didn't go in for the artful hip swinging that some women employed. No, it was her natural grace that he admired, the straight line of her back, the set of her shoulders, the way she held her head...

He groaned as his mind went flying off again along routes it wasn't permitted to take. The most disturbing thing of all was that he had never really noticed how a woman walked before. It was as though when he was with Claire he was aware of things that he had never paid any heed to in the past and it scared him. He was getting in way too deep and it had to stop.

'Here we are.'

Claire stopped when they came to some outbuildings and Jude made a determined effort to rein in his thoughts. Claire wasn't for him, he reminded himself, needing to keep that thought at the very forefront of his mind. Stepping forward, he tugged at the rusty old padlock that held the doors together.

'Is there a key for this?' he asked over his shoulder.

'Probably, although I've no idea where it might be.'

Claire stepped forward, bending so she could examine the lock, and Jude sucked in his breath when her shoulder brushed against his. Even though the contact was the most fleeting imaginable, he could feel waves of heat fanning out from where their flesh had connected. It took every scrap of control he could muster not to let her see the effect it had had on him, too.

'In that case, it needs drastic action.' Picking up a stout stick, he pushed it between the hasp and the padlock. A couple of sharp twists and the padlock fell away. He grinned as he kicked it aside. 'Either that lock was completely knackered or I'm stronger than I thought.'

'Hmm. I wonder which it is,' Claire retorted, dryly.

Jude chuckled. It felt remarkably good to be on the receiving end of her teasing, although if anyone else had made fun of him, it would have been a very different story. Once again it was unsettling to realise how differently he behaved when he was with her. He deliberately drove the thought from his mind as he prised open the door. The storeroom was packed from floor to ceiling, the thick layer of dust that coated everything making it impossible to tell what it contained.

'Heaven only knows what's in here,' he said, spluttering a little as he pulled at the edge of a rotting cardboard box, releasing a cloud of dust. 'The whole place will need clearing out before we can see what's what.'

'There's no way we can sort through this lot on our

own,' Claire observed with a grimace. 'It will need a whole team of people just to unload all this junk.'

'It will.' Jude huffed out a sigh. 'That knocks my idea on the head, doesn't it?'

'Not necessarily.' She moved aside as he backed out of the storeroom.

Jude raised a questioning brow. 'That sounds as though you have an idea.'

'I was wondering if Matt could come up with something,' she explained. 'Suffice to say that he has his contacts and it's just possible that he might be able to lay his hands on an awning or something similar.'

'Good thinking, Batman!' Jude exclaimed. He grinned at her. 'Shall we go and ask him? We may as well strike while the iron's hot, so to speak.'

'He was on duty last night, so he's not in work today,' she reminded him as they headed back to the hospital.

'Of course. I'll catch him later and see what he says.' He ran his hands over his face to wipe away the perspiration. 'I can't remember ever feeling this hot before.'

'It takes a while to acclimatise,' she agreed then paused. Jude had a feeling that she was debating what she'd been going to say and held his breath because it had to be something important if she was having second thoughts.

'How about a swim to cool you down?' she said finally. She gave a little shrug. 'There's over an hour left before evening ward rounds, so there's plenty of time and it should help to revive you.'

'Sounds great to me,' Jude said huskily. Would Claire join him in the water? he wondered, his heart racing at the thought. He cleared his throat, not wanting her to suspect how much the idea appealed to him. 'Right, which way do we go?'

'Just down here.'

Once again she took the lead only this time Jude refused to let his mind stray even the tiniest bit off course. He couldn't afford to indulge himself when he needed to behave with the utmost propriety. He took a deep breath as they set off through the trees. Claire was placing her trust in him and he wouldn't let her down.

Claire floated on her back, enjoying the sensation of the cool water lapping over her body. Sunlight filtered through the trees and she closed her eyes, letting the play of light and shadow flicker across her eyelids. She could hear the sound of splashing coming from the far side of the pool but she kept her eyes tightly closed. By tacit consent they had each chosen a section of the pool to swim in and she had to admit that she had been relieved. She still wasn't sure it had been a good idea to suggest coming here and it would have been so much worse if they had ended up swimming side by side. The thought of Jude's powerful body so close to hers was far too disturbing.

'This is great!'

Jude's voice carried across to her and Claire reluctantly opened her eyes. He was swimming towards her now, his arms cleaving effortlessly through the water. Sunlight glinted off the droplets of water beading his skin, highlighting the perfectly honed muscles in his arms and shoulders, and she felt her mouth go dry.

There was no doubt that the sight of him was having an effect on her.

He laughed when he reached her. 'I may just survive if I can come here and have a dip from time to time. Thank you so much for suggesting it. It was an excellent idea.'

'You're welcome.'

Claire bit her lip when she realised how uptight she sounded but it was hard to respond calmly when he was this close to her. She decided that it might be wiser if she got out of the pool and let her feet drift down to the bottom, but the water was deeper than she had thought. She coughed as she sank beneath the surface and swallowed a mouthful of water.

'Steady!' Jude gripped her arm and drew her safely back to the surface. He looked at her in concern. 'Are you all right?'

'Ye-yes.' She coughed again, trying to expel the water from her lungs, and his grip tightened.

'Don't try to speak. Come on, I'll help you out.' Before Claire realised what was happening, he caught hold of her around the waist and lifted her up onto the bank. Levering himself out of the water, he crouched down beside her. 'Try to relax. The tenser you are, the more difficult it will be to breathe.'

He put his arm around her, obviously trying to encourage her to follow his instructions, but it was impossible. In the absence of anything else, she had opted to swim in the top half of her scrubs. It was something she had done many times before but all of a sudden she was acutely aware of how the wet cotton was clinging to her skin, outlining the curves of her breasts and hips. It was two years since she had been naked in front of

a man and even though she wasn't naked now, it felt
as though she was. Unbidden her eyes rose to his and
she saw the exact moment when concern changed to
something else, an emotion that both scared and excited
her. To see such naked desire in Jude's eyes was something she wasn't prepared for. When he bent towards
her, she didn't move; she just sat there and waited…

'Hey there. Looks like you two have beaten us to it!'

Jude drew back abruptly when Lesley appeared
closely followed by the rest of the team. He gave Claire
a last searching look and she couldn't fail to see the
puzzlement in his eyes before he slid into the water.
Claire felt a rush of panic assail her. Was he wondering why she hadn't pushed him away? Why she
hadn't given any sign that she didn't welcome his advances? She knew it was true and it was the last thing
she wanted. She didn't want to give Jude the wrong
impression, certainly didn't want to encourage him,
but what had happened just now had shaken her. If
they hadn't been interrupted then who knew where it
could have led?

'It's a real scorcher of a day, isn't it? Perfect for a
dip,' Lesley declared cheerfully as she made her way
over to where Claire was sitting. The others had already jumped into the water and Claire was relieved
to see that Jude had joined them. She turned to her
friend, unable to disguise her anxiety.

'Can I borrow your towel? I didn't bring one with
me.'

'Of course.' Lesley handed her the towel, her face
filling with concern when she realised how tense Claire
looked. 'Are you all right, love? Nothing's happened,

has it?' She glanced towards the pool and her mouth thinned. 'Jude didn't try anything, did he?'

'No! Of course not.' Claire forced herself to smile. 'He's been the perfect gentleman.'

'Good. I'm glad to hear it.'

Lesley returned her smile but Claire could tell that her friend was wondering what had upset her. Shaking out the towel, she wrapped it around herself, not wanting to explain why she was so on edge. If she did that then she would have to tell Lesley why she could never have a relationship with Jude and that wasn't an option.

'I think I'll get changed,' she said hurriedly. 'There's a couple of things I need to do before I go off duty but I'll pop back with a dry towel for you.'

'Oh, don't worry about it. I'll borrow Kelly's spare.' Lesley stripped off her scrubs and dropped them on the ground. She was wearing only her underwear beneath, but she didn't let that worry her as she slid into the water. 'See you later,' she called as she set off across the pool to join the others.

Claire watched her for a moment then turned away and headed back to the hospital. How she envied Lesley and the other women, envied their confidence and their self-assurance. One of the worst things about what had happened was the fact that it had made her doubt herself. Had she given out the wrong signals that night? she wondered for the umpteenth time. She had wanted only to end the relationship but was she to blame for what had happened? Had she—as Andrew had claimed—brought it upon herself?

She bit her lip as the old doubts were joined by fresh ones. Had she done the same thing just now, led Jude to think that she had wanted him to touch her, kiss her? She couldn't put her hand on her heart and swear it wasn't true, not when she recalled the effect he'd had on her. Fear rose inside her. It would be so easy to make another mistake. Far too easy with Jude.

CHAPTER EIGHT

JUDE WAS DISAPPOINTED to find that Claire wasn't in the dining room when he went down for dinner. He hadn't seen her since she had left the pool and he had been hoping that she would be there that night. Jeremiah's X-rays had come back and he wanted to discuss them with her—or that was what he had told himself. It had seemed safer than admitting that he desperately wanted to see her.

Jude sighed as he went to the serving hatch. He had come so close to crossing the line today. If they hadn't been interrupted then he knew that he would have kissed her. He felt guilty as hell about it, too, and yet he couldn't rid himself of the thought that Claire might not have spurned his advances. Even though he knew it was madness, he couldn't get the idea out of his head. After all, she must have known what was about to happen, so why hadn't she stopped him? Why had she sat there, looking at him? It didn't make sense which was why he needed to speak to her. He mentioned her absence to Lesley as they carried their plates back to the table.

'What's happened to Claire tonight?' he said, deliberately keeping his tone light.

'She's gone back to the convent,' Lesley explained as they sat down. 'Apparently, the nuns have found some old cartoons and they're planning to show them to the kids tonight as a treat.'

'Oh, I see.' Jude dredged up a smile. He certainly didn't want Lesley guessing how disappointed he felt. That would only lead to questions and that was the last thing he wanted. 'Well, I'm sure the children will enjoy them. They've been through such a lot, from what I can gather. They deserve a bit of fun.'

'They do indeed.' Lesley forked up a mouthful of rice. She chewed and swallowed it then looked at him. 'Nothing happened today at the pool, did it?'

'Such as?' Jude said, feigning surprise although his heart had started pounding.

'I don't know. That's why I'm asking you. Only Claire seemed very…well, *uptight*, for want of a better word. I wondered if you two had fallen out about something.'

'No, of course not!' Jude exclaimed in dismay. 'Why? Did Claire say that we had?'

'No. On the contrary, she said you'd been the perfect gentleman.' Lesley sighed. 'Take no notice. It's just that she seemed very tense earlier on and I was wondering if there was a reason for it.'

'And you've no idea what was wrong with her?' Jude asked, overwhelmed by guilt. Had he completely misread the situation? Far from being receptive, had Claire been upset by what had so nearly happened?

'None at all. I love Claire to bits. She's one of the sweetest, kindest people I know, but she doesn't give much away. I know nothing about her past life, for instance, apart from the fact that she was working in London before she came out here.' Lesley grimaced. 'Still, we all have our secrets. I'm just being a nosy old bag!'

Jude laughed as he was expected to do but he couldn't deny that he felt dreadful. The thought that he had upset Claire was more than he could bear. He wanted to improve her opinion of him, not make it any worse!

They were halfway through the film show when five-year-old Bebe started crying and clutching her stomach. Claire hurriedly got up and went to her. Crouching down, she laid her hand on the child's forehead and was dismayed to discover how hot she felt. When Sister Anne came to see what was happening, Claire told her that she would take the little girl to the sick bay. She got Bebe settled in a bed and examined her. It was immediately apparent that the child was in a great deal of pain; she started screaming when Claire gently palpated her abdomen.

'Shh, sweetheart. I'm sorry. I didn't mean to hurt you.'

Claire stroked the little girl's cheek but she had to admit that she was extremely concerned. Although it wasn't possible to make a conclusive diagnosis, Bebe was exhibiting all the symptoms of appendicitis, and if that were the case then she needed to be seen immediately by a doctor. When Sister Julie came to see what was happening, Claire explained her concerns to her.

'So what do you suggest, Claire?' Sister Julie asked anxiously. 'Shall we try to get hold of a driver and take her to the hospital?'

'I think it would be far too much for her,' Claire replied, glancing at the little girl. 'She's in tremendous pain and being jolted over all those potholes will only make matters worse. No, we need to get one of the doctors to come here and see her.'

'In that case I shall radio the hospital and see what they can arrange.'

Sister Julie hurried away, leaving Claire to watch over the child. She fetched a bowl of tepid water and gently sponged Bebe's face and neck. The child's high temperature worried her most of all as it could signify that her appendix had perforated and that peritonitis had set in, and that was extremely serious. It was a relief when she heard footsteps coming along the corridor some time later, heralding the arrival of one of the doctors from the Worlds Together team.

Claire straightened up, the welcoming smile freezing on her lips when Jude followed Sister Julie into the room. For some reason she hadn't expected him to respond to their call for assistance and it threw her completely off balance to see him standing there. In a fast sweep, her eyes travelled from the top of his gleaming black hair to the tips of his expensively shod feet and she only just managed to bite back her groan as another image promptly superimposed itself on the reality before her. Now all she could see was Jude as he had looked that afternoon, his powerful body gleaming with moisture as he had sat on the edge of the pool, looking at her with such hunger in his eyes.

Her breath caught because she knew it was an image that was going to stay with her for a long time to come.

'There's a strong chance her appendix has perforated.'

Jude moved away from the bed and went over to the sink to wash his hands. He glanced round, doing his best to contain his feelings when Claire remained at the child's bedside. Maybe he should put it down to concern for their patient; however, he suspected there was a very different reason why she appeared so keen to maintain her distance from him. Once again he felt a rush of guilt rise up inside him so that it was an effort to concentrate when she spoke.

'I did wonder if it might be that with her running such a high temperature.'

Her voice was cool, in keeping with her overall demeanour since he had arrived, and Jude sighed. If he had upset her then he wished to heaven that she would come out and say so. Treating him with this icy politeness only made him feel worse!

'If peritonitis has set in then her temperature will be elevated,' he replied gruffly. He dried his hands and went back to the bed, taking care not to encroach on her personal space. He'd committed enough sins for one day! 'I'll need to operate immediately and see what's going on. If her appendix has ruptured, the longer the delay, the worse the outcome will be. Is there anywhere suitable here at the convent or will we need to transfer her to hospital? I'd like to avoid that if it's possible,' he added.

'Actually, the convent used to have its own hospital. Apparently, the nuns used to run it before the uprising. It was closed then but I know there was an operating theatre,' Claire explained then grimaced. 'However, it's not been used for years, so I've no idea what state it's in.'

'Then we'd better go and take a look.' Jude raised his brows when she failed to move. 'If you could show me the way, please, Sister?'

'Oh! Yes. Of course.'

A touch of colour stained her cheeks as she hurriedly led the way from the room. Jude forbore to say anything as he followed her along the corridor, but her reluctance to be around him was going to make life extremely difficult in the coming weeks. Although he appreciated why she was behaving this way, he couldn't help wondering why she hadn't made her feelings clearer that afternoon. If she had given him even the tiniest hint that she had felt uncomfortable then he would never have let things go that far. Once again the thought that there was something odd about her behaviour rose to his mind but he blanked it out. He wasn't going to complicate matters even further by going down that route again.

Claire stopped when they reached a set of double doors. Pushing open one of the doors, she felt for the light switch. 'I hope the lights still work,' she murmured.

Jude stepped inside when the lights came on, turning in a slow circle as he took stock. Although the equipment was dated, there appeared to be everything there they needed. The other plus point was that the whole place was spotlessly clean. 'This is fine,' he declared. 'I've brought my case with me, so we just need to make sure that the operating table and anaesthetic equipment are sterile before we start.'

He glanced at Claire, keeping his face free of expression. Maybe he was puzzled by her behaviour but it would be better to leave things how they were rather than go raking it all up. He didn't want to embarrass her and he certainly didn't want to explain why *he* had acted the way he had done. Heat ran through him at the thought of admitting how much he had wanted to kiss her. It was out of the question to do that.

'Have you anaesthetised a patient before?' he asked, deliberately focusing on the task at hand.

'Yes. Bill showed me what to do, although it was only the once when he wasn't feeling well. I'm certainly no expert,' she added quietly.

'So long as you understand the basics,' Jude replied curtly. 'However, if you're tied up doing that then I'll need someone else to assist me. Would one of the sisters be able to help, do you think?'

'I'm not sure.' She frowned as she considered the question and Jude's hands clenched. All of a sudden he was overwhelmed by the urge to smooth away those tiny lines marring her brow. It took every scrap of will-power he could muster not to give in to it.

'Sister Julie used to be a nurse—I remember her mentioning that she worked at St. Linus's Hospital in London, although I've no idea which department she was in.'

She looked up and Jude hurriedly adopted a noncommittal expression. The thought of running his fingertips over her brow was giving him hot and cold chills and it was alarming to realise how out of character he was behaving. He had dated many beautiful women over the years, not only dated them either but slept with them as well. However, he couldn't remember ever feeling this aroused before.

'Perhaps you could ask her if she would assist me,' he suggested, his voice grating. He saw Claire glance at him but thankfully she didn't say anything before she left.

Jude went to check on Bebe again, doing his best to ignore all the crazy feelings rushing around inside him. He had sworn after his experiences five years ago that he would never allow himself to become emotionally involved again but it was different with Claire—he couldn't seem to detach himself as he usually did. She wasn't for him; she never could be his, he reminded himself. But even though his mind understood that rock-solid, his heart refused to believe it. He sighed wearily. Maybe it was being here that was causing the problem. He was so far out of his comfort zone that everything was all mixed up: his thoughts, his feelings, what he wanted from life; every single thing. Once he was back in England it would be a different story. He would pick up the threads and carry on as before.

He frowned as he looked at the little girl lying in the bed. Once again the thought of continuing to live his life the way he had been doing held very little appeal. He had a feeling that nothing would be the same ever again.

Sister Julie agreed to help, so in a very short time the operation went ahead. Once Jude was satisfied that Bebe was properly anaesthetised he made an incision in her abdomen. Claire gasped because it was immediately apparent what had happened. Although the appendix had perforated, the infection had been contained by the omentum—the fold of membrane that hangs in front of the intestines. This had stuck to the appendix and formed an abscess which was why the little girl had been in such pain.

'She'll need antibiotics before I can risk draining this abscess and removing the appendix,' Jude declared. He looked at Claire over his mask and she could see the concern in his eyes. 'She's a very sick little girl and the outcome is by no means guaranteed.'

Claire nodded although she didn't say anything. The thought of the child's life being at risk after everything she had been through had brought a lump to her throat and she didn't want Jude to know how emotional she felt. For some reason she knew it would make her feel even more vulnerable.

They returned Bebe to the sick bay. Fortunately, Jude had brought antibiotics with him, so Claire set up a drip, although she suspected that the little girl would need something stronger to deal with the infection. She wasn't surprised when Jude announced that he intended to transfer Bebe to hospital as soon as possible.

'Can it wait until the morning?' Claire asked as she finished taping the cannula to Bebe's arm. She sighed when she saw him frown. 'I know how important it is to get the correct antibiotics into her, but it's too risky to drive into town at this time of the night. If it can wait till daylight, it will be much safer.'

'I suppose so,' he agreed with marked reluctance. 'But I'd like to leave at first light. The sooner we get the antibiotics sorted, the better her chances will be.'

'Of course.' Claire moved away from the bed, her breath catching when her hand accidentally brushed against his arm. She could feel the silky-soft hair on his forearm tickling her skin and swallowed as she was beset by a sudden rush of awareness. She hurried to the door, desperate to put some space between them. The last thing she needed was to be even more aware of him than she already was.

'I'll get onto Lola and make arrangements for Bebe to be moved in the morning,' she said, over her shoulder.

'Thank you.' There was something in his voice that made her heart race. Had he felt it too? Felt that flash of awareness that had passed through her? Common sense decreed it was impossible, that no one could experience another person's feelings, yet she couldn't dismiss the idea.

'I take it that I'll be staying here for the night.'

There was nothing in his voice to alarm her now, yet Claire still hesitated before she turned. Had she been mistaken? she wondered. Imagined something that simply hadn't happened? She searched his face and found her answer in the brooding intensity of his gaze. Her breath caught. She hadn't imagined it. Jude was every bit as aware of her as she was of him and it made the situation even more dangerous.

'Yes. I… I'll sort out a room you can use,' she said quickly, struggling to hold on to her composure. 'With all the children being here there isn't a lot of free space, but I'm sure we can find somewhere for you to sleep.'

'Don't go to any trouble,' he said quietly. 'I'll sleep in here if there's nowhere else. In fact, it might be better if I did. I can keep an eye on Bebe then. She is one very sick little girl.'

The concern on his face as he looked at the child was unmistakable. Claire felt a rush of warmth run through her. There was no doubt that Jude cared deeply about their small patient and it simply proved that her initial impression of him had been completely wrong. As she left the room, she suddenly found herself wondering if she should rectify the mistake he had made about her. Surely he deserved to know that she wasn't a nun? It didn't seem fair to let him carry on believing it and yet if she did tell him the truth, it could have repercussions.

She bit her lip as panic rose inside her. Recalling what had so nearly happened at the pool that afternoon, not to mention what had gone on just now, was it really wise to remove the final barrier between them? Maybe she did feel differently about him, but it didn't mean that she could cope with having a relationship with him.

CHAPTER NINE

MORNING DAWNED, CALM and clear, such a contrast to his state of mind that Jude found it hard to believe a new day had begun with so little fanfare. He had spent the night going over what had happened the evening before. Oh, he had tried to convince himself that he'd been mistaken, that Claire *hadn't* reacted to his touch, but he had failed. Miserably. Hadn't he felt that flash of awareness that had passed between them? Experienced that charge of electricity that had filled the air? Of course he had and there was no point trying to deny it either! Coming on top of what had gone on earlier at the pool, it was little wonder that he felt so confused.

He got out of bed and went to the window, resting his forehead against the glass as he went over it all once more. Why should Claire be attracted to him when she had sworn to forgo the pleasures of the flesh? Last night his thoughts had been in such turmoil that it had been impossible to think clearly, but he needed to set aside his own feelings if he was to make sense of it all. It was what he was good at, after all; disregarding emotions and rationalising a problem had always been his forte. With a bit of luck it would work this time too.

Jude wasn't sure how long he stood there, trying to

work out the answer to this particular puzzle, but the sun had risen above the horizon when he finally gave up. Maybe Claire had had her reasons but he couldn't explain them. That was certain.

He checked on Bebe, as he had done many times during the night. Although her condition hadn't changed very much, her temperature was slightly lower than it had been, which was encouraging. When Sister Anne came to relieve him, he made his way to the dining room, pausing in the doorway while he took in the scene that greeted him. There appeared to be children everywhere, some seated at tables, others sitting cross-legged on the floor. Every child had a bowl in front of him or her and every single one was tucking in to their breakfast. How the nuns had managed to get them all served was a miracle to his mind, but even the very smallest—little more than babies—were eating.

He spotted Claire at the far side of the room, helping a tiny tot scoop up cereal with a spoon. Jude felt a rush of emotion hit him as he watched her wipe the little one's mouth then drop a kiss on the child's upturned face. There was such tenderness in the gesture, such loving care, that he couldn't help feeling envious.

'Ah, Dr Slater. Good morning. Do come and join us.'

Jude swung round when Sister Julie materialised beside him. 'Good morning, Sister,' he replied then cleared his throat when he realised how choked he sounded. Deliberately, he turned so that he could no longer see Claire. Feeling jealous of a child really was beyond the pale!

'I hope you slept well,' Sister Julie continued as she led him over to where an elderly nun was serving breakfast.

'Very well, thank you,' Jude replied, deeming it

wiser not to admit to his sleepless night, let alone the reason for it. Heat rushed through him and he hurried on. 'Mealtimes must be very busy times for you.'

'They are indeed.' Sister Julie treated him to a gentle smile. 'Food is extremely important to the children. Most of them have gone hungry in their short lives and they attach huge importance to being fed.' She gestured towards the stack of empty bowls. 'As you can see, nothing is wasted. When you grow up not knowing where your next meal is coming from then you eat every scrap.'

'I see,' Jude said quietly. Oh, he had seen the appeals on television, even donated to them on many an occasion, but that was very different from witnessing the effects of poverty at first hand. He couldn't help feeling guilty about all the times he had turned up his nose at some perfectly good meal simply because it hadn't tempted his palate.

'There is no need to berate yourself, Dr Slater. None of us can fully comprehend what it must be like to go without food unless we have experienced it for ourselves.' Sister Julie smiled sympathetically. 'It hit me hard when I first came here too.'

'It makes me feel very guilty,' Jude admitted, even though he was surprised that he should open up to such an extent. He never discussed his feelings and yet here he was, admitting that he was ashamed of the way he had taken his good fortune for granted.

'It does.' Sister Julie looked calmly back at him. 'I found the best antidote for my guilt was to do something to help.'

She didn't say anything else as she filled a bowl with porridge and handed it to him. Jude took it over to a table and sat down, mulling over what he had heard. Dipping his spoon into the bowl, he tried a little of the cereal. It tasted very gritty and at any other time he would have left it, but he ate every scrap. How could he waste it after hearing about all these children who had gone hungry?

All of a sudden he was filled with a fresh resolve. Maybe he had come to Mwuranda for the sake of his pride but it didn't mean he couldn't help the people of this country. And not just while he was here either: he could help when he returned home by fundraising. He knew a lot of wealthy people and if he could get them to contribute then there was no end to the good they could do...

Was it only because he wanted to improve people's lives? a small voice suddenly whispered in his ear. *Or was there another reason?*

Jude's gaze went to Claire and he sighed. He couldn't put his hand on his heart and swear that his reasons for wanting to help were purely altruistic. The fact that it might improve his standing in Claire's eyes had a lot to do with it, even though he knew how pointless it was. No matter if he raised his status to sainthood level, Claire could never be his.

The ambulance arrived shortly before seven a.m. Claire helped to load Bebe on board then climbed in beside her. Jude was having a word with the driver before they set off and she shivered as she listened to him instructing the man to drive carefully and avoid the potholes. Far too many times during the night her sleep had resounded to the sound of that deep voice. It was as though it had imprinted itself in her mind and, try as she may, she couldn't shift it.

'Right. Let's hope we don't encounter the kind of problems we did when I arrived.'

Jude climbed in and slammed the door. Claire summoned a smile, not wanting him to suspect how on edge she felt. It wasn't just the sound of his voice that had disturbed her sleep but everything else that had happened yesterday—the incident at the pool, that flash of awareness that had passed between them. Heat flowed through her and it took every scrap of control she could muster not to betray how alarmed she felt.

'Hopefully, we'll have an uneventful journey today,' she murmured.

'Amen to that,' Jude replied, drolly, then grimaced. 'Sorry. No disrespect meant.'

Claire nodded, feeling infinitely guilty that he had felt it necessary to apologise. She turned away, checking Bebe's obs to give herself time to collect herself. Even though she felt bad about misleading him, surely it was better than telling him the truth? The fact that she was so vulnerable where Jude was concerned was worrying enough, but the fact that he obviously felt something for her made it even more dangerous. How could she hope to do the sensible thing if she had to contend with his feelings as well as her own?

The thought occupied her for the rest of the journey. It was a relief when the ambulance drew up outside the hospital. Jude and the driver lifted the stretcher out of the back and carried it inside. Claire led the way to a side room which was kept for emergency cases like this. Bebe would need intensive nursing and it would make it easier if she wasn't in a ward with all the usual comings and goings.

Following local tradition, the Mwurandan people

were cared for by their relatives while they were in hospital and it could be extremely noisy at times with so many people milling about. Although they had tried to instigate a *'no more than two people at a bed'* rule, it was rarely observed. Mothers, fathers, wives, husbands, aunts, uncles, cousins—the list was endless. At least Bebe would have some peace and quiet in the side room.

Claire made the child comfortable then went to the office to sign in. Lola grinned at her when she opened the door. 'Ah, so you made it back safely. I hope you brought Jude with you? I had visions of you leaving him at the convent!'

'Of course he's come back with me,' Claire said sharply then sighed. 'Sorry. I didn't mean to snap at you.'

'No sweat, honey. I should know better than to tease you about such a touchy subject.'

Claire flushed. 'There's nothing touchy about it.'

'No? My mistake.'

Lola tactfully let the subject drop but Claire was very aware that she had handled things badly. Just for a moment she found herself wondering if it would be simpler to tell Lola why she was so edgy around Jude before she thought better of it. Her hand shook as she signed her name on the sheet. It was the first time that she had been seriously tempted to tell anyone about her past but she was afraid that she would regret it. The problem was that she had no idea how people would react and she hated to think that they might view her in a different light afterwards.

Her breath caught as an even worse thought occurred to her. How would *Jude* react if he found out that she had been raped? At the moment he thought she was a nun and he probably conformed to most people's view of the women who had chosen that kind of a life. It would come as a massive shock if he discovered that she wasn't the innocent he believed her to be.

Tears welled to her eyes. She couldn't bear to imagine his reaction if he found out he was wrong.

It was late afternoon before there was any real change in Bebe's condition. Jude checked her chart, relieved to see that there was a definite improvement in her obs. He had to admit that he had been extremely concerned about having to delay the operation to remove her appendix. Although the circumstances were very different, he couldn't help thinking about Maddie and how delaying her surgery had had such disastrous consequences. However, it appeared that the broad-spec antibiotics he had prescribed were doing their job.

'Definitely an improvement, although it will be at least another day before I can risk operating.' He handed the chart to Claire, automatically batting it down when his pulse gave a familiar leap as their hands touched. He had done his best to avoid her, needing a break from all the soul-searching he had been doing lately. Maybe that was the key, he had decided: steer clear of her. From the moment he had arrived in Mwuranda they had been thrust together, but if he kept out of her way then surely he would get back on track.

In truth, he had never spent so much time with *any* woman before. Dates were usually confined to dinner and possibly a show beforehand. If he and his date ended up in bed then it was always at the woman's home too. It meant he could leave afterwards and not have to spend the night with her. He had never lived with anyone, never been tempted to forfeit his single life...

Up till now.

Jude's heart plummeted. It plunged right down to his boots then surged back up again so fast that he felt light-headed. Love. Marriage. Home. Family. They were mere words to him, words other people used and ones he avoided. He had no interest in exploring any of those options, had no desire to be a husband or a father or anything else that involved commitment. Oh, he had nothing against marriage per se but it wasn't for him. He had seen too many marriages end in disaster to go down that route, starting with his own parents.

A shudder ran through him as he recalled when his parents had split up. Although he had been only seven when they had divorced, he had recognised the hatred in their voices whenever they had spoken to each other. It had been a relief when he was sent away to boarding school, in fact. Unlike the other new boys he hadn't been homesick. He had been glad to be there, well away from those hate-filled voices. Although he had spent holidays with both his mother and his father after the divorce, he had never missed them when it had been time to return to school. School had had rules and regulations—he had felt safe there well away from all the emotional turmoil.

It was only after he had qualified that he had started to feel anything. Helping the people who had come to him had unlocked his emotions; he had found himself empathising with them. It had been Maddie's death that had made him see how stupid he was. Allowing himself to care about other people always ended in heartache—his parents, Maddie, Claire.

Panic ripped through him and he turned away, afraid that Claire would pick up on his mood. 'We'll continue with the antibiotics,' he said brusquely. 'We may need to change them but I'll decide that when the cultures come back.'

'Should we continue with twenty-minute obs?' Claire asked and the very coolness of her tone told him that she had recognised his change of mood even if she didn't understand the reason for it.

'Of course.' He stared aloofly back at her, opting for a technique he employed whenever he was dealing with a particularly obtuse colleague. Maybe it was unfair to use it now but it was better than letting her know how he really felt, how afraid he was. 'As I said, Sister, it could be another twenty-four hours before I can risk operating. None of us can afford to be less than vigilant during that time, including you.'

'Of course.'

Her tone was just as cool but he could tell that his sharp reply had hurt her. Jude felt like the lowest form of life as he left the room. The urge to go back and apologise was overwhelming but he forced himself to carry on, making his way to the office to sign out. He had to be strong. He couldn't allow his emotions to get the better of him. Even if he had been thinking about making a commitment, it wouldn't be to Claire. Her future was mapped out and, oddly enough, it was very similar to his own.

Like him, Claire wouldn't fall in love, she wouldn't get married, she wouldn't have children. She would dedicate her life to following her vocation. Even though

Jude knew that she was doing exactly what she wanted, he couldn't help feeling wretched at the thought of everything she was giving up. Someone as sweet and as gentle, as kind and as beautiful as Claire deserved so much more.

CHAPTER TEN

CLAIRE DECIDED TO stay the night at the hospital so she would be on hand if there was a deterioration in Bebe's condition. Although she knew the night staff would take good care of the little girl, she wanted to be there in case anything happened. Jude's parting comment had stung and she had no intention of giving him another opportunity to take her to task. Bill Arnold was duty doctor that night and he helped her move a chair into the side room.

'Are you sure about this?' he asked, his kindly face mirroring concern as they placed the chair beside the bed. 'I mean, you were working all day and it seems a bit much to expect you to work through the night as well.'

'I don't mind.' Claire summoned a smile, not wanting the older man to guess why she felt it necessary to stay. Admitting that it had been Jude's wholly unjustified rebuke that had made her decide not to leave would be tantamount to admitting that she cared what he thought. And that was the last thing she intended to do.

'Well, make sure you get some sleep. You'll be neither use nor ornament tomorrow if you're tired out.'

Bill patted her hand and left. Claire busied herself with Bebe's obs, noting them down on the chart with even more care than usual. No way was Jude going to find anything to complain about!

She sighed as she hung the chart on the end of the bed. She knew she was overreacting but she couldn't help it. It was as though every fibre of her being was attuned to his mood. If he was happy, she felt happy, and if he was annoyed, she felt unsettled too. Bearing in mind that they had met only days ago, it was hard to believe that he could have this effect on her, but there was no point pretending. Jude made her feel things she had never expected to feel. The key now was to learn how to moderate her response before it caused a problem—if it hadn't already done so.

Heat rushed through her as she recalled what had happened the day before. She had never expected to feel desire again after what had happened to her, but that was what she had felt, an all-encompassing need to touch Jude and have him touch her. Even now she could feel the echo of it resonating deep inside her and it scared her. How could she risk giving herself to a man again? How could she be sure that he wouldn't hurt her? The old fear might have faded but it hadn't gone away; it was still there, a dark shadow at the back of her mind.

She took a deep breath but the facts had to be faced. She couldn't be sure that it wouldn't rear up and destroy her life all over again.

Jude was first in the dining room for breakfast the following morning. Another restless night had left him feeling drained. He had kept harking back to how Claire had sounded when he had left her the previous day. He knew he had upset her and he felt guilty about it too.

Just because he was worried about getting involved, it wasn't an excuse to speak to her the way he had done and as soon as he saw her, he would apologise. Even if he did intend to steer clear of her in the future, it was the very least he could do.

His heart was heavy as he went to the buffet. When Moses offered him some of his specially brewed coffee, he accepted that too. Not quite the traditional hair shirt worn by the penitent but it would have much the same effect! He had just sat down when Bill Arnold appeared.

'Another early bird,' the older man observed as he loaded a plate with fruit. He added a hunk of bread and carried the whole lot over to the table and sat down. 'I don't know how you young 'uns do it. Matt turned up way before he was supposed to do, which is why I finished early. And Claire couldn't have had more than an hour's sleep last night, but there she was this morning, rushing around all over the place.'

'Claire's already at the hospital!' Jude exclaimed in surprise.

'She stayed the night there.' Bill broke off a chunk of bread and smothered it in some of the locally produced jam. Jude waited impatiently while he chewed it. 'I assumed you knew she was staying over.'

'No. I had no idea,' Jude replied, frowning. 'Did she say why she had decided to stay?'

'No. But she was with Bebe all night, so I assume she wanted to keep an eye on her. Typical of Claire. She always puts everyone else before herself.'

Bill carried on eating, obviously keen to get finished so that he could take himself off to bed. No wonder, Jude thought as the older man departed a few minutes later. Working twelve-hour shifts was exhausting enough and doubly so under these conditions. It made Claire's decision to work a double shift all the more difficult to understand—unless it was his comments that had spurred her into it.

The thought that he was responsible hit him hard. Jude stood up and carried his tray over to the rack even though he had barely touched his breakfast. Leaving the dining room, he hurried outside and made his way round to the rear of the building. One of the drivers had recovered the motorbike Claire had used to collect him from the airport and it was stored in the shed back there.

Jude wheeled it out, relieved to find that the key was in the ignition. He fired up the engine, grimacing as ancient pistons struggled to find some kind of rhythm. It was years since he had ridden a motorbike and it had been a modern version too, nothing like this heap of old junk, but he had no intention of letting that deter him. He needed to apologise to Claire and he needed to do it soon.

Claire had just finished sponging Bebe's face when the door opened. She glanced round, expecting it to be one of the local nurses coming to see if she needed help. The polite refusal was already hovering on her lips when she discovered that it was Jude.

'What are you doing here?' she demanded, unable to hide her dismay. 'The day staff isn't due for another half hour at least.'

'I wanted a word with you, so I came on ahead.'

He came into the room and closed the door. Claire shivered when she saw how grim he looked. Surely he didn't still believe that she was incapable of looking after Bebe properly, did he? The thought was like the proverbial red rag and Claire rounded on him, her grey eyes spitting sparks. Maybe she wouldn't have reacted so forcefully if she hadn't been so tired after working a double shift, but any thoughts of moderating her response flew straight out of the window as she let rip.

'Oh, did you? And what exactly did you want a word with me about? Or do I really need to ask that question?' She laughed bitterly. 'You made your feelings about my competence perfectly clear, Dr Slater, so I can only assume that you wish to take me to task once more. So come along, then. How have I failed to meet your exacting standards this time?'

'I haven't come here to take you to task,' he replied harshly. 'If you want the truth then I came to apologise, but obviously it would be a waste of my time as well as yours.'

He went to leave but there was no way that Claire was prepared to let him off so lightly. His scathing comment had hurt and she wasn't going to let him brush it aside with some trumped-up claim about apologising. From what she had learned, Jude Slater didn't go in for apologies. For any reason. To anyone!

She caught hold of his arm as he went to open the door. He was wearing a short-sleeved shirt and his flesh felt warm to her touch, warm and wonderfully vital. Claire had the craziest feeling that she could actually feel his life force pulsating beneath her fingers and it shook her. She had never felt this connection to anyone before, never experienced this feeling that she was within a hair's breadth of touching the very essence of another human being. It was a moment of such profundity that it cut right through her anger. Now all she felt was a deep sense of hurt. How could Jude believe that she wasn't up to doing her job? Even if he knew nothing else about her, surely he could tell how much her work meant to her, that it was the one thing that had given her life any meaning?

Tears blurred her vision and she let her hand fall from his arm. She'd had years of practice at containing her emotions yet she couldn't seem to contain them any longer. It was as though all the pain and heartache that had built up inside her was gushing out in an unstoppable tide.

'Here. Sit down.'

Jude's touch was infinitely gentle as he led her to the chair, his voice filled with compassion, and it just made everything worse. Anger would have been better, she thought wretchedly as she sank down onto the cushion. She could have coped with his anger; it would have firmed her resolve and helped her pull herself together. However, gentleness and compassion were very different emotions. They slid past her defences and found all the vulnerable places that she kept hidden.

'Don't cry, Claire. Please!' He knelt in front of her and she couldn't fail to see the anguish on his face. 'I can't bear to know you're so unhappy and that it's all my fault. I never meant to upset you. Truly I didn't. I don't have any doubts whatsoever about your competence.'

'Then why did you say what you did?' she said brokenly.

'Because I was upset.'

'Upset!' she exclaimed in surprise. She took a shuddery breath as she wiped her eyes with the back of her hand. 'Upset because of something I'd done, you mean?'

'No.' He hesitated, giving her the distinct impression that he was reluctant to explain. When he finally spoke, his voice was rough with emotion. 'I had a patient once, a young girl several years older than Bebe, who died after I had to delay operating on her. I... well, I couldn't help thinking about her and that's why I spoke to you so sharply. But you must believe me when I say that I have every confidence in you. You are a superb nurse.'

There was no doubt in her mind that he was telling her the truth and Claire felt her eyes fill with tears once more. The fact that he cared enough to talk about something that obviously distressed him touched her deeply. It was so long since anyone had considered her feelings that she was overwhelmed. Tears began to stream down her face again and she heard him sigh.

'I'm so sorry, Claire. You're the last person I wanted to hurt. Please forgive me.' Leaning forward, he gathered her into his arms. His body felt warm and hard as she rested against him, indubitably male too, but oddly that didn't worry her as she might have expected. Jude wouldn't hurt her. She could trust him.

Whether it was that thought which destroyed the final line of her defence, she wasn't sure, but she nestled against him, letting his strength fill her with an inner peace she hadn't felt in a very long time. Ever since the night she had been raped she had been running: away from Andrew; away from what had happened; away from herself. Far too often she had found herself wondering if she could have done something to prevent the attack, but not any longer. Now she could see that *she* wasn't to blame, that *she* had done nothing wrong, that *she* was the victim. And knowing it set her free.

Jude could sense a shift in the mood even though he didn't understand what had caused it. Claire didn't say anything but he felt the tension start to ease from her body. His breath caught when she settled against him so trustingly. He had wanted only to comfort her, yet all of a sudden he was filled with a sense of wonder. Holding her in his arms, feeling her heart beating in time with his, felt so right!

'Claire.' Her name was the faintest murmur, barely disturbing the air between them as he bent towards her. His mind was awash with so many emotions that he couldn't have put a name to even half of them. All he knew was that everything he felt seemed to be condensed into this single moment...

'I think Claire's in here. I'll go and see.' The sound of voices in the corridor broke the spell. Jude shot to his feet just a second before the door opened and Matt appeared.

'There's a phone call for you, Claire,' he announced cheerfully. 'Oh, hi, Jude. I didn't know you were in here. Anyway, it's Sister Julie. She wants to know how Bebe's doing.'

'I... I'll be right there.'

Claire stood up as Matt disappeared and Jude could see that she was trembling. She didn't look at him as she went to the door but there was no way that he could let her leave like this, he realised sickly. He had come so close to compromising her beliefs and making a mockery of everything she stood for. Apologising couldn't begin to make up for what he had done, but it was the only option open to him.

'I'm sorry. I didn't mean to embarrass you. I just wanted to…well, comfort you.'

'I know.' She gave him a tight little smile and left.

Jude followed her from the room and made his way outside. He stood on the steps, feeling his insides quivering as reaction set in. He felt guilty as hell about what he had done, but underneath it there was a deep sense of sadness, of loss. He would never make love to Claire, never experience the joy and fulfilment of their bodies becoming one. Sex had been little more than a mechanical process for him up till now, enjoyable enough but not exactly meaningful. However, he realised that it would have been far more than that with Claire. His mind as well as his body would have been engaged if he'd had the chance to love her, as he would never do. Tears suddenly blurred his vision. The future had never seemed bleaker.

CHAPTER ELEVEN

CLAIRE CAST A final glance in the mirror. It was Bill's sixty-fifth birthday and the team had decided to throw a party for him that night to celebrate. Moses had been enlisted to bake him a birthday cake and there was much speculation about how it would turn out. Birthday cakes weren't something the Mwurandan people went in for but Matt had found a recipe online and printed it out. Amazingly, Matt had also managed to source the ingredients and everyone was looking forward to a taste of home, everyone apart from her. Although she had tried to make her excuses, the others had insisted that she must be there and in the end she had given in. After all, she didn't have to talk to Jude if she didn't want to.

Her heart gave a little lurch as it had kept on doing whenever Jude's name had cropped up. They hadn't spoken again after they had left Bebe's room, not even to discuss their small patient's progress. Jude had made the decision to operate on the child and had drafted in Kelly to assist him, with Matt acting as his anaesthetist. When Claire had heard that, she had decided not to stay at the hospital. She'd been far too tired to be of much use anyway, so she had returned to the college with the rest of the night staff. However, from what she had heard, the operation had been textbook perfect and Bebe was expected to make a full recovery. Jude hadn't needed her help, which must have been a relief for him. He must be as eager as she was to keep his distance after what had happened that morning.

Her heart gave another jolt as she recalled how close he had come to kissing her. The worst thing was that she knew she wouldn't have stopped him if he had. She would have let him kiss her—even kissed him back!—and she couldn't help feeling guilty. Should she tell him the truth and admit that she wasn't a nun? she wondered for the hundredth time. It might make him feel better but if she did that then she would have to explain why she had misled him. Was she really prepared to do that? To lay herself open to even more heartache? The old fears raced round and round inside her head, making it impossible to decide. Maybe it would be better to ignore what had happened and hope that Jude would do the same.

Claire's heart was heavy as she made her way downstairs. Lesley had lent her the dress she had worn a few nights earlier as all the women had decided to dress up in Bill's honour. Bill himself looked positively resplendent in a crisp white shirt and a tie, a world away from his usual slightly scruffy self.

'I must say that you're looking very smart tonight, Dr Arnold,' Claire declared, kissing him on the cheek. She summoned a smile, not wanting anyone to suspect how downhearted she felt. 'Having a birthday definitely suits you.'

'Hmm, I don't know about that,' Bill grumbled, tugging at his tie. 'I feel more like the Christmas turkey—all trussed up and ready for roasting!'

Claire laughed. She moved aside when someone came to join them, her laughter fading when she discovered it was Jude. He, too, had dressed up for the occasion and her breath caught as she took stock of the pale blue shirt he was wearing, a colour which provided the perfect foil for his midnight-dark hair. It took her all her time to drag her eyes away but she had to stop staring at him. It wouldn't be fair to let him see how much he affected her after what had happened that morning. It was a relief when Lesley clapped her hands and called for order.

'OK, guys. I think it's time we drank a toast to our guest of honour.' Lesley raised her glass aloft. 'To Bill. Happy birthday. Here's to the last sixty-five years and to many more to come!'

Everyone raised their glasses, apart from Claire, who hadn't picked one up. She jumped when a glass suddenly appeared in front of her.

'Here. Have mine.'

Jude pressed his glass into her hand and she automatically took a sip of the liquid, sneezing when the bubbles fizzed up her nose. Jude took the glass back off her and handed her his handkerchief instead, a look of mingled amusement and apology in his eyes.

'Sorry. I should have warned you it was champagne, or something masquerading as champagne rather.'

'No, no. It's fine. Really.' Claire sneezed again and hurriedly apologised. 'Sorry. This always happens if I drink sparkling wine.'

'Something to remember for future reference,' Jude replied with a smile that disappeared abruptly when he realised the significance of that comment.

Claire gave him a tight little smile and turned away.

Jude sighed as he watched her walk over to Lesley and the other nurses. It was obvious that she felt uncomfortable around him and who could blame her? Would it help if he apologised again? he wondered. He had never been in this position before and he had no idea what he should do. He could end up by making matters worse and that was the last thing he wanted. Maybe it would be better to say nothing than say the wrong thing.

The evening wore on. Everyone was in very high spirits and Jude did his best to join in with the jokes and the laughter, but he was very aware that it was merely a front. Inside, in those secret places he had discovered only recently, he wasn't laughing or joking. He wasn't really sure what was happening in there except that he felt sort of flat and empty, as though he had lost something vital, something he had no hope of recovering. When Moses brought in the cake and everyone cheered, he was hard-pressed to dredge up a smile. Was this how he would continue to feel or would he get back to normal once he returned to England? His gaze went to Claire and his heart sank because he already knew the answer to that question. His life would never be the same now that he had met her.

'I don't know what to say…' There were tears in Bill's eyes as he stared at the cake. True, the icing was a rather lurid shade of green and the top layer had a decided list to starboard, but for a first attempt it was a remarkably good effort. Bill stood up and pumped Moses' hand. 'First-rate job, Moses. I really can't thank you enough for all your hard work. It's brilliant!'

Moses looked thrilled when everyone applauded him. He hurried back to the kitchen as Bill set about slicing the cake. Jude accepted a slice although the last thing he felt like was eating cake. He bit into the sponge and gagged at the overpowering taste of salt that filled his mouth. Everyone was in the same boat, all coughing and spluttering as they spat it out. Lesley wiped her mouth with a tissue and shuddered.

'Oh, yuck! I don't know what happened but something definitely went wrong. It's horrendous!'

'Yuck is right.' Amy grimaced as she pushed her plate away and turned to Matt. 'Are you sure you printed out the right recipe?'

'I think so. I mean it said all the usual things, flour, sugar, butter, eggs.' Matt looked decidedly put out at being blamed. 'I'm no cook but that's what usually goes into a cake, isn't it?'

'Maybe there was a mix-up in the kitchen,' Bill said soothingly. 'Not to worry, hey? It's the thought that counts and I really appreciate the effort you've all gone to tonight. The main thing now is to make sure that Moses doesn't find out that his masterpiece was a disaster. We don't want to hurt his feelings, do we?'

They all agreed that it was the last thing they wanted. Jude helped clear away the plates, scraping the uneaten cake into a paper bag that Kelly produced. The rest of the cake was carried upstairs to be disposed of discreetly the following morning at the hospital. Within a very short time the dining room was clear of any evidence and people were heading off to bed. Jude was the last to leave and he paused to switch off the lights.

It had been a strange night. He wasn't used to dissembling, mainly because he rarely felt so strongly about anything. He had changed so much since he had come here and he wasn't sure how he would cope when he returned home. Could he see himself going back to the work he had been doing, or would he find that he needed something more taxing that would not only stretch him but also make a real difference to people's lives?

Oh, he wasn't downplaying what he did in the private sector. Being rich wasn't a guarantee that one wouldn't experience discomfort and his patients were suitably grateful for his interventions. However, he was very aware that he hadn't pushed himself in the past few years, hadn't tried to develop his skills as he could have done. Maybe he had needed a break from the pressure of working for the NHS but it wasn't right that he continued to fritter away his talent. He didn't want to reach a point where he looked back at his life and wished he had done things differently.

It was a moment of revelation and it shook him. Jude switched off the lights, plunging the room into darkness. He glanced round when he heard footsteps on the stairs but he couldn't see who it was. It wasn't until she stepped down from the last step that he realised it was Claire.

Jude held his breath as he watched her cross the hall. He knew that he should say something to warn her he was there but he couldn't seem to speak. The words seemed to be jammed deep inside him and he couldn't push them out. She reached the door and he realised that he had to do something or risk scaring her half to death. Stepping forward, he switched on the lights again and heard her gasp.

'Sorry. I didn't mean to startle you,' he said hurriedly.

'I thought everyone had gone to bed!' she exclaimed, pressing her hand to her heart.

'I was on my way, but ended up standing here, woolgathering,' he replied lightly. He dredged up a smile, aware that he was probably the last person Claire wanted to see. The thought was almost unbearably painful and he hurried on. 'What brought you back downstairs? After another slice of birthday cake, were you?'

'Don't!' She shuddered. 'I still can't get the taste of salt off my tongue. No, I came down to look for a button.' She held out the skirt of her dress and showed him the gap in the row of tiny pearl buttons. 'It must have fallen off and I don't want to give it back to Lesley with a button missing after she was kind enough to lend it to me.'

'Oh. I see.' Jude peered under the table, deeming it safer than standing there and admiring how she looked in the borrowed dress. His pulse gave an appreciative little leap and he crouched down so he could no longer see her. 'Ah, there it is. Under that chair. I'll get it for you.'

Kneeling down, he quickly retrieved it. Claire smiled when he handed it to her. 'Thank you. I would have felt awful if I'd lost it.' She put it in her pocket and sighed. 'Lesley is always so kind about lending me her things. I'm going to miss her when I return to England.'

'I didn't know you were going back!' Jude exclaimed.

'My visa expires soon,' she explained. 'I'll have to leave then.'

'Can't you renew it while you're here?' he suggested, his mind racing. If she was returning to England then was it possible that he could arrange to see her again? Granted, they moved in very different circles but surely they could meet up? The thought buoyed him up even though he knew how pointless it was. After all, nothing would have changed. Claire would still be set on following a path that didn't leave any room for him.

'Unfortunately not. The Mwurandan government has tightened up the rules concerning foreign nationals. There's been trouble recently about undesirable elements getting into the country, so they've decided that nobody can apply for a visa without undergoing a rigorous check first. I'll have to return to England and contact their embassy if I want to come back here.'

'And do you?' Jude asked quietly.

'I'm not sure. Maybe it's time I went back home instead of hiding away here.'

Claire bit her lip as she realised what she had said. The comment had slipped out before she'd had time to think about it and it was obvious that it had aroused Jude's curiosity.

'What do you mean? How are you hiding away here? I thought you came here to help the people of this country,' he said, frowning.

'Of course I did!' She drummed up a laugh but it was a poor effort. It certainly did nothing to convince Jude.

'Are you sure about that?' He stared at her. 'Far be it from me to question your word, Claire, but I have to say that it doesn't exactly ring true.'

'No?' She gave a little shrug as she turned to leave. 'There's not much I can do about that, I'm afraid.'

'Oh, I disagree.' He stopped her by dint of placing his hand on her arm. Although Claire knew that she could pull away any time she chose, for some reason she couldn't move a muscle. It was as though the touch of his fingers on her skin had immobilised her. She could only stand there while he looked deep into her eyes.

'You could try telling me the truth, Claire. The real truth, I mean, not the version you've told everyone else.'

Claire's heart surged in alarm. That Jude had guessed she had been less than forthcoming with everyone came as a shock. She bit her lip, feeling fear unfurling in the pit of her stomach. She didn't want to lie to him but the thought of confessing what had brought her to Mwuranda and had kept her here was more than she could bear. How could she tell him the truth and watch his curiosity turn to revulsion?

She pulled away, her whole body trembling. Maybe she was the innocent victim but could she really expect him to see beyond what had happened to her? She couldn't bear to know that he would always think of her in future as a woman who had been raped—nothing more.

'You make it sound as though I'm hiding some dark secret!' She laughed, doing her best to feign amusement, not the easiest thing to do when her heart was aching. The thought of how Jude might react if he found out the truth made her feel sick. She knew instinctively that his reaction would affect her far more than anyone else's. 'I hate to disappoint you but there's no mystery about it. I simply decided that working here was what I wanted to do.'

'As simple as that, was it?'

The scepticism in his voice told her that he didn't believe her but there was nothing she could do. And in a way it was true. She *had* come to Mwuranda because she had wanted the job. The reason why she had wanted it was another story, and she wasn't prepared to go into that. However, the thought that it wasn't a total lie helped to appease her conscience.

'Yes. As simple as that.' She dredged up a smile, wanting to deflect his interest away from her. 'But what about you? Why did you decide to come here? It doesn't strike me that this is your usual kind of environment.'

'It isn't. I'm way out of my comfort zone and I don't mind admitting it.' He gave a small shrug, drawing her attention to the impressive width of his shoulders.

Claire took a deep breath when she felt her pulse leap. There was no point thinking about how attractive he was. No point at all. 'So what made you apply to work for Worlds Together?' she asked, needing a distraction. 'It seems a strange thing to do in the circumstances.'

'Pride.' He gave a rueful laugh. 'Someone accused me of taking the easy option and I decided to prove they were wrong. However, I'm beginning to see that they may have had a point. Suffice to say that I plan to do something about it when I get back to England.'

'I see.' Claire was intrigued by what she had heard, so much so that she longed to ask him about his future plans, but was it wise to become even more involved in his life when she should be keeping her distance? 'Well, I hope that everything works out the way you want it to,' she said, deeming it safer to let the subject drop.

'Thank you. I intend to give it my very best shot.' He hesitated. 'About this morning, Claire, I'd hate to think that you might feel awkward around me…'

'I don't,' she said quickly, not wanting to get into a discussion. Something told her that it would be the wrong thing to do when her emotions were in such turmoil. 'You were trying to comfort me and I understand that.'

'I was.'

He didn't say anything else apart from wishing her goodnight. Claire switched off the lights after he left and made her way upstairs. She knew she should be relieved to know that Jude had merely been trying to comfort her yet she couldn't deny that her heart was aching as she got into bed. Maybe it was foolish but she couldn't help wishing that he *had* kissed her, kissed her because he had wanted her, because he had desired her; because he simply couldn't help himself!

She pulled the sheet over her head, her cheeks burning. How crazy was that?

CHAPTER TWELVE

JUDE FELT VERY on edge the following morning and he knew it was his own fault. He never placed himself in the position of being vulnerable by revealing his feelings, yet he had done so with Claire. He had told her things he wouldn't have dreamt of telling anyone else and he regretted it. He needed to get back on track, shove all these thoughts and feelings back in their box and close the lid. He'd already come far too close to making a terrible mistake by nearly kissing Claire and he couldn't allow that to happen again.

It was all very unsettling. In the end, he decided to skip breakfast as he really couldn't face seeing Claire again. Matt had made good on his promise to get him some coffee and had even found him a battered old kettle as well, so at least he was able to brew himself a mug of that. He drank it standing by the bedroom window. It was another misty morning, the sun floating in a sea of red and orange as it rose above the horizon. Jude had never had much time for nature; he preferred man-made wonders, if he was honest. However, the sheer beauty of the scene unfolding before him brought a lump to his throat. Nature at her most beautiful was truly awe-inspiring.

He turned away from the view, downing the rest of the coffee in a single gulp. The sudden upsurge of emotion was yet another indication of how much he had changed and he didn't need any more reminders, thank you very much. He made his way downstairs and sat on the front steps to await the arrival of the truck, nodding as one by one the rest of the team joined him. Claire and Lesley were last to appear, Lesley giggling as she balanced a large cardboard box on her hip.

'It's the cake,' she mouthed when she saw Jude looking, and he smiled and nodded then realised with another little shock that he enjoyed being part of the conspiracy. He wouldn't have given a tinker's curse in the past but now he was as keen as everyone else to spare Moses' feelings. Was he completely changed and was it permanent? Or would he slip back into his old ways when he returned home to England?

His gaze went to Claire and he knew with a certainty that shook him that he wouldn't go back to the way he had been, that he, Jude Tobias Slater, was and always would be a very different person because of meeting her.

Claire hadn't been rostered to work in the clinic that day but when Kelly suddenly complained she was feeling sick, she immediately offered to swap places with her. While Kelly rushed off to the bathroom, Claire gathered together the notes for the dozen or so repeat appointments who would be seen first. Ten-year-old Jeremiah was the first on the list and he came hurrying over when she went to collect him from the waiting room.

'So how are you today, Jeremiah?' she asked, holding his hand as she led him to the screened-off area in the corner. She knew that Jude was duty doctor that day and steeled herself before pushing back the screen. No way was she going to react when she saw him, she told herself sternly. She was going to treat him the same as everyone else—politely and professionally. After last night, she would be mad to do anything else.

'I'm good, Sister Claire,' Jeremiah replied, his face breaking into a huge grin when he saw Jude sitting behind the makeshift desk. Letting go of her hand, he hurried straight over to him. 'Did you see the pictures of my bones, Mr Doctor, and can you make my leg better?'

'That's what we need to talk about.'

Jude stood up and came around the table. He barely glanced at Claire as he bent to look at the little boy and for some perverse reason she took exception to his lack of attention. Did he have to make it quite so clear how easy it was to ignore her?

'I've had a really good look at the pictures, Jeremiah, and I'm very sorry to say that there isn't anything I can do that will make your leg any better.'

Claire set aside her own feelings when she heard what Jude had said. Hurrying forward, she put her arm around Jeremiah's shoulders when he started to cry. She knew how devastated he must feel as he had been hoping that something could be done so that he would be able to play football—his passion—with the other boys.

'Don't cry, sweetheart. Maybe you can practise being goalkeeper. That way you won't have to run around as much, will you? What do you think, Dr Slater?'

'It's an idea,' Jude replied, although she heard the doubt in his voice. It was obvious that Jeremiah had heard it too because he pulled away from her.

'No! I can't be goalkeeper. I can't be anything with this stupid leg!'

He spun round and hurried out of the cubicle. Claire ran after him, quickly explaining what had happened to Sister Anne. She bit her lip as she watched the elderly nun lead him away. It seemed so unfair that nothing could be done to help a child like Jeremiah, who had been through so much in his short life. Her heart was heavy as she made her way back to the cubicle. Jude was seated behind the table again and he looked up when she went in.

'Is he OK?'

'Not really. I think he was pinning his hopes on you being able to do something.'

'I wish I could, but the fact is that I simply don't have the expertise to undertake such a complex operation.'

He sighed as he ran his hands through his hair. Claire felt a ripple of sympathy run through her when she realised how upset he looked. Being the bearer of such unwelcome news had taken its toll on him.

'It isn't your fault, Jude,' she said softly.

'No? Then whose fault is it? I'm a surgeon and I'm supposed to help people. Maybe if I hadn't wasted so many years then I might have been able to give that poor kid a better future to look forward to. But, no, instead of developing my skills, I've spent my time performing minor operations!'

Claire could hear the frustration in his voice. Jude may have had his own reasons for coming to Mwuranda but he genuinely wanted to help the people here. It made her wonder all of a sudden if he would feel the same about her if she told him what had happened, that she had been raped.

The thought was far too tempting. It was a relief

when he asked her to call in their next patient. They worked their way through the repeat appointments then started on the newcomers. There were dozens of them as usual, so they were kept busy for the rest of the afternoon, but Claire was glad. It was better to be busy than allow herself to explore that dangerously tempting idea. Once she told Jude there would be no going back; she would have to face whatever happened. She sighed. She wasn't sure if she was ready for that.

The day drew to a close but Jude was too restless to sleep. Claire had returned to the convent, so it wasn't her presence that was unsettling him. It was the thought of Jeremiah and how devastated the boy had been that was causing the problem. He had brought the X-rays back with him and he spread them on the dining room table after everyone had gone upstairs. There were half a dozen in total and he held them up to the light in turn. The boy's leg had been broken in several places and that was why it would be such a complex operation to repair it. Quite apart from his lack of expertise in this field, they simply didn't have the facilities here to undertake this kind of surgery. However, if Jeremiah could be treated in the UK then it might be a different story; there was a strong chance that his leg could be repaired or, at least, improved.

A rush of renewed optimism filled him as he gathered up the films and took them upstairs. He hadn't used his laptop since he had arrived and the battery was flat but he plugged it in, praying that they wouldn't have a power cut. Maybe he couldn't perform the surgery Jeremiah needed but he knew someone who could—

if he would agree. And if he could obtain permission to take Jeremiah *out* of Mwuranda and *into* England.

Jude took a deep breath and made himself stop right there. He would take it one step at a time, face any problems as and when they arose. Just for a moment he found himself wondering what Claire would think if he managed to set everything in motion before he drove the thought from his head. He wasn't doing this to improve her opinion of him. He was doing it for the sake of a ten-year-old boy who had been dealt a rotten hand. However, one thing was certain: he would never find himself in the position of being unable to help again!

Claire managed to get a lift to the hospital on the supply truck the following morning, so she arrived well before the others. Jeremiah had been inconsolable all the previous evening and she only hoped that the sisters could find a way to alleviate his disappointment, although it seemed unlikely that anything would help. She was feeling more than a little downhearted as she went into the office to sign in, only to stop in surprise when she found Jude bent over the computer.

'I didn't realise everyone had arrived,' she said in surprise.

'They haven't. I came on ahead on the bike as I wanted to email these to London.' He held up a wedge of X-rays and Claire frowned.

'Aren't they Jeremiah's?'

'Uh-huh.' Jude made a final check then pressed the send key. 'I'm emailing them to Professor Jackson, my old tutor. He's agreed to take a look at them and see if there's anything he can do for Jeremiah.'

'Really? Oh, that's wonderful!' Claire exclaimed.

'We'd better not count our chickens just yet,' he warned her. 'That leg is a mess and there's no guarantee that even the Professor will be able to do anything with it.'

'But you must think there's a chance he can or you wouldn't have contacted him,' she pointed out.

'Yes. If anyone can help Jeremiah, it's him. He's a brilliant surgeon—there's no other way to describe him. Some of the work he's done is staggering.'

'A bit of a hero of yours, I take it?' Claire said with a smile.

'I suppose so.' Jude frowned. 'I've never really thought about it but you're right. The Professor is definitely someone I look up to, even though he gave me a very hard time when I last saw him.'

'Really? Why was that?' she asked curiously.

'Oh, because he didn't think I was making full use of my training.' He sighed. 'It was the Professor who accused me of taking the easy option. The worst thing is that I agree with him. I might have been able to help Jeremiah myself if I'd not opted to work in the private sector for all this time.'

'I doubt if you've had such an easy ride,' Claire countered, hating to hear him berate himself. From what she had seen there was no question that Jude was a first-rate surgeon. 'I know how hard you must have had to work to qualify as a surgeon—it's one of the most exacting areas of medicine. The hours alone are crippling.'

'True.' He grinned. 'You're very good for my ego, Claire. Do you know that?'

Claire felt a little rush of pleasure and smiled at him. 'I'm only telling the truth.'

'Well, thank you anyway. I don't feel half as guilty

now for not being able to do anything for Jeremiah.'
His eyes met hers, dark and deep and filled with something that made a shiver run through her. When he took a step towards her, she didn't move, held by the intensity of his gaze…

'Hello! What's going on in here?'

Lola bustled into the office and the moment passed. Claire took a quick breath, struggling to pull herself together. However, she knew that if they hadn't been interrupted then she would have been in Jude's arms right now.

'I came in early to use your computer. I hope you don't mind.'

There was a roughness to Jude's voice that told her he was finding it as difficult as she was to behave normally. Claire shot a wary glance at him and felt her heart lurch when she saw how strained he looked. It was clear from his expression that he knew what would have happened if they hadn't been interrupted and it didn't make sense. He had explained that near-miss kiss by claiming he had been trying to comfort her and she had believed him. However, it didn't explain what had happened just now. As she filled in the sheet, she found herself wondering how far it would have gone if they'd been somewhere private. Would the desire to be held have progressed to something more?

Claire shuddered as she realised how easily it could have done. But how would she cope with intimacy after what had happened to her? Would it be the life-affirming experience it should be or a horrendous ordeal? There was no way of knowing until she took that final step and she wasn't sure if she could do that.

She glanced over at Jude, who was showing Lola the

X-rays. Although she knew in her heart that he would never willingly hurt her, was it enough to overcome her fear and help her find the courage she needed?

Jude managed to hold on to his composure but it was a close call. Javid was coming along the corridor when he left the office and he made some joking remark about Jude earning himself extra brownie points for his early start. Jude responded and he must have made sense too because Javid laughed, but he had no idea what he had said. His mind was too full of what had happened. Claire had been about to step into his arms—he knew she had! And once she'd been in them then who knew where it would have led? Hell's bells! That was enough to boggle any man's mind!

He about-turned and headed outside, needing some air. The sun had risen now and the temperature was mounting but he wasn't aware of the heat as he made his way to the pool. Although he had been invited to join the others for a swim on several occasions, he hadn't been back there. For some reason the thought of cooling off in the deep green water hadn't held any appeal. Now, as he gazed across the water, he understood why. He hadn't felt tempted to return because Claire wouldn't have been there. It was being with her that had made it so special.

Jude closed his eyes and let his mind wander, unsurprised when it started to conjure up a whole series of images. And every single one of them involved Claire: his first glimpse of her in that hideous old boiler suit; how slender her body had felt when he had put his arms around her yesterday; the look on her face as he had taken that single step towards her...

Jude opened his eyes and stared at the water. He needed to ask himself a question and it was such a momentous one that he needed every faculty in full working order. Was he falling in love with Claire or was it the fact that he was so far removed from everything he knew that he was misinterpreting his feelings?

He stood there for a long time, waiting for the answer to come to him, but it remained stubbornly out of reach. He sighed as he turned around and made his way back to the hospital. He would have to wait a while longer, it appeared, and in the meantime he would do what he'd said he would and stay away from Claire. Falling in love had never been on his agenda, and falling in love with a woman who could never love him in return would be a huge mistake. If there was any way to stop it happening then he would find it, so help him!

CHAPTER THIRTEEN

THE TIME FLEW PAST, one day running into the next without a pause. They didn't even stop at the weekends but worked straight through. It was a gruelling schedule which was why most people only remained in Mwuranda for three months at a time. Claire was the exception, although she knew that she would have to leave soon. She wasn't surprised, therefore, when a letter arrived, informing her that she must leave the country in two weeks' time when her visa expired.

She showed the letter to Lesley as they rode into town on the truck. She had stayed over at the college the night before as there had been no transport available to ferry her back to the convent. She had tried to avoid staying there since that morning in the office. The memory of what had so nearly happened between her and Jude was still very raw and it had seemed wiser to keep out of his way. However, she'd had no choice other than to stay, but as Jude had been rostered for the night shift, it had made it easier.

'So that's it, then. You must be looking forward to going back to England, Claire, even if it's only for a rest.' Lesley grimaced as she handed back the letter. 'I have to admit that I'm more than ready to go home and I've only been here for a fraction of the time you have.'

'I suppose so,' Claire replied as she slipped the letter into her pocket.

'Only suppose?' Lesley frowned. 'Aren't you looking forward to seeing your family and friends again?'

'Yes, of course I am.' Claire dredged up a smile, although the thought of being back in London was making her feel rather anxious. She still wasn't sure how she would cope if she saw Andrew again.

'Hmm. Well, I have to say that it doesn't sound like it,' Lesley retorted. 'Could it be the thought of leaving behind the handsome Dr Slater that's taking the shine off the idea?'

'No! Don't be ridiculous!' Claire exclaimed. She felt the colour run up her face when Lesley treated her to an old-fashioned look. 'Jude has nothing to do with it—that's the truth.'

'Methinks the lady doth protest too much,' Lesley misquoted with a grin. 'Come on, love, you know you fancy him something rotten. It's as plain as the nose on your face, as is the fact that he feels the same about you. What I don't understand is why you're so determined to keep him at arm's length. You're young, free and single, so why not do what comes naturally?'

'You're wrong. I don't fancy him,' Claire protested, although she knew that Lesley wouldn't believe her.

Fortunately, they had reached the hospital and she was able to make her escape, but the thought plagued her for the rest of the day. Was she making a mistake by avoiding getting involved with Jude? As Lesley had pointed out, there was nothing to stop her, so why didn't she come clean, admit that she wasn't a nun and have an affair with him?

Maybe it was what she needed to finally kill off the demons from her past. If she could prove to herself that she could cope with intimacy then what had happened would no longer rule her life. She didn't *have* to tell Jude about the rape either. It could remain her secret. There was no law that said you had to tell someone every little detail about your life, was there?

Her thoughts whirled as though they were on a merry-go-round but she still couldn't make up her mind what to do. The thought of withholding the truth from him if they did start a relationship didn't sit easily with her and yet the alternative was equally unpalatable. If she knew how he would react if she told him, it would be easier to decide, but that was something she couldn't foretell. She couldn't bear it if he looked at her with disgust once he found out. It would break her heart.

Jude only found out that Claire was leaving by chance when he overheard Lesley and Amy talking at dinner that night. He bent over his plate, struggling to get a grip as his emotions ran riot. He knew that Claire had been avoiding him since that morning in the office but he couldn't complain as he had been avoiding her too. Despite trying to pin down his feelings, he still wasn't sure how he felt. Oh, he was attracted to her—there was no question about that. He wanted her more than he had wanted any woman and not just physically either. He wanted to spend time with her—talking, laughing or even sitting in silence—and he had never felt that way about anyone before. But was it love? Real love? The kind that lasted for ever and ever?

The nagging thought that his feelings were intensified by the fact he was so far removed from his natural habitat lingered at the back of his mind and he was afraid of making a mistake, especially when it wouldn't make a scrap of difference to the outcome. He couldn't have Claire and even if he *was* falling in love with her, nothing would change in that respect, so why torture himself by wishing for the impossible? By the time he went to his room after dinner had finished, Jude's spirits were at an all-time low. He had come to Mwuranda to prove himself. What he had never expected was that it would turn his whole world upside down.

Claire had taken the morning off to pack. There was a plane due the following day bringing in fresh supplies and the plan was that she would fly back to England on it. Although there was another week left on her visa, it would only complicate matters if she booked herself onto a scheduled flight. Flights in and out of Mwuranda were dicey at the best of times and could be cancelled without warning. She didn't want to risk falling foul of the authorities by outstaying her visa. She had just finished packing the few clothes she planned to take back with her when one of the nuns came hurrying into the room and asked her if she had seen Jeremiah. Apparently, he hadn't turned up for lessons and no one had seen him since breakfast.

Claire abandoned her packing while she helped the sisters search the convent but there was no sign of him inside or out. He had become increasingly withdrawn since he had been told that nothing could be done about his leg and several times had gone off on his own. However, he had never been missing for this long. While

Sister Julie went inside to telephone the hospital in case
he had found his way there, Claire decided to check the
route he would have taken. She was worried in case
he had fallen and injured himself and was unable to
get back.

The air was stifling as she left the convent. She was
wearing one of the nuns' dresses again that day and she
could feel the sun burning through the light grey cotton. It was only a few miles to the hospital, although the
nuns never walked there. There were still rebel factions
operating in the area and it was safer to be driven there
and back. Claire kept a wary eye on the surrounding
scrubland as she followed the path, but she saw no sign
of the rebels. She also saw no sign of Jeremiah and her
concern intensified as she reached the trees that marked
the boundary of the hospital's grounds. Where on earth
had he got to?

She went to step out of the trees then stopped abruptly
when the sound of gunfire ripped across the clearing.
Dropping to the ground, she tried to make out where it
was coming from, her heart sinking when she spotted a
group of men at the opposite side of the clearing. They
were obviously rebel soldiers although she had no idea
why they had decided to attack the hospital. The Worlds
Together team had made it clear that they were impartial.
It meant that they had been able to carry out their work
in relative safety. What had happened to change that was
a mystery, but there was little doubt that the hospital was
under attack.

Claire remained where she was while she debated her
options. She was just trying to decide if the nun's habit
would offer her any protection when a movement caught
her eye. Alarm ran through her when she spotted Jere-

miah standing amongst the trees. It was obvious that he was about to make a run for it to reach the hospital and that was the last thing he must do. The rebels offered no concessions when it came to age; they would gun down a child as readily as they would a grown man. Claire knew she had to stop him and that to do so she had to put herself at risk. Stepping out of the trees, she shouted to him.

'Stay there! Do you hear me, Jeremiah? Don't move!'

There was another volley of shots and she gasped when she felt a burning pain in her right thigh. She fell to the ground, holding her breath when she realised that Jeremiah had ignored her and was attempting to cross the clearing. A man suddenly ran out of the hospital and her heart leapt when she recognised Jude. He picked up Jeremiah and carried him to safety then turned around and headed straight to her.

Claire watched in horror, sure that he would get himself shot, but, miraculously, he made it safely. He dropped to his knees beside her and her breath caught when she saw the expression on his face. She had never seen such fear on anyone's face before, but why? Because he feared for his own life, or because he was afraid for her? She had no idea, but the thought that he might care so much about her filled her with joy. In that second she finally admitted what she had been trying to deny for weeks: she wanted Jude to care about her. She wanted him to love her.

'Is it just your leg that's been hit?' Jude demanded, clamping down on the fear that was turning his blood to ice. He couldn't afford to fall apart. Claire needed him to be strong and he mustn't let her down. 'Claire, listen to me!' he instructed urgently when she failed to answer. 'Have you been hit anywhere else apart from your leg?'

Even before she could answer the question, his hands

began moving over her. Although her leg was bleeding copiously, he could tell from the flow that the bullet hadn't hit an artery. If that had happened then she could have bled to death right here in front of him. His hands shook at the thought.

'No. It's just my leg that's been hit.' She lifted her skirt and showed him the wound, shuddering at the sight of her torn flesh.

'Here, let me see.' Jude bent over so she couldn't see how terrified he felt. The thought of losing her was unbearable. 'Well, I'm no expert. The patients I normally treat don't go around getting themselves shot. However, from what little knowledge I do have, I'd say it's a flesh wound. Once we've stopped the bleeding, it shouldn't be too difficult to treat it.'

He tore a strip of cloth off the bottom of his shirt and balled it up then pressed it against the wound. He grimaced when she winced. 'Sorry. I know it must hurt like blazes but I need to put pressure on it to stop the bleeding.'

'It's all right,' she muttered, dashing away the tears that had sprung to her eyes. She gave a wobbly little laugh that tugged at his heartstrings. 'Take no notice—I'm just being a baby.'

'Of course you aren't,' Jude countered roughly. Reaching out, he pulled her into his arms, uncaring if it was the wrong thing to do. She was in pain and no matter if she was a nun, she was a human being and needed comforting.

He drew her to him, feeling a rush of emotions hit him. Her body felt so small and slender as she nestled against him, the soft curves of her breasts pushing against his chest, and he was overwhelmed by tenderness. He wanted to hold her like this for ever, to keep her safe in his arms and protect her from harm for the rest of his days. Was this how love made you feel? he wondered giddily. Did it make you put the other person's needs before your own, make you worry about *their* safety and *their* happiness at the expense of your own?

Jude knew it was true and the realisation filled him with both euphoria and despair. He loved Claire and he needed to face up to how he felt, face up to the fact that his love would never be reciprocated either. Claire would never love him in return and the thought was so raw and so painful that it spurred him on to do what he had sworn he would never do. Bending, he took her mouth in a kiss that was compounded of everything he was feeling, from the heights of joy to the depths of despair. It was a kiss that he knew should never have happened. It was a kiss he needed.

CHAPTER FOURTEEN

CLAIRE FELT DESIRE rush through her as Jude's mouth closed over hers. In that moment she realised how much she had been longing for this to happen. In some inexplicable way she had sensed that it would change her, make her feel differently, and it did. She felt like *her* when Jude kissed her, like the woman she had been who had enjoyed life and hadn't been afraid. It was such a wonderful feeling that she kissed him back, wanting him to know how much he meant to her...

The sound of gunfire brought them back to earth with a thud. Claire gasped when Jude pushed her away. His face was set as he stood up and stared across the clearing, and the first little doubt came trickling back. Did he regret what he had done, wish that he hadn't broken his promise? She bit her lip as the question was followed by another: had Jude kissed her not because of who she was but because it had been an instinctive response to holding a woman in his arms?

'We need to get back to the hospital. The rebels are starting to move and we won't stand a chance if they find us.' His voice was clipped although whether it was the precariousness of their situation that was causing it or what had happened, she wasn't sure.

'What do you suggest?' she asked, trying to keep the pain out of her voice. It wasn't his fault if he had acted out of instinct and she mustn't blame him.

'We need some kind of a diversion. If we can distract them then there's a chance we can get to the hospital.' He glanced at her leg which, thankfully, had stopped bleeding now. 'If I bind up your leg do you think you can walk on it?'

'I'll try.' She watched him tear another strip off his shirt. He bound it tightly around her thigh then helped her up. Claire gasped when a searing pain shot through her leg as soon as she put her weight on it.

Jude shook his head. 'You're not going to be able to get far on that leg. I'll have to carry you, so we definitely need to set up some kind of a diversion first.'

He helped her sit down again then went to the edge of the trees. Claire could see someone standing at one of the upper windows and realised it was Matt Kearney. Jude had seen him too and started signalling to him, and after a couple of minutes Matt gave him the thumbs-up sign and disappeared.

'Let's hope Matt manages to find something really good to distract them,' Jude said grimly as he helped her to her feet once more. He swung her up into his arms, his expression never altering as he settled her against his chest. He appeared so completely detached that Claire realised her suspicions had been correct. Jude may have kissed her but he would have done the same to any woman in the circumstances.

Thankfully, she had no time to dwell on that thought before there was a series of loud explosions from the rear of the hospital. She gasped when she saw dozens of rockets shooting skywards. More fireworks went off, sending out showers of brightly coloured sparks, but Jude didn't stop to watch them. He ran out from the trees, weaving from side to side so they wouldn't present such an easy target, but in the event not a single shot was fired at them. Willing hands reached out and pulled them inside when they reached the hospital.

'Put her on this trolley.'

Bill rapped out instructions in a wholly unfamiliar fashion and moments later Claire found herself being rushed to Theatre. Javid was already there, all scrubbed up and waiting. While Bill started the anaesthetic, she found herself wondering why Jude wasn't performing the operation. He was the lead surgeon, after all, but maybe he didn't consider her injuries serious enough to require his attention. Just because he had kissed her, it didn't mean that he thought she was special. The thought accompanied her as she slid into unconsciousness, a dark cloud at the back of her mind.

Jude paced the office, unable to sit still while he waited for news of Claire. The operation seemed to be taking an inordinate amount of time and it made him wonder if Javid had hit a snag. Even though he had agreed with Bill that it would be better if someone else performed the surgery, maybe he should go and check, he decided, flinging open the door...

And maybe he should leave well alone, an inner voice cautioned. *Hadn't he caused enough problems without creating any more?*

Jude's expression was grim as he closed the door. Walking over to the desk, he sat down while he thought about what had happened. Matt's diversion had proved highly effective. Not only had it allowed him and Claire to reach the safety of the hospital but it had brought the government troops racing to their aid. The rebel fighters had all been captured which meant they were safe for now. Apparently, a rumour had been going round that one of the highest-ranking generals in charge of the military had been admitted to the hospital which was why they had come under attack. Jude wasn't sure how it had started but it had caused a major disruption. And not only to the smooth running of the hospital either.

He put his head in his hands and groaned. To say that he regretted kissing Claire was a massive understatement. Not only had he made a fool of himself but he must have embarrassed her as well. How he was going to explain himself when he saw her, he had no idea. He couldn't tell her the truth; that he had fallen in love with her and wanted to spend the rest of his days with her!

'Ah, so here you are.' Javid suddenly appeared and Jude jumped up.

'How did it go?' he rapped out, unable to contain his anxiety. 'Was there a problem? It seemed to take an awfully long time.'

'Did it?' Javid glanced at the clock over the desk and shrugged. 'It didn't seem that long to me...' He broke off when Jude glared at him. 'Anyway, Claire's fine. It was just a flesh wound—the bullet must have clipped her thigh as it passed. I cleaned everything up, got rid of a few fibres from her dress that were lodged in the wound, and that was it, basically.'

'So she'll be fit enough to fly back to England tomorrow,' Jude said quietly, struggling to get a grip. He certainly didn't want to compound his errors by making Javid think that he doubted his ability.

'Oh, yes. Her leg will be painful for a week or so but it shouldn't cause any lasting damage, I'm pleased to say. No, she was incredibly lucky, all things considered.'

'She was,' Jude agreed. He thanked Javid then took a deep breath before following him from the room. He wasn't looking forward to the next few minutes but he owed Claire an apology and he needed to do it now because he wouldn't get another chance with her leaving in the morning. All he could hope was that he would be able to come up with something to explain his actions, something that wouldn't necessitate him telling her the truth. One thing was certain: Claire wouldn't welcome it if he told her that he loved her.

The effects of the anaesthetic had worn off fairly quickly. Although her head still felt a little muzzy, otherwise Claire felt fine. Bill had insisted on staying with her but now she chivvied him to take a break. It was the middle of the afternoon and, with one thing and another, lunch had been a non-starter.

She closed her eyes after Bill left. Whether it was the after-effects of the anaesthetic, the events of the day had taken on a surreal quality. She found it difficult to believe that she had been shot yet she had the dressing on her thigh to prove it. Her thoughts drifted on, inevitably coming back to that kiss. Had it been *her* Jude had wanted to kiss with such passion or would any woman have done?

The door opened as someone came into the room but it was a moment before Claire opened her eyes. She fixed a smile to her mouth as she turned to greet her visitor, not wanting anyone to suspect how much the idea hurt. It came as a huge shock to find Jude himself standing at the end of her bed.

'So how do you feel? Javid said everything went swimmingly,' he said coolly.

'I'm fine.' She gave a little shrug, determined to match his tone. She certainly wouldn't embarrass herself by letting him know how painful she found it to be treated so coldly. 'My head's a bit woozy from the anaesthetic but that's all.'

'Good.' Picking up the chart from the end of the bed, he skimmed through it. He hung it back in place and Claire felt a ripple run through her when she saw that his hands were shaking. Maybe he wasn't as indifferent as he was pretending, she thought. The idea made her head spin so that she missed what he said. It was only when she realised that he was waiting for her to speak that she pulled herself together.

'I'm sorry—what did you say?'

'I said that I owe you an apology, and I do. I should never have kissed you, Claire. Put it down to the heat of the moment, although that's no excuse. However, I want you to know that I bitterly regret my actions.'

Claire didn't have time to say anything before he swung round and left the room. But then what could she have said? she thought despairingly. That he hadn't embarrassed her, that on the contrary she had welcomed his kiss and wanted him to kiss her again? An admission like that was bound to have led to questions and she still wasn't ready to answer them and explain about her past.

Tears began to pour down her face. It was better to

leave things the way they were, to leave Jude still believing that she was someone she wasn't: a pure and innocent woman.

Jude had never felt more wretched in his entire life. He lay awake all night thinking about what had happened. Far from making him feel better, apologising to Claire had made him feel worse. He knew that he had been far too economical with the truth but what else could he have said? Surely it was better if she believed he was some kind of...*serial kisser* than embarrass her even more by admitting that he loved her!

Lesley was in the dining room when he went down for breakfast. She took one look at him and rolled her eyes. 'No need to ask how you slept,' she said wryly. 'You look dreadful!'

'I'm fine,' Jude stated huffily. He went to the buffet but the sight of food made his stomach churn. The plane was due to leave in an hour's time and every second that ticked past brought the moment when Claire would go out of his life for good that bit closer. That he would never see her again was guaranteed. She wouldn't contact him and he certainly couldn't contact her now. No, this was it, the not-so-grand finale, the end of any foolish dreams he had harboured...

'For heaven's sake, man, do something!' Lesley stood up and came over to him. 'You can't just let her go. It's obvious that you're crazy about her, so go and tell her that instead of mooning about here like some lost soul!'

'What's the point?' He couldn't even drum up any anger, although if anyone had spoken to him in that fashion in the past he would have had their guts for the proverbial garters. 'Claire isn't interested in how I feel. Her future is all mapped out and there isn't any place in it for me.'

'The *point* is that things aren't always what they appear to be,' Lesley shot back, glaring at him. 'I can't say anything more—it's up to Claire. But believe me when I say that you're making a huge mistake by letting her leave like this.'

Lesley stalked out of the room. Jude went to follow her and demand to know what she'd meant then suddenly thought better of it. It was obvious that Lesley had said everything she intended to say and now it was up to him what happened. The question he needed to ask himself was whether he was willing to risk making a fool of himself again.

His feet were already moving before the answer presented itself, carrying him out of the dining room and across the hall. By the time he reached the front steps he was running, racing around the building to where he had parked the motorbike. He swung his leg over the saddle, sending up a prayer that the engine would start. He didn't have time to coax it to life, not when the plane that was due to take Claire away was waiting on the runway.

The engine fired first time, rattling and coughing in protest, but working all the same. Jude set off in a shower of dust. It took forty minutes to reach the airfield which meant he had ten minutes to spare, ten minutes to change Claire's mind about the future she had planned. Was he right to attempt such a thing? He didn't know. But if he let her leave without telling her that he loved her, he would always regret it!

* * *

Claire had been ferried to the airfield in one of the trucks. Although her leg was extremely painful, she could manage to walk with the aid of crutches. Bill had insisted on waiting with her and they sat on a couple of empty packing cases while the crew ran through the pre-flight checks.

They didn't speak. Claire had nothing to say and Bill obviously recognised her desire for silence. It was as though every scrap of emotion she was capable of feeling had seeped away. In a few minutes' time she would get on that plane and she would never see Jude again.

The sound of an engine cut through the silence. Bill stood up and turned towards the road. 'What the devil's going on!' he exclaimed.

Claire glanced round, although she really didn't care what was happening. Her heart suddenly seized up when she recognised the man astride the motorbike. What was Jude doing here? Surely he had said everything yesterday? It had been the heat of the moment that had caused him to kiss her and he regretted it. What else was there to say?

She struggled to her feet, trembling all over as she watched him bring the bike to an unsteady halt. He propped it against the fence then came striding over to them. His face was set but there was something about the expression in his eyes that made her heart suddenly start beating again. If he regretted what had happened then why was he looking at her that way?

'I'll just go and check how the guys are doing.'

Bill hurriedly excused himself but Claire was barely aware of him leaving. Every fibre of her being was focused on the man in front of her. His face was pale beneath his tan, his eyes surrounded by heavy shadows. Jude hadn't slept from the look of him but why was that? Why had he lain awake all night when he had dismissed that kiss?

'I need to tell you something, Claire, although I'm not sure if you'll want to hear it.' His voice grated, filled with so many emotions that it was impossible to sort one out from another, so Claire didn't try. She simply stood there and after a moment he carried on.

'There was a reason why I kissed you yesterday and it had nothing to do with the heat of the moment either.'

He took hold of her hand and she had a feeling that he needed the contact to bolster his courage. The thought shocked her so much that the numbness which had enveloped her melted away. That this proud, self-possessed man needed her touch was humbling. It was an effort to concentrate when he continued.

'I had to kiss you, Claire—I couldn't help myself and that's the truth of the matter. I...well, I think I'm falling in love with you even though I know I shouldn't let it happen.'

Jude could feel the blood pounding through his veins. Claire hadn't said a word and her silence simply compounded his worst fears. Was she shocked by what he had said? Dismayed by such an unwelcome declaration? *Disgusted* even that he should dare to feel this way about her? He swung round, knowing that the only thing he could do was to beat a hasty retreat. He didn't want to put her under any more pressure, definitely didn't want her thinking that she had to try to spare his feelings...

'Wait!'

Jude stopped reluctantly, although he didn't turn

round. He couldn't bring himself to do that in case he saw pity in her eyes. His pride may have been battered to a pulp but he had something left, so help him! 'Yes?'

'You can't tell me that and then just walk away!'

The anger in her voice brought him swinging round and he stared at her in shock because it wasn't the re-action he'd expected. 'I'm sorry,' he began. 'I know I shouldn't have said anything…'

'No, you damned well shouldn't!' She limped over to him, leaning heavily on the crutches as she glared up into his face. 'I didn't think you were a coward, Jude Slater, but that's what you are, an out-and-out coward!'

She gave him a none-too-gentle poke in the chest with one of the crutches and Jude took a step back, try-ing to think of something to say in his defence. How-ever, it appeared she hadn't finished. 'You could have told me yesterday how you felt, or *any* day at all, come to that, but, no, you had to wait until I'm about to leave.'

'I'm sorry,' he began again then stopped when he realised he was repeating himself.

'And you think that's enough, do you? You hon-estly think that another apology is going to make ev-erything right?'

She shook her head, her silky blonde hair swirling around her shoulders, and Jude felt his body choose that particular moment to stir itself to life. He had never seen her so angry before and, hackneyed though it sounded, he couldn't help thinking how beautiful she looked.

'I hoped it would,' he said softly, wondering if she could hear the desire in his voice.

'Well, you were mistaken!' she shot back, but he saw the colour that rose to her cheeks and knew she had heard it. The strange thing was that she didn't look shocked or disgusted either.

Jude was just trying to get his head round that idea when Bill came over to them, raising his voice to make himself heard as the plane's engines started up.

'Sorry to butt in, folks, but the pilot's ready to take off, so you'll have to get on board.'

'Oh, right.' Claire swivelled round and kissed Bill on the cheek. 'Thanks for everything, Bill,' she said, pitching her voice to carry above the roar of the engines. 'You've been a wonderful friend.'

'My pleasure, love.'

Bill gave her a fatherly hug then moved away, obviously wanting to afford them some privacy. Jude held his breath when Claire turned to him. He wanted more than a perfunctory kiss on the cheek but after what had happened just now he'd be lucky to get that. She looked him straight in the eyes then suddenly leant forward and he froze when, instead of kissing his cheek, she kissed him on the mouth. Her lips clung to his for a moment before she turned her head and whispered something in his ear.

'What did you say?' he demanded, but she was already walking towards the plane. One of the crew helped her on board and the next moment the doors closed and that was that; Jude could only stand and watch as the plane took off.

'See you later, son.'

Bill clapped him on the shoulder then headed over to the truck, but Jude stayed right where he was. Closing his eyes, he tried to make sense of what had happened. The noise from the plane's engines had made it difficult to hear properly but he could have sworn that Claire had whispered, *'I am not a nun.'*

Jude's eyes flew open and he watched until the plane disappeared from sight, those five little words ringing in his ears. Was it true or had he misheard her? He had no idea but one thing was certain: he intended to find out!

CHAPTER FIFTEEN

A MONTH PASSED and Claire gradually settled back into life in England. Her leg had healed and she no longer needed the crutches to get around. She had moved into temporary accommodation, renting a bedsit on the outskirts of London until she found herself a job. She had applied for three nursing posts and was waiting to be interviewed.

On the surface her life was running smoothly but underneath the apparent order was a lot of uncertainty. Would Jude get in touch with her when he returned to England or would he decide that he wanted nothing more to do with her? After all, she had deliberately misled him, so who could blame him if he chose not to see her again? Then there was the question of how she felt about seeing him when it would mean her having to tell him the rest of the story. The fear of how he might react hadn't gone away; if anything it had grown stronger because she had so much more to lose. She couldn't bear it if his love turned to revulsion once she found out what had happened to her.

It was all very unsettling. Claire found herself going over and over it day after day. Lesley had given Claire her mobile phone number with strict instructions to text her with her new address, but she thought long and hard before doing so. Although it was tempting to simply disappear, she knew it would be wrong to take the easy way out. Apart from the fact that she wanted to stay in touch with Lesley, it wouldn't be fair to Jude. She had accused him of being a coward and she couldn't behave in the same way. The team was due to return at the end of the following month, not that there was any guarantee he would want to see her. Once he was back on home ground his feelings could change. She wasn't sure if that idea made her feel better or worse.

When her doorbell rang late one Friday night, she assumed it was a visitor for one of the other tenants ringing it by mistake. It came as a massive shock when she heard Jude's voice coming over the entryphone speaker.

'Claire, it's me, Jude. Can you let me in, please?'

Claire's heart began to pound as she pressed the button to unlock the main doors. She had no idea why he had returned early but that was less important than why he had come to see her at this hour. It was almost midnight and far too late for a social call. Whatever had brought him here had to be extremely urgent.

Jude could feel the tension that had gripped him for the past twenty-four hours reach a crescendo. He knew that he should have left it until the morning before he saw Claire but he couldn't stand the strain any longer. He had spent the past month thinking about what she had said and now he needed answers. What it all boiled down to was why had she let him believe that she was a nun?

His heart was racing when he reached the first floor. Claire was standing by the door and he sighed when he saw how strained she looked. Did she regret telling him the truth, wish that she hadn't said anything? He had no idea but the tiny ray of hope that it had been an encouraging sign flickered even if it didn't quite disappear.

'Come in.'

She led him inside, closing the door behind them. Jude took a long look around although there wasn't much to see. The whole place could have fitted into one room of his apartment and he felt a rush of anger at the thought. Claire deserved better than this shabby little room!

'I didn't think you were due back yet.' She sat down on the sofa which obviously doubled as her bed and Jude pulled himself together. He hadn't come here to dis her living arrangements.

'We weren't.' He opted for the single chair and sat down. 'Unfortunately, there's been a lot of unrest recently and it was deemed too dangerous for us to stay out there.'

'I see.' Claire frowned. 'I'm surprised Lesley didn't text to tell me.'

'I asked her not to.'

'Why on earth did you do that?'

'Because I was afraid that you would take steps to avoid seeing me if you knew I was back.' Jude leant forward, feeling the tension twisting his insides into knots. 'I need to know if what you said before you left was true, Claire. Was it? Are you a nun?'

'No. I'm not.'

Her voice was low but Jude felt its effects all the same. He took a deep breath, struggling to hang on to his control. 'Then why did you let me believe that you were?'

'Because I was afraid.'

'Afraid,' he repeated because it was the last thing he had expected to hear. 'Afraid of me, do you mean?'

'Yes. I realised that you had an…effect on me and I was afraid of what might happen.'

'What sort of effect?' he asked huskily, barely able to force the words out. This was more than he had dared hope for and it was hard to contain his joy.

'One that I never expected to feel.'

She looked him straight in the eyes and he went cold when he saw the anguish on her face. He wanted to tell her to stop then, that he didn't need to know anything else, that he had heard everything that mattered, only he didn't get the chance. The words came out of her mouth and it was as though he had suffered an actual physical blow as they pounded into him.

'I was raped, you see. And that's why I never wanted to feel anything for any man ever again.'

Claire could see the shock on Jude's face and stood up, unable to sit there and watch while shock gave way to anger and then to revulsion. That was what would happen, of course, she thought sickly. Once he got over his initial shock, he would react the way so many other men had done. She had read accounts written by other rape victims describing how their husbands and partners had reacted and they had been remarkably similar: shock came first; anger second; disgust next…

'When did it happen?' His voice grated and she winced. Jude was suffering because he cared about her, because learning what had happened to her hurt *him*. The thought made her feel even worse.

'Just over two years ago.' She plugged in the kettle, not because she wanted a drink but for something to do. She had to hold on to her control and make this as easy as possible for him. The last thing she wanted was him getting hurt.

'Before you went to Mwuranda.'

It was a statement, not a question, and she nodded. 'Yes. That's why I went. I wanted to get away from England.'

'I see. Did you report what had happened to the police?' he continued and she sighed, understanding his need to know all the details. He thought it would help, thought it would make it easier if he filled his head with facts rather than emotions, but she knew better than anyone that nothing could stop the pain.

'No,' she said quietly, hating herself for doing this to him. 'I decided not to go to the police in the end.'

'Because you were afraid of the publicity if the case went to court?'

'That plus the fact that the man who raped me said that nobody would believe me.' She gave a bitter little laugh, stopping abruptly when she heard the note of hysteria that had crept in.

'But that's ridiculous!' Jude leapt to his feet, his eyes blazing with anger. 'Of course they would have believed you, Claire!'

'Maybe.' She gave a tiny shrug. 'And maybe not. I wasn't raped by a stranger, you see. I had been dating this man for a couple of months. That could have made a difference to what the police thought, especially if he'd told them I was trying to get back at him for dumping me.'

'He threatened to do that?'

'Oh, yes.' Her voice caught but she forced herself to carry on. She couldn't break down now. She had to tell Jude everything, every horrible, awful detail. She owed him that. 'The fact that he attacked me because I told him that I didn't want to see him any more was irrelevant. He would have lied if it had meant he would escape punishment.'

'There's no saying the police would have believed him,' Jude said quietly, making an obvious effort to regain control. 'After all, it would have been his word against yours, Claire.'

'True. But he's a lawyer, well respected, apparently, and I wasn't prepared to take that risk.'

She took a quick breath, feeling the foolish tears burning her eyes. She had known how hard it would be to tell him the truth and she should be relieved that it was all out in the open at last. Yet the fear that Jude must view her differently now was unbearably painful. She realised that there was only one thing she could do; she had to make sure he understood that she didn't expect anything from him. Maybe he had said that he loved her but he must feel very differently now that he knew she wasn't the person he had believed her to be, that she was soiled goods, tainted by the past.

'So there you have it. I apologise for misleading you but it seemed the best thing to do.' She held out her hand, her heart aching at the thought of never seeing him again. But it wouldn't be fair to expect him to feel the same about her, to love her, to want her, to spend his life with her. Jude deserved better than her; he deserved a woman who didn't come with such terrible baggage. 'I hope you won't think too badly of me in the future,' she said, her voice breaking.

'And that's it, is it? You've told me the truth and now I'm expected to disappear?' He shook his head, his eyes holding hers fast so that Claire found she couldn't look away. 'Well, I'm sorry to disappoint you but that's not going to happen.'

He took a step towards her. 'You and I could have something really special, Claire. Are you willing to turn your back on that because you're afraid?' Reaching out, he ran the tips of his fingers down her cheek, smiling tenderly when she sucked in her breath. 'Because you do feel something, don't you, Claire? When I touch like this…' he repeated the gentle caress '…you feel the same way I do. Scared, excited, afraid of what's about to happen, afraid that it won't.'

'Jude—' She got no further as he drew her into his arms and cradled her against him.

'It's all right, my love. I understand how scared you must have felt, and how hard it's been for you to deal with what happened to you, but you're not on your own any more. I'm here and I'll always take care of you. You're safe with me.'

His voice was so filled with love that all the doubts which had consumed her suddenly melted away. When his hand moved to her hair and began to stroke it, she nestled against him, loving the feel of his body pressed against her own, so hard and strong and wonderfully reassuring. It struck her then that she had reached a turning point, that never again would she feel scared or ashamed. Telling Jude about the assault had stripped it of its power. Although she would never forget what had happened, she wouldn't let it destroy her life. And it was all thanks to Jude. He had given her back her future.

The thought unleashed all the feelings that she had tried to keep at bay. Reaching up, she drew his head down, kissing him with a passion she had never expected to feel again. But this was different. This was Jude. And he was the man she loved.

Jude gasped when he tasted the hunger on Claire's lips. After what she had told him, he had never expected this! However, there was no denying that she was kissing him as though she really meant it. He kissed her back, letting his lips speak for him. He loved her and he wanted her, and what he had learned hadn't made an iota of difference to any of that. Admittedly, he had been shocked but it hadn't changed his view of her. She was still the most beautiful woman he had ever met, beautiful inside and out too. Nothing that had happened to her in the past—no matter how appalling—would alter how he felt.

The need to tell her that was too strong to resist. He drew back, framing her face between his hands as he looked deep into her eyes. 'I love you, my darling, and I want you to know that what you've told me hasn't made any difference to how I feel about you.'

'Are you sure?' She bit her lip and he could tell that she was struggling to hold back her tears. 'I'd understand if you felt differently about me, Jude. It must be hard for any man to cope with what I told you, so please don't think that you have to stay with me out of kindness…'

'Kindness has nothing to do with it!' Jude didn't let her finish. He kissed her long and hungrily, wanting to erase any foolish ideas she had about why he wanted to be with her. He loved her so much and the thought of being without her was unbearable.

They were both trembling when they drew apart. Jude ran his knuckles over her swollen lips, filled with awe that she wanted him so much. If he was honest, he didn't feel worthy of her love. He had led such a hedonistic life before they had met, wasted his talents instead of using them to make a difference to people's lives. Surely he should confess all that and make sure she understood exactly what kind of a man he was before they went any further?

Taking her hand, he led her to the sofa, his heart thumping as they sat down. The thought of how she might react when she found out the truth about him wasn't easy to deal with, but it wouldn't be fair to play down his shortcomings after she had been so open with him.

'There's something I must tell you, Claire,' he began.

'It's all right,' she said quickly, her voice catching. 'I understand if you're having second thoughts.'

'I'm not.' He kissed her softly on the mouth then smiled into her eyes. 'Oh, I hate what's happened to you and wish with all my heart that you hadn't had to go through such a terrible ordeal. But it doesn't alter the way I feel about you. How could it when it's part of what has made you the person you are?'

'Are you sure?' She gripped his hand and his heart ached when he felt the tremor that ran through her. 'Sure that it won't make a difference in the future? I couldn't bear that, Jude. Really I couldn't.'

'I'm sure.' He kissed her again then forced himself to pull back before temptation got the better of him. However, he couldn't bear to think that *she* might regret staying with him if she found out about his not-so-glorious past. The thought filled him with dread but he forced himself to continue. 'I think it's only right that you know about my past, Claire. To be honest, I've devoted more time to pleasure than I have to my career in the last few years.'

'That might be true, but you did a brilliant job while you were in Mwuranda,' she protested. 'Everyone said so.'

'Did they? That's good to know.' Jude felt strangely heartened by that news and it helped enormously. 'However, despite those kind words, I know that I could have done an even better job if I hadn't wasted so much time these past five years. To put it bluntly, I've been coasting since I left the NHS.'

'Why did you leave?' she asked quietly, twining her fingers through his as though she sensed how difficult he found it to talk about the reason why he had quit.

'Because I was totally burnt out.' Raising her hand to his mouth, he gently kissed it. 'I was based at a hospital in the centre of the city and the workload was horrendous. There was never enough staff and we seemed to spend our time playing catch-up—I can't count the number of times we had to cancel a scheduled surgery because there weren't enough qualified staff available. Morale was at rock-bottom, so it wasn't only me who found it hard to cope.' He sighed. 'Despite all that, I probably would have carried on working there if it weren't for Maddie. Her death was the final straw.'

'Was she the child you mentioned when we were looking after Bebe?'

'Yes.' Jude took a deep breath, feeling the pain sear his insides even after all the time that had passed. 'Maddie was one of my patients, thirteen years old and born with a congenital heart problem. She had been in and out of hospital all her life yet, despite that, she was one of the pluckiest, bravest kids I've ever met.' He laughed softly. 'She loved playing tricks on us—you know the sort of thing, whoopee cushions placed on a chair, fake injuries. She just loved having fun.'

'She sounds lovely,' Claire said quietly.

'She was. A lovely, happy child who brought a lot of joy to her family and everyone she came into contact with.'

'What happened to her?' Claire squeezed his hand when he hesitated. 'You don't have to tell me if it's too painful.'

'No, I want to tell you,' he said slowly, realising it was true. Sharing this with Claire would help him put it into perspective, something he had never quite managed to do. 'Maddie was on the heart-lung transplant register as it had reached the point where it was the only option open to her. Anyway, we received notification that organs had become available, so we called her into hospital. She was so excited, not scared, just thrilled at the thought that she'd be able to lead a normal life after the operation.

'Everything was set up and ready, the harvest team was due to arrive and then the unthinkable happened. I had a call from the head of surgery to say that he'd been involved in an RTA on his way in and had broken his wrist. If that wasn't bad enough, he'd had our senior consultant with him, and *he* was suffering from concussion.'

'Oh, no!' Claire exclaimed. 'So what did you do?'

'There was no way we could go ahead with the transplant—we simply didn't have enough staff. As you probably know, time is of the essence in this type of situation. Organs for transplant soon start to deteriorate, so we couldn't wait until we managed to draft in enough staff. I had to contact the transplant team and tell them to offer the organs to another patient. Then I had to tell Maddie.' He lowered his head when he felt tears fill his eyes. 'She was devastated. I think that's when she gave up, because she'd lost all hope of getting better. She died three days later and there wasn't a thing I could do to help her.'

'It wasn't your fault, Jude.' Claire put her arms around him and hugged him. 'You did everything you could.'

'But it wasn't enough to save her.' He hugged her back, feeling a little better thanks to her closeness. He sighed. 'I handed in my notice the following month and went into the private sector, where I've stayed for the past five years. It's been the easy option, basically. However, it's time I thought about doing more with my life.'

'If it's what you want to do then I'm all for it. But don't do it for the wrong reasons, Jude.' She smiled at him. 'I'll admit that I had my doubts at first. You did seem a bit...well, *full* of yourself. But I soon realised what a superb surgeon you are.'

'Hmm. That's a backhanded compliment if ever I heard one. Full of myself indeed!' He kissed her, taking his time as he lovingly punished her for the comment. Claire sighed when he let her go.

'Sorry, but I did say you were superb at your job, don't forget.' She laughed when he rolled his eyes. 'Anyway, what I'm trying to say is that you shouldn't feel bad about the choices you've made. You needed a break from all the pressure from the sound of it. And as you just told me, your past has made you into the person you are today and I, for one, love every tiny bit of you.'

'That's good enough for me.'

He drew her into his arms, kissing her with a hunger he made no attempt to hide. Claire kissed him back, loving the fact that it felt so right. She had never expected to feel this way and it simply reinforced her decision to put the past behind her. When Jude gently set her away from him, she smiled into his eyes.

'Thank you. I didn't think I would ever feel this happy.'

'Neither did I.' He brushed his lips across her forehead and grimaced. 'I hate to do this but it's time I left. It's late and I'm in Theatre first thing tomorrow morning.'

'Really? I'd have thought you would take some time off before you went back to work,' she queried in surprise.

'I am, but I'm assisting Professor Jackson.' He grinned at her. 'He's agreed to operate on Jeremiah. We managed to get the paperwork all sorted, so we brought him back to England with us.'

'Oh, that's wonderful!' Claire exclaimed.

'Isn't it? However, if I'm to be any help at all then I'd better get some sleep.'

He stood up and Claire got up as well. She took a quick breath to contain the ripple of panic that ran through her. This was a huge step but she was determined to focus on the future and forget the past. 'You don't have to leave. You can stay here, if you like.'

'I'd love to but I don't know if it's a good idea, Claire,' Jude said quietly. Taking her hands, he drew her to him and hugged her. 'I know how difficult it must be for you to think about sleeping with me after what's happened and I don't want you to feel under any pressure. We can wait until you're ready and it doesn't matter how long it takes.'

'Thank you.' She kissed him on the lips, loving him more than ever for being so understanding. 'But I've wasted enough time and now I want to get on with my life, get on with loving you and showing you how much you mean to me.'

'Then why don't we take things really slowly?' He tipped up her chin and dropped a feather-light kiss on her mouth. 'If I spend the night here, we don't have to make love. We can simply sleep in one another's arms. It sounds wonderful to me. How about you?'

'It sounds wonderful to me too,' she said softly, her heart swelling with happiness at his thoughtfulness.

Jude kissed her again then helped her turn the sofa into a bed. Claire found the pillows and the duvet then hesitated, wondering if she should go and undress in the tiny bathroom.

'Here, let me help you.' Jude took her into his arms and kissed her hungrily before turning his attention to the buttons down the front of her blouse. He worked them free then slipped it off her shoulders and looked at her, studying the ripe curves of her breasts beneath the plain white bra she was wearing. 'You're so beautiful,' he murmured huskily. 'Even more beautiful than I imagined.'

Claire shuddered, more affected than she could say by the thought of him imagining how she looked. When he slid the straps off her shoulders, she stood proudly in front of him, glorying in the fact that he enjoyed looking at her. He didn't see her as soiled goods but as a desirable woman. The woman he loved.

He swiftly dispensed with the rest of her clothes and then it was her turn. Claire's hands were shaking as she grasped the hem of his sweater and drew it over his head. He was naked beneath, his skin deeply tanned underneath a light covering of hair. Reaching out, she ran her palms over the warm strong muscles, savouring the firmness of his flesh, its vitality. She could feel his heart beating beneath her fingertips and closed her eyes, wanting to store away the moment. She didn't feel afraid, as she might have expected. After all, this was the first time she had been intimate with a man since she had been raped. But touching Jude this way felt right; it was what she wanted to do. She knew then that what had happened in the past could no longer hurt her. Love had taken away its power to rule her life.

Jude could feel his desire building but forced himself to hold back. He didn't want to rush Claire. She needed time and he would give it to her. Tossing back the quilt, he held out his hand, smiling into her eyes when she immediately placed her hand in his. That she trusted him was plain to see and it meant the world to him. He would never betray her trust, he vowed as he drew her down on the bed. No matter what life threw at them, he would always be there for her, would always protect and cherish her until his dying day. She was his present and his future: she was everything to him.

Drawing her into his arms, he kissed her with heart-melting tenderness, feeling the tears running down his cheeks. He couldn't recall ever crying like this before but it didn't matter. He loved her so much that his heart seemed to be brimming over with emotion. When she cupped his face between her hands and began to kiss away his tears, he let her. He wasn't ashamed of her seeing them. If anyone had the right to know how deeply he felt, it was her.

'I love you,' he whispered, holding her close.

'And I love you too. So very much.'

They held each other close, not needing to do or say anything else. They both knew that from this moment on they would be together, that nothing could part them. They might not make love tonight but Jude knew that they would do so soon and that it would be wonderful too. More wonderful than anything they had ever known. They loved each other too much for it to be anything other than perfect.

EPILOGUE

Three years later...

'LADIES AND GENTLEMEN, please join me in welcoming our guest of honour this evening, Dr Jude Slater.'

Claire smiled when everyone started to clap. She knew that Jude had been a little nervous about tonight but he needn't have been. He had become something of a cult figure in the last couple of years as he had expounded his views on poverty in the developing world and what needed to be done about it. A lot of people admired his forthright approach, not least of all her. Jude was making a difference to a lot of people's lives and he deserved all the plaudits that came his way.

She let her mind drift back over what had happened while she listened to his speech. They had been married shortly after his return from Mwuranda. As Jude had said, there was no reason for them to wait. The service had been held in the church close to her parents' home in Cheshire. All the Worlds Together team had attended, along with her family and friends. It had been a wonderfully happy occasion. As she and Jude had made their vows they had both known that they meant every word. It was the start of their new life together and they wouldn't allow anything that had gone on before to ruin their love for one another.

They had gone to Paris for their honeymoon and it had been everything she had dreamt it would be. They had decided to wait until their honeymoon before they made love. It had been Jude's idea and she had been happy to go along with it, even though she'd had no qualms about how she would feel. In the event, their lovemaking had been everything they had hoped for, the confirmation of their love for one another.

Once they returned to London, she had accepted a senior sister's post at one of the large teaching hospitals while Jude had given up his job in the private sector and set about honing his skills by accepting a post with Professor Jackson's team. His natural talent for surgery had soon made itself apparent and he was much in demand both at home and abroad. However, he had continued to work for Worlds Together and had become a spokesman for them which was what had brought about this invitation to speak at tonight's dinner. They had both found worthwhile careers, although in her case there were to be some changes shortly.

A burst of applause announced that Jude had come to the end of his speech. Claire laughed as he mopped imaginary perspiration from his brow as he came back to their table and sat down. 'Phew! Am I glad that's over!' he declared, leaning over to drop a kiss on her cheek.

'Don't give me that,' she retorted, thinking how handsome he looked in his dinner jacket. 'You know you love the adoration of your fans. I mean, just listen to all that applause!'

'Oh, *please*!' He rolled his eyes. 'They're clapping because I didn't go wittering on for too long.'

'Hmm, if you say so,' she replied, still smiling. She took a quick breath, feeling excitement bubbling up inside her. She had been waiting for this moment all day and now it had arrived at last. 'Talking about fans, you're about to add another one to your club.'

'Am I?' he asked, frowning.

'Yes, you are.' Clare stood up, suddenly deciding that the crowded dining room was not the best place to continue the conversation. 'I'll tell you outside.'

Jude looked puzzled but he got up and followed her from the dining room. She led him across the hotel's foyer to the reading room, which was empty. Closing the door, she turned to look at him, unable to contain her joy a second longer.

'I did a test today while you were practising your speech,' she began, but he cut her off.

'You don't mean—'

'Yes, I do. I'm pregnant! We're having a baby, my darling, which means that in roughly seven months' time there'll be a new little addition to your fan club.'

'Oh, darling!' Jude could barely breathe as a wave of intense joy flooded through him. It was what they had both been hoping for and to finally have it happen was almost more than he could believe. He drew Claire into his arms, realising again how lucky he was. Not only had he found her, his soul-mate, but in a short time he was going to have a son or a daughter too. Life couldn't get any better.

Tilting her face, he looked into her eyes. 'I didn't think it was possible to feel any happier, but it is. I can't tell you how much this means to me, sweetheart.'

'You don't have to because I feel the same.' Taking

his hand, she placed it on her stomach. 'We're going to have a baby, Jude. Isn't it wonderful?'

'It is. Completely and utterly wonderful. Just like you.'

He kissed her softly on the mouth, letting his lips tell her just how much this meant to him. He'd thought he was happy before they had met but how wrong he had been. *This* was what true happiness felt like, he thought wonderingly, this feeling of complete and utter bliss. He had found the woman he would love for the rest of his days and they were going to have a child. Nothing could beat this!

* * * * *

If you enjoyed this story, check out these other great reads from Jennifer Taylor

THE GREEK DOCTOR'S SECRET SON
MIRACLE UNDER THE MISTLETOE
BEST FRIEND TO PERFECT BRIDE
ONE MORE NIGHT WITH HER DESERT PRINCE...

All available now!

SECOND CHANCE
WITH LORD
BRANSCOMBE

BY
JOANNA NEIL

MILLS & BOON

Published in Great Britain 2016
By Mills & Boon, an imprint of HarperCollins*Publishers*
1 London Bridge Street, London, SE1 9GF

© 2016 Joanna Neil

ISBN: 978-0-263-91519-8

Our policy is to use papers that are natural, renewable and recyclable products and made from wood grown in sustainable forests. The logging and manufacturing processes conform to the legal environmental regulations of the country of origin.

Printed and bound in Spain
by CPI, Barcelona

Dear Reader,

I've always loved coastal settings, and this book has one of my favourites—an English Devonshire village clustered around a sheltered bay. At the centre of this community is the Manor House and its estate, overlooking all—the proud heritage of the Branscombe family through generations. What could be a better, more perfect background for an enduring love story?

But, as you know, the path of true love never runs smooth, and Nate and Sophie have more than their fair share of troubles. How can their love survive the hostility that simmers between their fathers? Or overcome the overwhelming problems that cascade down upon Nate's head?

It takes a special kind of man to win against all the odds—and I hope you'll agree with me that Sophie deserves the best!

Happy reading.

With love,

Joanna

For my family, with thanks for their unfailing love
and support through the years.

Books by Joanna Neil

Mills & Boon Medical Romance

Dr Right All Along
Tamed by Her Brooding Boss
His Bride in Paradise
Return of the Rebel Doctor
Sheltered by Her Top-Notch Boss
A Doctor to Remember
Daring to Date Her Boss
Temptation in Paradise
Resisting Her Rebel Doc
Her Holiday Miracle

Visit the Author Profile page
at millsandboon.co.uk for more titles.

**Praise for
Joanna Neil**

'...a well-written romance set in the beautiful
Caribbean.'

—*Harlequin Junkie* on
Temptation in Paradise

CHAPTER ONE

'IT'S BEAUTIFUL OUT HERE, isn't it?' Jake smiled as he looked out over the sea and watched the waves rolling on to the shore. 'I never get tired of looking at that glorious view. I'm just glad I get the chance to come and sit here after work sometimes.'

'Me too.' Sophie returned the smile and then concentrated on carefully spooning golden sugar crystals into her coffee. It gave her a bit of time to think. She *ought* to be content, no doubt about it, but she couldn't get rid of this nagging feeling that before too long everything in her world was going to be turned upside down.

On the surface everything was running smoothly. What could be better than to be here on a late Friday afternoon, taking in the fresh sea air with Jake, on the terrace of this restaurant in the delightful little fishing village they called home? On the North Devon coast, a small inlet in a wide bay, it was an idyllic place to live.

A faint warm breeze was blowing in off the blue water, riffling gently through her long honey-blonde curls and lightly fanning her cheeks. From here she could see the rocky crags that enclosed the peaceful cove and she could hear the happy shouts of children playing on the beach below, dipping their nets into rock pools that had been left behind by the outgoing tide. She had every reason to be happy.

The truth was, though, that she'd been on edge this last couple of weeks...and there could be only one reason for that. Ever since Nate Branscombe had returned to the Manor House her emotions had been on a roller-coaster ride. Maybe she should have expected him to come back once he'd heard about his father's health taking a downward turn. Deep down, she'd known all along he would have to visit his father, Lord Branscombe, sooner or later, but when she'd heard he'd actually turned up she'd been swamped by a feeling akin to panic. She'd gone out of her way since then to avoid running into him.

'This is the perfect place to relax,' Jake said, oblivious to her subdued mood. He sipped his coffee and then glanced at his watch. 'I can't stay for too much longer, though...much as I'd like to—I have a meeting to go to.'

'Ah—the joys of working in hospital management!' She glanced at him, her mouth crinkling at the corners. It was what he was born to do, streamlining what went on in various departments of the local hospital.

Jake Holdsworth was a clever, likeable young man, good-looking, with neat dark hair and compassionate brown eyes. He was a couple of years older than her at twenty-eight, but they'd known each other for several years since he used to regularly come to the village to visit a favourite aunt. They'd become firm friends. Eventually, though, they'd gone their separate ways when they each left home to take up places at university—she went to Medical School and Jake went off to study Hospital and Health Services Management. It was one of her proudest moments when she was at last able to call herself Dr Trent.

'Oh, yes! Budget meetings, purchasing committees, dealing with the complaints of clinicians! It's all go!'

'But you love it.' Their lives had been busy, as each of them worked towards building their careers, and it was only lately they'd met up again. Jake had a keen sense of humour and she liked spending time with him. He always managed to put her at ease, to help her set aside her troubled family situation for a while, to make her forget that life could be a struggle sometimes. He was a restful kind of man and she enjoyed talking to him.

He was nothing at all like Nate Branscombe—the very opposite, in fact. She frowned. Somehow, Nate had the knack of stirring up strong passions in her—for good or bad—but, either way, they were feelings she would far sooner forget. More often than not, he left her in turmoil.

Nate had the kind of bone-melting good looks that sent her heart into overdrive the moment she saw him. Women couldn't get enough of him but, as far as he was concerned, it was all easy come, easy go. His girlfriends each thought they would be the one to change him, but she could have told them they were wasting their time. He would never make that final commitment.

Maybe that was why Sophie had always held back from him. He wanted her, there had been no doubt about it, and she'd been so…so…tempted, but she wasn't going to fall for him, like all the others, and end up being hurt. Nate liked women, enjoyed being with them, having fun, getting the most out of life, but she wondered if he'd ever meet the woman who was right for him. Or maybe Nate was aware that the women he'd dated simply didn't make the grade to be the wife of a future lord.

'Are you okay? You're a bit quiet today.' Jake studied her thoughtfully. 'Have you had a tough day at the hospital?'

'Oh—I'm sorry. I was miles away.' Jerked out of her reverie, Sophie made an effort to pull herself together. 'No, it was fine.'

'Is it some problem closer to home, then? Are you worried about your family?' Jake gave her a wry, coaxing smile before finishing off his coffee and resting his hands on the table, his fingers loosely clasped.

She shrugged her shoulders. 'The usual, I suppose. According to my brother, Rob, my mother's acting weird again, and Jessica's a bit upset because Ryan has to go away to work.'

He gave a sympathetic nod. 'It's not the best timing, is it? How far advanced is her pregnancy?' He hazarded a guess. 'Third trimester?'

She nodded, smiling. 'Thirty-seven weeks or thereabouts. The baby could decide to put in an appearance any time now.'

His mouth made a flat line. 'Not a great time for her to be on her own, then?'

'No.' Sophie frowned. 'Mum and my stepdad are fairly close by for her, though.'

She glanced around as she heard the sound of footsteps approaching. 'Your table's over here, sir,' the waitress was saying, showing Lord Branscombe to a table set in a quiet corner by the wrought-iron balustrade. As he followed her, Lord Branscombe was walking slowly, each step measured and cautious. He straightened, looking towards the table. A bright spray of scarlet surfinia

spilled over from a tall cream-coloured planter nearby
and beyond the rail there was a mass of green shrubbery, providing a modicum of privacy from some of
the other diners.

James Branscombe acknowledged the waitress briefly,
but came to a halt halfway across the terrace. He seemed
to be struggling for breath, a hand clutched to his chest,
and the waitress watched him worriedly.

'Are you all right?' she asked. 'I didn't think— The
steps up to the terrace are quite steep… Perhaps I should
have taken it more slowly…'

'Please, don't fuss,' he said in a gruff voice. 'Just bring
me a whisky, will you?'

'Of course. Right away.' His command had been pe-
remptory but, even so, the girl escorted Lord Branscombe to his table and made sure he was seated before
she hurried away to get his drink.

Around them, Sophie noticed the hubbub of conversation had died down. People cast surreptitious glances
towards the occupant of the table in the corner and then
began to speak in hushed voices. Lord Branscombe, for
his part, ignored them all, lost in a world of his own.
In his early sixties, he looked older, his hair greying,
his face taut and a deep furrow etched into his brow.

'Perhaps he shouldn't be out and about,' Jake murmured, echoing what everyone must surely be thinking. 'He doesn't look well.'

'No, he doesn't,' Sophie said, a touch of bitterness
threading her words. 'But when did that ever stop him?'

'True.' He sent her a quick worried look. 'I'm sorry.
Of course, you know that to your cost.'

'It's probably the reason Nate's back at the Manor
House,' she said, ignoring his last statement. She wished

she'd never said anything. After all, what was the point in raking up past history? 'He'll be worried about his father.'

'Hmm…about the estate too, I imagine.' Jake frowned. 'You must have heard the rumours going around?'

'About Lord Branscombe's business venture overseas?'

He nodded.

'Yes, I've heard them.' She winced. 'According to what I've read in the national papers, he's lost an awful lot of money.'

'Nate won't like that—the fact that the press have got hold of the story, I mean.'

'No, he won't.' Nate already hated the press after the coverage his father had received a couple of years ago when he was taken ill at the controls of a light aircraft. This new story would have stirred his dislike of them all over again. 'What makes it worse is that he didn't want his father to have anything to do with the so-called development out there in the first place, but Lord Branscombe wouldn't listen.'

'Oh?' Jake raised a brow. 'How do you know that?'

'I heard Nate and his father having a heated discussion one day when I was out walking the dog. Lord Branscombe wouldn't listen to reason…but then, he never has.' And it was James Branscombe's refusal to take heed of what people said that had left her father in the state he was now. Her lower lip began to quiver slightly and she caught it between her teeth to still the movement.

Jake laid his hand over hers, clasping her fingers in a comforting gesture. 'This must be really difficult for you, after what happened to your father.'

'It is.' She closed her eyes fleetingly. Her father had been a passenger in the single-engine plane that crashed nearly two years ago. James Branscombe had taken the controls against all advice and that decision had left her father with life-changing injuries. He'd suffered a broken back, shoulder and ankle, whereas Lord Branscombe had come out of it relatively unscathed.

Even now she had trouble coming to terms with what had happened.

Jake was concerned. 'You must be upset at the thought of Nate coming back. You and he had something going for a while, didn't you? Until the accident put an end to it.'

'Maybe I had feelings for him, years ago, when I was a teenager, and then later it all came to the fore again just before my father's accident…but we wouldn't have made it work. I realise that, now. We were both studying in different parts of the country for a long while, so I didn't see him very often…and, anyway, Nate could never commit to a relationship. Things went badly wrong for us after what happened to my father. I think Nate only stayed around long enough to make sure his father was okay. He's been back a few times since then, but I've kept out of his way.' She braced her shoulders. 'Do you mind if we don't talk about it?'

Right now she couldn't cope with having it all dredged up again. She steeled herself to put on an appearance of calm and she and Jake talked quietly for a while.

A few minutes later, though, her outward composure was all but shattered once more. She looked up and saw a man striding confidently across the terrace, heading towards the corner table.

'Nate?' The word crossed her lips in a whisper of

disbelief and Jake gently squeezed her hand in support. It was a shock, seeing Nate standing just a short distance away from her. When she'd seen him, soon after the crash, she'd been upset, out of her mind with worry, and they'd argued furiously over his father's actions. But when he went away, in her mind, in her soul, she'd still yearned for him.

Nate hadn't seen her yet as he stopped briefly to speak to one or two people along the way. Her mind skittered this way and that, trying to find some means of escape, but of course it was hopeless from the start.

He saw her and his eyes widened in recognition. For a moment or two he seemed stunned. Then he started towards her, a long, lean figure of a man, his stride rangy and confident, the muscles in his arms hinting at a body that was perfectly honed beneath the designer T-shirt and casual trousers he was wearing.

The breath caught in her throat. She couldn't think straight any more. All she could do was drink in his image—the broad shoulders, the sculpted cheekbones and the black, slightly overlong, unruly hair that kinked in a roguish kind of way.

'Sophie.' His voice was deep and warm, a hint of satisfaction there, as though he was more than pleased to see her. He stopped by her table and looked at her, his brooding green gaze all-encompassing, tracing the slope of her cheekbones and the soft curve of her mouth and lingering on the golden corkscrew curls that tumbled over her shoulders. 'It's good to see you again. You look wonderful.'

Unsettled by that penetrating scrutiny, she lowered her gaze. She didn't know how to react to him after all this time. She was distracted by a whole host of unfamiliar feelings that were coursing through her.

His glance trailed downwards, taking in the way Jake's hand covered hers. Then he lifted his head, making a faint, almost imperceptible nod. 'Jake.' He gave him a narrowed look and Jake must have begun to feel uncomfortable because he straightened, slowly releasing Sophie's hand.

'Hi there, Nate. We haven't seen you in a while,' he said.

'I've been busy, working away for the last few months.' Nate's gaze swept over Sophie once more, meshing with hers in a simmering, wordless exchange.

Images flashed through her mind, visions of times past when they'd walked together through the woods on the estate, when her feelings for him were growing with each day that passed. Nate had held her hand, that last day before she went away to Medical School, and led her into a sunlit copse. She'd been eighteen then, troubled about going away and perhaps not seeing him again. She recalled how the silver birch trees had lifted their branches to the clear blue sky and he'd gently eased her back against the smooth white bark. He'd lowered his head towards her and his kiss had been warm and tender, as soft as the breeze on a hot summer's day.

Even now, thinking about it, she could feel his body next to hers, remember how it had been to be wrapped in his arms, to have her flesh turn to flame as his lips nuzzled the curve of her neck.

Jake's voice broke the spell. 'I'd heard something about you being in the States for a while,' he said. 'You've been doing well for yourself, or so they say.'

'I guess so.' Nate turned his attention to Sophie once more. 'I was hoping we might run into one another.'

'I suppose it was inevitable.' Sophie pulled in a deep breath to steady herself. 'You're back here for your father, I imagine?' She looked up at Nate, amazed to find that her voice worked, with barely a trace of nervousness showing through.

'I am. He's not been doing so well these last few weeks, though he would never admit it.' He frowned, glancing to where his father was sitting alone at the table. 'I should go and join him.' There was a hint of reluctance about his mouth as he spoke. 'But I'd like to see you again, find out how you've been doing. I've tried to keep up with how things were going for you and your father, through Charlotte, mostly.' He looked at her intently. 'Perhaps we could talk later?'

She gave a non-committal movement of her head. Charlotte was the housekeeper at the Manor House and she might have expected her to let Nate know what was happening in the village. As to talking with him, surely it would be best, from her viewpoint, to steer very clear of both Branscombes, but especially Nate? Already she was conscious of a knot forming in her stomach and a fluttery feeling growing in her chest. In every way he was dangerous to her peace of mind. Her alarm system was on full alert.

Nate must have taken her gesture for agreement. He nodded once more to both of them and then left, walking over to the table at the corner of the terrace. As Nate went to sit opposite his father, Sophie saw that another man had come to join them—a man she recognised as Lord Branscombe's Estate Manager...

his most recent Estate Manager. Her father had done the job for a good many years before him. She sucked in a sharp breath.

Jake's gaze followed them. 'I wonder what will happen to the estate if Lord Branscombe really has lost most of his money overseas. That's what the newspaper articles are saying…that he's gambled his son and heir's inheritance on a doomed investment and lost.'

'I think there's a lot more to worry about than Nate's inheritance. There are more than two dozen houses on the estate with tenants who will be worried about what's going to happen to their homes.'

Jake's expression was sombre. 'And your father's one of them. It's understandable if you, of all people, feel angry about the way Lord Branscombe's behaved.'

'Maybe.' She frowned. 'But, like I said, I think I'd prefer not to talk about that right now.'

'Of course. But at least it sounds as though Lord Branscombe's finally getting his comeuppance.'

She didn't answer. The waitress came and refilled Sophie's coffee cup, glancing surreptitiously over to where Nate was sitting. Absently, she went to pour a refill for Jake.

'None for me, thanks,' he said, covering his cup with his hand.

'Oh, okay.' Still casting quick looks in Nate's direction, the girl slowly walked away.

Jake made a wry smile. 'He's lost none of his charm, has he?' he murmured, glancing at Sophie. 'He still has that charisma that had all the girls hankering after him.' There was a hint of envy in his voice.

'Mm hmm.' She was hardly immune to it herself— no matter how much she'd told herself in the intervening years that Nate didn't have any power over her feelings, it had taken only a few seconds in his company for him to prove her profoundly wrong. 'I suppose so.'

They chatted for a while, about Jake's work and her job as a children's doctor, until, reluctantly, he glanced once more at his watch. 'I should go,' he said. 'Do you want me to see you back to your car?'

She shook her head. 'No, that's all right. I still have to finish off this coffee. You go ahead. I'll leave in a minute or so.'

'Okay.' He stood up, leaning over to give her a quick, affectionate kiss on the cheek. 'I'll see to the bill on my way out.'

'Thanks.' Sophie watched him leave and then slowly sipped her coffee. It was hot, a new brew fresh from the pot, so she had to take her time. Lord Branscombe, she noticed, glancing idly towards his table, was picking at a plate of food with hardly any appetite, while his Estate Manager was tucking in to a steak and all the trimmings. Nate wasn't eating. The three men seemed to be having an avid discussion about something—the way forward, she supposed.

A short time later she pushed her cup away and picked up her handbag, getting ready to leave.

'You're going already?' Nate must have been watching her because he suddenly appeared at her side, his hand coming to support her elbow as she stood up. 'I didn't want you to leave without my having the chance to talk to you again. Perhaps I could walk with you?'

'I… Yes… I mean…' She was flustered, startled by the way he'd homed in on her, and she stayed silent as he accompanied her down the stairs. By the time they reached the lounge area of the restaurant, though, she had managed to recover her equilibrium enough to say, 'Won't your father be expecting you to keep him company?'

'I'm sure he'll be fine without me for a while. Besides, I've said all I need to say to him for now. He knows my opinion. I've no doubt he and Maurice will be battling things out for another hour or so yet.'

They walked out of the white-painted building and stood by the railings on the cliff path, looking out over the rugged crags to the beach below. 'I suppose I shouldn't have been surprised to see you with Jake,' Nate said. 'You were always good friends…but I saw that he kissed you. Are you and he a couple now?' He was studying her intently. 'Are things serious between you?'

She blinked at the suddenness of the question. She'd forgotten how direct he could be. 'Oh, we met up again fairly recently,' she answered cautiously. 'I think he's fond of me but, really, we're just friends.' She suspected Jake would like to take things further, but after a couple of ill-fated relationships over the last few years, she wasn't about to step into another one in a hurry. Perhaps *she* was the problem. She'd seen what had happened with her parents' marriage and she wasn't ready to put her trust in anyone any time soon.

'I see.' He studied her closely as though gauging her response. He didn't seem to believe the 'just friends' scenario. 'I've always cared for you, Sophie. You know that, don't you? It was hard for me to see you hurting so much after what happened to your father. I felt perhaps you blamed me in some way—perhaps you thought I should have tried to stop my father from flying—'

'You must have known he had angina.' She stared at him, and the pain must have been clear in her eyes. 'Surely there was something you could have done?'

His gaze travelled over her, searing her with its intensity. 'You know what he's like. He never admits to weakness. And I was working at a hospital in Cornwall at the time.' His mouth flattened. 'Sophie, I never wanted there to be this rift between us. You didn't seem to want me around but I always hoped—'

She stopped him before he could say any more. 'No—let's not go there,' she said quickly, anxious to ward off complications. He'd gone away to work abroad, leaving her to pick up the pieces. Perhaps, like he'd said, it was hard for him to see her pain, to witness the heartache his father had caused. 'A lot's happened in the last few years. I'm sure we're very different people now—leastways, I know I am. These past two years have changed me.' She braced her shoulders. 'So what's happening with you? Is there someone in your life these days?'

He pulled a face and shrugged. 'You know me,' he said. 'Can't settle—too much going on all the while.'

'Hmm. And it's going to take time, isn't it, to find the right woman...the one with the class and breeding to take her place at Branscombe Manor?' She said it with a smile, with the wry knowledge that he would most likely exhaust all possibilities before making his pick.

'Oh, you know me so well, don't you?' he said with a short laugh, reading her mind. 'Or at least you always thought you did.' He sobered, studying her thoughtfully.

'Oh, cryptic now, are we?' She let that one pass and

asked seriously, 'So…have you come back to sort out the estate?'

He raised a dark brow. 'Can you imagine my father letting me do that? He's never listened to any ideas that don't go along with his way of thinking, from me or anyone. That's why we argued and it's another reason why I left. He's always been a stubborn man, determined to do things his own way.'

'Yes, but you can be a bit like that sometimes,' she said, challenging him. 'Isn't there a bit of *like father, like son*? After all, you decided on medicine as a career and went your own way, even though you knew your father was set against it.'

'True,' he conceded, 'but I felt very strongly about becoming a doctor. I'm lucky, far more fortunate than a lot of people—I was able to dip into my trust-fund money to get me through university because he wouldn't support me in my choice. He wanted me to go in a completely different direction and learn everything there was about Estate Management so that I could take over one day, but I couldn't do what he asked. We settled the argument eventually, but it was always a sore point with him.'

'Some people around here think you don't care about the estate, or the village.'

'Is that what you believe?' He shot her a lancing green stare.

'I think I know you better than that…but I'd like to hear your side of things.'

He made a grimace. 'It's not true that I don't care. Of course I care. It's my heritage. The Manor has been in our family for generations and I want to keep it that way. I would have been fine with taking on the estate when the time came. I would have done whatever was needed, with the help of managers and estate workers, but my father wouldn't tolerate any of my ideas. Whenever I suggested changes that I felt would be for the better, he said things were all right as they were. He made things impossible for me. I wasn't prepared to be just a figurehead, keeping things ticking along in the same old way.'

She nodded, acknowledging the truth of that. Her father had often hinted at how difficult it was to work with Lord Branscombe. 'How are you getting along with him now that you're back?'

He shrugged. 'We still don't see eye to eye, but we get on fine. When I heard that his angina was worsening I had to come back, to make sure he's all right. I didn't see that I had any choice. My father can be difficult, but he's all I have and I'm his only son, so, despite our differences, we have a strong bond. We've come through a lot together over the years and we've learned to understand one another.'

'And how is he, really? He hasn't been looking too good lately.'

'Do you care?' His gaze narrowed on her, a muscle in his jaw flexing. 'After what happened to your father, do you actually care what happens to him?'

She winced as his shot struck home. 'If I'm honest, I'd like to be able to say…no, I don't care…but I'm a human being and I'm a doctor, so it's probably inbuilt in me to show concern for anyone who's suffering. I still blame him for what happened to my father, but I can't do anything to change the past, can I? Somehow, I have to try to accept it and move on.'

He sighed. 'I'm sorry, Sophie. I'd give anything for

it not to have happened.' He reached for her, his hand lightly smoothing over the bare skin of her arm. His touch disarmed her, sending a trail of fire to course through her body and undermine all her carefully shored-up defences. Against all common sense she found herself desperately wanting more.

She couldn't think clearly while he was touching her, holding her this way. She looked at him, absorbing his strong features, the proud way he tilted his head, and wished more than ever that things could be different between them. But it could never be. Not when his father was responsible for the accident that caused her father's terrible injuries.

'I know you're sorry...but it's too late for regrets now, isn't it? If you'd known about his angina earlier, you might have stopped him from taking off that day. But you didn't.' The words came out on a breathless whisper as she gently eased herself away from him. A look of anguish briefly crossed his face and she said quietly, 'I suppose Charlotte has been making sure you knew how your father was getting along?'

'Yes—if it had been left to him I would never have known how serious his condition had turned out to be. He's far too stubborn for that. But Charlotte has been keeping me up to date, especially after the newspaper stories came out about the investments failing and he took a turn for the worse. We all thought his angina was under control, but his condition has deteriorated and it's become unstable of late.'

She nodded. 'Charlotte's always been more than just a housekeeper to you, hasn't she—from when you were little?'

He smiled. 'That's right. She's looked out for me

ever since I was nine years old—from when my mother died. She was always there for me when I needed her. She always seemed to know what was going on in my head, the things that frustrated me or made me happy. Truthfully, she's been like a second mother to me. I'll always want to keep her close.'

She smiled. 'I know. I've always liked Charlotte.' She gazed up at him. From a very young age he'd had a number of pseudo-stepmothers foisted on him as his father brought home a succession of girlfriends, but Charlotte had stayed through it all, his salvation, the one fixed point in his young life that never wavered.

It had been hard for him back then. Going round and about the village with him and their friends as they grew up, Sophie had seen the effect the loss of his mother had on him. Perhaps seeing his vulnerability was what had drawn her to him in the first place. His father hadn't known how to deal with such a young, bewildered and frustrated boy and simply lost himself in keeping up with his contacts in the business world, in the City. Gradually, Nate had built a shell around himself. No one was going to penetrate his armour...no one except Sophie. Her parents had been going through a difficult time in their marriage and she and Nate had been like kindred souls.

Nate shot her a quick glance. 'She told me she hasn't seen your father in a while. Usually she sees him around the village, at the post office or the grocery store at least once a week, but lately she's missed him.' His voice deepened with concern. 'How is he? Is he still able to get about in the wheelchair?'

'Yes—he's not been out and about lately because

he's getting over a nasty chest infection but he manages very well, all things considered.'

'I heard he was having specialist treatment?'

'Yes, that's right. He was in hospital for a long time, as you know, and we were afraid he might never walk again—but thankfully he's making progress. His spinal cord wasn't cut right through, but it has taken a long time to heal, along with the broken bones—he still has physiotherapy several times a week. It's a struggle for him, but he's not one to give up. He generally tries to take things one day at a time. We're hoping that he'll be able to walk with a frame before too long.'

'I'm so sorry, Sophie. If there's anything I can do—' He tried to reach for her but she took a step backwards. It was far too unsettling to have him touch her. Frowning, he let his arms fall to his sides.

'It's all right; I know you would do anything you can to help.'

'My father said he tried to make amends but your father won't talk to him—all their communication is being carried out through lawyers.'

'That's right.' She shot him a quick glance. 'Do you blame him?'

'I suppose not…but nothing's ever going to be achieved by not talking to one another.'

Her back stiffened. 'The accident changed everything. He should never have gone up in that plane with your father—Lord Branscombe seemed unwell from the first but he insisted he was perfectly fit and able to fly. We'd no idea he was suffering from a heart condition. He should have been stopped. It wasn't even as though the journey was important. He just wanted to check out the site of a new golf course he was planning.' She wrapped her arms around herself in a protective gesture. 'It was totally Lord Branscombe's fault, but afterwards he replaced my father as Estate Manager and didn't even offer him a desk job overseeing things.'

Nate frowned. 'My father said he and the lawyers were talking about compensation.'

She gave a short humourless laugh. 'Compensation? What compensation? Your father had been having angina attacks for some time without telling the authorities. He knew it would affect his pilot licence if he said anything—and when the insurance company found out about that they wouldn't pay out. My father lost everything—his job, his house. He had to sell up and go into rented property.'

'I know—he's in one of the houses on the estate.' Nate's eyes darkened. 'It was me who made sure he had somewhere to go… As for the rest, my father said everything was being dealt with. I'm sorry if that wasn't the case… I've been working away quite a bit in the States, so I couldn't oversee things for myself. I wanted to, but…you didn't seem to want me around and then this job came up… I thought, perhaps, you would find it easier if I wasn't around…'

She turned her back to the sea and leaned against the railing, facing him. She wouldn't be drawn into that conversation again, not now. It was too difficult. 'Will you be going back there?'

'No, this last stint was just a six-months contract in the paediatric intensive care unit in Boston. I have a job lined up here in Devon, so I'll be able to keep an eye on things from now on. It's what I've been working towards. This business with my father just moved things forward a bit.' His gaze moved over her, gliding over her slender curves, outlined by the simple sheath dress she was wearing. 'Better still,' he said in a roughened voice, 'it means I'll be able to see more of you. Perhaps you and I could start over…?'

Her heartbeat quickened and her cheeks flushed with heat. 'Oh, I wouldn't be too sure about that,' she countered in a low voice, her throat suddenly constricted. If Nate thought he could erase the last two years and swoop back into her life, he had another think coming.

'Are you sure about that?' He was looking at her in that devilish way that had her nervous system on red alert and he was moving closer, the glint in his green eyes full of promise…

It was a promise that never came to fruition. Shouts came from above them, shocking her system and acting like a dash of cold water to propel them away from one another.

'Help, someone…come quickly—we need help here! Is Nate Branscombe still around? Is that his car in the car park?'

Startled, Sophie looked up to where the sound came from, up on the restaurant's terrace. She saw people getting to their feet, rushing towards the corner table, barely visible from this angle.

A man came to lean over the balustrade, looking down at them, waving his arms urgently. 'Nate, will you come up? It's your father. He's collapsed.'

'Call for an ambulance,' Nate shouted back. He was already taking the steps, racing to get to his father, but instead of following him Sophie hurried towards the car park. Her medical bag was in the boot of her car. Her instincts told her they might need it.

When she reached the corner table a few minutes later, she could see that James Branscombe was sitting propped up against the balustrade. His skin looked clammy, ashen as he groaned in pain. Sophie guessed he was having a bad angina attack, which meant his heart wasn't receiving enough oxygen and had to work harder to get what it needed.

Nate had loosened his father's shirt collar and was kneeling by him, talking to him quietly and trying to reassure him. 'Is your nitro spray in your pocket?' he asked, but James Branscombe was barely able to speak. Nate searched through his pockets until he found what he was looking for and then quickly sprayed the liquid under his father's tongue. The medication would dilate the blood vessels, allowing blood to flow more easily and thereby lessening the heart's workload.

Nate glanced at Sophie as she came to kneel down beside him. His expression was grim; his fear for his father was etched on his face. He seemed relieved to see that Sophie was by his side, though. 'You have your medical bag?' he said. 'That's good. Do you have aspirin in there?'

'I do—they're chewable ones, or he can dissolve them on his tongue.' She opened the case and handed him the tablets. They would thin the blood and hopefully would prevent blood clots from closing up the arteries.

After a few minutes, though, it was clear that Lord Branscombe was still in a lot of pain. His features were grey, his lips taking on a bluish colour, and beads of cold sweat had broken out on his brow. Sophie guessed this was more than a bad angina attack. She was worried for Nate; this must be something he'd dreaded, the real reason he'd come home.

'Morphine?' Nate asked, and she nodded.

'Yes, I have it. I'll prepare a syringe.'

'Thanks.' He administered the pain medication and soon afterwards wrapped a blood pressure cuff around his father's arm. 'He's becoming hypotensive,' he said, frowning. 'I'll put in an intravenous line—as soon as the paramedics get here we can put him on a saline drip to stabilise his blood pressure.'

They didn't have to wait too long. The ambulance arrived shortly, siren blaring, and the two paramedics hurried on to the terrace. They nodded to Sophie, recognising her from her work at the hospital.

Nate swiftly introduced himself and said, 'I think my father's having a heart attack. We need to get an ECG reading and send it to the Emergency department.'

'Okay. We'll make sure they're kept informed.'

'Thank you.'

One of the paramedics set up the portable ECG machine, whilst the other man began to give the patient oxygen through a mask. Nate helped them to lift his father on to a stretcher, and then together they carried him down to the waiting ambulance.

'His blood pressure's dropping.' The paramedic sounded the alarm and Nate reacted swiftly, setting up a saline drip and giving his father drugs to support his heart's action. Sophie stood by as the three men worked on Lord Branscombe.

'He's gone into V-fib. Stand clear.' Nate called out a warning as his father's heart rhythm went awry and the defibrillator readied itself to give a shock to the heart. He checked his father's vital signs. 'And again, stand clear.'

Her heart went out to him as he exhausted every effort to save his father's life. She saw the worry etched on his face and suddenly wanted to put her arms around him and comfort him, but of course she couldn't do anything of the sort.

'All right,' he said eventually. 'He's stable for now. I'll go with him to the hospital.'

The paramedic nodded. 'Okay, we're ready to go. The emergency team's alerted and waiting for him.'

'That's good.' Nate turned to Sophie, who was waiting by the ambulance doors. 'I want to thank you for all your help,' he said softly. He reached out and gently cupped her arms with his long fingers. 'I owe you. I'll make it up to you, Sophie, I promise.'

She shook her head, making her soft curls quiver and dance. 'There's no need for you to do that. I was glad to help.' No matter what bad feelings she might harbour about James Branscombe, she couldn't have stood by and done nothing to save him. Working alongside Nate, though, had been another matter entirely. She hadn't been prepared for that and the effect it had on her at all.

The paramedic closed the doors of the ambulance and climbed into the driver's seat. Sophie stood by the roadside and watched the vehicle pull away and it was as though the world was sliding from under her feet. She reached out to rest a hand on a nearby drystone wall.

Nate had been back for only five minutes and already she felt as though she'd been hit by an electric storm. How on earth was she going to cope, knowing he meant to stay around and once more make his home at Branscombe Manor?

CHAPTER TWO

'COME ON IN, then, Charlie.' Sophie let herself into her father's kitchen and then stood to one side to let the excited yellow Labrador follow her. He was carrying his lead in his mouth as usual—she always let him walk home the last few yards untethered. She went over to the sink and filled the dog bowl with fresh cold water. 'Okay, I'll swap you—you give me the lead and I'll let you have the water.' It was a ritual they followed every time they went out.

Charlie obligingly dropped the loop handle and she unclipped the lead from his collar and put it away. He drank thirstily and then dropped to the floor, panting heavily and watching her as she washed her hands and then filled the kettle and switched it on.

She gazed out of the window at the neat lawn and the garden with its bright flower borders. There were scarlet surfinias in tubs that reminded her of that day at the restaurant when she'd met up with Nate. It had been almost two weeks ago and she hadn't seen anything more of him since then but she guessed he was probably spending a lot of his time visiting his father in the Coronary Care Unit.

'He looks suitably worn out.' Her father wheeled

himself into the kitchen, breaking into her thoughts and smiling as he looked over at the dog. 'Just as well, if the physio's coming here later on. Charlie can be a bit too exuberant at times.'

Sophie smiled with him and pushed a cup of tea across the table towards him. 'He's not slowing down at all, is he? You'd have thought at eight years old there would have been a few signs of maturity by now, wouldn't you?'

'You would.'

Her father had bought Charlie as a pup, a couple of years after his marriage to her mother had broken down. He'd taken him with him everywhere, even to his work on the estate, and they'd roamed the woods and fields together, man and dog.

'How's the work going with the physio?' she asked now, as she slid bread into the toaster. Every morning before work, she came over to the house to have breakfast with her father.

'We're getting there, I reckon.' He paused, thinking about it. 'When she came yesterday I stood for a while with the frame, and I even managed to take a couple of steps.'

'You did?' He looked deservedly pleased with himself and Sophie stopped what she was doing and rushed over to him. 'Oh, that's wonderful.' She hugged him fiercely. 'I'm thrilled to bits for you. That's amazing.'

'Yes, it's definitely a step forward...' He chuckled at his own joke and she laughed with him. 'Seriously, with all the treatment I've been having at the hospital, and now these sessions at home with the physio, I feel as though I'm making progress. It's been a long job, but I'm getting there at last.'

They ate cereals and toast and chatted for a while, but Sophie soon realised her father had something else on his mind. 'I've been hearing rumours,' he said, 'about Branscombe losing all his money and the estate houses being put on the market. Do you know anything about that?'

'Not really.' She frowned. 'I don't suppose we'll know anything more until Lord Branscombe is out of hospital. Nate's looking after things in the meantime, but—'

'You've seen him again?' Martin Trent's voice was sharp, his whole manner on the alert all at once.

'No...no, not since I saw him that day at the Seafarer when his father was taken ill.' Sophie hastily tried to calm him. It was true. She hadn't *seen* him. She wasn't going to tell him that she'd phoned the Manor House the next day to find out how Lord Branscombe was faring. After all, it had been an innocent enquiry—she'd expected to talk to Charlotte, and it had been a shock to have Nate answer the phone.

'I haven't seen him,' she said again, calmly, concerned that her father was still looking tense, his fingers gripping tightly on the arms of his wheelchair, 'so I assume he's busy visiting his father and talking to the Estate Manager to see how they can keep things jogging along.'

'Hmmph.' He slumped back in his seat. 'I don't want either of us to have anything more to do with that family. James is an arrogant, self-centred womaniser and his son is likely no better.'

'We don't know that Nate is like that,' she said in a reasonable tone. 'He hasn't been around here for any length of time these past few years, has he, so how can we judge him?'

'He can't escape heredity,' her father said flatly. 'It'll be in the genes. That's all you need to know. Besides, he upset you… I know you and he argued but you were broken-hearted when he went away.'

'It was a bad time. You were injured and struggling to come to terms with being disabled and I was confused and lashed out.' Sophie sighed inwardly. She understood her father's dislike of the Branscombes and his hostility towards them. After all, he'd worked for Lord Branscombe for years and had suffered in the end because of it, but it was hard for her to share his animosity towards the son. Her mind drifted back to that last conversation she'd had with Nate.

He'd been more than pleased to talk to her that day when she'd telephoned the Manor House. Despite his troubles, his voice was warm and welcoming, sending little thrills to run along her spine. Just hearing him had made her feel that he was close by, almost as though he was in the room with her. She'd been concerned for him, though, wondering how he was bearing up, and tried to keep her mind on the business in hand.

'They're assessing my father in the Coronary Care Unit,' he'd said when she asked about Lord Branscombe. 'I think they're planning on removing the blood clot and putting a stent in one of his arteries. It's looking as though he'll be in hospital for some time.'

They'd talked for a while and he said, 'I'm sorry things turned out the way they did—both for my father and for selfish reasons… It was good seeing you again, Sophie. I'm sorry our get-together came to such an abrupt end.'

'Yes…though I wasn't expecting you to turn up that day or I—' She broke off.

'Or you'd have gone out of your way to avoid me.' She could hear the wry inflection in his voice and she flinched, knowing what he said was the truth.

Seeing him again had stirred up all sorts of feelings inside her that she'd thought were long since forgotten… or at least pushed to one side. But she didn't want to go there again—to start up something that would only end in distress.

Suddenly uncomfortable, she sought for a way to bring the conversation to an end. 'I'm sure your father's in good hands, Nate. He'll be glad to have you by his side as he recovers.'

'Yes, he seems calmer, knowing I'm here for him.'

'That's good.' She hesitated, cautious about getting more deeply involved with him, and then said, 'I should go. Maybe I'll see you around.'

'Sophie, couldn't we—?' Nate started to speak but she quickly cut the call before she could change her mind.

'Bye.' She had no idea what he must have made of her rush to get away, but he already knew she was trying to keep her distance from him.

'Anyway,' her father was saying, 'it looks as though the tenancies could be at risk if what the papers say is true.' His brow was furrowed with anxiety. 'I've grown used to living here since the crash—I have wheelchair access, handrails… I don't want to have to move…to have to go through the upheaval all over again…'

'It probably won't come to that,' she said, trying to soothe him. 'I suppose we're all in much the same boat—my place is rented too. But, as far as I know, the press stories are just speculation. It's too soon yet for anything to have been decided.'

'Yes, I suppose you're right.' He glanced at Charlie, snoozing in the corner of the kitchen. 'Thanks for taking him out for me every day. It's good of you and I do appreciate what you do for me—I know how hard you work.'

She smiled at him and stood up to clear away the breakfast dishes. 'I like to keep an eye on you. I was worried when you had that chest infection, but you look so much better now.' She finished tidying up and then glanced at her watch. 'I must go,' she said. 'I have a date first thing with those gorgeous little babies in the Neonatal Unit.'

'Ah…that's the bit you like best of all about your job, isn't it? Looking after the tiny infants.'

'It is.' She gave him a quick kiss and a hug, patted a sleepy Charlie on the head and headed out of the door.

She drove to work, following the coast road for a while, uplifted as always by the sight of the wide, sweeping bay and the rugged landscape of cliffs and inlets. After a mile or two she turned inland, driving along a country road until gradually it gave way to suburbia and eventually the local town came into view. She parked the car at the hospital and made her way inside the building.

There was one baby in particular she was eager to see this morning. Alfie had been born prematurely at twenty-seven weeks and had been looked after in Intensive Care for the last couple of months. She'd followed his progress day by day. Now that he was a little stronger and in a better stage of development, Sophie had been able to withdraw his nasogastric feeding tube and she was keen to see how he and his mum were coping with him taking milk from a bottle. They'd had a few attempts at feeding him over the last couple of days, but so far it hadn't been going too well.

'Hi there, Mandy,' Sophie greeted the young woman who was sitting by the baby's cot, holding the infant in her arms. She looked down at the tiny baby, his little fingers clenched, his pink mouth pouting, seeking nourishment. 'Isn't he gorgeous?'

Mandy smiled agreement, though at the moment the baby was squirming, crying intermittently and obviously hungry. The nurse on duty brought a bottle of milk and handed it to Mandy, who gently placed the teat in her baby's mouth.

Alfie sucked greedily, gulped, swallowed and forgot to breathe, causing him to choke on the milk, and Mandy looked anxious. 'He keeps doing that,' she said worriedly.

'It's all right, Mandy,' Sophie said softly. 'It's something they have to learn, to remember to breathe while they're feeding. Sometimes they stop breathing for a few seconds because the heart rate is a little slow—as in Alfie's case—but we've added a shot of caffeine to his milk to give him a little boost. There's supplemental iron in there too, because being born prematurely means his iron stores are a bit low.'

'Will he always have this low heart rate?' The young mother was full of concern for her baby.

'No, no. Things will get better as he matures. In the meantime, the caffeine will help. You can relax. He's doing really well.' Sophie lightly stroked the baby's hand. 'Look, he's sucking better already.'

She left the unit a few minutes later, after checking up on a couple of other babies, and then went along to the Children's Unit. An eleven-year-old girl had been admitted a couple of days ago, suffering from septicaemia, and she wanted to see how she was doing.

'Sophie—I was hoping I might catch up with you at some point today.' A familiar deep male voice greeted her and stopped her in her tracks. An odd tingling sensation ran through her.

She'd been lost in thought, but now she looked up to see Nate standing by the nurses' station, tall and incredibly good-looking, dressed in dark trousers that moulded his long legs and a pristine shirt with the sleeves folded back to the elbows.

She stared at him, her blue eyes wide with shock, her heart beginning to thump heavily. 'Nate—what are you doing here?' She was startled to see him standing there, and more than a little alarmed to have her sanctuary invaded. This was one place where she'd always thought she was safe.

'I've started a new job here as a locum consultant,' he explained. 'It's a temporary post for the next few months until they appoint a new person for the job. They tell me I'll be in the running for that too.'

She pulled in a steadying breath. 'I'd no idea you were looking for work over here. I suppose you must be pleased that you found something so soon…and so close to home.' Why did it have to be here, in her department? How on earth was she going to cope, having him around?

'I am; I'm very pleased. The opportunity came up and I decided to go for it. This will give me time to decide what I want to do—and of course it means I'll be on hand to visit my father in the Coronary Care Unit here, which is an advantage.'

'Yes, of course.' She looked at him in concern. 'I hope he's doing all right.'

He nodded. 'They went ahead and put a stent in the artery to prevent another blockage there. He's a lot better than he was.'

'That's good.' Her mind was reeling. It was difficult enough, knowing that Nate was back in the village… but to have him here, working alongside her…that was something she'd not contemplated. How was her father going to react to that news? But she didn't confide any of that to Nate. Instead she did her best to keep things on an even keel. 'I hope you enjoy your time here—I think you'll find it's a very friendly, supportive place to work.'

'I'm sure I will.' His green eyes glinted as he looked at her. 'Knowing that you're here too makes it even better.' His glance moved over her, flicking appreciatively over her curves, outlined by the close-fitting lavender-coloured top and dove-grey pencil-line skirt she was wearing. 'I'm more than glad to know that I'll be working alongside you.'

'I—uh…' She cleared her throat. 'Yes…well… I think I should make a start on seeing my patients. I was just about to do a ward round.'

He inclined his head briefly. 'I'll come with you and try to get acquainted with everyone. I've already met some of the doctors and the nursing staff…like Tracey and Hannah over there…' His mouth made a crooked shape and he gestured towards a couple of the nurses who had been watching him from a distance but who now felt dismayed at being discovered and quickly seemed to find a reason to be going about their work.

She acknowledged their reaction with a faint grimace. Nothing had changed, had it? No doubt the

nurses and female doctors had been falling over themselves to get to know him. He seemed to have that effect on women. They simply couldn't get enough of
him. And he probably liked things that way.

'Okay. I thought I'd start by looking in on Emma.'
She began to walk towards one of the wards, a four-
bed bay close to the nursing station.

He seemed to be searching his memory. 'That would
be the child with sepsis?'

She looked at him in surprise. 'You've looked through
the notes already?'

He nodded. 'I like to know who and what I'm going
to be dealing with, if at all possible. There isn't always
time but I was in early today, so I was able to take a
quick glance at the notes on computer. They only give
the bare essentials, of course.'

She had to admire his thoroughness. 'Well, she and
her friend apparently gave each other body piercings—
they wanted to wear belly bars but Emma's mother
wouldn't allow it, so they did it in secret. Emma's wound
became infected and the little girl was too worried about
what her parents would say to tell them what was happening. It was only when she started to feel ill that she
finally admitted what she'd done. Her parents brought
her to A&E but by then the infection was in her blood-
stream.'

He winced. 'You have her on strong antibiotics?'

'We do. We had the results of tests back from the
lab—it's an aggressive infection, so we've put her on a
specific treatment now. Of course she needs support to
compensate for failing internal organs while her body's
under attack.'

That was the reason the little girl was on a ventilator to help with her breathing and was receiving vital fluids through an intravenous line. Her parents were sitting by her bedside, taking turns to hold her hand. They were pale and distraught, and Sophie did her best to reassure them.

'Her temperature's down,' she said, glancing at the monitor, 'and her blood oxygen levels are improving, so it looks as though the antibiotics are beginning to have an effect. It will take time, but there's a definite improvement.'

'Thank you.' Emma's mother was still sick with worry. 'I just blame myself. I should have known.'

'I doubt anyone would know if a child made up her mind to keep something to herself,' Nate said, his voice sympathetic. 'It's all the rage to get these piercings, but I expect she'll be wanting to give them a miss for the time being, at least.' He smiled and the woman's mouth curved a fraction.

'Let's hope you're right about that.'

Sophie went on with the ward rounds, conscious all the time of Nate by her side. He talked to the young patients, getting a smile from those who were able and bringing comfort to those who needed it. He was a dream of a children's doctor. It was a role that could have been made especially for him.

'Shall we go and get some lunch in the hospital restaurant?' he suggested a couple of hours later, when she had seen all her patients and finished writing up her notes.

'Yes, I'd like that. I'm starving.'

He grinned. 'I thought you might be. You always

burned up energy like a racing engine. From what I've heard, the food's pretty good here.'

'It's not bad at all,' she agreed. 'That's mostly down to Jake's intervention, I think. Soon after he was appointed as a manager, he brought in new caterers and the whole place was reorganised. It's only been up and running for a few weeks. They do hot and cold food and there are sections where you can help yourself and get served quickly.'

He pushed open the door and slipped an arm around her waist as he guided her into the large open-plan area. She felt the warmth of his palm on the curve of her back through the thin material of her top and a sensation of heat spread out along her spine. Try as she might to ignore it, she couldn't get away from the fact that she liked the feel of his hand on her body... so much so that she was almost disappointed when he let go of her and led the way to the service counters.

There were several of them, each offering a variety of food—salads, sandwiches, cold meats, and then there were the hot food counters, serving things like jacket potatoes, chilli con carne and tomato-and-basil quiche.

Nate studied the menu board. 'Looks like today's specials are lasagne or shepherd's pie,' he said.

She pulled herself together and tried to concentrate. 'I think I'll have the lasagne,' she said, and added a rhubarb crumble to her tray. Nate opted for shepherd's pie and runner beans but didn't bother with a dessert. He added a pot of tea and two cups to his tray.

'No pudding... Now I see how you keep that lean and hungry look,' she commented.

'Oh, I prefer savoury food above all else.' His gaze

travelled over her. 'But the puddings don't seem to have done you any harm at all. You're as slim as ever—with curves in all the right places.' He smiled as a swift tide of heat swept over her cheeks. 'It must be all the exercise you get, working here and helping your father. Charlotte mentioned to me that you walk the dog and do your father's grocery shopping and so on.'

'I do what I can.' They chose a table by the window and sat down to eat.

'I imagine your father and Jake get on pretty well,' Nate said after a while. 'Jake's easy to get along with, isn't he?'

'I guess so. I mean, he and I get on all right. We always have done.' She frowned. They'd always been friends, a bit like a brother and sister, really. She looked at Nate. 'Actually, he hasn't had all that much to do with my father, up to now. They know one another, of course, from when we were younger, but I haven't had occasion to take him home as yet.'

'Hmm.' His green gaze was thoughtful.

'What's that supposed to mean?'

'I expect Jake wants to move things on… He'll want to be more than just friends.' He studied her intently as though memorising every one of her features. 'Any man would.'

She moistened her lower lip with her tongue. 'I don't know about that. I've been down that road before and I've discovered to my cost that things don't always work out too well.'

He raised a brow. 'Perhaps you've known the wrong people.'

'Perhaps.' The truth was, the only man she'd ever really wanted was Nate, but there had always been so many obstacles in their way that it just felt that maybe it was never meant to be. 'You must know from your father's experience that it isn't easy to find the right partner in life,' she said. 'My own mother and father couldn't make a go of it.'

'I think the truth is my father never really got over losing my mother,' he admitted. 'He was something of a lost soul after that. But, as to your situation, it always struck me—as a child growing up—that your father did his best. He wanted the relationship to work.'

'I'm sure he did.' She pulled a face. 'But, well, you know my mother... She could be...flaky, I suppose you'd call it. She was unreliable and her behaviour was odd sometimes. It made her difficult to live with, but of course we didn't know then that she was suffering from bipolar disorder.'

He slid his fork into his shepherd's pie. 'It must have been difficult for you when the marriage broke up and she took you and your brother and sister away to live in Somerset.'

'Yes, it was. It was hard leaving my father, and everything we'd ever known back here.' She frowned, thinking about it. 'Though it wasn't so bad for me because I was getting ready to go to Medical School. I was more worried about leaving Rob and Jessica behind at that time. They were still very young—nine and eleven by the time Mum remarried. It broke my heart to leave them.' Her mouth flattened. 'I still worry about them after all this time—eight years later.'

'But they come to stay with you quite often, don't they? Charlotte told me a long while ago that they're back here whenever they have the chance.'

'That's true. Jessica's married now, though, so I don't know if she'll be over here quite as much.'

His eyes lit up with interest. 'I heard about that—and that she's pregnant. Is she okay? Is it all going well?'

She paused for a moment to savour her lasagne. 'Yes, she's fine. Money's a bit tight—but she and Ryan managed to buy a small terraced house in an old part of town. They're young and they were impulsive, I suppose, in a hurry to be together. Only now Ryan's taken a job which means he has to work away for several days at a time. I'm just hoping they won't have too much of a struggle financially, with a baby on the way.'

He shrugged lightly. 'Young people are resilient. If the love's there I'm sure nothing much else matters.'

She smiled. 'I think that's what I've always liked about you—your optimism. Yes, I'm sure things will turn out fine, eventually.'

He poured tea for both of them. 'And Rob—how's he getting along? He must be sixteen or seventeen by now...'

'He's just turned seventeen. Rob's a typical teenager—full to bursting with teenage hormones right now.' She made a start on her dessert, enjoying the brief moment of sweetness as she tasted the creamy custard on her tongue. 'I think he worries about Dad.'

'I'm sure he does. The relationship between a father and his son is an important one.' He studied her closely. 'It applies to fathers and daughters too. Your father always looked out for you, didn't he? I had the feeling he didn't want you getting too close to me.'

'He was just trying to protect me. I guess he knew you weren't one to settle. And your family heritage is something you can't get away from—you lead a vastly different life to most ordinary people and I suppose he felt in your eyes and your father's eyes I would always be the Estate Manager's daughter.'

He shook his head. 'That's not true. I always thought you were special. I was miserable when you left to go to Medical School—I was glad for you that you were doing something you'd always wanted to do, but sad for myself. We were bound to be separated for a great amount of time, studying in different parts of the country.'

She smiled, unconvinced. As a teenager she'd longed for Nate to look at her the way he'd looked at other women, but it was only when her family was uprooted and she was desperately vulnerable that things had changed between the two of them. He'd reached out to her and offered her comfort, a shoulder to cry on.

But it had been too late. She'd made the decision to leave home to go and study medicine. Those last few times they had been together, he had held her in his arms and there had been the occasional stolen kiss, enough to make her long for more. How could she have allowed herself to get more deeply involved with him back then? He was often away, studying to be a doctor, and when he was home she was too conscious of the great divide between them to let it happen.

Perhaps it was true he had missed her for a while. But he must have known that they were miles apart in other ways. Nate's family, unlike hers, was completely orderly, old school, following age-old traditions, their ways of going on passed down from generation to generation. She sighed inwardly. She would never fit in.

Now, he reached for the milk jug and frowned as he caught sight of a newspaper lying abandoned and open on a nearby table. Sophie followed his gaze and scanned the headlines. There was a picture of Branscombe Manor with a larger image of Lord Branscombe in the foreground.

Lord Branscombe puts Village up for Sale! the headline screamed. *Villagers mount protest!*

'Wretched rumour-mongers,' Nate said under his breath. 'Why do they have to go talking to the press?'

Sophie studied the headlines in consternation. 'Is it true? Is the estate up for sale?'

'Nothing's been decided yet,' he answered shortly, his jaw tense. 'But that doesn't stop the rabble-rousers from going tattling to the papers, raking up trouble, does it?'

'People are worried about the future of the village,' she told him with a frown. 'They know what's happened with your father—how he lost a great deal of money—and they want to know what he's planning on doing about it. Surely you can understand that?'

'Of course I do. But my father is too frail to cope with estate matters right now, and stories like this aren't going to help. He made a mistake—he knows that now. He thought he was buying land with a huge potential for development but it failed spectacularly. He's lost millions of pounds. It's a tragedy for everyone concerned and I know how worried people must feel. Right now, though, he's too ill to deal with any of it and he's passed the reins over to me. Somehow or other I have to negotiate a way out of the mess.'

'I'm sorry.' She laid a hand on his arm, sympathising with his predicament and wanting to offer comfort. 'That's a huge burden for you to take on.'

'It's a headache, I grant you.' He squeezed her hand lightly, sending a warm tide of sensation to ripple through her.

As their lunch break drew to a close, they finished

their meal and headed back to the Children's Unit. When they reached it, they found everyone on high alert.

'A little boy's being transferred here from Emergency,' Tracey told them. 'I was just about to page you. He'll be here in a few minutes. His name's Josh. He's five years old—apparently, he ran out from behind an ice-cream van yesterday and was hit by a car. He was tossed in the air and hit his head on the ground.'

Sophie sucked in a breath. It was one of the worst things a doctor could hear...and as to the child's parents, they must be in torment. 'How bad is it?'

'His skull's fractured in four places and the CT scan shows there's a blood clot forming under the bone. The A&E team decided it would be best to keep an eye on things rather than operate. At the moment he's under sedation and on a ventilator.'

'Okay, we'll keep him that way for now. Let's make sure everything's ready for him.' Sophie quickly stifled her emotional response and switched to being professional. 'I'll take a look at him and then go and talk to the parents. Are they being looked after?'

'Hannah's with them at the moment.'

'Good.' Sophie started towards the side ward, getting ready to receive the little boy. She was very much aware of Nate walking along with her, silent and concerned, his expression taut. He'd been rigidly attentive, on the alert the whole time.

'Does this bring back memories for you?' she asked. 'I know you suffered a head injury as a child.'

'Ah...yes, that's very true. I was nine years old and fell from the roof of an old outbuilding near to the Manor House. One of the gardeners found me unconscious on the ground.' He frowned. 'Apparently, my mother was beside herself with worry back then… She stayed with me through two nights, thinking that I might not make it.'

Sophie was concerned for Nate. 'That must have made a lasting impression on you.' It must be one of the last major memories he had of his mother. She'd been killed in a car accident a few months later.

'My accident was the reason I wanted to study medicine. I was so impressed, even at that young age, by the way the doctors and nurses looked after me. I was convinced I had to be able to save lives the same way they saved mine. But my mother's death coming so soon afterwards—the car accident that killed her—was horrendous. It was such a shock. It had a tremendous impact on me and it's something I've struggled to come to terms with over the years…in order to carry on.'

She nodded, understanding. Sophie was almost four years younger than Nate, but even back then, as a little girl, she'd been aware of Nate's unhappiness, the way he'd withdrawn into himself. Now, as an adult, she could still feel terrible sadness for that vulnerable little boy.

'I can't imagine how any child could handle something like that.'

He made a brief faint smile. 'As I recall, you were very gentle and caring with me over the next few years. You talked to me and tried to bring me out of myself. I appreciate that, even now.'

'I'm glad if I was some help.'

She prepared herself as the injured child was wheeled into the side ward. He was deathly pale, breathing oxygen through a tube that had been inserted in his windpipe, and there were tubes and wires connecting him to equipment and monitors used in the transfer.

Immediately, she did a quick but thorough examination. 'Tracey, will you do fifteen-minute observations, please?—limb movement, pupils, blood pressure, temperature and verbal response and so on. We'll need to monitor intracranial pressure. A small blood clot might resolve on its own, but if the swelling gets worse he'll have to go up to Theatre to have it removed, so everyone needs to be looking out for that.'

'I'll see to it.' Tracey started on the first round of observations, noting the results in the patient's chart.

Sophie and Nate went to talk to the parents. They were sitting in the waiting room with Hannah, still very upset, but they were calm enough to recount the incident.

'I carried him to the ambulance,' his father said. 'He was bleeding from his ear and he was so quiet and limp in my arms. I was scared. I didn't know what was going to happen to him.'

Stressed, Josh's mother clasped her fingers together. 'We're still in shock,' she said.

'It's a difficult time for you,' Sophie agreed. 'But I promise you we're doing everything we can to make sure he's comfortable.'

'Is he…is he going to be brain damaged?' The father voiced what both parents must be thinking.

'I wish I could give you definitive answers,' Sophie said, 'but it isn't possible just now. The healing process takes time but he's young, and young people have remarkable powers of recovery. We have to be patient and wait and let nature do its work.'

'Dr Trent is very experienced in looking after children with these types of injuries,' Nate said, and Sophie absorbed his comment in surprise. Had he checked up on her qualifications? As the new locum consultant, he would probably have access to staff records. Or maybe the head of the unit had told him all about her. 'We'll let you know about his progress every step of the way,' Nate added. 'You'll be able to sit with him as soon as we have him settled, and we can arrange overnight accommodation in a room close by if one or both of you want to stay with him.'

'Thank you...thank you so much.' Josh's mother wiped away a tear. 'He's so tiny. I can't believe this is happening.'

They talked for a little while longer, and then Sophie and Nate left them in Hannah's care. The nurse would take them along to see their son in a few minutes.

Sophie spent the rest of the afternoon making sure that Josh's condition remained stable and that her other small charges were being looked after. She scanned lab reports and dictated her notes and then handed over to the doctor who was coming on duty to take her place.

'Are you off home now?' Nate asked, coming after her and watching her retrieve her bag from her locker. 'I expect you have plans for the evening?' He didn't ask her about Jake, but somehow she guessed that was on his mind. He just wouldn't believe that Jake was only a friend...

'Yes, I do, but I have to go and walk Charlie and pick up a few bits from the shops first of all,' she said. 'Aren't you about due to finish your shift too?'

He nodded. 'I'm just going to stay and tidy up a

few loose ends before I go. I'll walk with you to your car, though, if that's all right. I could do with a breath of fresh air.'

'That's fine.' They left the hospital together, walking out through the landscaped gardens to the car park beyond. All around them, stretching far into the distance, they could see the beautiful Devon moorland.

Nate took a moment to take it in as they came to stand by her car. 'I love this county,' he said, looking around. 'Whenever I've been away, no matter where I am in the world, I always want to come back here.'

'It's a wonderful place to live,' she agreed. 'I'm certainly glad I came back to the village.' She glanced at Nate, a small line creasing her brow. 'Your ancestral home is here, though, isn't it? How's that going to work out for you? Will the Manor House be safe, with everything that's been happening? You haven't really said anything about how you're going to be affected by all this.'

'I think the house at least should be secure,' he said. 'My father hasn't mentioned any problem with it.'

'But the estate *is* at risk, isn't it?' she persisted. 'I know you don't like to think about it, but the stories in the papers aren't unfounded, are they? Is there any chance that your father will sell up?'

His shoulders moved stiffly. 'He was approached by a would-be buyer—Peninsula Holdings—some time ago. He was considering their offer, but then he had his heart attack and everything's been put on hold. He's handed all the business dealings over to me, and I have to make a decision soon, but I still need to make up my mind on the best course of action.'

Sophie frowned. 'I've heard of that company,' she said, suddenly uneasy. 'They're a business conglomerate, aren't they—a company that likes to pull down properties and build hotels in their place?'

'It's true—they're a company generally interested in development, but that doesn't automatically mean they'll want to knock down the cottages on the estate. They might prefer to keep up the tenancies.'

'Really?' She raised a brow at that. 'From what I've heard of their other operations, if they do that they're quite likely to put up the rents—to a level that people can't afford.' Perhaps her father had been right to be worried all along.

'The rents are quite low, and have been for some time,' Nate said calmly. 'There was some talk of offering people the opportunity to buy their properties rather than rent.'

'My father wouldn't be able to do that.' Sophie shook her head, making her honey-gold curls dance. 'And I'm not sure *I'm* in a position to do that right now either. I'd need to come up with a substantial deposit, and that won't be easy at the moment. I've been doing what I can to help out Jessica—she needed funds when they bought the house—and now I'm helping my father. He's having private physio treatment at the moment, and that doesn't come cheap.'

She frowned. 'Is this development company going to put me out of a home, along with all the rest? Can't you do something to put this right, Nate?' Her blue eyes pleaded with him. 'There are too many people who stand to have their lives turned upside down the way things are at the moment.'

'You don't have any need to worry, Sophie. I won't let anything bad happen to you.'

'No?' She looked at him uncertainly. 'What could you do to make this go away?'

He smiled, a compelling, enticing smile that made her insides quiver with excitement and longing. He slipped his hands around her waist and drew her to him. 'You could always come and live with me at the Manor House. You could have anything you want there. You know I've always wanted to keep you close.'

He lightly caressed the curve of her hips and wrapped his arms around her, drawing her into the shelter of his long, hard body.

Her mind fragmented, her willpower crumbling as she felt the heat emanating from him, felt the powerful muscles of his thighs against her legs. 'I've always wanted you, Sophie,' he whispered.

A pulse throbbed in her temple, and a wave of heat ran through her from head to toe. Her wilful body was saying *yes, yes, please* to the temptation of being with him, locked in his seductive embrace, but the sensible part of her mind was telling her this was madness. What was she thinking of, letting him coax her this way?

'I can't,' she said huskily. 'There's just too much water under the bridge with us, Nate—you know that.' She closed her eyes briefly at the thought. 'Plus, my father would have a stroke.'

'Ah… I wouldn't want that to happen,' Nate murmured. 'But maybe you could bear my offer in mind… for some time in the future, perhaps? There is still something between us; I can feel it…'

She pushed against his chest with the flat of her hand. 'I think that's highly unlikely,' she said.

'Maybe.' A smile played around his mouth. 'But, like you said, I've always been an optimist.'

CHAPTER THREE

'OH, THAT'S GOOD to see. He's feeding much better now, Mandy.' Sophie watched in awe as the tiny infant lay in his mother's arms, suckling hungrily at the bottle of milk formula she was holding. He was wrapped tenderly in a beautiful super-soft Merino wool shawl. Alfie's eyes were wide open, the deepest blue, and he looked up at his mother with perfect trust.

A lump formed in Sophie's throat. She worked with babies and children all the time, but would she ever experience that profound joy of holding her own baby close to her heart? It was a difficult question to answer. The father of her baby would have to be the one and only man for her, the love of her life, because after the disasters that had occurred in her family she didn't want to make the same mistakes they'd made. She wanted a relationship that would stand the test of time…but was that going to be possible?

She closed her eyes briefly. Nate would make a wonderful father… She could see him holding their child in his arms…holding the baby against his bare chest. Unbidden, the image came through in startling clarity, along with a rush of heat that suffused her whole body. Nate was everything she was looking for in a man. He could turn her blood to flame with a single glance and just thinking about him in that way caused a wave of dizziness to engulf her. It could never be…he would never settle, and he wouldn't choose to spend his life with her, the daughter of a man who had worked for his father, would he? How could she contemplate such a thing? She must be out of her mind, even thinking along those lines!

She'd do far better to concentrate on the job in hand, wouldn't she? Chiding herself inwardly, she straightened, finished checking up on her tiny charges and with a new, brisk determination left the Neonatal Unit and went to look in on the rest of her young patients on the Children's Ward. Thankfully, Nate was nowhere to be seen. She didn't think she could cope with having him around just now.

'He's gone up to the Coronary Care Unit to see his father,' Hannah said when Sophie came across her a little later on. The young nurse frowned, pushing back a stray lock of chestnut-coloured hair. 'They were aiming to get Lord Branscombe out into the rehabilitation garden this morning but he wasn't well enough, apparently. He's been very breathless lately.'

'I'm sorry to hear it.' Sophie frowned. 'Nate must be very worried.'

Hannah nodded. 'He is.' She'd obviously been talking to Nate quite a bit lately. That was the way with him—he got on well with everyone, and the nurses especially had taken to him. Did he return their interest? Sophie wasn't at all happy with the way her thoughts were going—it was quite possible that he would start dating any pretty girl who caught his eye… Wasn't that warning enough that she should steer clear of accepting

Nate as anything other than a colleague? Her stomach churned uneasily.

She left Hannah after a minute or so and went to look through the patients' files in the wire trolley by the desk, searching for five-year-old Josh's notes. She and the rest of the team were worried about the little boy's head injury and she wanted to check up on his medication and observation chart. A further CT scan this morning showed there was a very slow bleed beneath the skull bones and the pressure inside his head was rising.

Looking at the little boy this morning had left her feeling worried. Pale and unmoving, his fair hair tousled against the pillow, he'd seemed incredibly vulnerable and her heart turned over at the sight of him. If the medication didn't resolve the problem, she would have to do something fairly soon to prevent a dangerous downturn in his condition.

'Hi there, Sophie.' Jake walked towards her and greeted her, smiling. 'I've been looking for you.'

Surprised to see him, she gave him a quick answering smile. As a hospital manager, he spent most of his time in his office, so she hadn't expected him to venture down here. He wasn't an impulsive man. 'Hello, Jake. Is everything okay?'

'Yes, absolutely fine.' He nodded. 'On the face of it, I'm down here looking for Tracey. I need to ask her to try out a new batch of disposable syringes—but I was hoping to see you. I wanted to tell you that I won't be able to come with you to the village fête on Saturday, after all.'

'Oh, that's a shame.'

'It is.' He looked genuinely downcast. 'I'm sorry—I was really looking forward to spending the day with you, but I have to go and talk to a couple of people I used to work with in Cornwall. They've been trying out a new supplier for things like cannulas and rubber gloves—equipment we use all the time—and they've supposedly made a huge saving in their hospital budget. I'm thinking of using the same supplier here, but I want to know how their trial went before I do that. Saturday's the only day we can all meet up.'

'That's all right. Don't worry about it.' She made an impish grin. 'I'll have Charlie for company. I dare say he'll drag me through all the mud in the playing field before we get to the enclosure where the dog show's taking place.'

'Playing field?' He lifted a brow. 'Oh, you don't know about the change of venue, then?'

'It's not going to be at the school?' She shook her head. 'No, I haven't heard anything...but then, I've been very busy lately, with one thing and another.'

'The school had to cry off—the mobile classroom unit is being delivered ahead of time, so the headmaster asked around to see if any other organisation could offer a field. Nate Branscombe stepped in and told the committee they could use the grounds of the Manor if they wanted. There'll be marquees if the weather turns bad, or the old stable block—it was a better alternative than the village common, by all accounts. Anyway, they're busy putting up notices all over the village.'

'Oh, I see.' That had come as a bit of a shock. She wasn't sure how she felt about spending the day in the grounds of the Manor. She studied Jake thoughtfully. 'How do you know all this—you're not on the committee, are you?'

He shook his head. 'Nate told Hannah and she told Tracey... You know how the grapevine works.'

'Hmm.' Apparently it didn't extend as far as Sophie, but in this instance that might be because they were worried about how she'd feel about going to an event at the home of her father's arch-enemy. They were probably right to have their doubts...but most likely they were waiting to tell her at the last minute.

'Is it going to be difficult for you?' Jake had picked up on her thoughts. Certainly, her father would be annoyed if she went there—he was already in a grumpy mood after she'd told him she was working with Nate, but she didn't see how she could get out of going to the event when she'd been roped in to open the proceedings on behalf of this year's charity—the Children's Unit.

'I think my biggest problem will be telling Dad,' she told him. 'He's already upset because Peninsula Holdings have sent out men to conduct land surveys on the estate—the tenancies could all be at risk—so any dealings I have with the Branscombes are likely to set him off.'

'Oh, dear.' Jake put an arm around her and gave her a hug. 'It's going to take a while for him to get over this latest blow, isn't it?'

'I think so, yes.' She nodded, comforted by the brief hug, until she looked up and saw with a faint shock that Nate had come into the room and was watching them, his green eyes assessing their clinch with obvious suspicion.

'Something wrong?' he asked.

Sophie eased herself away from Jake and braced her shoulders. 'Nothing I can't handle,' she said.

'That's always good to hear.' He studied Jake, his

expression taut. 'Is there something we can do for you, Jake?'

Jake took a step backwards as if he was getting ready to move away. 'No, no… I'm looking for Tracey—I need her to road-test some equipment I've ordered from a new supplier. Trying to save money wherever, you know…'

'She's taken a child down to X-ray,' Nate said curtly. 'I expect she'll be on her way back from there by now.'

'Oh, okay, thanks… I… I'll go and find her.' Jake raised a hand in a goodbye gesture to Sophie and headed for the exit doors.

'He's doing his best for this hospital, you know,' Sophie said, her blue eyes narrowing on Nate. He wasn't being uncivil towards Jake, but there was a definite friction in the atmosphere.

'Yeah, I know.' His green gaze lingered on her, dark and unfathomable.

She frowned. 'But you seem to have a problem with him…?'

'Mmm…you could be right…' His glance shimmered over her. 'It's what he's doing for you that bothers me.'

Her mouth made a faint wry quirk. Her relationship with Jake was none of Nate's business…but it kind of made her feel warm inside to know that he might be just a bit jealous. Perhaps he did actually care for her, deep down. Would there ever be a chance his feelings went further, and that she and Nate might get together? A strange tingling sensation started to run up and down her spine at the thought.

She gave herself a mental shake. She really couldn't afford to explore that notion, could she?

'Perhaps we'd do better to concentrate on the job in hand?' She gave Nate the file she'd been reading. He studied her, his eyes dark and brooding, but she ignored that and commented instead on the patient's folder. 'I'm concerned about Josh Edwards. I don't think the medication alone is going to be enough to resolve the situation,' she said. 'I think we should get him up to Theatre so he can be fitted with a drainage tube to relieve the pressure inside his head. The steroids and diuretics on their own aren't going to keep things under control.'

He glanced through the file and came to a swift decision. 'Okay. Notify the surgeon and ask Hannah to prep the boy.'

'Do you want me to talk to the parents?'

He shook his head. 'No, I'll do it. You might want to go and talk to the little girl with the belly piercing—she was asking for you.'

'Was she?' She smiled. 'From what she was saying yesterday, I expect she wants me to reassure her that there won't be a scar and that she can eventually go back to wearing crop tops. I looked in on her earlier this morning, but she was sleeping peacefully. The antibiotics seem to be dealing with the infection at last.'

'That's good. It's always nice to know when the treatment's working.'

'It is.' She glanced at him. 'Is there any news about your father? Is he making any progress?'

His mouth flattened. 'It's going to take time, I think. The heart attack caused damage to the heart muscle and he's finding rehab a strain. I'm booking him into a convalescent home so that he can rest and get the help he needs. We'll be transferring him there on Friday, so I should be able to check on him on Saturday morning and still do the honours at the fête in the afternoon. I've said I'll call out the winning raffle numbers.'

She nodded. 'I only heard about the change a little while ago. Jake was telling me that you're letting the organisers use the Manor. Aren't you worried about the damage that might be done to the grounds—your father's always been very particular about the way they look?'

'Not really. He's left everything up to me, and as far as I'm concerned, the old saying is true—what the eye doesn't see, the heart won't grieve over... Anyway, we have skilled groundsmen who know how to put things right afterwards. I'm more worried that villagers might boycott the event because of everything that's been in the newspapers about my father and the estate. There's been a lot of bad feeling, and word soon gets around. It would be a shame if that happened—it would be good to raise money for the Children's Unit. I certainly wouldn't want to jeopardise that in any way.'

'I don't think you need have any worries on that score. Everyone wants to contribute—I know a lot of people have been working very hard to try to make sure it's a success.'

'Well, let's hope it all turns out okay.' His gaze moved over her. 'I'll see you there, I hope?'

She hesitated, thinking about the implications of that, and his gaze darkened. 'Yes,' she said. 'I'll be there to represent the Children's Unit.'

'I suppose Jake will be with you?'

She shook her head. 'He has to go to a meeting with some ex-colleagues in Cornwall, so he cancelled on me. But I'll have Charlie with me. I've entered him in the dog show, and I'm just hoping he'll walk properly on the lead and not show me up! He gets excitable if there's a lot going on. He might try to head for the flower borders if I don't keep a tight hold on him.'

He grinned. 'Oh, I can imagine… Charlie's quite a character, isn't he? I remember when he was a pup I was back home for a couple of weeks in the summer, and he dug up the lawn at the back of the Manor. My father was apoplectic when he saw a dozen or so holes appear in his pristine turf, but I couldn't help seeing the funny side. Your father was chasing Charlie, trying to stop his antics, but Charlie thought it was all a good game and kept stopping to dig a bit more. As soon as your father caught up with him, he ran off. The more he was chased, the more fun it was.'

Sophie rolled her eyes. 'He's always been a handful. But hopefully he'll behave himself on Saturday. At least he's grown out of digging holes.'

He smiled. 'I'm glad you're going to the fête.' A gleam of anticipation sparked in his eyes. 'I'll look forward to seeing you there.'

A quiver of nervousness started in the pit of her stomach. 'Yes, you too.' She set her mind on her work and went off to sort out the arrangements for Josh's operation.

To her relief, everything went smoothly. The neurosurgeon treated the request as an emergency and the little boy was whisked up to Theatre. Once there, the surgeon implanted a small silicone tube into the subdural space in Josh's head to draw off blood that was forming there, and the pressure on the little boy's brain was instantly lessened.

Sophie went home that day feeling much happier about his progress. Josh was still sedated for the moment, but she knew he stood a much better chance of recovery.

The day of the fête arrived—a gloriously sunny afternoon—and Sophie set off early with Charlie to walk to the Manor. Their route took them along the cliff top, with moorland stretching away into the distance. Soon, Branscombe Manor came into view, situated high up on a hill, looking out over the landscape, a beautiful yellow stone mansion formed in an elongated U-shape with two gable-ended wings making the U. Over the years there had been side extensions added towards the back of the house, again with magnificent gable ends.

The house was architecturally superb, with stone mullioned windows fitted with leaded panes. The glass sparkled in the sunlight and she paused to gaze at the house in wonder as she approached it from the long curving driveway. But then her attention was distracted by the arrival of a large white catering van turning in off the lane.

There would be burgers and hog roasts and all manner of refreshments laid on for the hungry visitors. Stalls had been set up on the sweeping lawn at the front of the building, with striped marquees to one side where people could sit at tables and enjoy a cup of tea or coffee. Further along she saw another marquee where alcoholic drinks were being served.

Sophie looked around. As a teenager, she'd come here often with her father, helping him as he carried out various tasks around the Manor. All those memories came flooding back now, as she gazed once more at the imposing house and well-tended gardens. At the side of the house there was a walkway through a stone arch that led to a rose garden and beyond that there was a landscape of trees and shrubs.

'Hi, Sophie. Things are looking good, aren't they? We've a great crowd here already.' Tracey greeted her cheerfully, her fair hair tied up in a ponytail, her grey eyes lighting up as she saw Charlie. She bent down to stroke him. 'Shall I take him for you while you go and do the honours?'

'Oh, bless you. Thanks, Tracey.' Sophie handed over the dog, who went willingly, pleased to be fussed and patted and generally crooned over. His tail wagged energetically.

Sophie stepped up on to the dais and set about formally opening the proceedings. 'We want you to have a great time here today,' she told everyone. 'We've all kinds of fun things for you to see and do this afternoon—there's face painting for the children, a karate demonstration taking place in the South arena at two o'clock, and music from our favourite band all afternoon. Don't forget to look in on the flower and plant marquees while you're here, and there are all sorts of cakes, jams, pickles and chutneys for sale in the home produce section. Above all, remember that any money you spend here will go towards buying much-needed equipment for the Children's Unit at the hospital. Please—enjoy yourselves.'

'Well said. That's the aim of the day.'

Sophie glanced around, her stomach tightening in recognition as she saw that Nate was waiting to take his turn on the stand. He looked good, wearing casual chinos and a crisp open-necked shirt that revealed a glimpse of his tanned throat.

Gesturing to him to come and take the microphone

from her, she introduced him to the crowd and then stepped down. The atmosphere changed almost immediately as he took to the stage. People weren't sure how to react to him—it was clear in the silence that fell over them and in the way their expressions changed from smiling to sombre. His father's poor investments and lack of judgement had come down to haunt the son.

'Thank you, Sophie,' Nate said. He looked briefly at Charlie, who was busy trying to wind his lead around Tracey's legs in his efforts to get back to his mistress, and then he looked out at the sea of faces. 'Ah… I should mention there's a dog show too, for any of you who haven't yet had time to glance through your programme. It'll be held in the East Meadow at two-thirty.' He looked bemused as Tracey swiftly tried to untangle herself and Charlie began to pull her exuberantly towards Sophie and a child who was licking an ice cream.

'Among other things, there will be an obedience training exercise. I'm not sure if Charlie here will be a good candidate for that—he might be considered a bit of a disruptive element.' There was a ripple of laughter among the crowd as Charlie's ears pricked up at the mention of his name. The dog quickly turned tack, heading up on to the dais, pulling Tracey along with him. Worried, Sophie followed.

Nate grabbed hold of the leash from a relieved Tracey and then wound it firmly around his palm. 'Of course, he might do well in the sledge-pulling event.' Another murmur of amusement. He looked at the overexcited dog and said briskly, 'Charlie—sit!' To Sophie's amazement, Charlie sat, looking up at Nate with an expectant, adoring expression.

'Okay…' Nate turned his attention back to the audience. 'I'll call the raffle results at the end of the afternoon—we've a television as first prize, a hamper to be won, bottles of wine, and a whole array of wonderful things which you'll see on display when you buy your raffle tickets. Go and have a great time.'

Nate stepped down from the stage, bringing Charlie with him. 'Are you okay, Tracey?' he asked.

The nurse nodded. 'I just feel a little silly, that's all. I didn't expect him to go racing off like that.'

'I'm sorry,' Sophie said. 'Perhaps obedience classes would be a good idea, after all—except he's probably a little too old for them by now.'

'That's up for debate,' Nate said, laughing.

Tracey walked with them for a while as they wandered around the stalls and checked out the games on offer. Sophie tried spin-the-wheel and won a cuddly toy. 'That's one for the Children's Unit,' she said happily, holding on to the golden teddy bear. At the first opportunity she would pass it on to one of the organisers.

Nate had a go on the rifle range and hit the prime target, sending a spray of water to fall on Charlie's head. The dog promptly shook himself and showered everyone in the vicinity. 'Aargh, I'm sorry,' Sophie said, pulling the Labrador away.

'My fault,' Nate commented with a smile. 'I might have known he would try to get his own back.'

Tracey met up with a friend and went off with her to buy candy-floss, leaving Sophie and Nate to walk round the rest of the stalls together. They bought burgers from a van and walked along, eating them as they went. It was fun, until they began to be interrupted by villagers who stopped Nate and asked him about the tenancies on the estate and about the activities of Peninsula Holdings.

'What's going to happen to my home?' one man wanted to know. 'This company—Peninsula Holdings—has been sending men to measure up and ask a lot of questions. My tenancy's up for renewal in a few weeks. It always used to go through automatically, but what's going to happen now? Am I going to be put out of my home? Where am I going to go with my family?' He was understandably angry, disgruntled by the way things were going, not knowing how to plan for the future.

'Like I've told everyone else who's asked,' Nate said, 'nothing's been decided yet. Peninsula Holdings are looking into things to see if they want to do a deal. I may decide it isn't going to work. In any case, no one's going to be turned out at a moment's notice. It could be that you can go on renting, or any new buyer might want to offer the properties up for sale, but you would be given first option to buy. In any event, we'll make sure you're offered alternative accommodation.'

'And what if I don't want it? What if I don't want to move away? We've lived here in the village, in this house, all our lives.'

'I know…and I'm really sorry. I understand this is a difficult time for you.' Nate tried to soothe him, to calm all the people who came to complain or ask about what was going to happen, but nothing he said could appease them. Sophie could understand how they felt. It was all so unsatisfactory, with everything left up in the air, but she sympathised with Nate. She didn't see how he could tell them anything different if he was still awaiting the outcome of negotiations.

They headed over to the East Meadow for the dog

show and watched the dog trials taking place. Sophie sighed. 'They're all so clever, aren't they, listening to what their owners say and going where they tell them to go?' She glanced at Charlie, who was panting, eager to get involved. 'Not so with this one, though,' she said with a smile.

Nate chuckled. 'He's one of a kind,' he said, tickling Charlie's silky ears. 'I think dogs need to listen if they're to learn, but he's never seemed to have that connection between ears and brain.'

She laughed. 'Oh, well, here goes… It's the competition for the best-looking dog—that's one thing he *is* good at. He's always been beautiful to look at.'

He watched her get ready to walk the dog over to the line-up. 'You make a perfect team,' he said. His glance shifted over her slender figure, neatly clad in blue jeans and a sleeveless top. She was wearing her hair loose, the curls tumbling down over her shoulders.

Unexpectedly, he took his phone from his pocket and swiftly took a photo. 'Two beautiful blondes.' He looked at the image on the screen and a glint of satisfaction came into his eyes. Sophie was oddly still for a moment, the breath catching in her throat at the casual compliment. Then she collected her thoughts and set off with Charlie, conscious all the time of a warm glow starting up inside her.

She came back to Nate a few minutes later, but there was no rosette to show for their efforts. 'I can't believe you were outshone by an Afghan hound,' she told Charlie. 'Don't let it bother you—you're way better-looking than any dog here.'

Nate smiled. 'Better luck next time, maybe.' He glanced at Sophie, his expression sobering. 'I'm still being pounced on from all sides. Shall we try and get away from here for a bit, before anyone else comes up and tries to waylay me? Have you seen everything you want to see for the time being?'

'Yes, okay. Where do you want to go?'

'I thought we might take Charlie for a walk by the river—that might wear him out for a bit.'

She smiled. 'Okay. I think he'll definitely be up for that.'

They left the meadow and walked along a footpath until they came to the riverbank. The water was fairly deep at this point, flowing freely on its downward tilt towards the sea. It was fed by the lake in the grounds of the Manor, a favourite beauty spot when she had been a teenager. The lake was on private land belonging to the Branscombes and was supposed to be out of bounds, but she and her friends had often gone for walks there on hot summer days. Further along, she recalled, there was a weir, where they'd stood and watched the water tumble over stone and form white froth.

'You must love this place,' she said now, watching the ducks glide on the water, dipping their beaks every now and again among the reeds as they searched for morsels of food. 'It's so peaceful and unspoilt.' They were following a well-worn path by the river, where clumps of yellow fleabane grew along the banks and here and there were shiny deep pink blooms of musk mallow and star-shaped ragged robin. Charlie was sniffing among the blades of grass, seeking out the flower petals and sneezing when they tickled his nose.

'I do.' He sent her a sideways glance. 'It's even better having you here to share it with me.'

'Is it?' She was pleased but looked at him curiously.

'I wasn't expecting to see you at all outside of work, but I suppose when you opted to have the fête on the Manor grounds you felt you had to put in an appearance.'

'That's true…but I'd have turned up anyway, just so that I could spend some time with you.'

'Really?' Flattered though she was by his persistence, she wasn't about to fall for his charm the way countless other girls had in the past. 'That might have been awkward if Jake had been around.'

'Ah, but he isn't here, is he?' His eyes glittered. 'What was he thinking, choosing to go to a meeting and missing out on the chance of being with you?'

Impishly, she decided to play him along. She'd never said there was anything going on between her and Jake, but Nate seemed concerned about their relationship. 'He's very passionate about his work.'

'More than he is about you?' His dark brows rose in disbelief. 'Doesn't he know he's leaving you open to being chatted up by the likes of me?'

She smiled. 'We're just friends.' She sent him a fleeting blue glance. 'Besides, there's so much history between our families…'

'Yes, there is,' he said, trying to ignore the elephant between them. He checked his watch, a stylish gold timepiece that looked good on his strong tanned wrist. 'We've an hour or so left before I have to call the raffle results—we could go back to the house and get Charlie some water and I could show you round, if you like? You've never seen the inside of the Manor, have you?'

'Only the lodge, where my father had his office.' She smiled. 'I think I'd like that. I've always wondered what such a grand house was like inside.'

'Come on, then. We can take a shortcut from here across the field to the back of the house.'

He showed her the way along a narrow path that led to a hedgerow and a wooden stile. He held Charlie's lead while she swung her jeans-clad legs over the railing and stepped down into the field beyond. From here she caught a glimpse of the Manor House through the thicket of ancient trees that surrounded it.

'Are we going in through the servants' entrance?' she asked with a mischievous smile as they approached the back of the house. There were no stalls set up out here, and there was no sign of people coming away from the main event and wandering about. She guessed he'd had it temporarily fenced off.

'There's no servants' entrance nowadays,' he said, 'but it's not quite as grand as the archway at the front of the house.'

'Oh, I don't know about that…' She gazed at the covered portal. 'It's quite impressive.' The lawn and gardens here were beautiful, with wide flower borders and tall trees and a verdant shrubbery. Sophie went with Nate into the house through a pair of wide, solid oak doors and then stopped to look around in wonder.

She was standing in the kitchen, a huge room with gleaming pale oak floorboards and golden oak units all around. There was a large central island bar with a white marble top, and to one side there was a dining table with half a dozen chairs set around it. Above the range cooker there was a deep, wide cooker hood with a tastefully designed tiled splashback. All along one wall were feature windows with square panes and two of the windows were decoratively arched. The room was light and inviting—it was the most wonderful kitchen she had ever seen.

'Oh, I'm almost speechless,' she said, gazing around. 'I wasn't expecting anything like this. It's so traditional, yet completely modern.'

Nate smiled. 'I persuaded my father a couple of years back that it needed updating. I'm pleased that for once he took note of what I said.' He went to the sink and poured cold water into a large stainless-steel bowl and set it down on the floor for Charlie. The dog drank thirstily and then flopped down on the tiles, watching them, his head on his paws. 'What would you like to drink?' Nate asked Sophie. 'Something cold, or tea, coffee…? Something stronger, if you like?'

'A cold drink would be lovely, thanks. It's so warm today—it's left me with a real thirst.'

'Watermelon?'

She nodded and he took two glass tumblers from a display cabinet and filled them from a dispenser in the front of the tall double-door fridge. 'This is a mix of watermelon, a dash of lime and a hint of cucumber,' he said. 'I think you'll like it.'

She took the glass and swallowed deeply. 'Mmm… that's lovely. Thank you.'

'You're welcome.' He finished off his drink, tipping his head back. Sophie watched, fascinated as his throat moved, but she lowered her gaze as he put the glass down on the table. 'I'll show you the rest of the house,' he told her, 'the main part, at least. It would probably take too long to go through the East and West Wings.'

'Okay.'

There were several reception rooms, one used as a library and another as an office, all tastefully fur-

nished with the same pale oak used in carved, deco-
rative panelling on the walls and in the bookcases and
desks. The drawing room, though, facing out on to a
paved terrace, was very different.

'We went for a much lighter touch in here,' Nate
said. 'There's no panelling, as you can see, but we
chose a very pale silk covering for the walls.'

'It's lovely,' she murmured. 'It's all so restful.' She
looked around. 'You've kept the original inglenook
fireplace, but everything blends in perfectly.' The fireplace was a pale stone arch with a wood-burning stove
set into the recess. There were two cream sofas in
here, with splashes of soft colour in the cushions and
in the luxurious oriental design rug and floor-length
curtains. Again, the windows were tall, with square
panes, and there were glazed doors opening out on to
the terrace.

'I'm glad you like it.' He smiled. 'Let me show you
upstairs.' They went out into the large hall, almost a
room in itself, and Sophie looked up to see gleaming
pale oak rafters and a mezzanine floor set off by a
beautifully carved oak balustrade. 'I have my own office up there,' Nate said, following the line of her gaze.
'I like to sit up there in the room and look out over the
moors. You can see the lake from there, and a good
deal of the estate. Come on, I'll show you.'

He reached for her hand and led her up the wide
staircase to the open balcony that looked down on to
the hall. His fingers engulfed hers and instantly she
felt a thrill of heat pass through her at his firm touch.

The room opened out on to the internal balcony.
There were a couple of easy chairs up here, with bookcases to hand along with a small glass coffee table. She

imagined him sitting here, reading and being able to look down into the hall when anyone arrived downstairs.

Further back in the room, through a wide, square archway, there was a bespoke furnished study, with a built-in desk and units and glazed square-paned display cabinets above them. The main features, though, were the two wide arched windows that took up a good part of the back wall.

'Come and see.' Nate took her with him to stand by one of the windows. 'See what I mean?' He slipped his arm around her waist, holding her close. She knew she ought to move away but it felt good to have him hold her, to have him so close that she could feel his long body by her side, and she couldn't bring herself to break that contact. Instead, she wanted him to wrap his arms around her. His nearness was intoxicating.

'Oh…it's incredible!' She gasped softly in delight. 'You're so lucky to have such a wonderful view.' From here, with the house situated at the top of the hill, she could see all around for miles. She saw the lake and the copse, and beyond that she glimpsed some of the houses beyond, white-painted and nestled into the hillside. She looked at him, her lips softening with enchantment. 'It's all so lovely. I've never seen it set out like this before.'

'*You're* lovely,' he said huskily, his gaze lingering on the pink fullness of her mouth. 'It means so much to have you here with me like this. I've missed you, all those years we've been away from each other. I kept thinking about you all the time we've been apart.'

'Did you? Me too…' It was true. She'd never been able to stop thinking about him. And now she was lost in his spell, enticed by the compelling lure of his dark eyes and mesmerised by the gentle sweep of his hands as they moved over the curve of her hips, drawing her ever closer to him. He bent his head to her and gently claimed her lips, brushing her mouth softly with his kisses. Her whole body seemed to turn to flame and she melted into his embrace, loving the way his arms went around her. Her limbs were weak with longing. She wanted his kisses, yearned to know the feel of his hands moving over her.

'I've been desperate to kiss you ever since I saw you that day at the Seafarer,' he said, his voice roughened with desire. 'I wanted to hold you, to feel your body next to mine.'

She felt the same way about him, but his words made her stop and think about what she was doing. Her father had been upset when he'd heard about that meeting. He'd warned her about falling for Nate all over again. They'd never made any commitment to one another but, whenever he was around, she was drawn to him like a moth to a flame and, even though they'd argued, she'd been upset when he went to work in the States after her father's accident. How would she feel when his job here came to an end and there was the possibility of him leaving once more? It was better, surely, not to let things get out of hand?

'I wanted it too, Nate, but… I can't let this happen. I'm sorry if I led you on in any way. I'm very confused right now. I need time to think…'

'Why, Sophie? Tell me why.'

She looked up at him. 'I know you're not right for me,' she said quietly. 'It would be madness if I were to fall for you…again. We're worlds apart.'

'You don't know that.' His hands circled her waist.

'You seem absolutely perfect to me. I'd do everything I could to make you happy.'

She shook her head. 'But you can't. And what you're going to do will hurt my family and friends. Think about what you're doing—you're planning to sign away the homes of everyone who lives in property belonging to the Branscombe estate. It's no use saying you haven't made a decision yet. It's what you'll do to make sure that you can keep this house, isn't it? I understand that—the Manor has been in your family for generations; you said so. But do you really know the pain you will cause?'

He ran his hands lightly over her bare arms. 'If it came to that, if I have to sell the properties, I could negotiate a deal for you so that you could buy your house for a rock-bottom price.'

'And my father's home? What will happen to that? Can you tell me it won't be demolished to make way for a hotel or shopping mall? Isn't that what that company does? Will anything be left of our lovely tranquil village when they've finished?'

He winced. 'I'll make sure that your father gets a better place. He won't suffer.'

'He's already suffering. He's only just getting used to going around in a wheelchair and negotiating ramps. The last thing he needs is to be uprooted all over again.' She sighed heavily. 'It's as though you're moving chessmen on a board, deciding their fate.' She gazed searchingly at his face, studying the taut line of his jaw and the bleak sea green of his eyes. 'Nate, isn't there anything you can do to stop this?' She lifted her hand to his chest and ran her palm lightly over the warmth of his ribcage. 'Can't you find another way? Please?'

For a moment, his expression was agonised. 'I wish I could, Sophie, but a place like this, with all the land and outbuildings associated with it, costs a fortune in upkeep. I'll do what I can. You know I'd do anything not to hurt you.'

'I know you will. But things don't always work out the way we want them to, do they?' She eased herself away from him and took a couple of steps backwards. 'It's getting late. There's the raffle to draw and I should go and see what Charlie's getting up to. It's time we set off for home. He should be rested well enough by now. Thanks for showing me around.'

He walked with her to the kitchen. 'I could take you home in the Range Rover. Charlie could go in the back.'

'No, it's all right. We'll walk.' She needed to be alone right now, away from him, so that she could clear her head. With him around, it was impossible.

CHAPTER FOUR

'HI, JAKE. How did your weekend down in Cornwall go? Did things work out all right for you?' Sophie walked into Jake's office at lunchtime on Monday, greeting him with a bright smile. She was glad to see him. He was a calming influence—everything Nate was not.

She should never have gone back to the Manor House with Nate. That had been a big mistake, and she might have known he wouldn't be one to miss an opportunity. After all, he had nothing to lose.

Even now, she remembered how it had felt to be in his arms, to know the touch of his lips on hers. Her whole body tingled with nervous excitement at the memory.

'Oh, hi, Sophie.' Jake looked up from the mound of paperwork on his desk. 'Yeah, it went okay, thanks. We managed to get quite a lot sorted.' He frowned. 'The hotel was a bit crowded, though. There was some sort of event going on in town—a music festival—so it was quite noisy.'

'But it must have been good to meet up with your friends?'

He nodded. 'Yes…yes, it was.'

She hesitated momentarily. He seemed harassed and out of sync with things, not at all his usual self. 'I came up here to see if we might have lunch together?' she suggested. 'Maybe you can tell me all about it over a plate of spaghetti?'

He frowned again, glancing at his watch, and then started shuffling through papers. 'I'm sorry, Sophie. I've a stack of work to wade through and I have to get a report ready for a meeting with my boss this afternoon. Do you mind if we give it a miss and meet up later?'

'No...no, of course not... That's all right.' She tried to hide her disappointment. 'It was just a spur-of-the-moment thing... I hadn't heard from you, so I thought I'd come and see you on the off chance. It doesn't matter.'

'Ah, yes... I should have phoned you. Everything's been a bit hectic.' He grimaced. 'How about I give you a call when I'm free?'

'Yes, okay. That's fine. No worries.'

She had plenty of other things to occupy her mind when she went back to the Children's Unit after grabbing a quick bite to eat in the hospital restaurant. She checked up on her patients, taking time to look in on Josh, the five-year-old boy with the head injury, and she was thankful that his condition was at least stable now. He was still under sedation while they waited for the fractures to begin the healing process and while the swelling inside his head subsided. His parents were obviously worried about his prognosis and whether he would be brain damaged in any way, but Sophie reassured them as best she could before going in search of her next patient.

As she was walking by a side ward, though, she

heard a series of monitor alarms going off. Instantly concerned, she looked into the room to see what was happening.

Nate was in there looking after a young girl who appeared to be around ten years old. When Sophie walked further into the room, she could see that the child was thrashing around on the bed, her limbs moving uncontrollably, her head tipped back and her body arching. She was having a full-blown seizure and Sophie hurried over to Nate and said quietly, 'Can I help?'

He nodded, giving her a quick smile. 'Thanks, I'd appreciate that. The nurses are all very busy just now... Would you try to hold her still while I give her a shot of anti-convulsion medication? She only just seemed to come out of one seizure and now this...'

'Of course.' Sophie gently restrained the child while Nate drew up a syringe and inserted it into the intravenous cannula that was taped to the girl's arm. 'Are her parents around?'

'Her father had to leave to go to work. I sent her mother to take a break and get some coffee. These last few weeks have been a worrying time for her and she's stressed out. Luckily, she missed seeing these latest seizures.'

'Do we know what's causing them?'

He nodded. 'I think so. Lucy has been suffering from really bad headaches, nosebleeds and vomiting for some time now. Her blood pressure's frighteningly high—it's been getting steadily worse over a couple of years despite treatment. It isn't responding very well to antihypertensive drugs.' He withdrew the syringe and put it aside. Glancing briefly at Sophie once more, he said, 'It might be a good idea if you were to stay with us while I explain things to her mother. She's quite upset by what's happening to her daughter, and it might help her to have another woman present. I'll need to get her consent for angiography.'

'All right, I can do that.'

Slowly, as the drug took effect and as Lucy recovered consciousness, Nate began to speak to the child in a low voice, soothing her and trying to keep her calm. Even Sophie began to feel more relaxed under the comforting influence of his gentle tones.

'How do you feel?' he asked the girl after a while. 'Is your headache still as bad as before?'

'No, it's a bit better.' Lucy was silent for a moment and then her face suddenly paled, small beads of perspiration breaking out on her brow, and she said urgently, 'But I'm going to be sick again.'

Sophie quickly found a kidney dish and held it for the little girl while she vomited, and then gave her a tissue so that she could wipe her mouth when she was finished. 'I'll just get rid of this,' Sophie said, removing the dish and replacing it with a clean one. 'I'll be back in a minute or two.'

When she came back into the room, Lucy was resting, leaning back against her pillows and looking completely washed out. Her dark hair was damp with perspiration. Her mother had come back from the cafeteria and Nate was sitting on the end of Lucy's bed, gently explaining the results of tests that had been carried out earlier. 'As you know, we've done lots of tests, along with ultrasound scans and a CT scan, and from those results we can be fairly certain about what's causing the high blood pressure.'

Lucy's mother frowned. 'You said it might be something to do with her kidneys.'

'Yes, that's right. From what we can see on the radiology films, the blood vessels to her kidneys are narrowed and that's what's causing the problems she's been having.'

'But you can fix it with tablets, can't you?'

Nate shook his head. 'I'm afraid not.'

The woman stiffened and Sophie pulled up a chair and went to sit with her at the side of the bed.

'There's some sort of blockage in the arteries,' Nate explained, 'and that is what's making her have high blood pressure and causing the severe headaches and so on. It also means that the blood flow to her kidneys is not what it should be. We have to do something that's more invasive, I'm afraid. If we don't do anything, things could get much worse and there might be damage to the kidneys.'

The woman's hands started to shake and Sophie covered them with her own, wanting to comfort her and at the same time not wanting Lucy to see her mother upset. 'We need to do a procedure called angiography,' she explained. 'This will clear the blockage and open up the arteries, but Lucy will be anaesthetised so she won't feel anything or need to worry about what's going on.' The little girl was watching and listening through all this, wide-eyed, and Sophie glanced at her. 'How do you feel about that, Lucy?'

Lucy paused briefly to think about it. 'Will it make me better?'

'It should do. That's what we're aiming for.'

Lucy was quiet for a moment or two, thinking about it. 'If it's going to help, I think it's okay.' Seemingly older than her years, she glanced at her mother and said, 'I'd like to stop feeling this way, being ill all the time.'

Slowly, her mother nodded. She exhaled heavily. 'All right. I'll phone your dad and explain things to him.' She looked up at Nate. 'When will you do it?'

'Tomorrow morning, most likely. I'll speak to the radiology consultant who'll be carrying out the procedure. He'll want to see Lucy, and he'll explain things to you…but basically he'll thread a catheter from the groin through the blood vessels to look at the kidneys. Then he'll place a small balloon inside the artery and inflate it to open up the blood vessel and restore the circulation. When that's been done satisfactorily, he'll withdraw the balloon and catheter. He'll need to do the process for both arteries.'

Lucy's eyes grew even wider. 'Are you sure I won't feel any of it?'

He nodded and smiled. 'I'm quite sure. You might feel a little bit sore at the injection site afterwards, but you'll be given painkillers, so it shouldn't be a problem.' He studied her expression. 'Are you still all right with it?'

She nodded.

'Good.' Nate stood up and smiled. 'We'll leave you to talk to your mum and dad about it, and I'll let the nurse know what's happening so she can answer any of your questions.'

'Thanks.' Lucy's mother smiled at both of them as they went to leave the room. 'I'm really grateful to you for the way you're looking after her.'

They went over to the computer room so that Nate

could type up his case notes and confirm things with the radiology consultant.

Sophie wrote up her own notes on Josh, and when they had both finished, Nate swivelled round in his chair to look at her. He said, 'I'm glad we've finally managed to catch up with one another. It's been so busy here we haven't had a chance to talk…but it was good being with you on Saturday. I wanted to tell you I enjoyed the whole afternoon, walking with you, spending time at the house…especially spending time at the house…' He smiled, but she couldn't be persuaded to do the same. She was still struggling with anxiety at her lack of self-control after the way she'd responded to him that day.

'It's certainly a beautiful house,' she said, dodging around the issue.

His mouth tilted at the corners. 'You won't admit you liked being with me, will you?'

'How can I?' She sighed. 'I feel I shouldn't have let things get that far.'

'I don't see why.' His shoulders moved in a nonchalant fashion. 'Anyway, it was just a kiss.'

She sucked in a silent breath at that. Just a kiss? Had it meant nothing to him? She was shocked.

'It was exquisite…sensational…wonderful…' he added. 'But it was just a kiss, after all. I don't see that you've any reason to regret it. It was instinctive. We didn't plan it. It just happened.' His glance flicked over her, moving from her burnished shoulder-length curls to glide down over the simple sheath dress she was wearing and trace the long line of her shapely legs. 'Though I wouldn't have been sorry if it had gone further.' His green eyes darkened. 'I always wanted you,

Sophie…from back when we were teenagers. And I would definitely have staked a claim there and then if you hadn't decided to skip off to Medical School and disappear from my life for endless years.'

'Oh, really?' She pretended to be surprised. 'But you didn't try to find me, did you, and am I to believe you didn't go out and console yourself with any other girls in all those years?'

'If I didn't come after you it was because life got in the way. And as for any other women, trust me, no one could ever hold a candle to you.' All at once his expression was sincere, his gaze steady, and she almost faltered under the influence of that persuasive, utterly convincing guise until she managed to collect herself just in time. Was she a naive teenager?

'Well, that's good to hear.' She sent him a flashing blue glance. 'Although…you know I don't believe a word of it, don't you?' She frowned. 'There's no Irish in you, is there? I'm wondering because somewhere along the line you seem to have kissed the Blarney Stone.'

He tried to look offended but failed due to the faintly amused quirk of his mouth. His dark brows shot up. 'Not a drop. How could you say that to me? My ancestry is founded in the deepest combes—in the hills and valleys of ancient Devonshire—as you well know. I would never resort to such tactics.'

'Hmm. That's yet to be proved.' She pulled a wry face and might have said more but her phone rang and she unclipped it from the purpose-made jewelled clasp on the narrow belt around her waist. Then she glanced at the small screen and frowned. 'I'm sorry; I ought to take this,' she told him. 'It's my sister, Jessica. She almost never rings when I'm at work.'

'That's okay. Go ahead.' He was immediately serious but turned back to the computer while Sophie walked a short distance away to take the call.

'Oh, Sophie—' Her sister's voice came over the airwaves. 'I wasn't sure what to do—I didn't know whether to ring you or not. I don't know what to do.'

'It's all right—try to calm yourself.' Sophie used a soothing tone. 'I'm sure we can sort it out, whatever the problem is.' Intuitively, she asked, 'Is everything okay between you and Ryan?'

'Yes, except that he's had to go off to Canada on an engineering job—right now when my due date is so close.' Her sister pulled in a quick breath. 'I've been feeling so tired lately. I'm nearly full term, my back hurts, I'm getting these odd contractions—the midwife says they're Braxton Hicks—and he's away, working. It came up out of the blue and he said he had no choice but to go.'

Sophie tried to soothe her. 'I expect he's gone because he wants to boost your funds. Everything's been a struggle for you up to now, hasn't it, financially? He'd have known that Mum and Tom were close by if you needed them.' They hadn't counted on a baby coming along quite so soon.

'Yes, that's true. He's doing everything he can to make sure we're okay. It was all right till I had to stop working. I didn't realise how much we relied on my salary. We were doing all right, but then the boiler broke down and it's too old to be repaired, and now there's a problem with the plumbing that needs to be sorted but the plumber says he can't fix it for at least three weeks.' She sighed. 'I can't stay here but I don't know what to do. Can I come and stay with you for a while?'

'Oh, Jess…of course you can. Pack a case and catch the earliest train down here and I'll get the spare room ready for you. We'll book you in with a local midwife and arrange for you to have the baby in the local hospital. I'm sure everyone will be accommodating once we explain the situation.'

'Could I? Would you?' Jessica's words were tumbling over themselves in her relief. 'Oh, thank you, Sophie. Thank you. Oh—' She broke off suddenly and Sophie could feel there was something more to come.

'What's wrong?'

'Well, it's nothing wrong, exactly, but I think Rob wants to come and stay with Dad for a while. You know what he's like once he makes up his mind about something. He's very impulsive. He keeps saying he wants to help look after him. Mum's okay with it, and I know Dad will be happy, but I don't know where he'll stay—Dad's spare room is being used for storage at the moment, isn't it?'

'I'm sure we'll sort something out.' Sophie tried to stay focused on the situation in hand. 'See if you can get the evening train over here. I think there's one that gets into town at about nine o'clock. I'll come and meet you at the station. We'll work out what we can do about Rob, but the priority is to get you settled first. You have to think about your health and about the baby.'

'Okay, I'll do that… Thanks, Sophie. You're the best.' Jessica cut the call a minute or so later and Sophie frowned as she turned back to Nate, trying to work out what she needed to do. She would have to go home after her shift and make sure everything was ready for her sister.

'Trouble?' Nate was sympathetic, ready to listen.

'Not really. It's just that I need to get organised.' She

explained what was happening with Jessica and how Rob wanted to come over.

'I don't see how she can stay on her own in those circumstances...but I'm sure she'll be glad to have her big sister's support.' He gave her a brief smile before asking seriously, 'Is there any way I can help out with Rob?'

It warmed her through and through to know that he would do what he could for her. 'I'm not sure, to be honest,' she said. 'But thanks for offering.' It was good of him—there had been no hesitation; he was ready to help in an instant.

She paused for a moment, thinking about what she was going to do. 'I won't be at all surprised if my mother turns up at my place some time soon. This is just the kind of thing that would set her off. With all the changes going on, she'll probably forget to take her medication.'

He nodded. 'That could happen. She used to take off for days at a time, didn't she? I often wondered, back then, how you coped. You were only about sixteen when your parents' marriage broke up, as I recall, and your mother was in a bad way for a long time. I caught up with everything that was happening whenever I came home from Med School and Charlotte would phone me every week and let me know all the village news.' Nate's expression was pensive. 'Yet you seemed to take it all in your stride—you took on the role of mother to Rob and Jessica. They must have been...' he worked it out in his head '...seven and nine at the time?'

She nodded. 'That's right. They were very young, so I tried to be strong for them. It was hard because I was upset and hurting too. Dad was unhappy and not coping very well. It was still hard when Mum married Tom and we moved to Somerset. It was a new life, a new place, but we felt as though our roots had been torn.'

'I can imagine.' His gaze narrowed thoughtfully. 'I don't suppose there's room for Jessica at your mother's place?'

She shook her head. 'When Jess married they turned her room into an office. Anyway, she craves peace and quiet—mentally, if not physically.' She shot him a quick, amused look. 'A bit like you, really. You'd never be able to put up with some of the organised chaos we live in.'

His mouth curved. 'Probably not. I'm used to things running smoothly, like a well-oiled machine. I suppose Charlotte had a lot to do with that.' He glanced briefly at his watch. 'Your shift's about due to finish—why don't you go home and make a start on getting things ready? It's going to be a bit of a squeeze for you in your small cottage, I imagine—and you'll need to make room for a cot in case the baby arrives in the next couple of weeks, won't you?'

'Oh, heavens! I hadn't thought of that! What am I going to do for a cot?'

He was thoughtful for a moment or two. 'There might be one stashed away in the attic back at the Manor. In fact, now I think about it, I'm sure there is. My father has things up there going back generations. He never throws stuff out.'

'Oh, bless you! That would be marvellous.' She studied him cautiously. 'Is there any news on your father?'

He pulled a face. 'There's been no change, really. He's being well looked after at the convalescent home, but his recovery's going to be a long haul, I think. He's very breathless and needs a lot of rest.'

'I'm sorry. It must be difficult for you.'

'Yes. Thanks for asking.' He sent her a quick glance. 'Is your father making any headway?'

She nodded, smiling. 'He managed to stand and bear his own weight for a short time. It's a start. He took a couple of steps with support. I'm keeping my fingers crossed that he'll keep on making progress.'

'I'm glad.'

She left the hospital a few minutes later, her mind racing, full of things she had to do. It occurred to her that Jake had mentioned seeing her later, so she tried calling him. When he didn't answer, she sent him a text message telling him what was happening. He was probably in a meeting.

As soon as she arrived back at the village, she checked up on her father and heated up a beef casserole she'd made earlier.

'Rob told me he wants to come over,' he said as they ate together. 'I told him I'd love to have him stay with me but there's only the box room and that's filled with physio equipment and so on. It would take a bit of work to sort it out.'

'Don't worry about it, Dad,' she said. 'We can deal with that later.'

'And what about Jessica? Are you going to have room for her and perhaps for a baby as well at your place?'

'I'm sure we'll manage.' She looked at him thoughtfully. 'Anyway, how did you get on with the physio today—it was your day for the hospital workout, wasn't it?'

He grimaced. 'It was okay. I managed a couple of steps again, with a lot of help. Some days I don't seem to have the strength…'

'You're getting there—that's the main thing. A year

ago we wouldn't have thought you'd come this far.' She clasped his hand warmly and smiled at him and he brightened, seeming to absorb some of her optimism. 'Now—I'll take Charlie for his walk and then I'll have to love you and leave you. I've a dozen things I need to do before Jessica gets here.'

Charlie's ears perked up at the mention of a walk and they set off along the moorland path, heading for the local village shop. Sophie stocked up on extra provisions and then dropped Charlie back home.

She went back to her own white-painted cottage and put away the groceries. With any luck, Jessica would be arriving in the next couple of hours and by then she would have everything more or less in order. She put fresh linen on the bed in the guest room and made sure there were plenty of clean towels in the bathroom. When she had finished it was still light, so she went out into the garden to breathe in the fresh air and gather some flowers from the border. She loved her garden with its curving lawn and pretty display of colourful blooms. There were trellis panels covered in sweet peas in warm pastel shades, with deeper lavender, mauve and blue colours interspersed.

The sun was setting on the horizon when she turned back towards the house, carrying a wicker trug filled with bright pompon dahlias and a posy of delicate sweet peas.

'I thought I might find you out here.' Nate's deep voice startled her. He walked around the side of the house and came across the small terrace towards her, smiling. 'I rang the doorbell and knocked, but I saw your car outside, so I guessed you were still at home. I brought the cot and came to see if you needed any help.'

'Oh… I didn't expect you to look for it right away.'
She was a bit breathless all at once, seeing him standing
there. He looked wonderful, dressed in casual chinos
and an open-necked shirt with the sleeves rolled up. All
the nervous excitement of the last few hours seemed to
flow out of her as she looked at him, to be replaced by
a warm feeling inside. It was so good to have him here.

'That's really thoughtful of you,' she said. 'It's good
to see you, Nate.' She started towards the house once
more, heading towards the open square-paned French
windows. 'I was just going to put these flowers in
water. Jessica likes sweet peas, so I thought I would
put some in her room—and the dahlias will look good
in the living room.' She was babbling, startled by his
arrival, but thrilled to see him.

'Have you heard anything from your brother?' He
followed her into the kitchen.

'No, nothing. I tried calling him but I couldn't get
through. I expect his battery's low.' She set the trug
down on the white table, then switched on the kettle
and set out a couple of porcelain mugs for coffee. 'I'll
just put these flowers in water. Sit down—I can get
you some scones to eat if you're hungry.'

'No, thanks, I'm fine. Besides, you have enough to
do without bothering about me.' He watched her as she
arranged the sweet peas in a glass vase. 'Look—why
don't I go and meet Jessica at the station? She'll remember me from before your family left the village—and
we met up briefly in the village last time I was home.'

'Are you sure you don't mind doing that?'

'Of course not. I told you, I want to help.'

'Thanks. That would be such a relief. I'm really
grateful.' She made the coffee and slid a mug towards

him. 'I've been thinking about her, wondering if it will all go smoothly.'

He looked at her curiously. 'You don't show your feelings to the world, do you? You look very calm and composed on the outside, but I know you're a little anxious inside. That's probably what makes you such a good doctor. You get on with the job in hand—no panic, no fuss, just sheer concentration and doing the best you can.'

She gave a small broken laugh. 'You make me sound like a robot!'

'No! Never.' He stood up and laid his arm around her shoulders. 'It's all right to admit that you worry sometimes. I'm here for you, Sophie. I need you to know that.'

She reached up and touched his hand, and his fingers closed around hers. The warmth and gentle strength of that grasp encouraged her and somehow gave her a renewed burst of energy. With him around she could cope with anything. 'Thanks. I'm glad you're here.'

'Me too.' He released her and seemed to brace himself as though he was cautious about holding her for too long. Reading her thoughts, he said, 'Just being near you drives me wild. You can't imagine how difficult it is for me.'

'It isn't easy for me either...but, no matter what you say, I can't help feeling I need to keep my guard up. I don't want to fall for you, Nate. It's way too risky for my peace of mind.'

He looked at her, his dark eyes brooding. 'We need to work on that.' He started to walk away. 'I'd better go and get the cot—it's in the back of the Range Rover.

There's a nursing chair as well—it rocks gently, so Jessica will be comfy when she feeds the baby.'

She went with him, following him out along the path to where he was parked at the front of the cottage. She didn't know quite what she was expecting—perhaps a very old, serviceable child's cot—but what she saw made her gasp with delight.

'Oh, it's lovely! I didn't realise it would be a crib that swings from side to side.' The white cradle had beautifully carved spindle sides and was supported on a sturdy white wooden frame. The rocking chair was a perfect match, white-painted with spindle legs.

Nate carried them into the house and put them down in the guest room she had prepared. 'There, the cot looks good next to the bed, doesn't it?' He studied it, looking pleased.

'Oh, it's just perfect. I never imagined you'd bring anything as lovely as this.'

'It was mine, apparently. I remember my mother talking about rocking me in a cradle at the side of the bed. She said it sent me off to sleep every time.'

'Thank you. I'm so grateful to you.' Forgetting everything, without thinking, she turned towards him and hugged him tightly. He was there for her when she needed him without her even having to ask. That meant a lot to her.

His arms closed around her, folding her to him in a warm embrace. 'You're very welcome. Any time.'

She looked up at him, his handsome face just inches away from her own. She felt safe in his arms. He only had to bend his head a fraction more towards her and their lips would be touching. A surge of longing swept over her, filling her body with aching desire.

His green eyes shimmered with answering passion and he slowly lowered his head. He breathed in raggedly. 'Sophie,' he said softly, 'you need to think about what you're doing, about what you want…because I'm just a man and I'm finding it really hard to resist you. I don't want you to blame me afterwards for anything that might happen between us.'

His gentle words brought her back swiftly to reality. What was she doing? She pulled in a shaky breath. 'Ah… I wasn't thinking. You're right. I'm sorry.' Her hands were trembling as she dragged herself away from him. 'I don't know what's wrong with me. I haven't been able to think straight ever since you came back. It's like I'm eighteen again, as though the intervening years count for nothing.'

His hand lifted, his fingers tangling in the soft mass of her silky curls. 'I wish we could go back too… I want to turn the clock back and start again, and this time no bad things would happen to tear us apart. If I could write my own story, I'd make it one where you and I could be together and nothing would come between us.'

She gave him a tremulous smile. 'That would be good, wouldn't it? But this is real life, Nate. It never seems to go smoothly for either of us, does it?'

He shook his head and slowly took a step back from her. 'No, it doesn't.' He straightened and said quietly, 'I should go and pick up your sister.'

'Yes…thanks.' She nodded, taking a moment to get herself together. 'I'll send her a message to let her know you'll meet her instead of me.'

After he'd gone, Sophie looked once more at the room she'd prepared for her sister and the baby. She would have to buy bedding for the cradle, and maybe a mobile to hang above it, and she would find some soft cushions for the chair. They could be her gift for the baby.

It grew darker outside but there was no sign of Rob turning up and she busied herself with a few chores. At last the doorbell sounded and she opened the door to Jessica and Nate.

She greeted them with relief. 'Jessica, I'm so glad you're here.' She reached for her sister and put her arm around her. 'Come and sit down in the living room and put your feet up for a bit. You look exhausted.' Jessica's complexion was pale against the soft gold of her fair hair. Sophie glanced at Nate, who was following them along the hallway, and mouthed silently, 'Thank you.'

He smiled. 'I'll put the kettle on, shall I? I expect Jessica could do with a cup of tea...and maybe one of those scones you mentioned. From what she tells me, she hasn't been eating too well—too much heartburn lately.'

'Oh, it happens, doesn't it, when the baby gets bigger and presses on everything? It must be horrible.' Sophie helped her sister into a cosy armchair and pulled up a footstool for her. 'Perhaps you need to snack little and often. I have some of your favourite strawberry jam to go with those scones.'

Jessica smiled, her pretty face lighting up. 'Oh, it's good to be here with you, Sophie. I'm feeling better already.'

'I'm glad to hear it. We'll get you sorted out with a midwife and so on tomorrow. For now, you just need to rest.'

Nate pulled up a small side table and set down a cup of tea beside her chair. 'Why don't you girls try to relax for a bit and enjoy being with one another? I'll leave you to it. I'm sure you have a lot of catching up to do.'

Sophie followed him along the hallway to the front door. 'Thank you for everything.'

'You're welcome.' He leaned forward and dropped a light kiss on her forehead before opening the door and walking swiftly down the path to his car. She watched him go, hoping that nothing would cause their new closeness to fall apart. It meant a lot to her that he was around.

But how was she going to square that with her father's feelings towards the Branscombes? He, of all people, had reason to be hostile towards them and he would worry in case she was hurt again.

CHAPTER FIVE

A SHARP RAPPING sound startled Sophie just a few minutes later. She finished stacking plates in the dishwasher and went to see who was knocking at the door.

She hurried along the hallway. Jessica had gone to her room, exhausted, and she didn't want her to be disturbed by the noise. She opened the front door.

'Hey, Sophie.' Seventeen-year-old Rob stood on the doorstep looking tired, sheepish and dishevelled, his fair hair spiky. 'Can I stay with you for a bit—just till I clear out the box room at Dad's house? I didn't want to tell him I was coming over. I wanted to surprise him.'

'Of course you can. Oh, come here—let me hug you.' She wrapped her arms around him and held him close for a minute or two. 'How did you get here?'

'I thumbed a lift with a couple of lorry drivers. But the last one dropped me off a few miles from here and I had to walk the rest of the way. Then Nate Branscombe saw me and offered me a lift.'

'Nate saw you?' she echoed. 'But he— Where is he?' He wasn't here with Rob and she couldn't see beyond the tall hedge that obscured the road.

Rob carefully extricated himself from her arms and tilted his head towards the front gate. 'He's cleaning the headlamps on the car—we went through a bit of muddy water.'

'Oh, I see.' Gathering her thoughts, she ushered her brother into the house. 'Go and make yourself a hot drink, Rob. There's food in the kitchen. I'll just go out and talk to Nate for a minute.' She frowned, a sudden thought occurring to her. 'Did you and he get on all right?'

'Yeah, I guess. I wasn't sure how to react to him but he told me you knew I wanted to be with Dad.' He winced. 'I know Mum doesn't want us to have anything to do with him—she still cares about Dad even though they're not together any more. She's always saying how Nate's father caused Dad to break his back, but I don't think Nate had anything to do with that. He always seemed okay to me—a bit of an 'us and them' divide, sort of, but okay. But I suppose you never know. He comes from a different world to us and things are passed down in families, aren't they? It's all in the genes—character traits, some kinds of illnesses and so on?'

'Sometimes. Go in and get warm. I'll be back in a minute.' She suspected Nate was cleaning the headlamps to give her and Rob some time to themselves but she wanted to thank him for finding her brother.

She went out to greet him. 'Hi there.'

'Hi.' Nate smiled in the darkness. A streetlamp lit up his features and she had to resist the impulse to put her arms around him and hold him close. She was so glad to see him, and so grateful that he'd taken the trouble to bring Rob home.

'Thanks for bringing my brother back to me,' she said. 'I'm overwhelmed, the way things are turning out.

You must be tired by now. It's very late and we had a busy day at the hospital.'

'Yes, it is, but I'm okay.' He studied her, seeing that she was still dressed in jeans and a sweater. 'You're still up.'

'Yes, I wanted to make sure that Jess was comfortable. Do you want to come in for a coffee or tea or something?'

'Hmm…' He seemed to be thinking about that and his mouth curved. 'The "or something" sounds very tempting.'

Her cheeks flushed with warm colour. 'You know what I mean.'

'Yes…' He gave a soft, amused sigh. 'Unfortunately, I do.' He studied her, his eyes glinting, his gaze running over the tousled mass of her honey-blonde hair and the hot flare of her cheeks. 'I think, in order to avoid temptation, I'd better pass on the offer of a drink tonight. And, as you say, it's late.' He braced himself and came back to the matter in hand. 'Are you going to find space for Rob to bed down here?'

'He'll have to use the sofa.'

'I thought so. I offered to find him a room at the Manor House but he very politely refused. He said he didn't think it would be a good idea, given the way your parents feel about the Branscombes.'

'I'm sorry about that.' She pulled a face. 'He's probably right, though. If my dad found out, he would be very annoyed. I'd sooner not upset him right now or it could set his progress right back.'

He nodded. 'It's okay. I see your point. Actually, I think Rob will do better staying with you—he seems a bit down at the moment and I get the feeling he needs family around him. Too much going on in his life, perhaps…worries about college.'

She frowned. 'I know he wasn't enjoying the course he was on. I think he feels he chose the wrong subject. Or it may be something else altogether.'

'I'm sure you and Jessica will manage to help him get through it.' Nate smiled. 'I'll say goodnight, then, and leave you to go and look after your brother. I take it Jessica's okay? I told Rob she was here with you.'

'She's fine, thank you…and she absolutely loves the cot and the chair. She was amazed when she walked into the guest room and saw them there. She wants to thank you personally for giving them to her but she asked me to tell you if I saw you in the meantime. I think she's probably fast asleep right now.'

'I'm glad she's all right.' He slid behind the wheel of the Range Rover and started the engine. 'Shall I see you back at the hospital in the morning?'

'Yes, I'll be there. See you.'

She watched him drive away and turned to go back into the house. She was pleased Rob was home, and even more glad to know that Nate had been the one to find him.

What she had to do now was send her parents messages to say that Rob and Jessica were both safe and sound with her. With any luck, they would read them first thing in the morning so she wouldn't have woken them.

She went back into the house and found pillows and a duvet for Rob. Like Sophie, he was exhausted, and after he'd had a meal of a hot Cornish pasty and soup, along with a hot drink, she helped him to settle in the living room.

'You can bed down on the sofa for now,' she said. 'It's quite comfortable, so all being well, you should be able to get some rest. We'll talk in the morning before I leave for work, and then maybe we'll be able to have a proper chat later on. Nate said you were feeling a bit low.'

Rob sat down on the sofa and pulled a face. 'I'm always up and down lately. Sometimes life seems black and empty and yet other times I'm on top of the world. I don't understand it.' He sent her an anxious look. 'Sometimes I worry that I might be bipolar, like Mum.'

She knelt down beside him. 'I don't think you need worry about that, Rob. We would have noticed signs before this if you suffered from the illness she has. I think what you're feeling is just part and parcel of being a teenager. Maybe we need to find a better way of supporting you.'

He nodded absently, absorbing that. 'I hope that's all it is.'

'Well, Jessica's here, so you'll be company for each other—and it will make me feel better knowing you're here to keep an eye on her. You can let me know if she shows any sign of going into labour.'

His brows shot up and he said in a faintly alarmed tone, 'Is that likely to happen? She's not due yet, is she?'

'No…she still has a few days, possibly, but the baby seems quite big and there's not a lot of room for him in the womb, according to her last session with the midwife. Things could start happening any time.'

Rob looked worried and she laughed. 'It'll be fine, Rob. A first baby always takes a few hours, so there'll be no need to panic. Just ring me if anything seems to be starting.'

He nodded vigorously. 'I will—definitely.'

'Okay.' She smiled. 'Try to get some sleep.'

Despite having a disturbed night, Sophie was up early in the morning, preparing breakfast and getting ready for work. Rob appeared in the kitchen, bleary-eyed, as she was scrambling eggs at the hob, and he pulled out a chair by the table and sat down. 'Dad rang, didn't he?' He yawned and stretched his limbs. 'I heard him on the phone to you. You seemed to be trying to calm him down.'

'He wasn't happy because it was Nate who found you and brought Jessica here—he thinks I shouldn't have anything to do with him outside of work. I tried to explain but he wasn't really listening to anything I had to say.' She made a wry face. 'I suppose I'll still be in his bad books when I go round there to help out with Charlie. It'll give him another chance to have a go… But there was one good thing—he's really pleased that you're safe and sound.'

Rob gave a quick smile at that. Sophie guessed he missed living with his father. He went to see him as often as possible but that wasn't the same. 'I can give Dad a hand this morning if you want,' he offered. 'I know you normally have breakfast with him. It'll give me a chance to talk to him and I can take Charlie out for a walk, if you like.'

'Oh, that would be great, thanks. It will give me time to phone the midwife and sort things out before work. I'll let him know you're coming.' She was pleased he wanted to do that. It would do him good to talk to his father.

'Did I hear you say you were going to take Charlie

for a walk? How about I come with you?' Jessica came into the kitchen, blonde hair gleaming, her expression showing her delight at being with her family.

'Yeah, why not?' Rob smiled a greeting and they all sat round the table, tucking into toast and perfectly cooked eggs. They talked about things that had been going on in their lives, but most of all it seemed that Rob and Jessica were relieved to be back home in the village where they were born.

'I've set up an appointment for you with the local midwife for tomorrow morning,' Sophie told her sister as she was getting ready to leave for work a short time later. 'She lives in the village, so she knows our family well. She's going to arrange things with the maternity unit at the hospital.'

'Thanks, Sophie.' Jessica patted her abdomen. 'I wish baby would hurry up—it can't be much longer, surely?'

Rob's eyes widened in momentary panic. 'Just don't have him yet, okay? Just leave it till the weekend when Sophie's around...yeah?'

'Of course, bro—whatever you say!' Jessica laughed and ruffled his hair. Smiling, Sophie said goodbye and left for the hospital.

She did the rounds of the Neonatal Unit and then went on to see patients who'd been admitted to the Children's Unit. Josh's condition was less critical now as his head injury healed, and Sophie and Nate had decided it was time to gradually reduce his level of sedation. They had to wait and see what the outcome might be as he slowly recovered consciousness, but Nate had said he wanted to check on him later today when they brought the boy fully out of his induced coma.

She and Nate had both been busy all day and hadn't had time to stop and talk, but she met up with him by the nurses' station late in the afternoon. He was holding out a newspaper.

'Have you seen this in the daily paper?' He looked harassed and on edge, not at all his usual calm self.

'What is it?' She took the paper from him and scanned the article he'd been reading.

Villagers Protest about Homes up for Sale!

Peninsula Holdings are ready to make an offer for the Branscombe estate. Lord Branscombe, once involved in piloting a plane that crashed causing devastating injuries to his former Estate Manager, lost several millions of pounds in an ill-fated business venture overseas and now hopes to recoup his losses.

It's thought that he borrowed money to finance the investment. He suffered a heart attack recently and is now recovering in a convalescent home.

The villagers are seeking urgent talks with his son and heir, Nate Branscombe. Nate was unavailable for comment last night.

She sent him an anxious look. 'Is it true? Are the houses up for sale? Have you made a deal with Peninsula?'

'That's just it… I haven't spoken to the company yet. They finished their surveys last week and prepared a report for their head office. They're supposed to be getting in touch with me some time this week with a preliminary offer, but I've no idea what it will be.' His jaw tightened. 'They'd no right to leak this to the press and stir up trouble all over again.'

'What will you do?'

He pulled a face. 'The parish council has asked me to address an emergency meeting in the village hall later today. They've obviously been spooked by this article. I said I would do it providing there was no press intrusion, but I would have preferred to wait until I'd sorted things out. It all takes time—I have to meet with the accountants, try to set things up. They don't seem to realise that.'

She swallowed hard. 'I think people do understand… but everyone's nervous about the future. My own family's worried. I've just told Rob he can stay with me until we sort out better arrangements for him—he puts on an outward show of being okay but he needs stability. My dad said he can go and live with him once we clear out the spare room—but, even if he goes there, we don't know how long that set-up will be safe. They could both be uprooted before he has a chance to settle.'

'I told you, you don't have any reason to be concerned.' His mouth made a firm line and his green eyes were fiercely determined. 'I'll make sure the changes don't make things bad for you.'

She shook her head. 'I know you mean well, Nate, but once you sell out to Peninsula things could change. I'm sure their lawyers are clever enough to find ways to tear up any agreement. According to one of the men from the company, my dad's house will most likely be scheduled for demolition so they can build on the land. He's been worried about it ever since. Everyone's upset. No one knows how long they will be able to stay in their homes. Some people have lived in their houses since they were children. It's more than bricks and mortar that are at stake—it's the foundation of their lives.'

Nate cupped her shoulders with his hands. 'I do understand that, Sophie, and I'm doing my best to work things out…but there's a lot involved and it's not something I can do overnight.'

'I know.' She frowned. 'Perhaps it will help if you keep people updated with what you're trying to do. As things are, everyone's in the dark and coming up with worst-case scenarios.'

'I suppose you're right. I'll talk to them at this meeting.' His thumbs made soothing warm circles on her shoulders. It felt good and she wanted him to go on holding her, but he let his hands drop to his sides as Tracey appeared at the far end of the room.

She came over to the workstation and handed him a lab report. 'I thought you'd want to see this as soon as it came in,' the nurse said. 'It's the report on Lucy's angiography.'

'Ah, thanks, Tracey. That was quick.' Tracey smiled and walked away, leaving Nate to quickly read the lab's analysis. 'Apparently the treatment went well this morning,' he told Sophie. 'The blood flow to her kidneys has improved dramatically. There was a fibrous thickening causing an obstruction in both arteries, but that's been resolved now.'

Her mouth curved. 'It's all good, isn't it? When I looked in on her a little while ago, her blood pressure readings were getting back to normal. Do we know what caused the thickening in the first place?'

He shook his head. 'These cases are always difficult—there might be a genetic cause, but we can't know for certain. All we can do at the moment is try to put things right.' He glanced at his watch. 'It's getting late—there was an emergency with one of the patients and I missed out on lunch. Do you want to go and grab a coffee with me and maybe a snack?'

Her mouth turned down at the corners. 'I can't, I'm afraid. I said I would go and see Jake for a few minutes in my afternoon break. He's been so busy we haven't had time to get together for a while, but he sent me a text message this afternoon to see how things were going with Rob and Jessica. I think I need to let him know what's happening.'

A muscle flicked in his jaw and she guessed he wasn't happy about her seeing Jake.

She said cautiously, 'He and I are just friends, you know.'

'Hmm. Maybe.' Nate straightened. 'I'll see you later, then. Is there any chance you might come to the meeting at the village hall this evening? I'd like to have you there with me.'

She nodded. 'Yes, of course I'll go with you.'

She turned away to go and meet up with Jake, conscious all the time of Nate's narrowed gaze on her. Then Tracey came back and she heard her telling him about a problem that had cropped up with one of his patients, and he went off to deal with the situation. She guessed he wouldn't be getting the break he wanted.

Sophie took the lift up to the next floor. Jake would still be in his office. He'd told her earlier that he'd been busy all day, talking to suppliers and arranging new contracts.

'Sophie, it's good to see you.' His smile widened as she entered the room and he moved some of his paperwork to one side.

She gave him an answering smile. 'How are things going?'

'Oh, I've been deluged with work. The bosses want a lot of changes from the old system—more ways to save money and so on.'

'I suppose that's always going to be how things are. They're always trying to get a quart out of a pint pot. I don't envy you trying to make things work. You've put in a lot of overtime on this latest project, haven't you?'

'Yes, I have—it's taken a good deal of effort to put all this together.' He waved a hand over the files that were stacked up on his desk.

'Have you had time to eat? I could go to the cafeteria and bring you back some lunch if you can't get away?'

'Oh, that's okay—I went out to lunch with a couple of colleagues. We tried out the new restaurant by the river.' He glanced at her and said quietly, 'I'm sorry I haven't been there for you these last few days. You've a lot going on just now.'

'It's okay. You have, too.' She gave him a thoughtful look. 'You've been very busy.'

He frowned. 'Yes...yes... I was over in Cornwall again yesterday, talking to Cheryl and Matt about their systems and practices, or I'd have been in touch sooner.'

'Ah, yes, Cheryl...' Her brow creased as she tried to remember. 'I think I met her at one of the hospital's social functions. Nice girl. I seem to remember you liked her quite a lot.'

He looked at her oddly, seemingly nonplussed. Perhaps he'd thought she hadn't noticed. 'I... Well, she...'

She smiled. 'You'll have to let me know how things go with her.'

He shook his head. 'It's a non-starter. She only has eyes for someone else—a bit like you with Nate, I think… I can tell you both care for one another, but you must see that Nate never shows any sign of wanting to settle down. He's a heartbreaker, Sophie, and if he had his mind set on it, I dare say he would make a determined play for you. I suppose he's too involved with this estate business right now, though, and with his father being ill he's preoccupied.'

'That's probably true.' She started to walk towards the door. She didn't know what she thought about Nate, so she didn't want to talk to Jake about it just yet. 'I'll see you later, Jake.'

'I don't want to see you fall any further under his spell, Sophie. He already has you confused—I can tell. We should talk some more.'

'Yes, okay, we can do that. But I have to go now. I need to get back to work.'

'Shall I see you after work?'

'No, not today—I can't manage it. I have to go to a meeting at the village hall—about the estate being taken over. Tomorrow, perhaps.'

'Okay.'

She stopped to pick up a couple of coffees in disposable cups from the cafeteria, along with a pack of sandwiches for Nate. He'd said he hadn't eaten and he might appreciate some food.

Nate's expression was taut when she went back to the Children's Unit, and she wondered if he was still annoyed about the article in the paper and on edge about the meeting that was to take place later today. She approached him cautiously, not wanting to break into his introspection, but he acknowledged her with a brief nod.

'You weren't with Jake for very long,' he said, glancing up from the computer monitor where he was studying a series of CT images.

'No. We're both busy people,' she said. 'He just took a five-minute break.'

Nate seemed relieved. She pushed a coffee cup towards him and handed him the carton of sandwiches. 'I thought you might be hungry as you said you missed lunch.'

His eyes widened and he gave her a beaming smile. 'Bless you, Sophie. You're an angel.' He broke open the flip pack and bit into a chicken-and-mayo sandwich like a starving man. 'Mmm...this is great. Thank you—it was really thoughtful of you to do this.'

'You're welcome.' She turned the conversation back to work. 'You told me earlier that you wanted to look in on Josh before we finish here. Do you want to do that as soon as you've finished eating?'

He nodded. 'It's always a bit fraught, taking children off sedation after a head injury. I remember how it felt for me when I was a child, coming round a few days after my accident. I was intensely irritable and I didn't really understand anything that was going on. The nurses were great, though, incredibly patient.' He swallowed his coffee. 'My mother calmed me just by being there, talking to me and holding my hand. I don't remember what she said but it made me feel a lot better.' His features darkened momentarily as he recalled that time and for an instant his expression was bleak.

She wanted to reach out and hold him, to try to soothe his troubles away and make up for all the bad things that had happened in his life, but the fact that they were in a public place stopped her. 'It must bring back painful memories for you,' she said. He'd loved his mother and she'd been torn from him not too long after that.

'Yes, it does, even now.' He finished off his coffee and shrugged off his pensive manner. 'Let's go and see how Josh is getting along, shall we?'

'Okay.' She went with him to the side ward where they found Josh being looked after by Hannah. The five-year-old was agitated and restless, pulling at tubes and monitor cables, while his parents were looking on anxiously.

'What's happening to him?' his father asked, looking at Nate. 'Is this a sign that something's wrong?'

'Not at all.' Nate shook his head and drew up a chair so that he could sit down beside the parents. 'It's quite normal for a child to be agitated when he's coming off sedation. Hannah will make sure that he's comfortable and that he can't harm himself in any way. You don't need to worry—it looks alarming but, believe me, it's quite normal.'

He went on gently trying to reassure them. 'We need to check that he's not in any pain or suffering discomfort of any kind. Hannah will stay with him to see to that. We find it's best to keep everything reasonably quiet and dim the lights...but if you talk to Josh and try to encourage him, that might help to calm him down. He'll take a while to process information as his brain recovers, so don't expect a clear response from him just yet. You need to take things slowly.'

The man nodded. 'We will.' He reached out to hold his son's hand and spoke to him softly, and the little boy seemed to quieten at the sound of his father's voice. The child was very pale, his fair hair damp against his forehead.

After checking him over and conferring with Sophie as to his medication, Nate took his leave of the parents and thanked Hannah for doing a good job of looking after the child.

They started to walk back towards the desk but Nate's phone rang before they reached it. He listened carefully to the person at the other end of the line and then said curtly, 'Okay, I'll come over. Give me half an hour.'

He was silent and a bit grim-faced as he cut the call and Sophie said cautiously, 'Are you all right? Is something bothering you?'

He gave an awkward shrug. 'I just heard from the convalescent home that my father has taken a turn for the worse. He has a chest infection, so they have him on oxygen and high-strength antibiotics. I need to go and see him before I go to the meeting—it'll be a bit of a rush but I'll pick you up from your house at around a quarter to seven, if that's all right with you?'

'Yes, that's fine.' She laid a comforting hand on his arm. 'I'm sorry he's not doing so well.'

'Thanks.' He smiled at her and squeezed her hand in response. For a second or two he moved closer and bent his head towards her as though he might drop a kiss on her forehead, but at the last moment he straightened and gently disengaged his arm.

Sophie had to suppress an odd sensation of regret for what might have been. More and more lately, she found herself wanting closer contact with him. Instinct told her she could end up hurt and ultimately abandoned if she let herself get involved with him—his track record with women wasn't good but she couldn't help the way she felt.

She walked with him back to the computer station and prepared to go home. 'I'll see you later,' she said. 'I hope there's some good news about your father.'

'You too,' he answered. 'Good luck with Rob and Jessica. I imagine they're settling in all right?'

'I'm sure they'll be fine.'

She went home and phoned her father to make sure he was all right before hurrying to get changed for the meeting.

'Do you think Dad's still annoyed with you? How did he sound on the phone?' Rob asked. 'He's been on edge all day. Even Jessica had to try to calm him down. She took him a shepherd's pie a little while ago—it used to be his favourite.'

'It still is.' Sophie nodded. 'He told me to tell her how much he enjoyed it. Yes, he's still disappointed in me. I think he's also a bit apprehensive about this meeting tonight. He said he's going along to have his say. A friend's taking him.' She sighed. 'I wish the press hadn't stirred everything up. Nate says he's working on sorting things out but he needs time and no one's giving him that.'

'Well, good luck, anyway,' Jessica said. 'I'm glad I'm not going to be there to see sparks fly.' She had made dinner for the three of them and they sat round the table and talked for a while, enjoying being together.

Nate called for Sophie as he had promised. Jessica thanked him profusely for the cot and the chair, and Rob thanked him for giving him a lift to Sophie's house.

'I'm glad I was some help.' Nate gave them both a quick smile and then flicked a glance over Sophie, who was wearing a navy pencil-line dress teamed with navy stiletto heeled shoes. His dark brows shot up and he gave a silent whistle. 'Wow!' he said under his breath as they went out to his car. 'You look stunning.'

'Thank you.' She'd aimed to dress simply but stylishly for the occasion and she hadn't expected such a reaction from him. It felt good, though, to know that he thought she looked good. 'How is your father?' she asked.

He grimaced. 'He seems to be comfortable at the moment.'

They drove to the village green, where he parked his car near to the hall where the meeting was due to take place at seven-thirty. People were already going inside, but there were a lot more cars parked than Sophie had expected. The parish council had obviously been busy letting everyone know about the event. They stepped out of the car and Nate looked around, straightening his shoulders as though he was preparing himself for what was to come.

'There you are, Sophie! Your father said you would be here. I've been waiting for ages.' The familiar female voice startled Sophie and she looked around, her mouth opening in shock as she saw her mother standing by a bench seat that was set into the pavement.

'Mum, what are you doing here?'

Her mother looked animated, her eyes bright, her cheeks showing spots of bright colour, and her tawny, naturally curly hair was tousled as though she'd been running her fingers through it. Sophie's heart sank. Those weren't good signs. They were all indicators that her mother had been leaving off her medication.

'I wasn't expecting to see you until next weekend.'

'Well, I came to see you, of course.' She saw Nate standing beside Sophie and glared at him in recognition. 'Please go away. I want to talk to my daughter.'

Sophie looked at him in alarm, but Nate held up his hands, palms flat, and took a couple of steps backwards. He knew about her mother's condition and wasn't going to argue with her.

Her mother seemed satisfied with that for the moment. She clearly had other things on her mind. She quickly turned her attention back to Sophie and said, 'No one was at the cottage when I got here this afternoon, so I phoned your father.' She rolled her eyes. 'He wasn't any help at all. He told me to go back home. As if I would! I want to see Rob and Jessica—I thought we could all go for a picnic on the green to celebrate us being together.' She was talking fast, full of excitement about her plans.

'Mum—this isn't a good time. We're just about to go into a meeting.'

'Oh, who cares about meetings? I've a basket full of food in the car—I thought we'd spread out a cloth on the grass and enjoy ourselves.'

Sophie sucked in a swift breath. Beside her, she felt Nate stiffen and she couldn't help worrying about what he might be thinking. It was embarrassing when her mother had these manic episodes because to her everything seemed normal and she didn't see that she was doing anything out of the ordinary.

All the times before in the past when her mother had gone off her medication came flooding back, making her stomach churn. Her mother could either go into a deep depression or feel so full of energy that she could take on the world. It was difficult to know how to deal with her sometimes. From experience, Sophie knew that any attempt to turn her mother off her goal would only end in her taking offence. Despite her seeming confidence, her illness meant she was in a highly vulnerable state.

'All right,' Sophie said, trying to talk in a soothing manner. 'Let's think about this. It's going to be dark by the time we get things sorted—so perhaps this isn't the ideal place for a picnic. How would it be if I take you back to the cottage to see Rob and Jessica? I'm sure they would love to see you and take a look at the food you've brought with you. They could help you set it out and you could have a picnic at the cottage.'

Her mother moved her head from side to side as she thought about that. 'Okay,' she said at last, and Sophie gave a silent sigh of relief.

'Good. Where's your car? Is it close by?'

'Yes, it's over there.' Her mother waved a hand towards a side street.

'Ah, I see it.' Sophie swallowed carefully, conscious all the while of time passing by and of the village hall filling up with people. She was worried about the effect this disruption must be having on Nate but he stayed silent, simply watching her with her mother, his mouth making a flat line. He was clearly disturbed by the turn of events but he wasn't going to interfere and make the situation worse. Sophie had said she would go with him to the meeting and she didn't want to let him down, but she had to take care of her mother. 'Mum, have you brought your tablets with you—are they in your bag?'

'Tablets? I hate taking them…and I don't need them. I feel great!'

'I know you do…but do you have them with you? Can I look at them?'

'Oh, this is wasting precious time.' Even so, her mother searched in her bag and triumphantly produced a bottle of capsules. 'Here, you might as well throw them away.'

Sophie took the plastic bottle and slipped it into her own bag. While her mother was preoccupied with the contents of her leather purse, she glanced at Nate and said softly, 'I'll drive her to the cottage—Rob and Jessica will look after her. It shouldn't take too long—I'll try to be back for the start of the meeting.'

'You'd better send them a message to let them know you're on your way.'

She nodded. 'I'm sorry about this.' It seemed she was always having to apologise. 'I did tell you my family is always going through problems of one sort or another.'

'Yes, you did, and I remember how it was from when you all lived here before, but it's okay. It can't be helped. I'll follow you in my car and make sure everything's all right.'

She hadn't expected him to do that. 'Are you sure? What about the meeting?'

'With any luck, we should be back in time.'

'Thanks.' She exhaled slowly. She felt better already. She turned back to her mother. 'Come on, Mum,' she said, taking her arm and leading her away. 'It's been disturbing for you lately, hasn't it, with everything that's been going on at home? But it's all working out fine.'

'Yes, it's good now. Rob and Jess are with you. They'll be all right.'

Sophie settled her mother in the car and took a moment to phone Jessica and tell her that they were on their way.

'Don't worry,' Jessica said. 'I'll make sure she takes her tablets. She'll probably sleep for a while afterwards. They often have that effect on her after she's left them off for a while.'

'Thanks.'

Back at the cottage, Jessica and Rob welcomed their mother and settled her in the recliner armchair. They started to talk to her about things that were on her mind. Over the years, they'd all found this was the best way to deal with her wild mood swings.

Satisfied that she was being well looked after, Sophie went out and slid into the passenger seat of Nate's car.

'Is she okay?'

'I think so. Rob's setting out the food and Jessica has persuaded her to take a tablet.'

'Good.' He started the car and they set off once more for the meeting.

Nate pulled up opposite the village hall. He cut the engine and looked about him, frowning. There were men and women outside the hall, holding cameras aloft, and some had recording devices. These weren't villagers.

'It's the press,' Nate said through his teeth, his mouth making a grim line. 'Who would have told them about the meeting?'

'Isn't that the chairperson from the parish council speaking to one of them?' Sophie murmured. 'He looks quite pleased with himself. I think we can guess who told them.'

'He's gone too far this time.' Nate stepped out of the car and went towards the gathering of people. Sophie followed him.

'There he is.' The crowd surged towards him, cameras flashing, following him as he walked into the hall.

'Are you selling out, Branscombe?' a reporter shouted.

'Are you going after the money like your father?' another called out.

Nate tried to speak to the assembled people but was cut off by another journalist. 'Sins of the father,' the man said. 'What do you say to that, eh? Makes a good headline, don't you think?'

Nate tried to go on with what he wanted to say. People seemed disturbed by what was going on and Sophie caught a glimpse of her father in his wheelchair at the side of the hall, being kept back out of harm's way by his friend. He looked concerned by the turn of events.

'I agreed to come here this evening to talk to all of you and try to put your minds at rest,' Nate began. He didn't get a chance to go on.

'How can you do that? Your father's landed you right in it, hasn't he?' one of the reporters interrupted.

'Yeah, how are you going to sort out his mess?' another one enquired. 'Are you going to make a mint from selling out to Peninsula?'

Nate braced his shoulders. 'Okay, that's enough,' he announced in a brisk tone. 'Either you back off or this meeting is not going ahead.'

'Peninsula Holdings are going to put this place on the map. They'll build hotels and a shopping mall. That'll all be down to you, won't it?' A man with a camera stepped up to Nate and took his picture.

Another held out his recording device. 'What do you say to the people who want to keep their village exactly as it is now?'

Nate's jaw clenched. 'That's it. I'm leaving. If the

people who are villagers or tenants on the estate want to talk to me, they can come to the Manor House tomorrow evening at seven. The press are not invited.'

He looked at Sophie. 'Are you coming with me? I'll understand if you don't want to.' He swivelled around and walked swiftly back to the car.

Sophie followed him, eyes wide, anxious about the disastrous way things had erupted and desperate to talk to him. As she turned to go, she couldn't be sure but she thought she saw Jake among the crowd. Had he gone there to take part in the meeting?

Then, as she hurried away, she caught sight of her father's expression. 'I'm sorry,' she mouthed silently. He was taut with disbelief at the way things had gone. She didn't like to dwell on what he thought of her being with the son of the man who'd caused his disability, but at that moment she felt like a traitor.

She slid into the car beside Nate and he gunned the engine into life. The journalists were blocking the road back to the cottage, so he reversed quickly, turned the car around and headed out along the main highway.

'Where are we going?' she asked.

'To the Manor House.' He shot her a quick glance. 'Is that okay with you?'

'I suppose so.' She frowned. 'I can't help thinking it would have been better if you'd stayed to talk to the villagers.'

'You're probably right, but I wasn't going to take part in a circus. I told the organisers "no press" but they didn't keep to their word.'

'They'll probably be on their way to the Manor right now,' she said quietly. 'You could be heading right into another confrontation.'

'Yes, I expect that's true. I could drive to the Wayfarer's Inn instead—it's out of the way, no one will guess we're there, and we can talk over dinner. What do you think?'

'Sounds good.'

The Wayfarer's Inn was off the beaten track along a country lane and served the residents of another small village further inland. It was set against a backdrop of tall trees and had a garden where people could sit outside at rustic tables lit by old-style lanterns. Sophie and Nate chose to go inside and found a table in a corner made private by a wooden trellis and strategically placed tubs filled with greenery.

Sophie was surprised to find she had an appetite despite the fact that she'd shared a meal with her brother and sister less than three hours ago, but Nate was making up for missing out on a proper meal earlier that day. They ate chilli con carne with pilau rice and sour cream, and finished off with apple-and-raspberry crumble. They talked about his father, who was struggling with lung problems after his heart attack.

It was only later, when Nate's mood had mellowed a little, that Sophie asked him about his plans for the estate.

'What would you have said at the meeting?' she asked him as they drank rich dark coffee. 'Do you think you would have managed to appease them?'

'Some people might have been satisfied, but others possibly not. The thing is, I don't have a lot of options. My father borrowed money to finance his investment abroad and that has to be paid back.'

She frowned. 'I can see why it's been such a worry.'

'Yes.' He made a wry face. 'I've been trying to organise ways to save the estate, but they won't be to everyone's liking. For a start, I would have to terminate short-term leases so that I can sell those properties. That would only apply to newcomers who rent property for the holiday season. We get a few people who come over from France or Spain, wanting a change of scenery. In the winter, the houses are difficult to let unless business people want to stay while they're over here for conferences and so on.'

He refilled his cup from a cafetière and spooned brown sugar crystals into his coffee. 'I'll see if I can start some kind of farming project, and I thought we could make more use of the lake—maybe restock it with fish and organise fishing weekends. I'm sure they would go down well.'

'You'd have to have somewhere for them to stay locally.'

He nodded. 'I could get some log cabins built by the lake…have facilities put in and so on, but it will cost quite a bit initially. I'll put my own money into that but it will be some time before the venture pays for itself.'

'So, all in all, it would have been simpler for you to sell up and have none of this problem?'

'It would. It's taken a while for the accountants to look into everything but I'm fairly sure we have some viable options now. I think I can safely turn down any offer Peninsula makes.'

She smiled. 'That's such a relief. It sounds as though you've tried really hard to find a solution.'

'I have.' He reached for her hand across the table. 'Above all, I'm doing this for you, Sophie. I told you I would do everything I can to make sure you and your father can keep your homes. I'm going down this route because I feel we—my father and I—owe it to your father to help him any way we can to make up for what happened to him, and I'm doing it because I care about you and I want you to be happy.'

'Thank you. I… I don't know what to say. I'm so grateful to you.' She leaned forward in her seat and placed her free hand in his palm. He cupped her hands and bent his head towards her, brushing her lips with his own, sending an instant wave of heat to course through her body.

'You know I want you, Sophie…more than anything. I'd move heaven and earth for you. I want to take you in my arms and kiss you right now and let you know just how much I'm aching for you.'

She kissed him, closing her eyes, oblivious to their surroundings. Her lips were aflame, her blood fizzing with excitement. Hidden by the screen, they were in their own secluded world, and in that moment she wanted him every bit as much as he wanted her.

'We could get a room here,' he said softly, his voice rough around the edges, his hands trembling a little. 'I need you so much. Tell me you feel the same way.'

'I want you,' she said huskily. 'I do…but… I'm not sure it would be the wisest thing… There are so many reasons why this would be all wrong… You and me— we're from different worlds.'

'That doesn't matter. Why should it matter?'

She thought about it. He was offering her a night of bliss, of joy and ecstasy, the fulfilment of all her longings…but that was all he was offering. Could she put her uncertainties about everything that had happened between them and the problems between their families to one side and give in to temptation, take what he was prepared to give, for now?

Her musings were short-lived. A waiter approached and they broke apart, just as her mobile phone started to trill. Still shaken by her need for Nate, she did nothing, but took deep, slow breaths, trying to bring herself back to normal.

The phone kept on ringing. 'They're persistent, whoever they are,' Nate said drily. 'Perhaps you'd better answer it. It might be to do with your sister, or your mother.'

She nodded. The waiter asked if there was anything they needed and Nate asked for the bill. He had himself under control, as if nothing had happened between them. Either that or he was very good at hiding his feelings.

He'd had to remind her about the worries over Jessica and her mother. What had she been thinking? How could she possibly spend the night here with him when her family needed her? She couldn't leave them to their own devices so soon.

She looked down at the screen on her phone. 'It's Jake,' she said flatly. 'I thought I saw him outside the village hall earlier. He's probably worried in case the press caught up with us.'

Nate's head went back a fraction and his gaze narrowed on her. He didn't like the fact that Jake was calling her.

Jake's voice was brisk and matter-of-fact. 'I had to ring you,' he said. 'I tried to get to the Manor House in case you were there, but there are a dozen reporters at the gate. I know you're with Nate—I saw you leave the meeting with him—but I don't feel I had any choice but to get in touch. Your father's very concerned about what happened at the hall tonight. I spoke to him and he's in a bad way, very shaken up. I think he might be suffering a panic attack of some sort.'

'Thanks for letting me know, Jake. I'll go and see him.'

'I told him you would.'

'Yes…okay.'

She cut the call and told Nate what was happening. 'I'll have to go over to Dad's house and try to calm him down. You can stay here, if you want—Jake said the journalists are at the Manor. I'll get a taxi to take me home.'

He shook his head. 'I'll take you, and then I'll go to the Manor House. I'm not going to let a bunch of reporters keep me away.'

She frowned. 'So we could have gone there earlier?'

'I guess so.' He nodded. 'It's just that when you suggested there might be a problem, I thought this place might be more romantic—I suppose I leapt at the chance to spend time with you somewhere you might feel comfortable. I didn't have an ulterior motive, but I wanted you to be able to relax.'

'Hmm…and I did. You're right—this is a lovely inn.' She made a wry smile. 'And I was relaxed enough to be very tempted by your offer of spending the night, until I started to think about everything that's happened. My family has to come first. We've had more than one chance but it's just not meant to be.'

'I won't let you down again, Sophie,' he said.

'I'd like to believe that.' She stood up and he went with her towards the exit door.

'And you know I won't give up trying to win you over, don't you?'

'Mmm… I guessed as much. You always were persistent.'

He studied her as he held open the door to let her through. 'You don't believe I can be good for you, do you?'

She returned his gaze. 'No. There are so many reasons why I should steer clear of you, and an equal number of reasons why I can't—my head and my heart are at war and I've no idea what to do about that.'

He smiled. 'That's easy. Listen to your heart every time…and let me take care of the rest.'

CHAPTER SIX

'YOU WERE THERE with him at the meeting—you were there with Nate Branscombe.' Sophie's father glared at her angrily next morning. 'How could you do that? How could you ally yourself with him when you know how I feel about that family?'

'Nate's okay—he's not done anything wrong. He wasn't the one who hurt us.' Sophie tried to defend Nate but her father wasn't having any of it.

'He's in charge now and if things don't go his way he'll sell us out, plain and simple. He's a Branscombe through and through. And all this time you and he have been getting close again—I can see it in the way you look at him, in the way you talk about him… Don't fool yourself that he cares about you, Sophie. He'll do the same as he's always done with women and drop you as soon as things start getting serious. Didn't you learn anything when he left after my accident? He didn't stay around to help you pick up the pieces, did he?'

'I made it too difficult for him. I was angry and upset and I wouldn't listen. I thought someone—he— should have known his father was having angina attacks. I lashed out at him.'

'You weren't to blame for him leaving. He'd have

gone anyway. I worked for his father, remember? I know how his kind think. They simply move on.'

'Nate's different, Dad. He's a decent man.'

'He's messing with you. James Branscombe always made it clear to me that his son was to marry aristocracy. It was always uppermost in his mind that his son would carry on the line and keep that upper-crust heritage. His family's place in society means everything to James. And his son won't go against him.'

Sophie flinched at the things he was saying. She'd probably known it all along, but having it spelled out for her so graphically made her stomach churn. Her father was upset and angry but she understood he was only trying to look out for her. He wanted to warn her there was no future for her with Nate, but deep down she already knew it, didn't she? Her problem was that she had trouble accepting it.

'I'm not looking to marry him,' she said. 'No one said anything about that.' But if she had the chance to be with Nate for ever, wouldn't she grasp it with both hands? Wasn't she lying to herself if she said anything different? But she couldn't say any of that to her father, could she? He wouldn't understand. 'Try not to upset yourself. You'll only end up having another panic attack like you did last night.' She knelt down beside her father's chair. 'Look, Dad, I'm sorry you feel this way… but I told you how Nate plans to put things right about the estate. He's doing the best he can in difficult circumstances. If you're not convinced, you'll be able to talk to him at the Manor House tonight.'

'Hmmph. We'll see.' He frowned. 'You'll be there, I suppose?'

She nodded. 'I'm going with Rob. He said he wants

to know what's going on. Do you want me to take you, or will your friend be driving you there?'

'I've already made arrangements.'

'Okay.' She stood up. 'If there's nothing else I can do for you, I'd better get back to the cottage. Jessica was having some kind of cramps in her abdomen this morning. They may be nothing, but I need to take her for her check-up at the hospital.'

He nodded. 'Let me know how she goes on. Where's your mother staying? I don't suppose there's room for her at the cottage, is there? Is she any calmer?'

'She seems to be all right now. We're making sure she's taking her tablets and she's booked herself into a room at the village pub. Tom will come over when he gets the chance but it's difficult for him because he has to go to work every day and can't get away easily. Anyway, Mum says she's going to stay there until Jess has the baby. Don't worry. We'll look after her.' She laid a hand on his shoulder and bent to kiss him lightly on the forehead. 'I'll see you later, Dad. Rob will be along in an hour or so to make a start on clearing out the spare room. He's really keen to get things organised.'

She went out by the kitchen. Charlie's tail thumped happily on the floor as she stroked him before leaving the house. She'd spent a fraught half hour with her father and she was almost relieved to be going home.

Jessica was still feeling uncomfortable when Sophie arrived back at the cottage, and she did her best to reassure her. 'We'd perhaps better take your overnight case with us to the hospital,' she said. 'They might want to keep you in.'

Some half an hour later, she took her over to the maternity unit. 'Stay with me when I see the doctor, will you?' Jessica asked. 'And I want you to be there when the baby comes—I don't even know if Ryan will be able to be here for the birth. I need to have you with me.'

'That's all right. Of course I'll stay with you—and once we know that you're in labour, we can get in touch with Ryan. With any luck, he'll be able to fly home at short notice.'

'Thanks, Sophie.'

The obstetrician examined Jessica carefully and looked at the ultrasound scans. 'I think we'll admit you for observation,' she said. 'If things don't start to happen overnight, we'll induce labour in the morning.'

They found a bed for Jessica on the ward and Sophie helped her settle in. 'You can walk about if you want, use the day room and talk to the other mums-to-be,' the midwife told Jessica. 'But make sure you get some rest if you feel you need it. We'll be checking your pulse and blood pressure and listening to the foetal heartbeat and so on at regular intervals.'

'I'm leaving you in good hands,' Sophie told her sister a little later. She glanced at her watch. 'I'm here on borrowed time—I need to go over to the Children's Unit and get to work, but I'll come over to see you later.' She left Jessica making a phone call to Ryan.

The rest of the day passed without anything untoward happening, and after checking on Jessica once more in the late afternoon, Sophie spent some time getting ready for the meeting at the Manor House. She missed Nate and wanted to be with him, but she hadn't seen much of him all day. They'd both been busy with their own lists of patients, and now she was edgy with anticipation at the thought of seeing him again at his home. Last night at the Wayfarer's Inn, he'd kissed her and made it very clear how much he wanted her. How would it have been if she'd spent the night there with him? A frisson of nervous excitement rippled through her at the thought.

A crowd of reporters had gathered outside the gates of the Manor by the time Rob and Sophie arrived, but security staff were on hand to make sure none of them had access to the grounds. They'd been told to expect Sophie and her brother, so they were allowed in without any fuss, and Sophie was able to drive up to the house without restriction.

Nate met her and Rob in the wide hallway and immediately took them to one side. 'Hey, I'm glad you came.' He greeted them cheerfully, but after a moment or two of general chit-chat, Rob excused himself and went to find his father. Nate drew Sophie into a side room.

As soon as they were alone, he put his arms around her and held her close. 'I wish there wasn't such a crowd here tonight,' he said. 'I'd much rather it was just you and me—I'd like to have the time to show you properly just how glad I am to see you.'

'That might not be such a good idea.' She felt warm and safe in his arms, but even so, she looked at him uncertainly, her father's warnings echoing in her head.

'No?' He took no notice of her doubts, folding her to him and sweeping away her qualms with a kiss that was passionate, fervent and full of pent-up desire, as though he'd been holding back and couldn't resist any longer. His kiss left her breathless, clinging to him in startled wonder, definitely wanting more.

'Oh, wow!' she said. 'I wasn't expecting that.' He held her so that her body meshed with his and she smiled up at him, loving his nearness. She was all too conscious of the way his hands were moving slowly over her, shaping her curves, exploring the soft hills and valleys of her body. It made her feel good, made her tingle all over with longing.

'I can't get enough of you,' he said, his voice ragged as he bent his head to nuzzle the silky-smooth column of her throat. He nudged aside the flimsy fabric of her top, exposing her bare shoulder. 'I've been thinking about you all night and all day, waiting until I could get you alone.' He ran the flat of his palm lightly down her spine, moving ever lower until he drew her against him and his strong thighs tangled with hers. 'You're so, so beautiful,' he whispered. 'You tantalise me every time I'm with you.'

She kissed him, a deep-seated need growing in her. She wanted this, was desperate to be with him. And yet, even as she returned his kisses and ran her fingers over his taut biceps, at the back of her mind the doubts were creeping in. Why did it have to be so difficult for her to give in to her heart's desire?

Perhaps it was because she knew, deep down, that she would never be satisfied with a relationship that was going nowhere. She wanted more, much more from Nate, but was he prepared to give it? Her whole life had been torn apart when her parents' marriage broke up, and her own relationships with men had been fraught up to now. Perhaps those experiences had made her afraid. She couldn't face being hurt again and if Nate let her down she would be devastated. More than anything, she needed to experience a love that would last—and she was coming to realise that it was *his* love she wanted above all.

She ran her hand lightly over his ribcage as though

she would memorise the feel of him. She wanted him and needed him, but… When she looked up into his eyes, she knew he read the uncertainty in hers. 'I won't let you down,' he said. He kissed her passionately, his hand moving to the small of her back, crushing her soft curves to blend with his.

A clock chimed the hour and he sighed, releasing her slowly. 'We should go,' he murmured reluctantly, resting his head lightly against her temple, and she nodded. 'I didn't want any of this,' he said quietly. 'This business of the Manor and the estate. I simply wanted to be a doctor.'

They broke apart and she spent a moment tidying herself up, straightening her camisole top and smoothing a hand over her jeans. 'Is my hair a mess?' she asked and he gave her an amused smile.

'You look fantastic,' he said. 'You always do. That's part of the problem.' There was a faint note of regret in his voice.

They went into the main hall, where people were beginning to take their places around a long, rectangular solid wood table, and Sophie slid into a seat next to her brother and her father. The walls in here were panelled in oak and the evening light filtered in through leaded panes, casting a warm glow over everything.

Nate welcomed everyone. He'd provided them with tea and coffee and soft drinks or wine, and there was a buffet table at the side of the room behind Sophie, where a selection of finger food had been set out. Sophie guessed that his housekeeper, Charlotte, had been busy organising things. She noticed that as well as a variety of tiny sandwiches, there were mini Yorkshire puddings with rare beef and mustard and horseradish sauce, bruschetta with goat's cheese, basil and tomato, and blinis with smoked salmon. He'd done his best to make sure his guests were treated well.

His efforts certainly helped to put his audience in a better mood and encourage them to listen to what he had to say. He told them of the plans he'd outlined to Sophie, and added that he was hoping to start an organic farming business on the land that up to now had been left to pasture. 'I'll need skilled workers to help me with that,' he said.

There were some dissenting voices. Some people didn't like the fact that he was planning to organise fishing weekends. 'There'll be a lot of strangers roaming around, and they'll start up competitions and so on,' one man said. 'The village won't be the same.'

'It's better than having to sell the houses to Peninsula, though, don't you think?' Nate pointed out the advantages but added, 'The costings aren't all in yet, so I'm making no promises...but this is what I'm aiming for. I'll do my best to hold off any sale.'

When the meeting finished, people stayed to eat some more and talk for a while and ask questions but gradually they started to drift away. Sophie's father spoke to her briefly. He seemed slightly appeased by what he'd heard but said tetchily, 'I'm going home. I can't be in this place without remembering all my dealings with James Branscombe. He was a difficult man to work with. I don't know if his son's going to be different—let's hope he is.'

Rob frowned, watching his father leave. 'He's very bitter still, isn't he? I can't blame him. His whole life changed after the accident. I just don't know why he stayed with Lord Branscombe so long if he felt that way about him.'

'I think the money was probably good, and the work suited him. It kept a roof over our heads. People put up with a lot to have a secure life.'

'Perhaps he'll feel better when I go to live with him. I'll be able to help him out if he's struggling.'

'That's true.' Sophie nodded. 'Though sometimes it might do him good to struggle a bit.'

Rob frowned. 'How can that be?'

'It might help him to do things for himself as much as possible.'

'But he can't, can he? He's in a wheelchair.'

Nate came to join them. 'I couldn't help overhearing the last bit of your conversation,' he said. 'I think Sophie means that if your father has to try to do some things within his ability, it will help strengthen his muscles. Being able to pull himself up to a standing position, for instance, will help—though he'll need someone to be there with him to make sure he doesn't fall.'

'Oh, I see.' Rob nodded thoughtfully. 'Yes, I can do that.'

Nate studied him. 'How are you doing these days, Rob? Are you feeling any brighter in yourself?'

Rob pulled a face. 'I think I'm better now I'm a bit more settled. I have mood swings and I don't understand why I feel that way. I worry about it sometimes.'

'That's understandable.' Nate was sympathetic. 'Sophie told me you were afraid you might be suffering from bipolar disorder like your mother but, to be honest, seeing you and hearing how you react to things, I think you're going through what every teenage boy goes through. Your hormones are all over the place. It's a difficult time for you.'

'I think Nate's right.' Sophie joined in. She was glad Nate had taken the time to try to reassure her brother. 'You've been better in yourself since you came here and met up with some of your old friends. You said a few of them are studying at the college in town—perhaps you might want to look into signing up for one of the courses that start soon. You've already done a year of Psychology—why not try to finish your studies?'

Rob gave it some thought and then nodded, seemingly invigorated. 'Yeah, I might do that. My mate has to go to an Open Day in a couple of weeks. I could go along with him.'

'That's a great idea.'

Nate glanced at Sophie. 'How's the rest of the family doing?'

'They're fine, thanks.' He already knew about Jessica being admitted to hospital. 'Jess's still having odd abdominal cramps—they're not really contractions as such but she's quite uncomfortable. Her back's aching and she doesn't like being on her own in hospital. And I checked on Mum before we came here and made sure she took her tablets.' She sent him a quick concerned glance. 'Is there any news of your father?'

'He's much the same. He's been readmitted to hospital so he can have intensive treatment. They have him on antibiotics and diuretics to try to reduce the fluid in his tissues, but he seems to be struggling.'

'I'm sorry.'

She and Rob had to go soon after that so that Sophie could drive to the hospital and check on Jessica. She was reluctant to leave Nate—she wanted to stay and talk some more—but her sister was uppermost in her mind just then.

Jessica was thrilled to see her and Rob. They spoke for a short time and Sophie rubbed her back for her, but Jess was tired and soon dozed off. It looked as though they would go ahead with inducing labour in the morning.

Everything went as planned. A whole day went by after the midwife inserted the pessary that would hopefully start things off. By then the weekend was almost on them and Sophie was glad because it meant she would be able to spend time at the hospital without worrying about having to take time off work.

She went to the village High Street on Saturday morning to buy things that Jessica might need, like baby bottles, nappies and wipes. She found a lovely congratulations card and some of Jessica's favourite chocolates. Lost in thought, she came back out on to the street only to be pulled up short in surprise as she saw Nate coming out of the post office. Her pulse quickened.

'Hi there. It's good to see you.' He smiled and gave her a hug. 'I wasn't sure if I would see anything of you over the next couple of days, with Jessica being in hospital, but here you are. It's my lucky day.' He waved a hand towards the post office. 'I had to send off a registered letter—' He glanced at her packages. 'It looks as though you've been stocking up on essentials in preparation for the baby.'

She nodded. 'Jessica brought a few things with her on the train, but there was a limit to what she could get in her case. As it was, it was a good thing it had wheels on it.' They walked along the street together to where she had parked her car.

'Are you headed for the hospital now?'

'Yes, I—' She broke off, frowning as she noticed a small boy walking with his mother. They were going towards the pharmacy nearby and the child was coughing quite badly, dragging his feet as though being out and about was too much for him. He was a thin little boy around seven years old and he was breathless and didn't look at all well. His mother looked at him worriedly, supporting him, and as Sophie and Nate looked on, the little boy's knees started to buckle under him.

Nate reached them and helped to catch the child before he collapsed completely. 'Can I help you?' he asked the mother. 'He looks quite poorly.' He held the child, kneeling down and cradling him in his arms as his mother nodded anxiously.

'Oh, yes…please can you help?' She knelt down beside him, saying urgently, 'I recognise you—you're Nate Branscombe, aren't you? Can you do something for him? You're a doctor, aren't you? I tried to get to see our GP but the surgery's closed.'

She dragged in a shaky breath. 'My little boy's had a cough for about a week but the antibiotics the doctor gave him don't seem to be working. I'm on my own this weekend. I've been so worried. I'm new to the village and I have no transport and no one I can leave him with while I try to sort out what to do. I was going to the pharmacy to see if anyone could help, but he suddenly got worse. I knew he was ill but I didn't think it was so bad—I think I need to call for an ambulance.'

'Yes, that would probably be best,' Nate said. He glanced up at Sophie but she was already dialling the number. 'He's feverish and not breathing properly,' Nate went on. 'He needs oxygen.' He looked at Sophie once more. 'Do you have your medical kit in your car? I have mine but I'm parked further down the road.' He checked the boy over, feeling for a pulse. 'His lips are a bluish colour already. I'm afraid we may need to intubate him fast.'

'Yes, I'll go and get it.' Finishing the call, she hurriedly opened the boot of her car and hauled out her copious medical bag. Taking off her jacket, she rolled it up into the shape of a pillow and placed it under the boy's head. She placed an SpO2 monitor on his finger and connected it to the portable machine that gave an oxygen read-out.

'What's his name?' Nate asked the mother.

'Shaun.'

'Okay.' He spoke directly to the boy. 'Shaun, I'm going to listen to your chest.' The boy didn't respond but Nate reached for a stethoscope and was quiet for a moment, running the diaphragm over Shaun's ribcage. 'It sounds like pneumonia,' he said after a while. He checked the SpO2 reading. 'His blood oxygen saturation is very low,' he told Sophie. 'The most important thing right now is to get a tube into his windpipe and give him the oxygen he needs.'

Sophie helped him, introducing a cannula into Shaun's hand and giving him a sedative and anaesthetic so that Nate could get easier access to insert the tube into his throat. They worked quickly, taping the tube in place on the boy's cheek. Nate connected the tube to the bag and mask device and then attached this to an oxygen canister. He began to squeeze the bag rhythmically, getting life-saving oxygen into Shaun's lungs.

Sophie explained the procedure to the mother and then said, 'When he gets to the hospital he'll most likely be given an X-ray and possibly a CT scan to take a better look at his lungs. They'll want to do tests to see what's causing the problem and they'll give him a stronger broad spectrum antibiotic in the meantime.'

In the distance, they heard the sound of the ambulance siren. Nate looked up, frowning slightly as he saw that a crowd of onlookers had gathered around them. They were mostly silent, just watching, but Nate was too busy to take much notice. 'I'm going to give him nebulised adrenaline,' he told Sophie. 'Will you take over here while I set it up?'

'Of course.' She squeezed the oxygen bag while he prepared the nebulised solution. It would help to relax the child's airways and allow him to breathe more easily. After a while, when the boy was still unresponsive, he gave him a shot of corticosteroid, aiming to reduce any inflammation that was causing a problem. Sophie went on squeezing the oxygen bag and Nate spoke quietly to the child's mother, trying to reassure her.

The ambulance drew up close by. 'Hi, Doc—hi, Sophie…' The paramedics arrived and listened carefully as Nate outlined the situation.

'We need to have a team waiting for us at the hospital. He should go straight to Paediatric Intensive Care.'

'Okay, we'll let them know.'

They transferred Shaun to the ambulance and connected him to the monitors that would tell them his heart and respiratory rate, along with the level of oxygen in his blood. It was improving but it was still very low because of the infection in his lungs. Shaun's mother sat alongside her son and Nate climbed into the vehicle to make the journey with them.

He glanced at Sophie. 'Thanks for everything you

did back there, Sophie. Maybe I'll see you at the hospital later?' He was looking at her packages, abandoned on the pavement.

She nodded. 'Yes, I'll be there most of the day, I expect.' She watched the ambulance pull away and then went to gather up all her equipment.

The small crowd of people were still watching. 'You and the other doctor did all right, there,' one man said. 'Do you think the boy will pull through?'

'Well, we've done everything we can and he'll be in the right place to get the care he needs,' she answered carefully.

'I never thought of Nate Branscombe working as an emergency doctor,' another bystander said. 'I only ever saw him coming and going from the Manor House.' He nodded slowly, deep in thought. 'Just goes to show, you never really know someone.'

Sophie collected her supplies and put them back into her medical bag. She stowed it away in the boot of her car, along with her shopping. A woman who Sophie recognised from around the village picked up one of the bags from the pavement and handed it to her. 'Baby things,' she said with a smile. 'I guessed your sister would be due any time now. I hope things go well for her.'

'Thanks.' Sophie smiled and slid into the driver's seat. She and Nate had spent a worrying half hour or so with the boy and she was almost looking forward to enjoying a more relaxed time in the maternity unit with Jessica.

Perhaps she ought to have known it wasn't to be. Life was never that easy for her, and when she arrived on the ward Jessica was nowhere to be seen.

'Oh, she's been taken to the delivery suite,' a nurse

told her. 'She's not doing too well, poor girl. The contractions have been painful and they've been going on for quite a long time through the night. The doctor's given her an epidural to give her some relief.'

'But she didn't tell me... Why wouldn't she have phoned me?'

'She said if it was going to be a long haul she didn't want to worry you. I was about to call you, though. Things are beginning to speed up quite significantly.'

'I'll go and see her.'

Sophie hurried away to find Jessica. She was lying on the bed looking very pale, with a sheen of sweat on her brow. 'Oh, Jessica, you were supposed to ring me,' Sophie said, going over to her to give her a hug. 'Did you change your mind about wanting me here?'

'No! Never!' Jessica smiled tiredly. 'It's just that it all started to happen in the night and I guessed you'd be asleep. I didn't want to disturb you. And Mum was here earlier. She can be a bit exhausting when she's in full flow. I'm not sure she's taken her tablets.'

'Oh, heavens! Where is she now?'

'She's gone to get a cup of coffee. Do you think you might be able to persuade her to swallow her meds with a bun or something?'

'I will...but shouldn't I be here with you?'

'You will be. They say it will be a while yet.' Jessica smiled, laying a hand on her abdomen as another contraction swept over her. 'I can feel it but since I had the epidural there's no pain. I'll be fine. I think Ryan's on his way to the hospital. He said he was going to catch a flight last night.'

'That's good. All right, I'll go and see if I can find Mum and calm her down—though I suppose you can't really blame her for being excited with a grandson on the way!'

Jessica smiled. 'Yes, maybe.'

Sophie found her mother in the cafeteria, happily sending messages from her phone to all her friends. 'I can't believe it's actually happening,' she said. 'But she's been in labour for ages.'

'It's taking a while, isn't it?' Sophie agreed. 'But a first grandchild is something special…worth waiting for.'

'Oh, I can't wait to hold him!'

'I know. I feel the same way.'

They chatted and she persuaded her mother to eat something and swallow her tablets. Tom phoned a little later and Sophie took the opportunity to slip away while her mother was preoccupied with the call. 'I'll see you in a little while,' she mouthed as she left the cafeteria and her mother smiled.

She went back into the delivery room and saw, to her relief, that Ryan had arrived. He was holding Jessica's hand.

She and Ryan greeted one another and then Sophie went to stand at the other side of the bed. 'I'm so glad you made it in time,' she told him. But, even as she said it, things started to happen all at once. Another major contraction started.

'I can see the baby's head,' the midwife said. 'Try to give a big push.'

The baby's head appeared, but instead of being followed by the appearance of his shoulders, everything seemed to stop. They waited for Jessica's next contraction, but even then the baby's shoulders stayed firmly in place and when the midwife intervened it was no use.

'The shoulder's stuck,' she said, looking worried. The baby's face was turning grey and Sophie was becoming more alarmed with every minute that passed. If the baby stayed in this position for too long, the umbilical cord would be squashed and oxygen wouldn't get through to him.

The midwife had signalled for help and the room filled with people: obstetricians, paediatricians, midwives, an anaesthetist. They all had a specific job to do but seeing them all there, trying to bring this baby into the world, was terrifying. As a doctor, Sophie knew the dangers but this was different—this was her sister at risk, along with her unborn baby.

Two midwives helped Jessica to get into a better knees-up position to facilitate the birth, the doctor made a deeper episiotomy cut and another midwife pressed down hard on Jessica's abdomen. The baby was in distress and Jessica began to haemorrhage. It was horrifying to stand there and see it happen, and for Sophie to know that she had to keep out of the way and let the doctors and nurses do their jobs. This was her sister and her nephew who were in danger and she was frightened for both of them.

In the next minute the baby was born, but he didn't make any sound. He was a bluish colour and floppy, and immediately the paediatrician took him and began to try to resuscitate him. A midwife wrapped him in a blanket to keep him warm and then the doctor suctioned him to clear away the secretions that were blocking his airway. They placed him in an incubator and started to give him oxygen, attaching vital monitor leads to him before wheeling him away to the Neonatal Intensive Care Unit.

Sophie wanted to rush after him and do anything

she could to help, but her sister needed her too. Ryan was white with shock and looked about ready to pass out, while Jessica was clammy with exhaustion and loss of blood. She was still bleeding and the midwives were doing everything they could to stem the flow. Sophie tried to stay calm, urging Ryan to sit down and put his head between his knees for a while to restore his blood pressure, and then she went to hold Jessica's hand once more.

Over the next hour, as the doctors and the nurses did everything they could to bring the bleeding under control, Jessica kept vomiting. All Sophie and Ryan could do was to try to make her comfortable. Sophie spoke to her mother and tried to reassure her—they'd been allowed to take it in turns to be in the delivery room.

'I believe things have calmed down finally,' the doctor said at last. 'She's stable, and the best thing to do now is to let her rest.'

Sophie and her mother left Jessica alone with Ryan from time to time over the next couple of hours, to give them some space. Her mother went to fetch coffees for everyone and Sophie went outside for a breath of fresh air.

Her phone rang. It was Nate, and relief washed over her at the sound of his voice. Everything seemed better when he was close by, even if he was only at the end of a phone line.

'I wondered how things were going,' he asked. 'I've been thinking about all of you.'

'She's had a really tough time and I'm worried about the baby,' she told him. 'I don't know exactly how he's doing, yet, but I think he's out of the woods. Jessica's still retching. They're giving her oxygen through nasal tubes and she's on intravenous fluids, so she's gradually improving.'

'I'm sorry, Sophie. It sounds as though it's been rough on her and the baby. Are you going to stay there through the night?'

'No, Ryan's the only one who can be with her then. The rest of the time they're not allowing more than two visitors at the bedside and Mum's going to be there for a while. Actually, I was almost expecting her to be overexcited despite her medication, but she's been remarkably subdued.'

'She's probably worried, like everyone else. I guess when she takes her medication she's fine.'

'Yes.' She frowned. 'I'm glad you understand, Nate.' Somehow, it was becoming more and more important to her that he accepted her family as they were. 'I was afraid you might be uncomfortable around my family. They can be difficult to handle at times.'

He gave a short laugh. 'I'm hardly likely to feel that way—there are skeletons in most family backgrounds, mine included, and my father isn't exactly a prime example of how to behave.'

'I suppose not.' She wished he could be here with her right now. She yearned for his soothing presence but it wasn't to be. He was probably going to spend time with his father.

Sophie cut the call a little later, after telling him, 'I'll stay with Jessica for another couple of hours and then I'm going to see Dad and Rob and let them know what's happening. After that I'm going home. It's been a traumatic day.'

Before going back to Maternity, Sophie looked in

on the Children's Unit and checked up on Shaun to see how he was getting on. He'd been in a bad way when the ambulance brought him to the hospital earlier that morning and she was worried about his condition.

'He's on powerful antibiotics,' Tracey told her. 'He'll stay on the ventilator for some time, but he seems to be responding to the treatment.'

'That's something, anyway,' Sophie said. 'Thanks, Tracey.' She checked on Josh, the five-year-old who had the head injury, but he was doing fine. He was almost well enough to be discharged home.

She went to see her sister one more time. Her mother was keeping her company, concerned for her youngest daughter and holding her hand.

'I feel so dizzy,' Jessica murmured, glancing at Sophie. 'The baby—is he all right? I wish he was here. Have you been to look at him? Ryan's gone to see him.'

'Yes, I looked in on him in the Neonatal Unit,' Sophie told her. 'They're keeping him warm and giving him oxygen. When you're a little stronger and the baby's more up to it, you'll be able to hold him.'

'I wish I didn't feel so tired,' Jessica said. 'I feel so weak—the room's spinning.'

Sophie gently squeezed her hand. 'It's because you haemorrhaged—you're very short on iron, so they're going to give you a transfusion. You should start to feel much better after that.'

Sophie's mother left to go and meet her husband and tell him what had been happening, but Jessica asked Sophie to stay. 'I feel better having you and Ryan with me,' she said.

Jessica had the blood transfusion soon after that,

and an hour later Ryan wheeled the baby into the side room where she was recovering. The baby was a much healthier colour now and looked none the worse for his ordeal. He was well wrapped up in a shawl and had a soft wool hat on his head to keep him warm.

Ryan carefully laid the baby on Jessica's chest and she wrapped an arm around the sleeping infant. 'We're going to call him Casey,' she said with a smile, and her husband kissed her tenderly. She was still very weak, but the three of them were together at last and Sophie breathed a sigh of relief, watching them. It looked as though mother and son were out of danger. She took some photos for posterity and then slipped out of the room to give them some privacy.

She went to see her father and tell him about the new addition to the family. Rob was with him, getting the spare room ready while they waited for news, and he and her father were both glad to hear that disaster had been avoided. 'I think the baby is a bit jaundiced,' she told them, 'so the medical team might have to deal with that, as well as making sure that Jessica recovers her strength.'

'Maybe we could go and see her if she's going to be staying in hospital for a few days,' her father said and Sophie nodded.

'Yes, I'll take both of you. Ryan's going to stay with her until they let her come home and then she'll come back to live with me for a while, until he finishes this project he's working on. As soon as that's done, he's going to take paternity leave to be with her and the baby.'

'I'm glad he made it back here in time.' Rob was

proud to be an uncle and pored over the photos with his father.

She left them a little later and went home. It was late evening by then and she realised she had missed out on a meal. Her stomach was rumbling and she set about making a quick broccoli, pasta and cheese bake.

The doorbell rang as she set the table and she wondered if Rob had forgotten his key.

'Hi, Sophie.' Nate stood outside her front door, looking wonderful, his dark eyes glittering as he gazed at her in the evening light, his body honed and full of vitality. He was wearing smart casuals, chinos and a dark shirt.

'Come in.' She smiled at him and showed him along the hallway to the kitchen. 'I wasn't expecting you, but you must have smelled the food. There's plenty. Would you like to eat with me?'

'Mmm…smells good. It'll have to be a quick bite, though,' he said regretfully. 'I've been with my father most of the day and I need to go back to the hospital in a while.'

She frowned. 'It's bad, then?'

He nodded. 'I came away for a while so that the nurses could tend to him. I thought I'd check up on you—see how you're bearing up. I guessed you'd be back by now.' He folded her into his arms. 'I've been thinking about you all day, wondering how you were getting on, missing you.'

'I'm fine—we're all doing great after all the worry.'

'I'm glad about that.' He kissed her tenderly, holding her close and making her body surge with heat.

She kissed him, loving the way his hand rested on

the swell of her hip, until all at once there was a loud beeping sound that erupted on the airwaves and destroyed the moment.

'Oh…it's the oven timer,' she said in dismay. 'My broccoli bake is ready to serve.'

He laughed. 'We'd better go and see to it, then, before it spoils.'

'Okay.' She pulled herself together and fetched hot plates from the oven and served out the food. 'Sit down. Help yourself to extra cheese and there's hot crusty bread and a green salad to go with it, if you want.'

He sat across the table from her and began to eat. 'Mmm…it's delicious,' he said, and she smiled.

'Rob and Jessica like this—it's one of their favourite meals. They always ask for it when they come to visit.'

He studied her thoughtfully. 'You've always looked after them, haven't you? I suppose with your mother's condition affecting her so badly in those first few years they turned to you?'

'Pretty much, yes. Sometimes Mum would go off for days at a time, so we had to manage as best we could. I felt so guilty when I left to go to Medical School. I came home whenever I could—most weekends and sometimes in the week if my shifts allowed for it. And of course I spent my holidays with them. They were still so young and things were topsy-turvy for them.'

'But now things seem to be turning out all right— Rob is back with your father and planning on going to college, and Jessica is a mother herself.' He speared a forkful of salad and glanced at her. 'That must seem strange to you—it's happened so soon, while she's still so very young. Do you ever think of having a family of your own?'

She nodded. 'One day, yes, I'd like that. I hope it will happen. Seeing Jess's baby has made me feel even more maternal. He's so soft and warm and beautiful.' She drew in a deep, happy breath. 'They let me hold him and it's the best feeling in the world.' He smiled and she said quietly, 'What about you, Nate? Have you thought what it might be like to have your own babies up at the Manor House?'

He was still for a moment, his fork poised in mid-air. Then he let it settle once more on his plate and flicked a glance over her, his gaze searching, intent. 'I've thought about it,' he said at last. 'Sometimes, especially of late, I wonder what it would be like. I'm not sure, though. It's becoming more difficult for me to contemplate as time goes on.'

She studied him cautiously. 'Because you haven't found the right woman or because you don't want to deal with that aristocratic heritage and all that goes along with it?'

'It's neither of those things, really. I suppose, in my heart of hearts, I'm afraid to open up to any woman. It's only happening now because of you, I think. I never understood it before, but of late I've been thinking things through, trying to sort out my feelings. I don't feel I can trust things to work out right. I think the way I am has a lot to do with my mother dying when I was so very young... When you have that wonderful relationship with your mother, you have a right to expect it to last for ever, and as a child I was shocked to the core when it was taken from me.'

'You didn't ever get over it?'

He shrugged. 'You do, of course—not get over it, exactly, but you learn to adjust. There was a void in my life. But then, after a while, my father started to bring girlfriends back to the Manor... He was determined never to marry again—no one could replace my mother in his eyes, I think...but those relationships would last at most two, three years, maybe, and during that time I grew attached to a couple of the girls. They were decent women and I think they meant well—they were each affectionate and sweet towards me and I liked having them around, being able to confide in them...but then the relationship with my father would come to an end and they would disappear back where they came from and I never saw them again. I felt...empty...and lost.'

He shook his head, deep in thought. 'Bringing children into the world is a huge responsibility. They need stability but I don't know what it's like to have a lasting, loving relationship and I'm almost afraid that for me it doesn't exist. The experience has left me feeling that I can't risk putting all my faith in one woman. I tend to think that, somehow or other, I'll always be let down.'

'So it's best not to care too much in the first place?' She gave him a regretful, sympathetic look. 'That's a sad way to go through life but I understand how you feel. I have the same fears sometimes. Maybe we should both try to be braver and learn to take a bit of a risk in our lives.'

He gave her a wistful smile. 'Maybe.' His eyes darkened. 'I'm beginning to realise there's only one woman who could persuade me to take a chance on love...and that's you, Sophie. You mean more to me than I can put into words. I couldn't bear to lose you but I... After what my father put your family through, I'm not sure I deserve you.'

Sophie's eyes widened at the revelation. It wasn't exactly a declaration of love but it was probably as near as he'd ever come to it. 'You mustn't think that way,' she said. Her heart burned with longing. Would he one day be able to tell her what she wanted to hear—that he loved her every bit as much as she loved him?

'I wish—' He might have been about to say more but his phone began to trill and he looked down at the screen and read the text message there. 'It's my father,' he said. 'The doctor thinks I should go to see him. It sounds urgent.'

'I'm sorry.'

He stood up. 'Thanks for the meal, Sophie. I'm glad Jessica and the baby are all right.'

She went with him to the door and opened it to let him into the night. She didn't want him to go but knew that he had no choice. Then, as he walked away from her along the path, she saw to her dismay that Jake was heading towards her. The two men crossed by each other on the path and she saw Nate look at Jake and frown before nodding to him and going on his way. What must he be thinking?

It was more than likely he would be disturbed and concerned, jealous, even, but after what he'd just said to her, would he ever be persuaded that he could trust in her love? Could she ever hope to have a future with him?

'Sophie,' Jake said, coming over to her. 'I hope you don't mind me dropping in like this. I bought a present for Jessica's baby—and some course notes for Rob. He was asking me about working in a hospital and what kind of courses he should follow.'

'That's brilliant, Jake. Thanks.' She gave an inward sigh and braced herself. 'Come in.'

CHAPTER SEVEN

'DO YOU THINK Casey's skin's a better colour now, Sophie?' In her room in the Maternity Unit Jessica held her baby close to her, unwrapping his shawl and lifting his vest to show his chest. 'He was so yellow before with the jaundice but I think the treatment's working, don't you?'

Sophie smiled. 'Oh, yes…he looks much better now.' He was a beautiful baby, with a sweet rosebud mouth and perfect little fingers that curled into fists.

Jessica looked relieved. She wrapped the baby up warmly and held him against her. 'I've been so worried. The last thing you want is for your baby to have to stay in hospital for treatment when he's so tiny. Poor little man—having to have his eyes covered while he's under the special lamp for two or three hours at a time.'

'I would think he only needs a few more hours of phototherapy and then his levels of bilirubin will be back to normal,' Sophie said. 'I know it's been difficult but he's slept through it for the most part, so I don't think it's bothered him too much.'

The midwife had explained the problem of jaundice to Jessica but as a new young mother she was understandably worried. Quite often in newborn babies it was possible that the liver didn't work all that efficiently for the first couple of weeks, so the level of bilirubin could build up in the blood. Usually, it cleared up on its own, but if that didn't happen the baby could be given phototherapy. The light used in this treatment helped to change the bilirubin to a form that could be more easily broken down by the liver.

'I'm so glad you and Ryan have been able to be here with me,' Jessica said. 'It's made everything so much better. I know you have to work, but it's been good having you come in several times a day to see us. And Mum will be coming again at the weekend. It's all worked out far better than I expected.'

'Of course it has. And I have everything waiting for you back at home when you're ready to be discharged.'

Her day's work had ended some time ago and Sophie left her sister and the baby a little later, to go back to the cottage once more. If only the rest of her worries could be so easily resolved.

She was anxious for Nate. While she and her family had celebrated a wonderful new addition to the family, his own situation had become tragic. His father's health had steadily deteriorated and a few days ago Nate had broken the bad news to her that his father had passed away.

'He had another heart attack,' he'd said flatly. 'I have a lot of things to deal with, so I probably won't be able to see you for a while. I'm going to take a few days off work to make the funeral arrangements, and I have to get in touch with all my relatives. They're scattered far and wide over the country, so I expect a good many of them will want to come and stay at the Manor for a while.'

'Are you coping all right? Is there anything I can do?' Sophie asked, but he'd been determined to manage by himself. She wanted to be with him but he'd shut himself away to grieve alone. Sophie's only consolation was that Charlotte was with him and would do her best to comfort him and steer him through this difficult time.

Back at the cottage Sophie prepared for the funeral that was being held next day. Nate had said he hoped she would be there. She'd picked out a black suit with a fitted jacket and a pencil-line skirt that she felt would be suitable for the occasion. Teamed with a grey silk blouse and black stiletto heels, she felt the outfit would give her a bit more confidence.

Her father had received a formal invitation too, because he had been for a long time a trusted worker on Lord Branscombe's estate. He showed the beautifully embossed card to Sophie. 'It came with a letter too,' he said. 'I suppose that was thoughtful of Nate Branscombe—that personal touch—knowing how I felt about his father.'

'Will you go to the service?' Sophie had asked.

To her surprise, he nodded. 'Rob said he'll take me. I thought about it long and hard before I made the decision. I've been bitter and resentful for such a long time, feeling that I was treated badly. All along, I blamed James for insisting I went on that flight with him, for not listening to reason when people told him he shouldn't pilot the plane while he was feeling unwell…but the truth is, I should have refused to go with him. It was my own weakness in not standing up to him that led to me being in the position I'm in now. I only have myself to blame.'

'Oh, Dad...' Sophie's voice broke in a sob as she knelt down beside her father's wheelchair. 'You're not to blame for anything,' she protested, laying a hand on his arm. 'I think most people would have accepted his word for it that he felt he was up to it. He was your boss and in the end you went along with what he said because ultimately you trusted him to do the right thing.'

She gently squeezed his arm, wanting to show her support. 'You always did everything you thought was for the best...and you've worked so hard to try to walk again; you've been so stoical this last couple of years. I'm proud of the way you've pushed yourself. And you're getting there... It's taking a while but you *will* walk again. Rob's told me how hard you've been working with him at your physio. You're making progress all the while. Please don't blame yourself for any of this.'

He patted her hand. 'You're a sweet girl. You've always been there for me. I'm sorry I've given you such a hard time these last few weeks over James's son. I suppose I've been harsh in judging Nate. None of this is his fault.'

She looked at him in surprise. 'Are you telling me you've changed your mind about him?'

He shrugged awkwardly. 'Let's say I'm reserving my opinion of him. I heard the talk in the village about how you and he saved that little boy—the one who collapsed and couldn't breathe. I know the child's still in hospital but he's a lot better, isn't he? It made me think about Nate in a different way. And then I heard he got in touch with the mother's family to make sure she had some support. Apparently her cousin has come over here to stay with her. They were good friends before they eventually lost touch with one another, the woman said.'

Sophie's eyes widened. 'I hadn't heard that—Nate didn't say anything to me about it.'

'Ah, well, the boy's mother's been chatting in the post office.' He smiled. 'You know how word gets around.'

She nodded. 'I do.' It made her feel warm inside to know that Nate had done what he could to help the boy's mother.

The weather blessed them on the day of the funeral. Summer was drifting into autumn and the leaves on the trees were turning to red and gold. There was a faint breeze blowing but the sun put in an appearance through puffy white clouds so that the mourners could gather in peace. The service and the rest of the proceedings went without a hitch.

Nate was immaculately dressed, surrounded by a host of relatives Sophie had never met before. He introduced her to them but the names soon became a blur. She smiled politely and made sympathetic comments and hoped that she was being of some help to Nate by being there alongside him.

'I hadn't expected so many people from the village to turn up,' he commented as they ate canapés at the reception afterwards.

'No, nor did I.' She made a slight smile. 'But I think your standing in the village has gone up lately, since you helped young Shaun…and since you outlined your plans to save the estate.'

'Hmm… I only hope I'll be able to live up to what I said back then.' He was frowning and she looked at him curiously.

'Is there a problem?'

'I think there might be but I'm not sure how much of a setback it's going to be. My father's solicitor wants an urgent meeting with me. All I can say is that from the initial conversation I've had with him, the situation doesn't sound promising.'

She sucked in a quick breath. 'Will you let me know if things change?'

'Of course.' He was solemn but his expression became taut all at once, and when she followed the line of his gaze, she saw he was looking directly at Jake. Jake was there as a mutual friend but it seemed Nate didn't want to speak to him just then. 'I'll leave you two alone together,' he said, excusing himself and moving away from her as Jake came towards them. 'I should go and talk to some of my relatives.'

'But Jake will be wanting to speak to you,' she protested. 'He'll want to offer his condolences.'

He shook his head. 'I don't think so. He's looking at you, Sophie. He's been looking at you for the last half hour. Besides, I ought to circulate a bit.'

Jake had been watching her? She was startled Nate had noticed something to which she'd been totally oblivious, but it was clear he wasn't intending to stay around. Nate left her and went to speak to an uncle who had taken up a position by the buffet table.

Sophie exhaled slowly and greeted Jake with a slight nod of her head. 'Hi, Jake. I'm sorry we have to meet again on an occasion like this.'

'Yes, me too.' Jake studied her. 'I hope you know what you're doing with Nate. He let you down before and he'll quite likely do it again.'

'He didn't let me down. I think he went away because he had to come to terms with what his father had done and he couldn't bear to see the pain it caused our family. He tried to talk to me about it but I wasn't ready to listen back then.'

She laid a hand on his arm. 'Thank you for looking out for me. You've always been a great friend to me,' she said quietly. 'One I'll always treasure.'

'Likewise.'

She smiled. 'Have you heard any more from Cheryl?'

He shook his head. 'A couple of emails. That's all.'

'Hmm. I think you were wrong about her wanting someone else. I happen to know that she's very keen to meet up with you again.' She lifted her brows. 'I heard she was desperately hoping you might want to take her to the annual get-together next month.'

He laughed. 'You're joking with me! How would you hear something like that?'

'The hospital grapevine, you know? She confided in a friend, who told another friend, who spilled the beans to someone who works in Accounts.'

A faint smile curved his mouth. Sophie knew she had set him thinking about a particular course of action but she said no more about it. Instead, she let her glance wander across the room to where Nate was standing. He was looking at her intently, frowning, but when she caught his gaze he turned away and spoke to his companion. He didn't look at all happy, seeing her with Jake. Perhaps he'd misinterpreted their smiles and gestures. No matter what she'd told him to the contrary, he clearly believed she and Jake were an item.

She didn't see Nate again for a few days. When she tried phoning him, he was too busy to say much and she was left feeling dissatisfied and unhappy. She desperately wanted to be with him, to be able to comfort him, but it seemed he simply wanted to be left alone.

He went to London to meet with his father's solicitor and to have further talks with Peninsula. He hadn't told Sophie what the talks were about, except to say that he wanted to clarify things after his father's passing…but when she walked Charlie by the Manor one day and saw valuable paintings being loaded on to a prominent art dealer's van, she guessed something was very wrong. This was a legitimate fine-art dealer from London. Selling the paintings had never been part of Nate's plan to recover the estate.

Whatever the outcome of those appointments in London, Sophie was shocked, along with everyone else in the village, when Peninsula announced just a few days later that they were holding a meeting in the village hall on Saturday afternoon. 'We want to discuss possibilities for the area,' their spokesman said. 'Come along and listen to what we have to say.'

Sophie went to the hall with her father. Nate was nowhere to be seen and it took only a few minutes, less than half an hour, for the spokesman to cause uproar among his audience.

'We've great plans to make changes that will benefit everyone in this area,' the spokesman said. 'If everything goes ahead as we hope, we'll be in a position to make all your lives better, so we're looking for your support.'

A man from the audience stood up. 'What plans are you talking about? Why are you back here telling us how you want to change our village? Has Nate Branscombe sold out to you?'

'He hasn't signed the papers yet but our offer is definitely back on the table,' the spokesman answered. He clicked a computer mouse and brought up on the screen in front of them an enlarged photo of their village, nestled in the valley around the beautiful blue bay. 'There's a prime position for a five-star hotel,' he said, pointing to an area on the cliff top to the east. 'Just think how that will boost the prosperity of the area.' He clicked the mouse again. 'And here's the outline of what the proposed shopping mall will look like. There will be restaurants, a leisure centre, a gymnasium, cinema...'

A woman stood up, angrily voicing her thoughts. 'And along with all that there will be tourists with their cars and takeaway food cartons littering the country-side...broken bottles on the beach... What next—a casino open all hours?'

People stood up, shouting, anxious for their voices to be heard. Some remained seated, Sophie noticed. Not everyone was against change but the majority were adamant that it shouldn't happen, not in their idyllic part of the world.

She left the meeting with her father, taking him back to his home. 'Do you think Nate meant for this to happen?' he asked as she wheeled his chair up the ramp into the house. Charlie woke up from his snooze in the kitchen and came to greet them, tail wagging enthusiastically.

'I don't think so.' She flicked the switch on the kettle. 'But there was some kind of problem—he had to go to see his father's solicitor in London, so I suspect there are financial problems he didn't know about. He hasn't told me anything about it, but I'm guessing it's serious.'

'So you think he'll sell to Peninsula after all?'

'I don't know. I know he doesn't want to.'

Her father was obviously worried as they talked about the possibilities of Peninsula Holdings taking over. 'This place will be the first to go,' he said, looking around the kitchen. 'What are they going to offer me in its place? A ground-floor retirement flat in the suburbs? Their representative seemed to think that would be perfect for me—a place in a warden-assisted block, he said. I could look out on to the street on the front with the shops directly opposite and a communal garden at the back. How would I look after Charlie in a situation like that?'

A look of despair crossed his face. 'I'm used to being in this beautiful place, with trees and shrubs and countryside and the sea not far away, neighbours who pop in to say hello whenever they have five minutes to spare. I can't bear the thought of moving.'

'Perhaps it won't come to that.' She handed him a mug of coffee and slid a plate of his favourite cheese straws towards him. 'I'll go and see Nate—see if he'll talk to me. Maybe together we can come up with some ideas that will help him keep the estate.'

'Bless you, Sophie. I hope there's some way out of the situation.'

The kitchen door opened just then and Jessica came in, wheeling the baby in the pram. Sophie wedged the door open temporarily to allow her into the kitchen and then stopped to coo over the baby. 'Oh, isn't he gorgeous?' He was fast asleep, his little pink hands curled into fists either side of his cheeks. 'He's perfect.'

Jessica smiled. 'He would be if he managed to sleep for more than two hours at a time. I thought if I walked him over here the motion of the pram would rock him to sleep.' She looked down at her baby. 'Oh... I might have known. He's awake again.' She chuckled and carefully lifted him out, wrapping his shawl around him once more. 'I think your grandad wants to see you, young man.'

Her father nodded. 'Oh, definitely. I'll grab my chance to hold him while Rob's spending time down at the beach with his friends. I might not get a look in otherwise.'

'Here you go.' Jessica gently placed Casey in her father's arms. 'Sophie gets to hold him a lot,' she told him with a smile, 'so you get first dibs.'

They sat around the table and talked, taking turns in holding the baby until Charlie began to get restless. He came and laid his head on Sophie's lap, looking at her with big eyes.

Sophie reached for his lead. 'I'll take him out for a walk,' she said. 'Maybe I'll go along the cliff path and up by the Manor. Nate came back from London yesterday, so he might be home. Perhaps I'll get the chance to talk to him.'

'Good idea. Thanks, Sophie.' Her father watched her leave with Charlie. His expression was sad for a moment until he turned back to Jessica and Sophie heard him ask her about Ryan's job and how much longer he would be away.

Sophie loved walking along the cliff top, looking out over the sparkling blue water below. She stood and watched as the waves rolled in to shore, leaving behind bands of white foam and forming rock pools among the shells and pebbles on the sandy beach. Whenever she could, she loved to walk down there, collecting pretty white spiral shells or glossy cowries and periwinkles.

Today, though, she kept to the path and clambered steadily up the hill towards the Manor House. She hoped the gates would be open so that she could simply walk up to the main door, but since the press had taken to bombarding Nate with questions, and generally intruding on his everyday life, he'd taken to using security measures.

She pressed the buzzer and spoke into the intercom. 'It's Sophie,' she said, when Charlotte answered. 'I wondered if I might see Nate.'

'Oh, hello, Sophie.' There was a pause and then she added, 'He says you're to come right in. Is that your dog I can hear alongside you?'

'It is.'

'Ah, he's a lovely dog, is Charlie.' The wrought-iron gates started to swing open and Sophie set out to walk along the long sweeping drive up to the house.

Nate met her halfway. 'Hello, Sophie,' he said. 'It's good to see you.' He hugged her, looking into her eyes with hungry intensity as though he would absorb every part of her. 'I've missed you.'

She clung to him, needing that close, warm contact. 'I missed you too.' She sent him a troubled look. 'I wanted to come and see you before this, but I know you've been busy with family visitors staying over... as well as the business in London. And the press were here a lot, I heard.'

'Yes. Actually, some of them were sympathetic for once, so I spoke to a couple of them briefly. They wanted to concentrate on the fact that I'm a doctor and how it feels to take over the title.'

She smiled. 'There was a beautiful aerial photograph of the Manor House and the estate in one of the national papers.'

'Yes, I saw it. It was a good article too, considering I hadn't given an interview.' He sent her a thoughtful look. 'I was going to come and see you later today—but you've beaten me to it. I expect you're worried about this business with Peninsula?'

'I am. Leastways, my dad's really concerned about what's going to happen.'

'Yes, I guessed as much. I feel bad that you're having to go through all this worry.' He bent down to stroke an eager Charlie and tickle him behind the ears. 'Shall we walk for a while or would you rather go up to the house?'

She smiled. 'I think Charlie would appreciate the walk. I think he was born for the hills and dales—he can go for miles.'

He chuckled. 'Okay. We'll take a stroll by the lake.' He put an arm around her shoulders as they turned on to the perimeter path. It felt good being this close to him, having the warmth of his fingers filter through the fine material of her cashmere top. He pointed out a few changes along the way. 'If you look closely through the trees, you'll see a few log cabins have sprung up here and there. We're still in the process of getting facilities connected—it'll take time, but at least we've made a start.'

She looked at him curiously. 'You're going ahead with your plans, then? I thought everything might have been put on hold when Peninsula started talking about what they wanted to do.'

They were walking through the copse towards the lake, a silver expanse of water bordered by ancient willow trees that dipped their branches gracefully into the water and where spreading oaks mingled with elderberry and blackberry brambles that were luscious with ripening fruit.

'I'll do as much as I can to hold on to the estate, but I'm afraid things are much worse than I realised. Unfortunately, my father hadn't told me the full extent of his liabilities. That's what the solicitor wanted to talk to me about.' He led her to a bench seat set back from the water, close by a landing stage. They sat down and Charlie flopped to the ground at their feet, his tongue hanging out as he panted happily. Sophie looked around. A boat, a small motor launch, was moored by the wooden jetty.

'So the projects you hoped would put things right and cover the debts won't be enough?'

He nodded. 'That's right. My father's financial situation was far worse than he'd said. I think he didn't tell me because he hoped his other investments would come right, but that isn't happening as yet. I'll do what I can to sort out the mess but I'm still working through my options. I've submitted a plan of action to the bank manager and he's going through it with his advisers.'

She reached for his hand and covered his fingers with hers. 'I don't know what to say. I wish there was something I could do to help.'

He smiled. 'It helps just having you by my side, Sophie. I know you're only here because you're worried for your father, but at least I have you for a little while.'

She frowned. 'I don't understand. Why would you say that? I'd be here anyway—don't you know that? I want to be with you.'

'You're seeing Jake, though, aren't you?' A knot formed in his brow. 'There have been rumours. I saw the way you and he acted together on the day of the funeral. He was smiling, relieved almost, after you spoke to him. Up till then I thought I might be in with a chance but after that I realised it could never happen, you and me.'

'Oh, no… I think you misunderstood the situation completely. As to rumours—you know how people get things wrong. They see me having coffee with him in the cafeteria and suddenly it's a full-blown relationship.' She smiled, a small glow starting up inside her. He'd said it—he wanted to be with her. 'There's nothing going on between me and Jake. I told you—we're friends. He was just pleased because I told him someone else is interested in him.'

He drew in a quick stunned breath, his eyes widening.

She said gently, 'I only have feelings for you, Nate. I love you. It's always been you. I just need to hear that you feel the same way towards me.'

He lifted a hand, stroking his thumb lightly across her cheek. 'I wish it were that simple, Sophie.' His eyes darkened, becoming unfathomable like the rippling surface of the lake. 'I love you too, with all my heart, with all my soul, but I can't give in to my feelings for you.'

Anguished, she lifted her hands to his chest, laying her palms flat against the top of his ribcage. 'I don't understand, Nate. I've waited so long to hear you say that you love me. If you feel the same way, why can't we be together?'

He shook his head. 'How can I let it happen when my family has been responsible for so much heartache heaped on your father, on you—perhaps ultimately on everyone who is a part of this estate? My father was responsible for the accident that crippled your father. I can't ever hope to make up for the horror of that.'

'You don't have to…'

'I do.' He straightened. 'I owe you so much but right now I may be about to lose everything I have. Everything I am, my whole existence, my heritage, my family name, is tied up in this place and it's all coming crashing down around me. I can't… I won't…ask you or your family to suffer any more because of my failures. I love you, Sophie, but I can't ask you to be with me, to marry me, until I've restored the family pride and I can offer you the future you deserve.'

She looked at him in shock. 'But I love you, Nate. Isn't that enough to see us through this? Surely, nothing else matters? We can work this out together, can't we?'

'No, we can't. I'm sorry, Sophie.' He clasped her hands in his. 'When I saw you with Jake, when I didn't see anything of you these last few days, it hit me like a ten-ton truck that I want you more than anything else in the world—I want to be with you, I love you, it's going to be unbearable without you…but I won't put you or your family through any more hardship because of me.'

He kissed her gently, briefly, on the mouth, as though he daren't linger a moment longer for fear of losing himself entirely. Then he stood up. 'I'll walk you back to the gates. Perhaps it's best if we don't see each other for a while.'

Sophie scrambled to her feet and went blindly along beside him. 'You can't do this, Nate. There has to be another way. We can work through this together.'

He didn't answer and that silence made things a hundred times worse. She couldn't feel, couldn't think. She was in shock, her whole body trembling, but she knew there would be no point in trying to speak to him about it any more. He wouldn't talk about it. He had made up his mind and there was nothing she could do to persuade him otherwise.

CHAPTER EIGHT

'YOU'VE JUST COME from the Neonatal Unit again, haven't you?' Hannah smiled as Sophie went over to the coffee machine in the staff lounge. 'I can always tell. Either that or your sister brought the baby in to work to see you.'

'Ah… I can't seem to help myself,' Sophie said, reaching for a mug. 'There's just something about those tiny babies that gets me here, every time.' She pressed the flat of her hand over her heart. 'They're so vulnerable, with tubes for this and that and all the monitoring equipment. I've been doing screening tests today—checking nutrient levels and urea and electrolytes. If there was time, I would spend most of the day in the unit, to be honest.' She smiled. 'But my other patients can be just as adorable. It's so satisfying to see them getting stronger day by day.'

Hannah washed her cup out at the sink. 'I bet you've loved having your sister and her baby staying with you. To look at him you wouldn't think he had such a hard time being born.'

Sophie nodded. 'I've loved every minute of it, and yes, he's doing really well now. He's gaining weight—still not sleeping through the night, of course.'

'Ah—now I know why you've had that peaky look

about you of late.' Hannah grinned and started towards the door. 'I'd better get back to work,' she said.

'Okay.' Sophie concentrated on pouring hot coffee into her mug. Peaky? There was only one reason for her being under par lately and that was because of Nate. Why was he so determined that things couldn't work out between them?

'Hi—how are you doing?'

She gave a small start of surprise as she realised Nate had come into the room as Hannah was leaving. The kitchen area was slightly hidden from the entrance. 'Hi. I didn't see you there,' she said as he came to stand alongside her, reaching for a porcelain mug. 'Shall I pour you a coffee?'

'Thanks.'

'How does it feel to be back at work?'

'It feels okay.' He accepted the mug she slid towards him. 'I wasn't sure how it would be, but it's actually good. The chief called me into his office this morning and for a minute I wondered if something was wrong— I was only here on a temporary contract and I'd had to take time off—but he offered me a permanent post.'

Her eyes widened. 'Will you take it?'

He nodded. 'Yes, I like working here. I like the people and the set-up.'

'I'm glad for you.' She sipped her coffee, looking at him over the rim of her cup. 'I suppose at least being here helps take your mind off all your other problems.'

'True.' He searched in the fridge and found a box of doughnuts. 'I brought these in to share out—would you like one?'

'Thanks.' She helped herself, biting into the cake and carefully licking the sugar off her fingers. Nate watched her, as though fascinated by her actions, until he gave himself a shake and put the box back in the fridge.

'So, what's happening with everyone at home?' he asked. 'I feel as though I've been a bit out of touch these last few days while I've been busy trying to sort out problems with the estate.'

'Oh, we're all doing fine. Rob's started a psychology course at college and my dad's doing really well with his physiotherapy. He's taking a few steps on his own now, with the aid of a walking frame. He says he's going to progress from there to walking with elbow crutches.'

'I thought he would manage it, given time. He's always been a determined man. He just needs to strengthen his muscles now.' He studied her. 'I expect Jessica will be going home soon—how will you feel about that? You've enjoyed being with her and the baby, haven't you? I heard you telling Hannah a bit about him.'

Her mouth turned down at the corners. 'I'll hate it when she leaves but Ryan's coming back next week and they'll want to be together in their own home, of course. I'm taking a few days off work to go there with her to help her settle back in...just until Ryan's home.'

'That sounds like a good idea.' He frowned. 'She doesn't like it there, though, does she? She mentioned something to me about it, and I remember you telling me her house is not up to much and there's no garden, just a small yard out back.'

'That's right. It was all they could afford at the time.' She sighed. 'She says she wants to move back to the village. It was where she was born, after all. Ryan's happy to do that but they have to find the right place, some-where within their budget.'

'Won't Jessica miss your mother if she does that?'

Sophie nodded. 'I'm sure she will…but it's only about an hour away on the train—a bit longer by car. Up to now we've taken it in turns to make the journey, so we all get to see each other at least once a week. It seems to have worked out reasonably well, so far.'

Nate was deep in thought for a minute or two and she looked at him questioningly. 'Is everything all right?'

'Yes, absolutely. I was just wondering whether they might want to live at the Manor. The place is far too big for me. It takes me all my time to use the main part of the house, and then there are the East and the West Wings that can be more or less turned into self-contained units if necessary. If they had part of the East Wing, for in-stance, they would have access to a terrace and the gar-den, and there's a kitchen there that used to be the old scullery. They could stay as long as they wanted, make it their home or use it while they build up their finances to get a place of their own.' He sent her a cautious glance. 'What do you think?'

She gasped, her eyes widening. 'What do I think? Oh, Nate!' She flung her arms around his neck and kissed him soundly on the mouth. 'I think you're wonderful, fantastic, beyond words.'

He looked at her in stunned surprise, laughing uncer-tainly as his hands went automatically around her waist as though they belonged there. She kissed him again, a longer kiss this time, equally fervent. 'No wonder I love you so much,' she said in a contented whisper. She clung to him, her soft curves crushed against his hard body.

'Sophie… I… We said we wouldn't do this…' He

gently tried to push her away but his hands were trembling and the knowledge that he was so affected by her made her blood sizzle with renewed vigour.

'You've got to be kidding,' she said, smiling up at him.

He shook his head, a look of anguish on his face. 'It's too difficult for me if you wrap yourself around me this way,' he said in a distracted, ragged tone. 'I'm only flesh and blood—you're making it way too hard for me to resist you.'

'Good. I'm glad.' She looked at him with sparkling, mischievous eyes. 'It was a silly idea in the first place. Why on earth would you want to keep me away when I can help you get through this awful time? I won't stay away. That's not what love's about, is it? Love is about being there for each other through the hard times. Why should you struggle on your own when I can share your troubles with you? You know what they say—a problem shared is a problem halved?'

'Ah... Sophie...that's not always the case but...' At last he gave in with a small shuddery sigh that seemed to ricochet through his whole body. Joy surged in her at his capitulation, and when he bent his head and rested his forehead against hers, she knew the sweet scent of success. 'I hope you don't come to regret this,' he said huskily. 'Don't say I didn't try to warn you.'

'Yeah, you did...but it didn't work.' She smiled impishly and he kissed her feverishly, with growing passion until she was breathless with longing.

They came up for air just as they heard the door open and someone came into the room. By the time Tracey came over to the coffee machine and saw them there, they had managed to compose themselves once more.

'Oh, hi there,' Tracey said, pausing to look in the fridge. 'Did I hear there were doughnuts to be had?'

'There certainly are—in the white box.' Nate smiled at her. 'They say an army marches on its stomach. I think the same goes for hospital staff—we can't work properly if we're hungry.'

Tracey laughed and bit into the doughnut. 'Mmm... delicious. Just what I needed.' She looked at Nate. 'I saw an article on the Manor House in the paper the other day—the photo that went alongside it was beautiful with the sun glowing on the stonework...and the stable block at the back through the courtyard...and the grounds looked so lush. I can't imagine living in a place like that... I'd never want to come in to work— I'd want to go out and explore it every day. It makes me think how it might have been in Regency times— peaceful and perfect and genteel.'

'There is that, I suppose.' Nate thought about it. 'There are portraits of the ancestors in the West Wing— women in their ballgowns or day dresses, and the men rigged out in their finery. I take it for granted, probably, and I tend not to think about it too much—I'm too busy trying to be a doctor.'

'Yes... I can see you have your priorities sorted.' Tracey smiled and helped herself to coffee while Sophie and Nate excused themselves and prepared to go back to the Children's Unit.

'You didn't send the ancestral portraits to auction, then?' Sophie said quietly as they walked along the corridor. 'I saw some of the paintings being collected one day when I was walking Charlie.'

He shook his head. 'No, only some that I really didn't like. Quite a few were stored in the attic and hadn't seen the light of day for many years. The proceeds will go towards the work on the fishing lodges.'

She glanced at him. 'You know, Tracey may have come up with something when she mentioned the Regency period of the Manor House. You often get film companies or TV production companies wanting to use historic houses as locations. It might be worth thinking of that as an option. I don't know whether it would make much of a difference to your situation.'

To her surprise, he nodded. 'Actually, ever since that picture appeared in the paper I've been receiving requests from companies interested in using the property. I wasn't sure how much of a disruption it would be—but I'm told it would be the ideal location for a TV drama series set in the mid-nineteenth century, and also there's a company looking to make a period adventure film with a grand mansion at its centre. I'm not sure. They won't need to use the whole house, but they're happy that there's plenty of space for the trucks and equipment. They won't be there for too long, I imagine. What do you think?'

Her eyes widened. 'I think it sounds really exciting, and I can't see too many problems as long as you're dealing with companies that have good reputations. I think you need to give it some deep thought. It's your home, after all.' She frowned. 'Perhaps you could persuade them to keep the disruption to a minimum—have them use separate entrances, maybe? And I guess the vehicles might be hidden by the trees and shrubs if they used the West side of the house. What matters is that you feel comfortable with your decision.'

'Thanks, Sophie. I knew you would put it all into perspective for me.' He put his arm around her and briefly hugged her. 'You're right. I need to give it a lot of thought.'

They went their separate ways, attending to their small patients. Sophie's mind was buzzing with questions yet to be answered as she checked lab reports and studied X-ray films and CT scans. What would he decide?

Sophie was away from home for the next few days, so she didn't get the chance to be with him and work through the choices he might make. Instead, she helped Jessica get her house organised and pristine once more after the boiler and central-heating repairs.

'I can hardly believe Nate is being so generous, offering us a place in his home,' Jessica said excitedly. 'I talked to Ryan about it on the phone and he thinks it's a great idea…though, with all the business of the film-company offer and so on, Nate probably has too much on his mind. He might have had second thoughts about it.'

Sophie shook her head. 'No, he called me this morning and said you can move in whenever you want.' She looked at the baby lying in his cradle. He opened his eyes and looked at her, making little gurgling sounds and blowing tiny bubbles from his perfect mouth. Sophie lightly stroked his soft palm and he gripped her fingers tightly in response. She smiled down at him. 'Nate said there's a room that can be turned into a nursery,' she told Jessica. 'You just need to let him know how you want it decorated and he'll get things organised.'

'Oh, I can't wait!'

Ryan came home next day and Sophie left the two of them to spend time together with their baby. She arrived home and a bit later she went over to her father's house, to find him and Rob preparing for another meeting at the Manor. It was Friday evening and Nate had phoned her earlier to make sure she would be able to come along.

'He's invited all the villagers from the estate, plus any others who are interested in knowing what he plans to do,' her father said. 'Do you know what he has in mind?'

She shook her head. 'I don't. He was sifting through various options, talking with the bank manager and so on, last time I spoke to him about it.' She looked at her father, spruce in a dark grey suit and shiny polished shoes. 'You're looking very smart,' she said. 'It's not a formal do, is it? Nate didn't mention anything like that.' She was a bit concerned that she might not be dressed for the occasion. She was wearing a soft wool dress with a slightly off-the-shoulder neckline and three-quarter sleeves. It was comfortable and classic and she felt good in it.

Her father laughed. 'No, it isn't a formal do... I just wanted to celebrate being able to get out of the wheelchair and stand up for a while. See?' He stood up carefully, taking his time, and Rob came over to him and handed him a couple of elbow crutches.

'One step at a time, Dad,' he said. 'Remember how we practised this...'

Sophie watched as her father slowly walked across the room, straight-backed and proud. 'Oh, Dad,' she cried, going over to him. 'It's wonderful. I'm so happy for you.' She hugged him, and hugged her brother. 'Now look what you've both done,' she said, choked up. 'I'm all tearful and at this rate I'll have to do my make-up all over again!'

They both laughed and a few minutes later they all set off for the Manor House.

Nate greeted them and showed them into the long panelled room where everyone was assembled, helping themselves to refreshments. There was a variety of food, as before, with southern fried chicken, spring rolls and salsa dips, and a range of desserts that included strawberry bruschetta and dishes of Eton mess.

Nate drew Sophie to him and dropped a kiss on her mouth. 'I'm really glad you're back,' he said, grabbing her hand and leading her over to the side of the room where a bar had been set up. He handed her a glass of wine and murmured, 'I have to go and talk to everyone—help yourself to food and sit down close by me, will you? It's good to have you here. I can't tell you how much I worried while you were away. I thought you might have changed your mind about us, knowing what might lie ahead.'

She looked at him thoughtfully. 'You're still worried I might disappear out of your life?'

He moved his shoulders awkwardly. 'I wanted so much for things to work out for us. I hardly dared hope...'

'You know I'll be here for you, always. The way I feel won't ever change, Nate.'

He exhaled slowly and gently squeezed her fingers. 'I'm glad. Hearing you say it makes me feel so much better.' He braced himself. 'Here goes, then.'

He called for everyone to take a seat, and when they were settled, he said, 'Thank you for coming here today. I know you've all been worried about what might happen to the estate…to your homes. I'm here to tell you what's been decided and how we'll be going forward from now on. None of it involves Peninsula Holdings. I turned their offer down and they won't be coming back.'

A cheer went up and he smiled. 'Yes, I thought you would like that. But I have accepted a couple of other offers that might affect you in a roundabout way. I've agreed to let a TV company use the West Wing of the Manor House in order to make a period drama series, and I've also signed an agreement to allow a film company to use the house at a later date.'

There were gasps of astonishment from the villagers and a buzz of excited conversation started up. People started asking questions and Nate held his hand up for quiet. 'I know there are things you want to ask,' he said, 'and there will be time for that. Let me just say that the activities of the companies will take a matter of months and there shouldn't be any impact on the village—apart from perhaps a few more customers in the shops or the pub for a while.'

'Will we get a visit from Colin Firth?' one woman called out hopefully.

'Does Daniel Craig do period drama?' another asked with a wistful expression.

Sophie laughed, and Nate smiled. 'I wouldn't know about that,' he said. 'All I want to say, to finish, is that your houses are safe and you need have no worries for the future on that account.'

Everyone started talking at once and Sophie took a

moment to quietly say to him, 'Has it really solved all of your problems? Are you out of the woods now?'

He nodded. 'Oh, yes,' he said. 'They're paying me an embarrassing amount of money—a lot of it up front, so I can categorically say the future's looking rosy.'

She laid a hand on his arm, her fingers curling around his sleeve. 'I'm so happy for you. I know how much all this means to you.'

'It means everything to me to know that your father's house is safe and his way of life won't be disrupted any more. He's doing so well, isn't he? And you and I... Now we can have a future together, can't we, Sophie?'

'We always could,' she said. 'You know I don't need a Manor House and all the trappings of an estate to keep me happy. I just want you—the man who saves a little boy's life when he collapses in the street, or feeds a baby in Neonatal—the man who brings my sister to me and gives my brother a lift late at night. You're everything I want, Nate.'

He bent his head to her and kissed her. 'I can't wait for everyone to go,' he said under his breath. 'I want you all to myself.'

She chuckled and went with him to mingle with the crowd and answer questions about the TV production and his plans for the estate.

Her father hugged her as he said goodbye a while later. 'You and Nate are obviously very happy with one another,' he said. 'I'm pleased for you. Does your mother know?'

'I mentioned it to her when I went over to Jessica's

house. She seemed to accept it. I think she'll be happy as long as you're happy with it.'

He nodded. 'I'll give her a call.'

He and Rob left to go home, and gradually the rest of the villagers began to take their leave. Nate and Sophie saw them off, and when the last one had gone, Nate gave a soft sigh of relief.

'Come into the drawing room with me,' he said, taking Sophie by the hand and leading her into a room off the wide hallway. 'I have something for you.'

Sophie looked around. She remembered this room from before, with its pale silk wall coverings, cream sofas and luxurious oriental rug. The curtains were drawn now, beautiful brocade drapes that elegantly skirted the floor. Several lamps were lit in here, casting a golden glow over the room, and the wood-burning stove flickered with gentle heat in the inglenook fireplace.

Nate went over to a bureau in the corner of the room. He took a small box from a drawer and turned to her. 'I wanted to give you this,' he said, going over to where she stood in the middle of the room and getting down on one knee in front of her. He carefully opened the box to reveal an exquisite sparkling diamond ring nestled on a bed of silk. Brilliant light was reflected from every perfect facet.

Sophie gasped. 'Oh, Nate...'

'Will you marry me, Sophie?' he asked. 'Will you accept this ring as a token of my love and as my promise that I will always be yours?'

'Oh, Nate...yes.' Her voice broke with emotion. 'I will. I'm overwhelmed.'

He exhaled slowly as though he'd been holding his breath in preparation for her answer. He stood up and placed the box on a table, taking out the ring and turning towards her once more. He reached for her left hand and carefully slid the ring on to her finger. 'It fits perfectly, doesn't it?' he said. 'I asked Jessica your ring size.'

'Ah...that's how you knew. Yes, it does... Wait till I see her—she didn't say a word to me about this! Nate, it's so beautiful.' She looked at him, her eyes shining with happiness.

'It's where it belongs—on your finger. There's a wedding ring made to go with it. Perhaps we could make it a short engagement? I know it's traditional to have a summer wedding, but I was thinking maybe Christmas would be a good time? We could be married in the village church and then come back here for the celebrations. What do you think?'

She lifted her arms to him and wound them lightly around his neck. 'I think that sounds wonderful,' she said.

He wrapped his hands around her waist and drew her to him. 'We could honeymoon in the Caribbean, after the festivities. Do you think you would like that?'

'Anywhere would be lovely,' she murmured, 'as long as I'm with you.'

He smiled and kissed her tenderly, with growing passion. 'I've a feeling that life is going to be sheer bliss from now on,' he said after a while, his voice roughened.

She came up for air briefly. 'Oh, yes, definitely.' She

kissed him again and neither of them spoke for a long, long time after that. They were far too busy showing their love for one another.

* * * * *

If you enjoyed this story, check out these other great reads from Joanna Neil

**HER HOLIDAY MIRACLE
RESISTING HER REBEL DOC
TEMPTATION IN PARADISE
DARING TO DATE HER BOSS**

All available now!

MILLS & BOON®

MEDICAL ROMANCE™

THE ULTIMATE IN ROMANTIC MEDICAL DRAMA

A sneak peek at next month's titles...

In stores from 3rd November 2016:

The Nurse's Christmas Gift – Tina Beckett *and*
The Midwife's Pregnancy Miracle – Kate Hardy

- **Their First Family Christmas** – Alison Roberts *and*
The Nightshift Before Christmas – Annie O'Neil

- **It Started at Christmas...** – Janice Lynn *and*
Unwrapped by the Duke – Amy Ruttan

Just can't wait?
Buy our books online a month before they hit the shops!
www.millsandboon.co.uk

Also available as eBooks.

MILLS & BOON®

EXCLUSIVE EXCERPT

Could a miracle in maternity reunite paediatrician
Max Ainsley with his estranged wife, Annabelle
Brookes, in time for Christmas?

Read on for a sneak preview of
THE NURSE'S CHRISTMAS GIFT
*the first book in the heart-warming
festive Medical quartet*
CHRISTMAS MIRACLES IN MATERNITY

"It's still there, isn't it, despite everything?"

Annabelle frowned, moving under one of the street
lamps along the edge of a park. "What is?"

"That old spark."

She'd felt that spark the second she'd laid eyes on
Max all those years ago. But he wasn't talking about
way back then. He was talking about right now.

"Yes," she whispered.

She wished to hell it weren't. But she wasn't going
to pay truth back with a lie.

"Anna…" He took her hand and eased them off the
path and into the dark shadows of a nearby bench.

She sat down, before she fell down. His voice…
She would recognise that tone anywhere. He sat beside
her, still holding her hand.

"You've changed," he said.

"So have you. You seem…" She shook her head,

unable to put words to her earlier thoughts. Or maybe it was that she wasn't sure she should.

"That bad, huh?"

"No. Not at all."

He grinned, the flash of his teeth sending a shiver over her. "That good, then, huh?"

Annabelle laughed and nudged him with her shoulder. "You wish."

"I actually do."

When his fingers shifted from her hand to just beneath her chin, the shiver turned to a whoosh as all the breath left her body, her nerve endings suddenly attuned to Max's every move. And when his head came down, all she felt was anticipation.

THE NURSE'S CHRISTMAS GIFT by Tina Becket

Available November 2016

www.millsandboon.co.uk

Give a 12 month subscription to a friend today!

Call Customer Services
0844 844 1358*

or visit
millsandboon.co.uk/subscription